Choose your Lane to love!

Readers love *Shades of Henry* by AMY LANE

By Amy Lane

All the Rules of Heaven
An Amy Lane Christmas
Behind the Curtain
Bewitched by Bella's Brother
Bolt-hole
Christmas Kitsch
Christmas with Danny Fit
Clear Water
Do-over
Food for Thought
Freckles
Gambling Men
Going Up
Hammer & Air
Homebird
If I Must
Immortal
It's Not Shakespeare
Late for Christmas
Left on St. Truth-be-Well
The Locker Room
Mourning Heaven
Phonebook
Puppy, Car, and Snow
Racing for the Sun • Hiding the Moon
Raising the Stakes
Regret Me Not
Shiny!
Shirt
Sidecar
Slow Pitch
String Boys
A Solid Core of Alpha

Three Fates
Truth in the Dark
Turkey in the Snow
Under the Rushes
Wishing on a Blue Star

BENEATH THE STAIN
Beneath the Stain • Paint It Black

BONFIRES
Bonfires • Crocus

CANDY MAN
Candy Man • Bitter Taffy
Lollipop • Tart and Sweet

DREAMSPUN BEYOND
HEDGE WITCHES LONELY HEARTS CLUB
Shortbread and Shadows
Portals and Puppy Dogs
Pentacles and Pelting Plants
Heartbeats in a Haunted House

DREAMSPUN DESIRES
THE MANNIES
The Virgin Manny
Manny Get Your Guy
Stand by Your Manny
A Fool and His Manny
SEARCH AND RESCUE
Warm Heart
Silent Heart
Safe Heart
Hidden Heart

Published by DREAMSPINNER PRESS
www.dreamspinnerpress.com

By AMY LANE (CONT)

FAMILIAR LOVE
Familiar Angel • Familiar Demon

FISH OUT OF WATER
Fish Out of Water
Red Fish, Dead Fish
A Few Good Fish
Hiding the Moon
Fish on a Bicycle • School of Fish

FLOPHOUSE
Shades of Henry
Constantly Cotton

GRANBY KNITTING
The Winter Courtship Rituals of
Fur-Bearing Critters
How to Raise an Honest Rabbit
Knitter in His Natural Habitat
Blackbird Knitting in a Bunny's Lair
The Granby Knitting Menagerie
Anthology

JOHNNIES
Chase in Shadow • Dex in Blue
Ethan in Gold • Black John
Bobby Green
Super Sock Man

KEEPING PROMISE ROCK
Keeping Promise Rock
Making Promises
Living Promises
Forever Promised

LONG CON ADVENTURES
The Mastermind • The Muscle
The Driver

TALKER
Talker • Talker's Redemption
Talker's Graduation
The Talker Collection Anthology

WINTER BALL
Winter Ball • Summer Lessons
Fall Through Spring

Published by Harmony Ink Press
BITTER MOON SAGA
Triane's Son Rising
Triane's Son Learning
Triane's Son Fighting
Triane's Son Reigning

Published by DREAMSPINNER PRESS
www.dreamspinnerpress.com

CONSTANTLY COTTON

AMY LANE

REAMSPINNER PRESS

Published by

DREAMSPINNER PRESS

5032 Capital Circle SW, Suite 2, PMB# 279, Tallahassee, FL 32305-7886 USA
www.dreamspinnerpress.com

Trade Paperback ISBN: 978-1-64108-287-7
Digital ISBN: 978-1-64108-286-0
Trade Paperback published April 2022
v. 1.0

Printed in the United States of America

This paper meets the requirements of
ANSI/NISO Z39.48-1992 (Permanence of Paper).

Mate—always. Mary—you continue to save my life. Kim Fielding—
midnight texts are the best. Kids—thanks for.

AUTHOR'S NOTE

STILL ALL fiction. Still making up shit as I go along.

THE LONG AND WINDING ROAD

"MR. JASON, what was that?"

Lieutenant Colonel Jason Constance, Commander of Covert Operations, self-named Desert Division, wondered if it was possible for his stomach to sink past his balls.

He hadn't been in this much trouble out on the field, looking at a trained assassin through his sniper's scope. And even then he hadn't felt fear.

But then, his ass had been the only one on the line.

"Hang on, Sophie!" Jason called to the back seat of the "borrowed" medical shuttle. He blinked hard to clear the grit of sleep from his eyes. He had managed to pull over to catch a nap for an hour or so, but his internal monitor was pinging danger, and he'd started the bus up when he was certain the kids had all dropped off to sleep.

He couldn't shake the thought that someone was on their tail.

Around lunchtime, his life had seemed so simple.

Stressful—yes. Lonely—*hell* yes. But... fuck.

Simple was relative.

He was in charge of one of the most complicated, gawdawful tasks on the planet. For years, a powerful man—a commander in the armed forces named Karl Lacey—had utilized his ties to the covert ops community to try to create the perfect assassin. He'd used everything from psychics to behavior modification to outright torture to get men to forget their better angels and to find joy only in the hunt... and the kills.

The results had been predictable. To everyone but Lacey.

He'd set a batch of highly trained serial killers loose on an unsuspecting world.

Jason and one of his best operatives, a man named Lee Burton, had stopped the operation before it went international. They'd had help. Burton's boyfriend, Ernie Caulfield, a psychic Lacey had trained up and then tried to have Burton assassinate, had been their compass, and a batch of civilians who'd seen Lacey's psychological Frankenstein's monsters in action had become weapons.

The fallout had left Jason in charge of Lacey's old hidden military base in the desert outside of Barstow, with Lee Burton. Jason and Lee had spent the better part of the last eight months tracking down Lacey's abominations, and it was grim, dangerous, dirty work.

And painful.

They called it Operation Dead Fish.

Not every man Lacey had turned loose on the world had started out a monster. So many of them were left with tortured bits of soul and heart mangled in the wreckage. But it was hard to bring a patient in when that patient was trained to dismember people with his teeth and a plastic fork. Not a lot of their targets were brought home alive to fix.

The only thing that had kept Jason from hollowing out, becoming the man he and his small contingent of fifty or so operatives, agents, and trackers hunted, had been the other part of that fallout.

Burton's boyfriend, Ernie, was so psychic he really couldn't function in a crowded city or urban area, but he was also sort of a sweet, goofy angel who liked to feed people their favorite pastries and could pull a future out of thin air with a rather spacey look into the clouds. Burton's best friend, Ace Atchison, and Ace's psychotic boyfriend, Sonny Daye, had proved staunch and loyal friends and good soldiers, as had Ace's friend and employee, Jai, no last name, a mobster who had been "given" to Ace because Ace had risked his life to save Jai's boss's granddaughter.

And Ellery Cramer and Jackson Rivers, the lawyer and his PI boyfriend, who had not only stopped one of the first serial killers to escape Lacey's control but had tracked the man to Lacey independently, had proved invaluable, both in a fight and as allies in a dangerous secret war.

And all of them, in one way or another, had become something Jason Constance had never thought to have when he'd signed his name on Uncle Sam's bloody dotted line:

Friends. Family. People who knew who he was and cared about *him*—not what he could do for the juggernaut corporation that was the US military.

So Jason had started his morning depressingly early, resolving a crisis that had been brewing for a week and then checking with his far-flung agents, who were currently tracking a number of the rogue operatives through various countries, including their own, and then making contact with his field agents, who were keeping tabs on dangerous targets and trying to find a way to take them out without alerting—or hurting—the civilian population, and then finally with his wetwork agents to make sure that killing people for a living hadn't turned them into killers who did it for fun.

By lunchtime, all he'd wanted was a goddamned tuna sandwich. That was all. The limit of his ambitions.

And then Ernie had called him, out of the blue, and complicated his world.

Ace Atchison and Jai were chasing down an RV of trafficked children, he'd said. They would need help. "Jason, you know we can't just let this happen," he said.

And Jason, so desperate to do something *good*, and do something *real*, had agreed. He'd had Anton Huntington, his transport guy, fire up the old helicopter and take him out to I-15, that long stretch of nowhere between LA and Vegas, and he'd gotten there just in time to watch the big Russian ex-mob guy and a staff sergeant with a high school education take out the guy ferrying kidnapped children from Sacramento to Vegas.

Literally without trying.

That didn't stop Ace and Jai from being glad to see him. No. But it did feel anticlimactic. Right up until Jason had called his own CO, Brigadier General Barney Talbot, and told him that he'd intercepted some trafficked children and would like permission to use military transportation to take them back up north to Sacramento.

It was a basic request—a courtesy, really. Jason, whose real rank was actually heftier than the silver-leaf Lieutenant Colonel insignia he wore on his uniform, had sort of thrown it out there in the name of keeping to protocols in case he ever had to act civilized.

And Talbot, one of the coldest fuckers Jason Constance had ever dealt with, including the assassins in his charge, said, "My division is, at this moment, tracking the group trafficking these minors. We need to see where they're going and follow the money trail. Please put them back on their original transport and designate a soldier to continue to drive them to their original destination."

Jason remembered a feeling of blankness blowing through him, a cold desert wind scouring the duties and the paperwork and the must-dos and the protocols right out of his blood, like the abrasive cleanser used in plumbing.

Every nerve ending was suddenly pristine and alert and awaiting a different set of orders from Jason's tattered, thin soul, as opposed to the ones he usually followed from Washington.

"No, sir," he'd said, his voice sounding tinny, far away, shouted from a mountaintop, even to his own ears. "No, sir. I'm not putting these kids back in that piece-of-shit tin wagon and shipping them back to hell."

The conversation had devolved from there.

And when it was over, Jason turned to Huntington almost as though he was surfacing from a deep pool—or a deep sleep.

"Sergeant Huntington?"

"Yessir?"

"I'm about to do some things my superiors don't approve of. Doing what I ask may get you called in on a court-martial. Let me know if that bothers you."

"You go, I go, sir," Huntington had replied smartly. He was young—late twenties or so—with thick blond hair, Iowa farm-boy blue eyes, and a chest almost too big to fit behind the helicopter controls. Jason had been nursing a crush—a very, very secret crush—on his transport sergeant almost since Anton had joined covert ops, but since he was pretty sure Anton Hungtington was straight (and even if he wasn't, Jason wouldn't hit on someone in his unit, ever), he'd indulged in the crush like other officers indulged in nudie magazines.

He only brought it out at night, when nobody else could see.

But still, it did his heart good to know that he inspired loyalty in somebody.

He'd had Huntington radio for a military transport bus and taken responsibility for the kids, while Jai and Ace had driven off to meet Burton and take out the people on the receiving end of this horror perpetrated against children.

Jason felt like his job was more dangerous.

As soon as the transpo arrived—with cases of water, thank God—Jason had sent the driver back to the base with Anton and hopped behind the wheel.

The trip from the middle of the desert had gone fairly quickly, or as quickly as the old bus could go, given that it overheated if Jason pushed it past fifty miles an hour.

Ernie called him halfway to the I-5 interchange and told him to stop off at a hospital close to the freeway in East Los Angeles. Apparently Jai's boyfriend worked there, and he'd volunteered to take a look at the kids and make sure nobody was suffering from heatstroke or lingering effects from their imprisonment in the back of the sweltering RV.

Jason had pulled into the ambulance bay and been directed toward the side of the big building that was closest to the parking structure. A small, almost hidden, employee entrance sat there, and Jason turned off the laboring engine while he and the kids waited in the shade.

And then the door had opened, and Jason had gotten a good look at another member of Burton and Ernie's hidden family.

He had only the occasional glimpse of Jai, the giant Russian who had been helping Ace Atchison tend to the children as they were moved from the horrible, stench-ridden RV to the slower, air-conditioned military transport bus, but he knew the man existed. When he had dinner with Burton and Ernie, Ernie gossiped to him about all of the denizens of Victoriana, and Jason started listening to their stories like some people paid attention to television shows. Jason Constance, covert ops, living in a hole in the world and tracking down people the US government denied creating, had no family. Or at least in his uniform, he pretended he didn't. His sister was alive and well and living outside of San Diego, teaching, and his parents had retired to Arizona. He texted them from a secure phone reserved for family interactions and exchanged pleasantries because he'd been brought up right and he was loved. But he didn't talk about them to anybody but Ernie and Burton. Ernie was semiofficially dead, and he liked it that way, so Jason felt safe there, but that was the only place. He hadn't had a lover since he'd gone into covert ops ten years ago. Back then, the stigma against being gay was such that any contact, any at all, would have compromised him and the people he worked with beyond forgiveness and redemption.

Things were different now, and even if they weren't, watching Burton and Ernie build their private bastion of tender civilization in the middle of the unforgiving desert would have inspired him to find somebody, anybody, to make the world a warmer, more welcoming place for his stripped-bare, desiccated soul. But his emotional centers felt battered and rusty, like a once-functioning piece of equipment that had been dipped in salt water and left in the sun to rust and gum up with sand.

He wasn't sure he could even touch a lover right now, not with the reverence and joy he seemed to remember that involved.

So seeing George, Jai's boyfriend, jumping into the military bus to smile gently at all of the children and tell them that he had meals prepared and was going to take everybody's temperatures and make sure nobody was sick—that was like watching a movie star walk into his life and invite him to the party.

And to realize that this perfectly average slender blond man with gray eyes and an engaging smile belonged to Jai, the almost terrifying ex-mobster who stayed very intentionally on the periphery of Jason's vision whenever they met? If Jason hadn't just flushed his entire career down the toilet, he would have been almost giddy.

As it was, he'd been up since 4:00 a.m., following an op going down in Europe, and it was nearly eight in the evening by the time George and his boss, Amal, managed to sneak Jason and the children onto a medical transport, practically under Barney Talbot's nose.

He was too tired for giddy. He'd settle for relieved.

Jason pulled out into the thick of Los Angeles weekend traffic, knowing the only way to get the kids away from the military and the mob was to take the 14 through the mountains and then turn back toward I-5 north of Palmdale.

Which would be like a flea taking a tour on a hairless cat. Sure, it could get from nose to tail faster, but it could also get caught and squashed. There wasn't much up in that area—lots of bare stretches of road with housing developments parked in acres of succulents so the wind didn't scour the dirt from the mountaintops.

And not a lot of places to stop.

But the kids had been fed—twice, because he'd stopped for fast food while he'd been clawing his way through traffic to get to the hospital—and they had water, fuel, and AC. If he could tough it out over the mountains, he could find a place to park in Palmdale or Lancaster, before driving the relatively short six hours to Sacramento, where hopefully he could find the authorities to get the kids home.

It was a plan. He liked this plan. There was sleep in this plan; there was another chance to feed the kids. Hell, because it was a medical transport, there was even a bathroom in this plan. This plan was a go!

And it had been a go as he'd made his way through the mountains and found a small town before Palmdale with a gas station.

It wasn't that he needed the fuel—as far as he could see, he had plenty to get him to Sacramento—but having the level place to park the bus was a plus. Once they'd descended from the mountains, and the temperature had leveled out a little from ice fucking cold to warm night breeze, the level place was pretty much his only requirement. There were thin polyester blankets in the compartments above the seats. He, Sophie, and Maxim broke those out and distributed them to the other young people, aged around ten to fourteen as far as he could see, and he had Sophie and Max tell the other kids they were stopping to sleep before he finished the drive. It should be easy, right?

A few hours, that's all. Four hours of sleep, right? He was a soldier; he'd run on less, certainly. But he'd been running on two hours at a time for the last four nights, and it wasn't like he wasn't used to being perpetually tired, but this was stretching it.

He was trying to pilot a land yacht through a traffic tsunami, and the kids in the back were depending on him.

A few hours of sleep.

So he parked the bus and had the kids crack the windows to let in some of the night air, and then he wadded up one of the blankets under his head and leaned against the window and closed his eyes.

He dreamed about the desert.

Not this one here, the one at home, but the one far away, where his job had been to kill people in a war he didn't understand. Half the reason he'd risen up the ranks, really, was so he could understand why he was ordering young soldiers to their death and making them kill people they didn't know.

But back then he'd been barely out of OTS and trying to get the attention of his CO. He remembered all of them in the coms tent, the beginnings of an epic windstorm gathering around the barracks.

"But look," he'd said, pointing to the blips on the screen. "General, these aren't our guys. I know you think they're our guys, but they're not moving in our patterns. We need to get eyes on them because if they get any closer—"

About then the first missile was launched at their fortification, from what they later discovered was the back of a captured Humvee.

He'd seen the trouble, all right—but only when it was right on them.

He woke up in the front of the bus with a strained breath. Fighting his way to consciousness, he knew the one thing he had to do was listen.

He heard the grumble of a big vehicle—a badly tended SUV, he thought—as it exited Highway 14 and rode the hairpin offramp toward their current location.

Where the big medical bus was sitting like a fat bird.

Quietly, so as not to disturb the children, he hit the starter and watched as the warm-up light glowed on the dashboard. These things usually took about two minutes to warm up. Two minutes. That was enough time for the SUV to see them on the way by and to turn around and come back and check on them. Was it enough time to fire? Was it enough time for the men inside to see who was sleeping there and come back to kill them?

"Sophie," he hissed.

The girl—wide gray eyes, a pink stripe in her hair, and a razor-quick mind—had apparently been sleeping as lightly as he had.

"Mr. Jason?"

"Tell everyone to get on the floor. We need to pull out as soon as the engine's ready."

"Yessir," she said. No questions, no whining. God, it was too bad she was twelve years old; he'd like to recruit her.

The SUV passed them, and for a moment he wondered if he wasn't getting on the road too soon. It was an SUV for God's sake. Somebody lived out here, right?

But he got behind the wheel and started up the bus as soon as the light went out.

And as he was pulling away from the gas station, the first bullet zinged by, and the second too. The third didn't zing. Fired from a silencer, he figured, the third bullet ripped through the side of the bus and then tore through the seat where Sophie and Maxim had been sleeping, before it lodged itself solidly in Jason's shoulder.

"Mr. Jason," Sophie said breathlessly from the floor. "What was that?"

And as pain tore through him, every synapse declaring a magnesium fire in his shoulder, and now in his side, all at the same moment, he realized they were fucked.

"Hang on, Sophie!" he called, stomping on the accelerator and going straight. Not toward the freeway, which would take him right by the people shooting at them, but straight, which would take him into some of the least populated places of California and possibly Nevada.

But hopefully, it would not take them to where there would be bullets.

LAUNDRY DAY

COTTON ROLLED over and shoved his head under the pillow, hoping for the banging on the door to go away.

The best thing about self-imposed celibacy was he actually knew he was waking up in his own bed. The worst thing was he'd been used to getting fucked to sleep, and now he had to lie awake in his own bed, reflecting on his life choices and his uncertain future, and he didn't close his eyes until the wee hours of the morning. And now somebody was banging on the door to the flophouse *in* the wee hours of the morning, and it appeared he was the only one awake enough to hear.

"Go away!" he mumbled, stuffing the pillow over his head. Then he heard Henry's voice through the door.

"Please, guys! I can't get my keys. Someone out here needs your help!"

Cotton looked around and tried to take stock. He and Billy were in this room now. Vinnie, the new guy, was on the couch, and Randy and Curtis were next door. Randy got the big bed—not because he paid for it, like they were supposed to, but because the kid had a seven-foot wingspan and size fifteen feet. At one point, Henry had just ordered, "Give him the big bed! Zep and Fisher moved out. It's his. 'Nuff said."

Henry was sort of commanding that way. People listened to what he said.

Which was why Cotton didn't understand why he was the only one stumbling toward the door.

He opened it anyway, not caring that he was wearing a pair of assless briefs. It was late August for God's sake. He might be celibate, but it wasn't like he was going to accidentally roll over onto someone's dick!

"Henry?" he muttered, still blinking sleep out of his eyes. "Is that guy bleeding?"

"Cotton, is your bedding clean?" Henry asked, busting through the door. His doctor boyfriend, Lance, came with him, as well as a guy they were hoisting between them, using their arms as a sling.

"Did laundry yesterday," Cotton said blankly. "No, seriously, is he bleeding?"

"Yes, Cotton," Henry muttered. "Yes, he is. Now move so he doesn't bleed on the carpet."

And with that, Lance and Henry hauled the stranger into the second bedroom of the small apartment and apparently dumped him on Cotton's bed.

After Cotton shut the open front door, which led to the stairwell, and followed them, he heard Billy—who hated mornings, particularly after he'd had a hard workout day at the gym—growling, "Hey, is that guy bleeding?"

"Yes!" Henry barked, and Cotton seriously had no idea what to do next.

Henry may have been ex-military, a blond, blue-eyed, square-jawed wet dream of a soldier, in Cotton's opinion, but ever since he'd shown up at the flophouse back in March, he'd worked hard to be gentle with all of the guys there. Henry had never worked in porn, but he'd never disrespected the people who did.

"Whoa," Billy said, and Cotton heard Henry's deep breath even as he entered the room.

"Sorry, man," he apologized. Sincerely, it sounded like. "It's been something of a morning."

"Who is this guy?" Cotton asked, looking over at the bed. Lance, who had only worked porn to get through med school, really, and to help his sister through law school, had also brought his black bag with him. As Cotton watched, Lance, one of the most beautiful men he'd ever seen in porn or out of it, with coal black hair, delicately gold-toned features, and almond-shaped brown eyes, sliced through the stranger's black T-shirt and heavy-duty uniform cargo pants with a handy little cutter that looked like it was made for the job. The man's clothes screamed military, and the man himself had a body fit from hard use, much like Henry's. Yeah, sure, this guy had hit the weight machines, but that was probably so he was ready for whatever his job held in store.

He had a square jaw—go figure—and a somewhat narrow, appealing face. If Cotton had to guess, he'd say the man's eyes were brown, to match the hair that had grown just long enough to curl across his brow.

Someone was too busy for his weekly military cut. Interesting.

But the man's eyes were closed, and his jaw was clenched in pain, and the body that was revealed as Lance threw what was left of his clothes toward the foot of the bed had been damaged in more than one place.

"God*dammit*!" Lance swore.

"What?" Henry asked. "Cotton, could you go get—"

"On it," Cotton said, running toward the kitchen for trash bags and the kitchen towels he'd laundered the day before. He kept his ears peeled, though, because he wanted to hear what Lance was saying about the mysterious stranger currently on his bed.

"It's more than his arm," Lance snarled. "Here, help me turn him—*fuck*!"

Cotton rushed back to see that Lance had half rolled their mystery military man and was lifting the remnants of his T-shirt off of what looked like a lot of crusted blood on his side.

"Did it hit anything vital?" Henry asked, concerned.

"I don't know. *Cotton*!" Lance's voice rang sharply. "Here, grab some gloves from my bag before you throw that away." He flexed his hands, and Cotton could see the sterile poly gloves that Lance used automatically when he was helping to doctor their small hurts.

"Sorry, Lance," he murmured, rooting through the black bag until he found a box of them. Sliding a pair on, he tried to make himself invisible again while he helped clean up.

"No worries," Lance told him gently. "Just want my guys protected, right?"

Cotton nodded, although he sighed inwardly. Yes, the entire flophouse got the memo: Cotton was fragile. Don't yell at him, don't say boo to him. He was having a hard time figuring out life right now, and they all had to be careful or he'd flip out on them and probably cry himself sick.

Gah! He would really like to be a grown-up at the table.

But this wasn't about him.

"Is he going to need surgery?" Henry prompted. "Because that could be bad at the moment."

"No, it's a through-and-through," Lance murmured, probing the wound. "And it appears to have missed all the fun things—intestines, kidneys, liver, other important organs—but it's crusted over with blood, and the risk of infection here is hellific." He grimaced. "Billy, is the spare key to our apartment still hanging in the kitchen?"

"Yup," Billy said, moving from his huddle on his own bed and reaching for a pair of basketball shorts hanging off the dresser that sat between the two beds making up most of the room. Billy slept naked. "What do you need?"

"Well, we have a guest bedroom and about eight sets of twin-sized sheets," Lance muttered. "If you could grab half of those? We're going to need to keep his bedding clean. Also, I've got big bed pads in my bag. Once we resheet this bed, we're going to need to spread one under him or he'll seep into the mattress."

In spite of the gravity of the situation, Cotton couldn't help what came out next. "Ew."

He expected sharp words again, but Lance and Henry both nodded.

"Seriously," Henry said. "Sorry, Cotton. We'll replace the mattress if it's bad."

"And we may want to lay down mats," Billy said, sliding into flip-flops and heading out to the hall.

"We've got some in the same closet," Lance called, and Billy grunted, his dark hair sticking up all over his head, his pale brown skin even paler from lack of sleep. He hadn't made it into the military, but he still walked like a soldier, shoulders swinging, stride crisp—even when he was wearing flip-flops and neon orange basketball shorts and heading through the flophouse on an errand.

"What happened to him?" Cotton asked, drawn to the man's face—slack in unconsciousness but still very appealing—again. "It looks like he's been shot twice and beaten by a baseball bat."

"I'd say beaten with the butt of a pistol," Henry said clinically. "But yeah. He was driving a busload of kidnapped kids back to Sacramento, and apparently the mobsters who stole them wanted them back."

Cotton grimaced. "A busload of kids?" That didn't make sense! Did someone just drive off with them? Had this wounded man been caught in a Tom-and-Jerry military game where people kept trying to grab the bus back? He couldn't wrap his brain around what Henry was saying.

"The kids had been taken from their families in Sacramento," Henry clarified. "They were being shipped down to Vegas to be auctioned and—" He couldn't hide his shudder. "—sold. Some friends of ours intercepted them on the way to Vegas, and this guy—Colonel Jason Constance—volunteered to drive them home."

"And the mobsters attacked him on the way back?" Cotton finally felt like he was getting the picture. "That's horrible! Why didn't he have help? Why isn't he in the hospital?"

The face Henry turned toward Cotton was bleak. "Because at least one person in the military branch Constance was in contact with was making money off the sale. Someone was giving the mobsters guns, and they were supposed to pay him with the proceeds from this shipment of kids. So Constance is in danger of being court-martialed, he's in all sorts of trouble in Washington, and the mobsters probably want to clean up what's left of him since he stopped the sale from going through. The whole world wants this poor guy's scrawny ass, and the only way to give him a chance to fix it is to—"

"Wait, I got this one," Cotton said, his heart actually aching for the unconscious officer currently bleeding on his bed. "To keep him away from the hospital and keep him hidden."

Henry smiled in obvious relief. "Got it in one," he said. He looked to where Lance worked, motions crisp and defined like someone who knew what he was doing. "Now it's up to God and Lancelot."

"Lancelot's busy," Lance snapped, interrupting his own muttering. "Go talk to God."

THE NEXT few days were, as Lance said, touch and go. Cotton was aware—peripherally—that the flophouse apartment was being watched. He wasn't sure by whom, but it was supposed to make him and the others feel safe and guarded.

He mostly just forgot that anything outside the apartment was real.

Inside the apartment, or inside his and Billy's room, there was only Jason Constance and the endless round of things that needed to be done to keep his tired body from failing completely.

The flophouse had an inflatable mattress for emergencies. They never knew when John would send a new model to the flophouse itself, whether for a night, a week, or a month, so they had some place to stay before their checks started coming in. Billy had started sleeping on the mattress because Billy was a nice guy, and sometimes Cotton was too exhausted to move.

Lance had given everybody in the flophouse nursing lessons, starting with "Never forget the gloves" and ending with "Wash your hands until they crack. Here's some butter to make sure that doesn't happen." In between there was "Here's how to give a sponge bath" and "Here's how to use the touchless thermometer" and "Here's how often he can take these medications."

Cotton didn't film scenes anymore. Supposedly he still worked for Johnnies when John needed a guy to hold lights or remake sets, but there was almost always somebody at the office to do that, so Cotton rarely got called. In addition to residuals from his old videos, he collected a small paycheck, essentially for breathing, he figured, and because John knew that he was having trouble figuring out what to do with himself now that he was no longer—could no longer be—a sex worker.

Something in his heart or his brain broke, and he just couldn't anymore, and he didn't know what to do. It was the only thing he'd ever been good at. He'd been kicked out of the house before he finished high school and had lived on the streets, turning tricks to eat, until he'd hit on one of the Johnnies boys—Reg. He'd just turned eighteen, but Reg had been less interested in banging him and more interested in making sure he was okay, so he'd turned Cotton's care and feeding over to his boss, John Carey.

John had cleaned him up, fed him, gotten him tested—gotten him *healthy*—and set him up at the flophouse. At the time, John had been pretty strung out, but even then, even before his recovery, John had taken care of Cotton, and not once had he taken Cotton up on an offer of sex for trade.

Cotton had lived in the flophouse for months on John's dime before he begged to be put on the roster to film scenes. He'd spent two years as one of John's premier performers, but then Henry had come to the flophouse, and something in Cotton had started breaking.

At first he thought it was a crush. But then, he'd crushed on almost every guy he'd slept with after John had pulled him off the streets, and that had included the guys he'd done scenes with. And then one night Henry had pulled him aside for a private talk, and Cotton had started to undress excitedly, thinking, "Yay! Henry finally wants me!" But Henry had just stared at him and asked him to put his clothes on.

And had then done something extraordinary.

He'd *parented* Cotton, in a way that had nothing to do with being Cotton's Daddy. John had done this to some extent—insisting Cotton eat, politely declining his offers of sex, making sure he slept at the flophouse, and checking in on his roommates. Lance had tried, sort of begging Cotton not to get his hopes up as he threw himself into crush after crush, hoping each time he'd find true love, discover the Daddy who would take care of his Boy.

But Henry had sat him down and said, in essence, "This isn't good for you. I've had sex that wasn't good for me, and I had to quit so I could find the kind that didn't hurt me inside."

Cotton would always regret not etching his actual words on gold foil and putting them above his bed. That conversation had been the beginning of his breaking.

He'd continued to work scenes, though, having what appeared to be gleeful sex on camera with whomever showed up in the roster. He'd thought it was something he was good at. And hey, he didn't expect anything from it, right?

But one day he'd walked onto the set—a bed with a super firm mattress so the models didn't sink down to their balls in fluff, well-washed cotton sheets and comforter, a sturdy dresser and sturdy chairs for acrobatics, and artwork that got changed around a lot, not to mention a shag carpet that was steam-cleaned frequently—and sitting on one of the chairs, stroking his cock, was…

A stranger.

But one who looked like… well, a bad memory, really. Cotton had some super shitty memories, and he'd thought he was okay with that, but this stranger hit his shitty-memory sweet spot, and that was the end.

Cotton started crying and couldn't stop. He sat in John's office for two hours, silently weeping, while John and Dex, who was John's business partner and the "mom" of the operation, both tried to calm him down.

Finally John crouched in front of his chair—classic dad move, Cotton had thought then, and he hadn't changed his mind—and taken Cotton's hands in his.

"Buddy," he said, voice gruff, red hair a spiky mess from anxiously tunneling fingers, eyes red-rimmed and sad, "Cotton.…" He took a deep breath. "Carson," he said softly, surprising Cotton with his real name, the one he never used. He'd left Carson Harris behind when he'd been kicked out of the house.

"John," he'd whispered back. "I don't have anywhere else to go."

"Baby," John told him, green eyes sober. "You can always be here. Don't worry about food. Don't worry about rent. If the guys at the flophouse don't cover you, I've got your rent. I know Henry has been trying to feed you all right out of porn anyway. Let him." He'd pushed Cotton's brown hair back from his forehead like Carson's—*Cotton's*—mother used to. "As long as you want, as long as you need, we will take care of you." He gave half a cracked laugh. "Hell, if me *or* Dex had a spare room, you would have been living there for the last three years. So don't worry about food or rent. Just… whatever is going on in your heart? It's been broken a long time. Honey, you need to fix that. And you can't do that working here. Some guys can. Bobby can. Reg could."

Cotton nodded, because Bobby still did the occasional scene for the joy of it, and his boyfriend enjoyed watching him. Reg had been a legend in his time. Not the strongest or the brightest, but his heart, his pleasure at getting to do something somebody else enjoyed, that had translated onto the screen.

"But I'm not.…" A sob tore at his throat.

"No," John said, squeezing his hands. "And you shouldn't have to be. Kid, I know you wanted to pay your own way in the world. It's the only reason I let you start working here. But I was fucked-up then, and my reasoning was fucked-up, and my backbone was made of coke, and we all know it. I'm clean now, and I'm a grown-up. I don't want you working here anymore. It's hurting you. This business, it comes with all sorts of pain. There's drugs—although I try to keep them out 'cause they almost wrecked *me*. There's depression. And there's brokenness. You've got the second two, Carson—"

"Cotton," he said gruffly. "I... I'm Cotton now."

John nodded. "That's fair," he said. "And you can still be Cotton even if you never come back here again." He gave a crooked smile then, his pointy canine teeth making it charming even though John was not particularly handsome. "You are always welcome to come back. You can work lights, you can clean the showers, do the laundry. There's always work here to do. Just not...."

"Naked," Cotton had said, and they'd both smiled.

And Cotton realized that he'd stopped crying, because apparently John Carey really was a decent guy for a porn mogul, and he'd known it was time for Cotton to quit.

That had been in early June, and since then he'd applied to junior colleges, but it had been too late in the year for him to get in by fall semester. On the one hand, it had been fine. He'd cleaned the house and cooked for everybody. Done the shopping and even looked into getting a job. Henry had a contact who could get him a bonded job cleaning houses—he thought that might be a thing he could do.

But whatever he'd planned for the rest of his life after he got his shit together got a shock to the heart the moment Jason Constance was rushed through the door of the Johnnies' flophouse and Cotton allowed his bed to be converted to a hospital cot.

He'd never worked so hard in his life.

He changed bandages, took and recorded vital signs, sponged down fevered flesh, and monitored fluids. Lance showed him how to install an IV and then how to change the ports, how to read a chart to see if someone else had given the patient medication while Cotton had been catching a rare couple hours of sleep. In a million years, Cotton had never dreamed he could do these things, but Lance and Henry had needed him.

This man—this tired man tossing on Cotton's bed, bleeding—had been a hero. Cotton felt like the absolute least he could do to reward that was to help Lance make sure the man was okay.

For three days "okay" was not a thing. Lance had to work shifts, but he trained the Johnnies guys on the fly, and Henry helped too when Henry wasn't at his job as a private investigator. But for three days, with Cotton taking point because he was home the most, they watched as their patient thrashed about in pain and fever. They gave him his medicine through the IV because he couldn't wake up enough to swallow pills, and they cleaned his wounds almost constantly because infection could not—*could not*—be allowed to take hold. For three days, they fought to make sure that didn't happen.

The third day after Jason Constance had arrived, his temperature finally dropped below 100. In celebration, Cotton had stripped him naked and put bed pads underneath him so Cotton could clean him, stem to stern.

He'd soiled himself once in the three days, but that seemed to have taken care of the last thing he ate, and Cotton and the others had no problem with poop. They worked in an industry in which they all had to monitor their food and fluid intake to the last gram before they worked a scene so they didn't poop on camera, and accidents still happened. Skin and sheets washed. It was a fact of life.

After that one accident happened, though, most of his fluids seemed to be sweated away, although Cotton had needed to clean up after that too. And it was funny, he thought, wiping down the unconscious man between the crease of his ass and under his balls. Nobody really thought porn could prepare a person to do something as important as nurse someone back to health, but not having a problem with body fluids—and having the upper body strength of a small bull—had really been a help during the last few days. He very carefully, because he respected that these bits were tender, wiped down the patient's testicles and then pulled back his foreskin and made sure his penis was clean too.

That was the last part of the tour; he'd started at the head and sponged down the hair so the oil didn't build up and worked his way to the feet and then rinsed out the water and done the privates. Lance hadn't told him that, but he'd showered enough times before going on set to know how to wash all the parts for a close-up so that he gave serious thought to what you didn't want touching what with only a soapy washcloth between them.

He finished up with a towel to all the points that could get moist and yeasty. Lance had used that word, and it had made every guy in the apartment go "Ew!" so Cotton was particularly careful not to let it happen on his watch.

And finally he was done, pleased with the fact that while he'd been fascinated with the patient currently taking up his bed, he hadn't ogled or objectified—or counted scars, although the temptation had definitely been there.

Jason Constance, hero and badass, was an exceptionally well-made man.

Cotton's gaze went up to his face, to take in the high cheekbones, square jaw, and the dark fringe of lashes one more time, and he gasped when he encountered wide brown eyes instead.

The man who'd been exhausted and feverish for three days was staring at Cotton, eyes fastened on his face hungrily, like Cotton was food when they all knew he hadn't eaten in quite a while.

"Hello there," Cotton said, surprised. "You're awake? *Are* you awake? Do you need anything? I should call Lance. He's asleep, though, and he's *wrecked.* I mean, since you're not dying, maybe we could let him sleep. Should we call Henry? Should we call Henry's bosses, because they're the ones who stashed you here?" Cotton stared back at those big brown eyes, eyes going liquid and half-mast in a face that seemed—under the beard and the lines of pain around the mouth and nose—almost sweet.

"Wow," the patient rasped. "You are really pretty."

Cotton grinned, surprised and delighted. "Thank you!" Carefully he stowed his sponge-bath supplies on the dresser they'd been using as a surgical table. He stood and stretched and then looked at Jason and sighed. "I hope you still feel that way in a few minutes. I put bed pads underneath you for the sponge bath, and they're wet now. I need to change them, and if your pain meds are wearing off, that might not be fun for either of us. Are you up for that?"

Jason Constance's eyes sharpened, and he took a deep breath—and coughed. Infection, Lance had said. Fluid in the lungs was a sign. But apparently Henry hadn't been full of shit when he'd said Jason was a hero.

"Yeah. Knock yourself out."

"Excellent!" Cotton gave the man his best smile. Anybody who could wake up after three days and tell Cotton he was pretty got all the good things.

Cotton had done this a couple of times during the last few days. He hadn't stopped working out just because he no longer worked porn, so it had been relatively easy, once Lance had shown him the trick to it. It was *easier* if he had help, but he was pretty sure he was the only one in the apartment at the moment.

"Okay," he said, mostly to himself. "Here. I'm going to roll you over to your side, the one with the bandage on the arm."

"Left," Jason said, and when Cotton put one hand on his shoulder and the other on his hips, he felt Jason tightening his muscles to help Cotton out.

"Yup! And when I get you there, I'm going to pull out all your bed pads and replace them so we don't have to burn my mattress. Then I'm going to rock you to the side with the bandage around the waist—"

"There's a bandage around my waist?" Jason mumbled, and it looked like he raised his head to see, but it fell back down again weakly.

"Yeah. You got shot there. Everybody's going to want to talk about it. Anyway, I'll rock you back on that side and straighten the pads."

"Everybody?" Jason asked as Cotton rocked him to his left for the first turn.

Cotton tugged at the pads, pulled them out from under his side, and told him, "Stay there." He bagged the used ones and spread the next set onto the bed. "Yes, everybody," he said as he rocked him back. Jason was a good patient—allowed his body to be moved and held the position he needed to. Maybe it was just a change after the unresponsiveness of the last three days, but Cotton was grateful.

"Who's everybody?" Pause. "Wait—did you say I'm in your bed?"

Cotton spread the pads, making sure there was some extra on the side to pull toward him after Jason rolled the other way. "Everybody is Jackson Rivers and Henry, I think. They'll confab with your guy, Burton, and decide whether or not we've got snipers and assassins pointed here." He put his hands on Jason's hip and shoulder again. "Okay, pulling on this side usually hurts. Your arm doesn't like moving more than it doesn't like getting smushed up against the mattress. Are you ready?"

"Yeah, sure." Jason helped this time too, and Cotton rolled him so he was facing the wall and pulled the bed pad straight.

"God, this is *so* much easier when you're awake. Seriously. I mean, if we can get you to stand up to pee, my life will be *gravy*!"

Jason made a choked sound. "Jesus! What have I been doing instead?"

"Oh, honey," Cotton said, rolling him so he was lying on his back again. "Don't ask." With that, he reached to the bottom of the bed and pulled up the medical-grade sheets and blanket that Lance had smuggled out of the hospital when it became clear that Jason was running through their linens faster than they could keep up with in the apartment complex's four-machine laundromat downstairs.

"Gah!" Jason covered his eyes with his hand. "So embarrassing. First time in ten years I'm in a pretty boy's bed, and I've been soiling his sheets!"

Cotton paused in the act of covering him up, and a number of things occurred to him in the span of a heartbeat.

The first was that Jason Constance was thin and pale and exhausted, and he was still worried about his behavior in Cotton's bed.

The second was that even thin and pale and exhausted, he was *very* male, *very* attractive, and *not* the featureless heroic Ken doll that Cotton had been caring for over the last three days.

The third—and most obvious—was that Jason Constance was gay.

He finished shaking out the sheets and tucked them up under Jason's arms, aware of the man's wide brown eyes drinking him in.

"What?" Jason mumbled, probably falling asleep. He'd been really sick. Sick enough that the only thing keeping Lance from dialing for an ambulance had been Henry's assurance that the minute *somebody* knew where this man was sleeping would be the moment somebody would show up there with a gun. Cotton could forgive him for falling asleep right after saying something that momentous; it had taken the wind out of Cotton's sails too.

"You think I'm pretty," Cotton said, hating himself because he sounded a little starstruck. "That's—I mean, a lot of guys think I'm pretty, but… but you care what I think back. *That's* amazing."

Jason yawned again and closed his eyes. "So pretty," he murmured.

Cotton tucked him in tightly, because the fever wasn't completely gone and he'd started to shiver during the last part of the bath. And then, while his patient and new occupation fell almost immediately asleep, Cotton leaned over and kissed his forehead. "You're pretty too," he said.

It wasn't his imagination. The deeply etched lines of worry and pain next to Jason's mouth eased, and his lean lips tilted up into almost a smile.

SIT-REP

JASON HAD attended a lot of situation reports in his time, but never as a patient as naked under the hospital sheets as he was confused on top of them.

His pretty nurse with the amazingly wide sepia-colored eyes and dimples in the corners of his cheeks had brought in extra pillows and now sat cross-legged on the floor, wearing nothing but cargo shorts. Apparently it was full-blown end-of-August outside the apartment, and while Jason struggled with fever and chills in a tiny room with white walls and the occasional poster, two twin beds, and a dresser on a four-foot strip of cheap beige carpet between them, the rest of the residents were setting up extra fans over ice chests in the rest of the apartment to keep the temperature down during the heat.

Jason had met everybody. He was sort of sure he'd met everybody.

His brain had already sorted the people who lived here into their own personnel files, complete with skills and weakness.

Curtis—African American with a square face, penetrating brown eyes, a crisp military haircut, a no-bullshit way of taking his turn nursing, and a stack of textbooks in kinesiology and nursing he was reading in order to get ahead of the local state college start time.

Billy—Latinx with an almost vulpine clean-shaven jaw, brown eyes, and hair long enough to be silky against his collar. He had a sarcastic sense of humor that bordered on bitter, was terrifyingly competent, and detailed every last thing he ate in a diet diary, including carrots.

Randy—translucently white, freckled, red-haired, gangly, clumsy as fuck, easily panicked, and had trouble remembering his indoor voice. Also nearly six-and-a-half-feet tall and seemed to get hurt walking through doors.

Vinnie—Caucasian, tanned, brown hair and hazel eyes, with a shy smile and a habit of deferring to anybody else in the house. Frequently heard asking the other roommates what they were doing outside of Johnnies—whatever that was.

And then there was Cotton.

Cotton—dark haired, sloe-eyed, Caucasian with a faint tan. Taller than Vinnie and Billy, shorter than Randy, he spoke quietly and seemed to be a born caretaker.

All of the boys—men?—*all* of them were between eighteen and twenty-four, built like they'd been sculpted from marble, and pretty as hell, even Randy, when he wasn't practically shouting things like "Oh my God, the hair on my balls itches!"

Jason hadn't had the nerve to ask where exactly he'd been taken to recover, but he was really close to having a heart-to-heart with God and inquiring pointedly to see if the big guy was having him on.

He'd been celibate for ten years and he woke up *here*? Wherever here was, if it wasn't a cosmic joke, it should have been.

Because of course all of the young men—every last one of them—had helped to care for him, change his dressings, change his *bedding*, and sponge him down when he was out of his mind with fever. All he'd wanted was a date, maybe. An average-looking guy. Some wine. A chance to talk about something besides his job. That was it. It had been his fantasy for ten years.

But no, he had to wake up in a boarding house for gay male angels. And the guy who seemed to have the most responsibility for him—Cotton— was the prettiest one of all.

But that wasn't what he was going to say to the people gathered around his bed.

Henry Worrall was five feet eleven inches of solid all-American-boy soldier. Jason wasn't sure what branch of the military, but he recognized the posture and the haircut and even the way he ground his teeth. There were ways to do that your CO wouldn't see. Henry knew them all.

He was standing boyfriend-close to Lance, the doctor who had given orders to all the other guys in the house, telling them how to care for Jason. He didn't remember much from the past three days, but he remembered that: the barked orders and the instant deference to both Henry and Lance.

But Henry and Lance weren't the ones dominating the room right now, and Cotton, sitting quietly between the dresser and the bed Jason was lying in, was certainly not in charge.

The guy in charge was a little older than everyone else—although still younger than Jason!—with dark blond hair, arresting green eyes, and a face that bore both ancient scars of childhood acne and more recent bruises and scrapes from what looked like a rough couple of days. He was wearing cargo shorts and a bright blue T-shirt with otters on it and stood like he was in pain. Jason didn't need a sign or a dossier to remember exactly who this was.

"Jackson Rivers, I presume?" he said, extending a hand.

Rivers gave him a blinding grin and took the hand in a hard shake. "Colonel Constance," he replied. "It's a pleasure. I've been sending my thanks to you through Burton for far too long."

Jackson and his boyfriend, Ellery Cramer, had helped Burton and Jason through a lot of shit—and then apparently repaid the help in spades.

Jason managed a one-shouldered shrug. "Thanks are good," he said, and then, remembering, he felt a grin taking over his expression. "Staying out of the fucking trees would have been better. And oh my God, I cannot *tell* you how happy you would have made me if you'd managed to keep your mother-in-law in one place that week."

Rivers threw back his head and laughed. "Oh my God! I'd almost forgotten about that!" he said in delight. "Here I was remembering when you and Burton saved my brother's life, and I'd forgotten that week Lucy Satan visited and you two had to track us over half of creation so you could try to stop a hit!"

"There was a hit on Ellery's mother's life?" Henry asked, and Jason heard the horror in his voice. Well, Henry had gotten to meet the old girl in person, then. She'd had a big enough force of personality through the end of a scope when Jason and Burton had been trying to protect her.

"Longest century of my *life*," Jackson confirmed, shaking his head. "About a month before you and I met. God. But yeah, Colonel Constance here—"

"Jason," he said, feeling like his rank was overkill in this little room.

"Jason," Jackson said with a nod. "He's kept Ellery and me alive on more than one occasion. If I'm not mistaken, the entire reason Ellery didn't die when we got tangled up with that thing in the desert was thanks to Jason's help with transpo and running interference with the authorities." He met Jason's eyes again, grave and grateful. "There really aren't enough thanks in the world." Those green eyes gave a twinkle. "But I can't promise you about staying out of trees. My brother's adopting the kid I chased up there. I have the feeling shitty grades aren't going to be the only reason he climbs trees."

Jason groaned and felt a warmth in his stomach. He'd followed this man and his family often enough that he felt... attached to them. He'd told himself it was a stupid, pointless attachment. It wasn't like they knew who he was or cared.

But apparently Jackson and Ellery didn't take their safety for granted.

Jason didn't get a lot of thanks in his job—it was nice, right now, to know he'd helped a good man.

"Well," he said, trying not to get too sentimental, "let me know if you're going to be doing it when I'm on guard duty. I'll be sure to send Burton instead."

Rivers laughed and then sat on the bed across from him. "By the way, I'm not sure if your nurse told you when you woke up, but Burton isn't here because he's staking you out. Did you know that?"

Jason nodded. "Smart man," he rasped. "Tell me what went down the day I got here, and I'll tell you who we have to worry about."

Jackson gave a snort of laughter. "Okay, so what you need to know is this. The kids in that bus were abducted by a guy named Ziggy—"

"Seriously?" Jason interrupted. He wasn't usually chatty, but... Ziggy?

"Right?" Rivers said, and Henry exclaimed almost at the same time. "Fuckin' Ziggy!"

"Anyway, Ziggy was bad news," Jackson continued. "And part of being bad news was starting a gang war between Alexei Kovacs and Dima Siderov. And the shit Ziggy did to make that happen would"—his voice dropped a little—"break your heart."

By his side, Henry nodded soberly, and Jackson continued. "Ziggy had a partner in mayhem—two, in fact. Dietrich and Karina Schroeder, both of whom wanted the gang war to happen so they could take over Dima's branch here in Sacramento. The shipment of kids that you helped to intercept was meant as a payment to Alexei for sending his guys up here to help take over Dima's operation. You all with me here?"

Everybody in the room nodded their heads, except Henry, who said, "Now tell him about the monkey wrenches."

"Monkey wrenches?" Lance asked, full of suspicion.

"*So* many monkey wrenches," Rivers confirmed. "The first monkey wrench was that Ziggy killed off Dima's nephew to cover his tracks. That put Ellery and me on his ass because he tried to pin it on an innocent kid, and stopping that shit is what we do."

Jason *hmm*d, knowing that was true. It was one of the reasons he and Lee Burton kept an eye on Jackson Rivers and Ellery Cramer—good men were hard to find.

"The other monkey wrench you know about," Rivers said. "That was the shipment of kids getting intercepted and lost in the desert. Or, you know, returned to their homes, as it were."

"Were they?" Jason asked hungrily. God—please. Please let that terrible drive through the desert not have been in vain.

"Yeah," Rivers told him, voice dropping like he knew why this was important. "They were returned to their families. You did good. What you may not know is that after Jai and Ace left you in the desert to transport the kids, they went and met Burton."

Jason closed his eyes, remembering. "They were supposed to get rid of the RV the kids came in," he said.

Rivers nodded. "They did. They blew it up. They blew it up right as it crashed into Alexei Kovacs's mansion, killing Kovacs and his second-in-command. So remember that power takeover that was brewing up here?"

Jason stared at him. "Oh my God."

Jackson nodded one more time. "Yeah. By the time you got to Sacramento, Ziggy's guys and Alexei's guys were trying to stop you because you and those kids could tell not just the DA and the authorities, but also all of organized crimedom what was going on."

"So that explains all the bad guys when I got to town," Jason muttered. "Fantastic. I was wondering."

"Well, yeah." Rivers made a curious stretching gesture, like he was trying to work all the space between his neck and his ass, and Henry let out a huff of exasperation.

"Jackson, would you like an ibuprofen today? You're talking about that shit like you weren't involved."

Rivers gave a grunt. "Yeah, sparky—I'll take some painkillers. I've got about another hour here before Ellery needs me home or he'll have my head."

"Both of you?" Jason asked, horrified. God. These men!

"Long story," Rivers told him, waving it off. "But here's the thing. That's what happened to *us*. And that's why you were surrounded by mobsters and Burton needed to save everybody's asses as you drove in. What we need to know is what happened to *you*. Your wounds were old, Jason, and it took you a helluva long time to get here."

Jason nodded. Now that he wasn't wondering about his welcome to Sacramento, with the chaos of car accidents and people in SUVs chasing him and the kids around with semiautos, he could concentrate on what had happened to *him*.

"Well, originally," he told the people hovering around his bed, "I'd planned to get in about noon the day before. We pulled off to rest. I was getting punchy, and by that time I was driving a medical shuttle that... uhm, somebody from a hospital in LA let me borrow."

"Jai's boyfriend," Rivers filled in dryly. "We all know who George is by now. Okay, so you stopped and got the kids checked out and fed. George told us that. Then you left—we thought for Sacramento."

"Yes, but when I got the shuttle from the hospital, my CO, Barney Talbot, was already there. I had told Sergeant Anton Huntington, my chopper pilot, to be straight with whoever asked him questions after he got me my original transportation. He told Talbot where I was heading and then told me that Talbot was on my tail. So I figured getting back on 5 or the 405 was going to get me caught. Instead, I go up around the mountains toward Lancaster, and the road is slow and twisty, and by the time I got to right before Palmdale, it was nearly two in the morning. I pulled off underneath an overpass to nap, and about two hours later, I woke up hearing an SUV."

The story came back to him completely then, and his heart started beating a little faster, the fever sweat he hadn't been able to shake drenching him again.

As an operative, he'd faced worse situations many times.

But never, *never*, with a busload of kids.

"We were attacked," he said, remembering the giant shadow of the looming SUV. "I woke up just as they pulled off the road. They strafed the side of the bus with semiauto fire and got me, because I'd had the kids lie down on the floor. I assumed it was the mobsters the kids were supposed to go to in the first place."

"Well, they were probably Kovacs's guys at the beginning," Rivers said, nodding. "So you got hit through the bus?"

"Yeah, but worse than that." They'd been on a tight, winding road, in a sparsely populated area. He remembered swinging the bus around and using it as a cudgel, feeling the tires going off the road but knowing in his gut that if the people in that other vehicle pushed him off the road and forced him to stop, he and the kids would be doomed. They'd end up shoved in a sand dune somewhere, a mass grave nobody found. "The bus got hit. It was starting to die, so I got desperate. I fired through the window and took out the driver. They swerved away, but everybody in the SUV was armed. I took a side road to fuck knows where and pushed the medical transport until it coughed and died." He let out a sigh, his entire body sheened in sweat, that moment of complete desperation washing over him. To his surprise, strong fingers grasped his own, calming him down a little, and he managed to breathe enough to keep going.

"We all got out of the bus. I had the kids wrap up bottles of water in their medical blankets. We got out of the bus and started walking. I...." He wasn't proud of this. "I called Huntington back—bless the kid. I told him we needed mass transpo and directions. He... he said he'd track my phone, but he told me he wanted to wait. He had the feeling *he* was being traced. They were afraid he was helping me. I told him I didn't want to get him in trouble, and I remember what he said...." He'd hated hearing that note of fear, of betrayal, in young Anton Huntington's voice.

"He said, 'Colonel, the coms unit caught chatter from our people. They're not sure who, but someone higher than us at another HQ was complaining because they were supposed to get money from the sale of the kids. They were going to give Kovacs guns.'"

"You monitor your own coms?" Henry asked, and Rivers looked surprised, like this hadn't occurred to him.

"We're tracking down government-trained serial killers," Jason said bleakly. "We monitor fucking everybody."

The people in the room shuddered, but that grip, that kindness-affirming grip on Jason's hand—that didn't ease up one iota.

"So someone was giving the mobsters directions?" Rivers confirmed.

"Yeah. That's what Huntington and I figured." Jason gave half a laugh. "So now that I've involved my transport sergeant in something that may or may not end his career, he turns around and involves our sat-com guys. He gave me directions overland, and I'm talking *over* land. Around farms, around sandpits, through saguaro. We saw rattlesnakes. I shit you not. And those kids—man, they were troopers. We had the food George gave us and as much water and as many protein bars as we could carry. We slept during the day, because we found some shade and an irrigation ditch, and then walked again in the evening when it got cooler. We had to stop again in the dark of night—I was afraid of the rattlesnakes, of tripwires—there were some militia camps out there that were fucking armed that we had to skirt." He shuddered. "It was supposed to be a ten-mile walk, but we probably went twenty-five. Took us a full day."

"Where were you heading?" Henry asked, sounding enthralled.

Jason gave a laugh. "Remember that bus we were driving?"

"Johnson's Independent Church of the Christian Republic," Rivers recalled in horror.

"Yep." Jason gave a dry laugh and started coughing. To his surprise, Cotton spoke up for the first time.

"Lance, he's getting tired. We need to let him rest."

Jason finished coughing, looked across the bed, and realized that Cotton was the person holding his hand, and his eyes were fastened on Jason's face, not because of the story he was telling, but because he was worried for Jason's health.

He gave a distracted smile and tried to finish the story. "We had to wait until nightfall. The church was a lot busier than anybody thought, and most of the parishioners were, uhm—"

"Domestic terrorists?" Rivers supplied.

"Religious extremists?" Henry asked.

"White supremacists?" Lance asked.

"Carrying guns!" Jason half laughed, before coughing again. This time, Cotton stood up and used the touchless thermometer on his head like a pro.

"Lance, he's topping 102. I'll get him medicine, but this needs to end."

"Cotton, it's important," Henry said, and Jason heard a layer of gentleness in his voice.

But Cotton wasn't listening for gentleness. "I know it is!" he said, his voice pitching. "It's important and it's relevant, but Jason's sick. We've worked all this time to get him good enough to talk—was that bullshit? Do we just throw him away now?"

There was a stunned silence, but oddly enough, it was Rivers who spoke next. "No," he said gently. "But we need to know what he knows so we can keep him alive while he recovers. And you too, Cotton. I know it seems unfair to push him on this, but I promise you, we want everybody, including Colonel Constance, to be okay."

Jason was close enough to hear him swallow. "Okay," Cotton muttered. "Sorry."

"Don't be." Jason could see Jackson catch his angel's eye and smile winningly. "You're right, he needs an advocate right now. You're good at it. But let us finish up and we can get out of your way, all right?"

"Okay. Thanks, Jackson."

Cotton sat back down next to the bed, and over his head, Jason mouthed, "Thanks."

Of all things, Rivers winked.

"You keep sticking up for him—he needs it." Jackson turned his attention to Jason. "So you guys waited in the desert until the church emptied out, and then you hotwired that hideous monstrosity with all the bullet holes."

Jason gave a soundless laugh.

"Is that where you got the bruising on your face?"

Jason snorted. "Would you believe domestic terrorist religious extremists aren't excited when you try to steal their property?"

"I'm stunned," Rivers said, face deadpan. "Was he breathing when you left?"

Jason nodded. "But he probably had a nice sleep out there with the rattlesnakes. Anyway, the kids were starving by then. I pulled off at the first generic rest stop and had Sophie and Maxim go in and get about two hundred dollars in fast food. Shakes, cookies, fries—the works. And then two flats of water. God, those kids…." He shook his head. "All of them. So brave. But Sophie and her brother—we would have been lost without them."

Rivers responded, surprising him. "You should know that it was their brother's case that tipped us off that something was wrong. He got knocked on the back of the head and framed for murder, then put into gen pop at seventeen by a corrupt guard. Dietrich and Karina Schroeder managed to recruit half their family into this attempted takeover, and now they're in the wind with Dima Siderov."

"What about the other half of their family?" Jason asked, fairly alarmed.

"Well, a lot of them are dead or in prison," Rivers answered frankly. "And a lot of Siderov's operation was taken out in that massive traffic clusterfuck you got to witness. But that just makes those who are left more desperate. And their contact in the military is going to want you taken out in case you know something, because they'll be breathing down his neck."

"What are you going to do?" Jason asked, feeling that fever pounding his head and scorching over his skin now. "I don't want to put anybody in danger." He glanced at Cotton, who squeezed his hand in return.

"Burton's staking you out," Rivers told him. "You know that—and he brought friends. But beyond that, I think he's putting people on it in your unit. We know you can trust Anton Huntington. That's a start. He's got a couple of people on the inside who he's tapped too. I think as soon as you're well enough to move, we do it—"

"Not alone!" Cotton protested, and Rivers nodded slowly.

"Of course we'd move a nurse with him," he said, and Jason caught his dark look at Henry and Lance to make them not protest.

"I don't want anybody in danger," he repeated, and without thinking about it, squeezed Cotton's hand. "Angel," he mumbled. "Nobody can hurt you, okay?"

"I'll take care of you," Cotton told him. "Don't worry."

"He's not getting it." Jason's voice sounded petulant to his own ears, and he gave a hard shiver. "Make him get it."

"Oh no, brother," Rivers murmured. "It's you who's not getting it. Okay, Lance, you do your doctor thing. Cotton, you can stay in here with him now, but as soon as he's asleep, come get me."

"Okay, Jackson."

"Good. We need to talk."

And with that, Lance put his gloves on, working from the TV tray someone had moved in as his surgical table, and started to inject something—probably a febrifuge—into the IV still in Jason's arm. "Okay, Colonel," Lance said, no bullshit. "Time for some night-night juice and some rest."

"Protect him," Jason mumbled. "Make sure you protect my angel."

"I'm right here," Cotton said, still sitting on the floor by his side.

"Why is that?" Jason asked, rolling his head so he could look into Cotton's pretty eyes. "It's the most amazing thing."

And that was the last thing he remembered saying for a while.

ANGEL LESSONS

COTTON WAITED until Jason's breathing was even—or as even as it was going to get, now that the infection threatened to settle into his lungs—before he let go of his hand and stood. While Lance cleared the medical area, including giving everything a spritzing with disinfectant, Cotton started rummaging through his drawer for a shirt.

"That was embarrassing," he muttered. "I didn't expect everybody to come in and confab right after I got out of the shower."

Lance gave a gentle chuckle. "You managed pants. I think you can be forgiven, since we've sort of stolen your and Billy's room."

"It's nice of Billy to let me have the bed," Cotton told him, finding a clean white tee and slipping it over his head, where it stretched slightly over his chest. Some guys liked their T-shirts loose, but he was a fan of the subtle stretch. His build was wafer-thin as it was, and a little bit of negative ease between himself and the cotton made him look bigger.

"All of you—you in particular—have been doing your best to keep this guy alive over the last few days," Lance said, admiration thrumming through his voice. "I'm really proud of you guys."

"Kids," Cotton said. "He was protecting kids." He could imagine the school bus pulling up under the fluorescent lights of one of the rest stops on I-5, and two teenagers running out with cash or a card in their hands while Jason rested and bled in the driver's seat of the garishly painted vehicle. It was a needless move—probably cost them time, probably cost Jason Constance blood—but he'd done it so the kids who had walked miles in the desert and then sat under scavenged shade could eat.

Cotton's eyes burned and his heart squeezed in his chest thinking about it.

"I mean, don't we all wish someone had protected us when we'd been kids?"

Lance knew his story, so he was forgiven for the depthless compassion in his golden eyes. "Yeah, Cotton. We all do. You're right. He deserves someone on his side."

Cotton nodded and gave Jason one last, lingering look as he lay on the bed, the hospital sheets and blankets pulled up to his chin while he sweated out his fever and shivered underneath.

Someone strong, he thought. Jason Constance deserved somebody strong, who could fight for him. Because he'd fought so hard for others.

On that thought he walked to the tiny kitchen where Henry was shoving two ibuprofen at Jackson Rivers with a can of soda to go with them.

"And you've eaten?" Henry asked.

Rivers grimaced. "Henry—"

"Crackers," Henry muttered, going for one of the six boxes of saltines in the cupboard. "Look, your boyfriend has been texting me for the last half hour to make sure you're not overdoing it while he had to stay home. Shut up and—literally—take your medicine."

Rivers groaned. "Fine. You both suck." With that he grabbed the painkillers and the soda, washed one down with the other, and then held his hand out for the saltines. He shoved one in his mouth and sat down with the package. "This is wonderful and horrible by the way. Dr Pepper and saltines were what I lived on in school, but I thought I'd outgrown this meal by now."

"I'll get you a sandwich when I drop you off. I have to go in to the office."

"A case?" Rivers asked, perking up.

"For *Galen*," Henry specified. Rivers's boyfriend, Ellery, was a partner in a defense firm with Galen Henderson, John Carey's boyfriend. This made Cotton happy. For one thing, Galen and John were good for each other, and he didn't worry about John falling out of recovery with Galen in his corner. For another, Henry was pretty tough, and he could protect Galen and John if they needed it, like Jackson protected Ellery.

Cotton had grown very used to having people to care about in his life over the past couple of years. After those months on the street, feeling so alone, he was a little paranoid about making sure they weren't going to get hurt.

"Well, hell." Rivers munched on another saltine. "Just as well, I guess. Ellery needs to stay home."

Henry rolled his eyes. "So do you. Somebody wants to kill you."

Rivers met the news with raised eyebrows. "Is that you? Do *you* want to kill me, Henry?"

"Yes. Now hurry up and talk to Cotton so we can go."

Rivers gave Cotton a tired smile. "Sit down here, Cotton," he said. "Have a saltine."

Cotton pulled up one of the worn vinyl chairs that went with the cheap Formica table. Everything about the flophouse was temporary. He and Billy had hung posters on the walls of their room recently after a quiet conversation and a tacit agreement that they would probably be there longer than other people, because they didn't seem to have anywhere else to go.

Cotton's posters were getting tattered. He needed more sci-fi stuff. Tyler Hoechlin—be he werewolf or be he Superman, Cotton was still a fan.

In fact, funny that he thought about that, because Jason looked a lot like Tyler Hoechlin, only his face was a little narrower, and he probably shaved all the way clean when he wasn't at death's door.

He pulled his wandering thoughts back to Jackson Rivers, who was looking at him kindly. "Not a lot of sleep lately?"

Cotton yawned in response and then gave a laugh. "Yeah. I'm usually sort of the housekeeper/cook here since I'm not filming scenes right now. Last three days, I've been doing a lot of the nursing. Billy's sleeping on the air mattress so I can stay in there with Jason."

"Not filming scenes?" Jackson sounded only mildly curious, but Cotton saw him make eye contact with Henry and gave an exasperated snort.

"Did Henry tell you I had a breakdown? Because I did. Embarrassingly enough."

Jackson's gaze sharpened. "He told me you'd had enough," he said, voice firm. "That's nothing to be ashamed of."

Cotton blew a raspberry. Sure. Because Jackson Rivers just started crying for no reason at all and noped out of *his* job.

Jackson's bottle-green eyes never left his face. "A long time ago, I was working undercover. Did you know that?"

Cotton shook his head, *more* than mildly curious.

"When I was on the force—right after I'd joined. I reported my partner to IA because he was as dirty as fuck and I was still idealistic, and the DA made me wear a wire. For three months."

Cotton's mouth went dry. "Three months?"

"Every day. I developed an ulcer, lost about fifty pounds, and every day I would go home, take my weapon off, and very carefully lock it away in the gun safe so I didn't use it on myself. And then I'd cry. For hours. *Hours.* Because your body knows shit sometimes that your mind doesn't. My body knew that I was not going to survive much longer if I kept doing what I was doing."

"What happened?" Cotton asked, horrified.

"The DA was dirty too. He hired a hitman to take both of us out so he could take over my partner's operation. I spent a year in the hospital, and my partner died on-site."

Cotton sucked in a breath, but Jackson's quick, jerky nod silenced his pity.

"You need to hear this story for you, Cotton. Not for me. It's okay if your body told you—and told you hard—that it was time to stop. The fact that you listened to it is a good thing. It means you're smart, intuitive. It means you can protect yourself like you protected Jason in there when you knew he needed to quit. And that's why I wanted to talk to you, because I've got a big ask."

"What do you need?" Cotton couldn't say no to Jackson any more than he could say no to Henry or John. But Jackson was the first person to ask him to do anything that required responsibility, so he was definitely not going to fuck this up.

"I need you to make sure he's never left alone. Ever. And I need you to be no more than the weight room or the laundromat away. So if you need supplies, call up one of the other guys. Don't go yourself. And pack a go-bag."

Cotton stared at him, stunned, as Jackson pulled another cracker out and scowled at it.

"Eat," Henry prompted. "And then explain."

"I'm not sure when, but I do know that it's going to happen," Jackson said. "Burton is going to get a lead on the imminent threat to Jason's life, and he's either going to eliminate it for good or neutralize the threat and move Jason. If he moves Jason, I want Jason to have someone he can trust by his side. Lance can't go. Lance is going to earn himself a big fat investigation if he does any more here, and Henry and I refuse to let that happen. And you're the guy here Jason trusts the most… and the one most capable of taking care of him if he's still sick when he's got to leave. So pack a go-bag with a couple of changes of clothes, some cool-weather gear just in case, and a travel kit, yada yada yada. Like if you were going to the mountains for a few days, or the ocean. A go-bag. Pack one for Jason too. In fact…." He paused long enough to reach into his pocket, and he came out with a stack of bills. "You've got department stores across the street and some thrift stores too. Send the guys over there for some clothes for him, and some boots too, since the ones he wore in are still covered in blood. Same deal as for you. Some for cool weather, some for hot like it is outside. Toothbrush, travel kit—you get the idea. You understand?"

Cotton took the money in wonder. "So you're trusting me to just pack up and go with him? To be ready to be his… travel nurse?"

"Well, yeah," Jackson said, half on a laugh. "Is that a problem?"

And Cotton thought about Jason, sick and being transported some place to be all alone while there was a threat to his life out there in the world.

"No." He was actually the perfect candidate. *He* wasn't starting school. *He* didn't have a job outside or inside of porn. And nobody in the flophouse would miss him if he was gone. "I'd be happy to," he said.

"Jackson!" Henry protested. "You can't just kidnap him!"

Well, maybe Henry would miss him, like a little brother or something.

Jackson turned to Cotton. "It's not kidnapping," he said levelly. "It's accepting a mission. You up to do this, Cotton?"

Cotton bobbed his head up and down without hesitation. "Absolutely."

"Good." Jackson stood stiffly and handed what was left of the crackers back to Henry. "Let me know if you guys need more money. I'll have Henry stop by an ATM so I can pull out some more cash for you guys in general. You two are going to need resources, and cash is good because it can't be traced. Henry can show you how to hide it around your person so you never lose all of it. Deal?"

"Deal." Cotton stood and took Jackson's offered hand. "Thank you," he said, feeling foolish and needy. A mission? Possibly risky? Following a man he hardly knew into danger? Why sure! He'd be happy to! Didn't have anything else on his platter, right?

"For what?" Jackson said, rolling his eyes. "We're thanking you, right now, for being willing to do this. Let me know if you need anything, though, and see if you can't get those go-bags packed by tomorrow at the latest. I have no idea when Burton's going to decide to move him, but when it happens, it's going to be fast."

Cotton understood. "I'll be ready." But that didn't feel honest. "I mean, I'll *try* to be ready. I'm not really a… you know. Action hero or anything."

"Who is?" Jackson asked with a shrug that apparently pulled something he'd recently injured. He sort of hunched his back and muttered, "Ouch. More to the point, who wants to be? Jesus!"

"All right, boss, let me get you back home, okay?"

"Yeah. Fine. Whatever. I'll call Burton on the way and you can add your shitty two cents' worth."

"My opinion's worth a buck at least," Henry countered, opening the door so Jackson could lead the way out.

"Ha! You're still an intern. Fifty cents, maximum."

Cotton didn't hear what Henry said in return, but he didn't have to. Everybody at the flophouse had seen the two of them together, and some members had seen them in action as partners. As lovers, they'd rip each other to pieces, but as friends and investigative cohorts, they were pretty much perfect.

But Cotton had other things to worry about, and with a moment's hesitation, he texted Billy to see when he'd get home. Jackson had told him he needed to stay put, so he needed his own partner in crime.

"WHATCHA DOIN'?" Jason slurred. He still had a fever, but he was obviously waking up from his nap.

Cotton looked over from Billy's bed, where he was folding clothes and making sure the toiletry bags held all the essentials.

"Packing for us," he said.

Jason squinted. "You're bigger'n me."

Cotton laughed a little. "Possibly. That's why we've got two bags—my clothes and yours. You've got everyday muscles. I've got show-pony muscles." He sighed. "Which are going to melt away pretty soon, since I'm only working out enough to keep fit."

"You'll still be pretty." Jason's voice had taken on a dreamy tone, and Cotton set the last of the requirements of the two bags neatly on top and went to sit on the edge of Jason's bed so he could check his vitals. He sounded particularly out of it, and Cotton was worried.

"Yes," he said. "Always pretty. But am I useful? Am I wanted? Pretty fades." He'd meant it as sort of a joke, but he wasn't aware of how plaintive he'd sounded until he felt Jason's dry, hot hand on the inside of his wrist as he lifted the touchless thermometer.

"Pretty on the inside doesn't," Jason said, and Cotton's chest warmed even as he panicked. He wielded the thermometer, heart stuttering when he saw the spike go over 102.

"How do you know I'm pretty on the inside?" he said softly, putting the back of his hand on Jason's forehead. "I could be a real dick." Or a sex worker. Which was not something he'd ever been ashamed of before. He'd made his own damned living, hadn't he? But for some reason, when Jason Constance had called him an angel, he hadn't wanted to counter with "Sadly, no, but I am a whore."

"Because you're nice to me." Jason shivered, hard and uncomfortably. "And you touch me. I miss touch."

Cotton nodded. "Everyone deserves to be touched," he said softly. "By someone who matters."

"Who touches you, angel?" This man was feverish and exhausted; his eyes shouldn't have been so penetrating, boring straight down to Cotton's soul.

"Lots of men," he said with a grimace. "But nobody who's mattered." And that was the truth, both parts.

Jason's gaze grew sorrowful. "Poor angel."

Cotton captured his hand at his cheek. "Poor hero," he corrected. "And super sick hero to boot. I'm going to get you your medication, and maybe another sponge bath, but we need to get your fever down before you worry about touch, okay?"

Jason nodded, and his eyes closed like he couldn't keep them open.

"Dream about you, angel."

Cotton closed his eyes, thinking about the kind of man who would do what Jason Constance did for a living. He was a sin-eater, someone who cleaned up the sins of others, allowed the government to function without the onus of facing what they'd done. He'd gotten hurt trying to save a busload of children—but also trying to save his own government from committing one more sin.

That kind of man didn't need a nonfunctional porn star in his life.

"Dream about someone better," he murmured, but he wasn't sure if he was talking about Jason or himself.

TWO HOURS later, he was less worried about being good enough for Jason's dreams and more worried about Jason's body holding out long enough for him *to* dream.

The fever wasn't going down. He'd given all the medication Lance had left, but Jason's fever was still raging, and the wounds—particularly the one on his side—were swollen and red. He knew Lance was giving him antibiotics, but obviously he needed something stronger.

He texted Henry, because they were all trying not to get Lance in trouble, and Henry was worried enough to leave work to stop by, Jackson at his heels.

Jackson had taken one look at the wounds and scowled.

"Okay, we need to clean these some more, and it's going to hurt. Henry, go to the store across the street and fetch some more hydrogen peroxide and some of those scrub brushes that people use on their nails. Cotton, start a pot of water boiling so we can sterilize them. Lance left his scalpel, so as soon as Henry gets back, I'm going to lance the infection here and let it drain. It's going to be super gross, but it might let his body fight the infection if it's not all clotted up in there."

"Is that real medicine or hoping for the best?" Cotton asked, not sure himself.

"Little of both," Jackson told him frankly. "But if it makes you feel better, Lance was the one who said the wound might have to be punctured. He also said that you can give him the extra dose of painkiller and antibiotics ahead of time. Lance is bringing home the super powerful antibiotics to take their place but we need to tend to him first."

Cotton nodded, thinking he was glad—so glad—he wasn't going to be the one who had to scrub at Jason's infected flesh and poke a hole in him when he already felt like crap. He just had to run around and keep the supplies stocked and get rid of the trash. He was good at all of that other stuff, but inflicting pain he wasn't sure he could do.

They ran around: Henry to go get supplies, Cotton to prep to make sure they had a sterile tray—one of their large dinner plates that they'd passed through the dishwasher recently—with a sterilized scalpel, some clamps, some gauze fresh out of the package for wiping the wound down, and a pad and tape to bind it. When Henry got there, they boiled the scrub brush for two minutes before Jackson had everyone put on a fresh set of gloves and they got down to business.

Henry picked cleanup duty, and they both told Cotton that his job was to hold Jason's hand and keep him calm.

"Is that really a job?" he asked, feeling stupid and useless.

"Since we don't have any anesthetic, it's the most important fucking job we've got," Jackson said, voice low and terse with urgency. "He's going to try to move, and you calm him down. Tell him what we're doing so he doesn't have to concentrate on anything besides keeping still."

"We do have some of that lidocaine that Henry made us buy," Cotton said. "The kind in the aloe gel. Would that help?"

Jackson blinked. "Henry, go get that shit." He looked at Cotton. "Absolutely," he said. "If nothing else, it will make *me* feel better because we're not simply attacking him in the sore side without a barrier."

"Goddammit," Henry muttered. "I'm going to have to glove up again."

"Since you are," Jackson told him, "maybe push the bed out a little from the wall. I can barely fit in here."

Cotton gave a little laugh. "You weren't supposed to, Jackson. The bed's supposed to be flush. You sort of bulldozed your way in there."

Jackson gave him a tense smile. "Having a scrawny ass has its uses."

A few minutes later they were situated again, but this time Jason's wounds had been thoroughly numbed and cleaned. Jason only mumbled a little as Jackson had attacked them with a scrub brush and hydrogen peroxide, opening his eyes to a slit.

"Angel, they're hurting me."

"Baby, they have to. Your hurts are making you sick."

"Okay. Okay. Do what you gotta."

Cotton gripped his hand, the one with the IV tube, and smoothed a cool cloth over his forehead. "God, Jackson, I think he's getting hotter."

"Well then, it's time for the big guns." Jackson made a sound in his throat that was suspiciously like gagging, but it was over so quickly Cotton thought he must have imagined it. "Henry, I'm going to go through a whole lot of gauze here. Be ready to get it off the bed and away."

Jason let out a low moan as Jackson lanced the wound on his shoulder, and everybody buried their faces in their shoulders as the smell of infection filled the room.

"Well, that's pleasant," Jackson muttered. Cotton could see him busy with the gauze, and Henry was picking up as fast as he could. In a few moments, the welling pus was cleared, and they moved on to the next one.

This time Jason bucked and cried out, and Cotton held his hand tightly and murmured, "Hang on, baby. They're almost done."

This time the smell was so bad Henry had to run out of the room to be sick.

But not Jackson, and not Cotton. Jackson kept cleaning, irrigating, and cleaning some more, and Cotton held Jason's hand and cried, telling him everything would be okay, it had to be okay, because they were working so hard to save him, and what kind of angel would Cotton be if they let him slip away now.

AN HOUR later, Jackson, Henry, and Cotton all sagged, exhausted and sweat drenched, around the kitchen table.

"The smell is still out here," Henry mumbled, and Cotton brightened.

"Hey, we've got an oil infuser!" He remembered this from one of the guys; there'd been so many. "I think this was Bobby's. He left behind a lot of his stuff. Anyway, it's in the closet, and there's some lavender and eucalyptus oil there, and...."

He had the thing plugged in and sitting on the kitchen counter, where the coffee maker usually went, and as Henry and Jackson both took deep breaths of air that *didn't* smell positively vomitous, Jackson smiled tiredly at him.

"You," he said distinctly, "are absolutely awesome to have around. This was genius."

Cotton gave a faint smile. "Yeah, but you lanced the wound."

Jackson shuddered. "God, I hate hospitals. I mean, it's a phobia. After that, I'm going to start having nightmares about your apartment too. Sorry. That's not fair, but I'm saying."

Henry grunted. "That sucked. Cotton, you get points for staying in the room."

At that moment, Lance walked in, and the smell of humid August night air was almost as sweet and fresh as the infuser.

"Oh God," Lance muttered. "Shit, guys, I'm going to jump in the shower so I don't share any of my super-grade hospital bugs with the guy in there, and then I'll have a look. I know this smell. Fuck. How's he doing?"

"Better," Jackson said, looking around the table and getting a consensus. "His fever dropped to 100 again, and he's got some color back in his face. We cleaned and squished saline in his wounds, like you told Henry, but yeah. He's going to need you."

"I'll shower after Lance," Cotton said. He looked around. "Where is everybody? The place should be bustling about now."

"Our apartment," Henry told him. "I texted everybody and told them to go there instead. Once we can open some windows and air this place out a little, everyone will come back." He sighed. "But we might let Billy sleep in our guest room tonight. Poor guy—the inflatable is hell on his back."

Jackson grimaced. "You have a guest room? That's almost human of you."

"I know," Henry said with a snort. "I was prepared to let it be vacant with a few boxes, but suddenly it's vacuumed and there's a bed and a nightstand and a lamp. It's fucking scary."

Cotton smiled, because he was in on this joke. "Henry did it," he said gleefully. "Don't let him fool you that it was Lance. He put in a queen-sized bed for overflow, in case it was needed."

Jackson quirked an eyebrow. "Well done, grasshopper. Next step, personal hygiene."

"Fuck you," Henry muttered, obviously embarrassed. He stood. "I'm going to go check on everyone and shower downstairs. See you at the office tomorrow?"

Jackson shrugged. "We were going to get K-ski from the hospital first."

"I might stop by," Henry said. He gave a dirty chuckle. "Giving him shit could be the treatment he never knew he needed."

He left, leaving Cotton to ask, "Who?"

"A friend of ours," Jackson told him, looking tired. "A lot of people got hurt last week."

Cotton sighed. "I'm so very, very useless."

"Stop it," Jackson snarled, so angry Cotton jumped. "Henry and I wouldn't have had you in that room if we hadn't needed a steady hand. Cotton, I know you're at a loss right now, but don't go there with those thoughts. You're amazing. And maybe you're feeling like you're going to be still a kid forever, or fragile and hurt forever, but trust me, anyone who can come out of that room and say, 'Hey, how about lavender?' is a person we need in this world. You will find a place in it. Have some faith."

Cotton nodded, warmed but also near tears and not trusting his words at the moment. He wanted to go back to Jason, who thought he was an angel. For some reason, that made him feel better, and he wasn't sure why. It wasn't something he could live up to, was it?

STILL, WHEN Lance was done with the shower, Cotton took over, pleased to sluice the sweat and care of the evening off his skin. He dressed in basketball shorts and a tank top and went in to where Lance was finishing up.

"Is he okay?" Cotton threw his dirty clothes in his personal basket and thought achingly about all the laundry he had to do tomorrow.

"For the moment," Lance murmured. He looked at the clothes and said, "I'll have one of the guys come in and make a trip to the laundromat tonight. They want to help too."

Cotton's eyes burned, and he realized he was exhausted. "That would be *awesome*," he said fervently. "I'm beat!"

"Yeah, well, what you guys were doing tonight was hard." Lance carefully taped a new bandage over the wound on Jason's shoulder. "I sedated him so he can sleep and maybe help fight the infection, and reirrigated both wounds. I think they should heal now, but God. That was bad. He might have gone into sepsis if you'd waited for me to get home." He let out a breath. "I know we all trust Henry and Jackson, but I swear, I have to keep reminding myself of what could happen if we admitted him to the hospital."

"They wouldn't take care of him like we do," Cotton mumbled, pulling back the sheets on Billy's bed and climbing in. He hadn't eaten, but then, going hungry was sort of par for the course when you were modeling, and he wasn't particularly excited about food yet anyway.

Lance *hmm*d and tore off his gloves before pulling the blankets up to Jason's chin and double-checking the IV levels. They kept "banana bags" in an ice chest next to the bed because Lance insisted keeping Jason hydrated—and having a medium to inject the antibiotics and painkillers into—was essential.

When he was done there, he walked over to where Cotton was stretched on his side and pulled the sheet up to his chin just like he had for Jason before giving a gentle kiss to his forehead. "Don't get too attached, okay?"

"He calls me his angel," Cotton protested.

"Well, you are. But, Cotton, he's not like anyone you've ever met before."

Cotton knew this translated into "He doesn't know you were in porn" but decided not to buy in to that. "Sure he is. He's like Henry and Jackson. But, you know, he hasn't had a life in years."

Lance straightened. "He said that?"

"Yeah. Said he hadn't had a pretty boy in his bed in ten years, and now he was soiling the sheets."

Lance's snort of laughter reassured Cotton no end. "Well, at least we know all the gay guys in the flophouse won't weird him out."

"I thought that too," Cotton murmured, his eyes closing.

"Get some rest, baby. I'll have Curtis check his vitals in an hour and Randy do the laundry. If Vinnie does his vitals at midnight, you should be able to sleep for a good five hours, and you need it."

"Okay. Thanks, Lance."

"For what?"

"Trying to protect me. It's nice."

"Wasn't done enough," he said. "Night." He turned out the lamp by Cotton's bed and the overhead light, leaving only the reading lamp by Jason's bed on but directed at the wall so Jason could get some sleep too.

"Night, Lance," Cotton mumbled. "Night, Jason."

"Night, angel," Jason murmured. "Sleep tight."

Cotton smiled, one of those secret smiles to himself that felt like hugs. "You too."

PROGRESS INTERRUPTED

"NO OFFENSE," Jason said, looking unhappily at the young man at his elbow, "but I would really rather try this without you."

Randy, the enormously tall, gawky, red-headed teenager who had been on "duty" that morning, gave him a sympathetic grin. "Look, dude, I know you don't want anybody watching you wee. I get it. But if you fall down in the bathroom, that's bad mojo. You're swimming around in your own piss on the tile. Don't do it. Bad luck. So you need a bathroom buddy, okay? Lance made us promise."

Oh Lord. This kid had a heart of gold, but he had size fifteen feet, and if they didn't end up in his mouth at least three times a sentence, the kid was going nowhere.

"I swear I can go piss by myself," he said, hoping his age and occupation would give him some oomph with this kid.

Unfortunately, age and occupation didn't seem to be the currency of the realm.

"Dude, I know you think you can, but Lance and Henry made me promise. Cotton's in the weight room, and dude, he really needed the break, you feel me? Billy moved in to some other dude's place because he needs nursing, and now I guess that's what we do, right? And Vinnie and Curtis are both at their wait-jobs. You got me until Cotton gets back. You really gonna risk a burst bladder or something 'cause you got pee-shy?"

Jason resisted the urge to groan and bury his face in his hands. "I've spent the last fourteen years of my life in a military barracks, dammit. I do *not* get pee-shy!"

Randy rolled his eyes. "So! Every dude in this apartment has seen every other dude naked at some point in time, and if you think we leave the door open when we crap, you're way wrong."

Jason gaped at him. "There's an image."

"I'm just saying. You don't need to be worried around us, 'cause we've seen it all. I mean, unless you got some weirdo hook, or—oh, hey! Are you diphallic? 'Cause that would be *awesome*! I would totally do you if you were diphallic. Hell, I'd ride you twice!"

"Don't worry about the bathroom anymore, Randy," Jason said in horror. "I think the pee has crawled back up."

Randy gave him an openmouthed grin. "It can do that? But maybe I help you into the bathroom, you sit down and contemplate Dog or your navel or something, and I go put the teakettle on. Lance said we gotta keep you hydrated, and he left this good tea shit for you, so, you know, if you go to the bathroom, you'll get tea."

Jason was abruptly tired. "Sure," he said. "Help me to the john, and you can go make tea. Makes total sense."

Randy nodded. "Henry's always telling me to use that. You know, the commonsense thing. Anyway, don't worry. I'll wash my hands after I sit you on the pot."

"Good to know," Jason muttered, and he found himself manhandled to the small bathroom in the apartment shared by more young men than he could keep track of and sat naked on the toilet, his newly acquired boxers around his ankles.

Randy washed his hands, using lots of soap, then told him to take his time, he'd be back in a few, before disappearing.

Not for the first time, Jason wondered where in the fuck he'd ended up.

As a young man growing up in Seattle, he'd had fantasies about a place like this. Nothing but young, hot gay men for as far as the eye could see. They ran around in their boxer shorts and had amazingly muscled bodies and wanted nothing more than to manhandle his body—scrawny and developing back then—and to see to his every need.

As an adult with nearly ten years of celibacy behind him, someone who had been in the world's most violent places and seen some truly awful things one human could do to another, landing in his teenaged fantasy felt a bit like a cosmic joke.

It wasn't that the young men were all too young for him—although they were. The closest one in age that he could see was Lance, but Lance and Henry were very much together, and that wasn't a viable option anyway. Lance was opinionated and liked giving orders, and that was so much like Jason that he figured they'd kill each other.

But more than the age thing—or the opinionated thing—there was the fact that they weren't too young for him, he was too *old* for them. Randy's goofy joy, Vinnie's sweet willingness to please, Curtis's crisp competence and surprising bursts of humor—they were all the traits of young men who were fully prepared to go out and see what the world had to offer.

Jason had already seen that; it wasn't pretty. He needed a companion who seemed to understand that the world was a hard place and that the safety another person could give you—to lick your wounds, to find tenderness in a hard desert land—was sometimes the most wonder you could hope for. Someone who would understand that Jason did awful, painful things, and he couldn't always save the day, and who could hold him when there was nothing else he could do to fix a broken world.

Which brought him to Cotton.

Cotton was every bit as terrifyingly young as the rest of the house, but there was an age to Cotton, a depth in his eyes. Whatever had happened to Cotton in his young life, he had the markings of a very old soul.

The other men in the apartment were amazingly kind to Cotton, as though he were fragile or somehow damaged and needed to be treated gently, and Jason was curious.

Given that Cotton had stayed steadfastly by his side through some of the worst moments of this last week in recovery, and had obviously been getting his medical training on the fly, Jason thought he might be one of the strongest people he'd met during his career in the military.

But still—that haunted look in his eyes.

Jason wanted to make that better.

Which was stupid, because Jason was the last person in any world who could make *anything* better.

Besides, he thought uncomfortably, all of these young men seemed to be exceptionally… well, sexually savvy. They were unashamed in their bodies, and it wasn't that Jason hadn't spent his time in frickin' communal showers or close proximity to other men in the past fourteen years, but this was different. In those situations, he had needed to school himself constantly that sex, touching, sensuality, was a thing to be stomped on, squashed, hidden, because the alternative was a whole lot more painful than being horny.

With the exception of a few gloriously hedonistic years in college, sex had been very much off the table.

Not so in his living situation at present.

Sex was very much *on* the table here. It was joked about, it was referenced, it presented the subtext for all everyday activity. Lance and Henry had their own apartment together so *they could have sex*. The young men were constantly preparing for dates in which *they would have sex*. There was talk of modeling, and while they were all beautiful, and he had no doubt they could wear clothes, shoes, or hair products with panache, he got more of a feeling from the guys that modeling was *all about sex*.

Sex wasn't merely on the table here, it was being served up for an appetizer, tossed as a salad, carved up for dinner, and offered as dessert, and the fact that Jason hadn't so much as had a taste of this particular meal made him *very* self-conscious.

And, yes, it made him extremely loath to sit on the commode with Randy watching to make sure he could wipe himself.

He sighed and sagged a little onto the toilet and realized, with surprise and gratitude, that he actually had to go.

Would wonders never fucking cease.

He finished and had managed to stand up and wash when a tentative knock sounded at the door.

"Jason? Are you done?"

His knees went a little weak. "Yeah, Cotton. I'm sorry. Lost in thought."

"No worries. Just wanted to shower. Here, if you're washed up, I'll help you back to the bed, if you don't mind my gym-stink."

Jason opened the door for him and Cotton stood there, flushed and sweaty as promised, dark hair slicked back behind his ears, his perfectly muscled, slender body looking profoundly defined.

God, oh God. He was so pretty. And suddenly Jason wanted a seven-course meal of sex with sex wine thrown in, as long as it was Cotton in the bottle.

He allowed Cotton to take his arm, irritated and frustrated that he needed the support, and tried to think of something to say.

"So, uhm, Randy said that Billy is staying somewhere else?" God, he was nervous—like a school kid, if truth be known. Life was so unfair. What was the use of being thirty-six years old if he couldn't at least pretend to some maturity?

"Yeah." Cotton gave a bit of a laugh. "I guess last week was a big one for people getting hurt. Another friend of Jackson's got out of the hospital a few days ago, I guess, and he's going to need some help. Billy signed on because the inflatable mattress was killing his back."

Jason smiled a little, relieved when they rounded the corner and he could sink onto his mattress. "You guys seem pretty on board to help. That's sweet of you."

Cotton shrugged. "Some of us are just happy to have a place to stay and people who will miss us."

Jason blinked at him, his curiosity a living thing. "Why... how did everybody come to be living here? And where is here, anyway?"

Cotton glanced away, avoiding Jason's eyes while he went rooting through the big dresser that sat between the two twin beds. "We all model at the same place. Somebody—I mean, we think we know who, but nobody's said anything to him—somebody leased this apartment about five years ago, and it's been sort of a revolving flophouse for guys who need a place to stay since. If someone shows up needing an apartment, sometimes for a night, sometimes for years, John or Dex sends them here, and we figure out rent and food and bills every month. It's very...." He squeezed his eyes shut like he was searching for something inside his brain. "Communal," he said, popping them open. "It's very communal."

Jason blinked, frowning a little. "That's... that's sort of odd. Wonderful, I guess, but...." Cotton was still not looking at him, but he had rounded up a clean set of clothes, which he rested on top of the dresser. Maybe it was that those fathomless old/sad eyes weren't on him anymore, but he suddenly thought of a question. "Who do you all model for, anyway?"

Cotton sucked air through his teeth. "Uhm... nobody told you?"

Jason yawned and stood to pull the covers back on the bed. "No, but—"

"Here, let me do that." Cotton helped him into bed, shucking the covers and helping him lie down, and he cursed the fact that he was too weak to so much as go to the bathroom himself without needing a nap.

After a moment of shuffling and pillow plumping and pulling the covers up to Jason's chin, Cotton stepped back and grabbed his clothes.

"Cotton," Jason said softly, "I didn't know it was a sensitive question. I'm sorry. Is there a mystery there or—"

Cotton blew out a breath and turned to face him, his eyes shiny and bright. "Porn models, Jason. We're all—or some of us *were*—pornography models for Johnnies. That's who we think leased the apartment: John Carey, the owner. Because he didn't want his models out in the rain or living homeless." He sighed and looked away. "It's why we're all so eager to help, you know? Because John gave us a break when we needed it, and we want to give back."

And with that, Cotton fled the room—even Jason could see it was a retreat—leaving Jason only a little surprised but very confused.

WHEN COTTON returned, freshly showered and smelling so good, he had a tea tray with him.

"I guess Randy started the pot and then weenied out because he didn't understand any teabagging that didn't come with a testicle."

Jason snorted. "Oh my God!"

"Sorry," Cotton mumbled, sounding embarrassed.

"Don't be! You guys have been so much fun to listen to over the last couple of days, but I couldn't figure out why every reference was sex. Now I know."

Cotton gave him a sideways look. "You don't really think that."

"Think what?" He was so tired, but he didn't want things like this between them. Cotton was the one person he felt comfortable with here, in this place where everybody was young and happy and well-laid. So, well, yeah—his magic fantasy flophouse was *exactly* the flophouse of his dreams, including the oozing sexuality that practically permeated the place, but that wasn't Cotton's fault.

He had no claims on Cotton, on his person or his body. He was just lucky the kid—or kids, really—had such a developed sense of service, of kindness.

"That it's no big deal. I mean… everybody judges."

Did they?

"I…." Jason gave a helpless little laugh. "Maybe they do. I know I'm in no position to judge. When I was in college, this place would have been my holy grail, right? No mountain too high, no valley too far to land in the magic place of porn models wandering around in their boxers."

Cotton smiled slightly as he made busy with the TV tray and the tea. "That would make a shitty song."

"But a true one," Jason told him, making his voice as wise as he could. "It would be the height of hypocrisy if the porn palace of my dreams as a kid is a place of moral turpitude now, you know?"

"Here, let me help you sit up." His hands were, as always, professional and efficient as he plumped some extra pillows behind Jason's back and set a tray up over his lap, but that didn't stop Jason from enjoying their touch.

"Thank you," Jason murmured, and he took the mug of tea gratefully. "I miss coffee, but this tastes like vitamin C and grandma, and, you know, when you can barely walk to the john, that's appreciated."

"Well, it's rosehip tea with chamomile. It's supposed to be good healing mojo. I guess Galen sent it over."

Jason closed his eyes and tried to remember who was who. "Wait— Galen is… Henry's boss."

"Yes," Cotton told him, smiling approvingly. "And John's boyfriend."

"Wait—John is *your* boss?" Jason asked, and against all the nice stuff he'd spouted, he felt a burst of anger for the porn mogul who made his living from exploiting young guys on camera.

"Yeah. He's a good guy." Cotton gave him a benign smile, and Jason tried to keep that unexpected shaft of fury to himself.

"What makes him good?"

"Well," Cotton said, taking his usual seat on the bed across from Jason's. "He set up the flophouse, we're pretty sure, and he gives us health and dental, including mental health, which he doesn't have to do. I mean, technically, we're contracted labor, and even more technically, we're not really legal in California. But he runs the place like a business, and he treats his employees really good. Rehab's in the contract, and there's a flat fee for filming a scene and residuals for how many hits it gets on the website. We have the option of leasing the facilities, which are all set up for cameras and internet, if we want to do the webcam business, and he hosts us on his site and promotes us at a very reasonable fee. He sets up promotional events where we can go sign posters and host clubs in the area. Not every guy wants to do that, but some of them really enjoy the attention." He sighed, and Jason realized he'd been holding something back.

"And what else?" he asked gently.

"And once, about three years ago, when I was living on the streets and he was struggling with addiction, I offered a friend of his a blowjob for twenty dollars, and after Reg said no, he literally drove me to John's house and said, 'This kid needs your help.' And then John drove me here and paid my rent and threw in for food and made sure the other guys took care of me and took me to the doctors and the dentists and made sure I was healthy. And when I asked if I could film scenes and earn my keep, he said no."

Jason's heart did a stupid little dance. "So you didn't film scenes?"

Cotton shook his head. "Eventually yes. I did. Because he was being really nice, but I can pay my own way." He sighed. "I mean, I thought I could."

Jason fought against the stupid disappointment. Oh. Jason had answered the question of what kind of hypocrite *he* was, hadn't he?

"You thought you could?" he asked, not understanding.

Cotton shrugged, and in the silence that followed, Jason could hear the sadness in him like the tolling of a bell. "I... I couldn't. I mean, I walked in to film a scene almost three months ago, and I'd... I mean, two months earlier, Henry and Lance sort of convinced me to stop dating. They said I kept hoping for some guy to rescue me, but that wasn't a reason to sleep with someone. And they were right. And I felt better. Like, I wasn't dragging around this constant disappointment in life, you know? Because the guys I'd fallen hopelessly in love with had ghosted me after sleeping with me once."

"Ouch," Jason murmured, chest aching. Nobody deserved that.

"So there I was, thinking, 'Hey, I've got this maturity thing licked!' and I walked in to film the scene and… and the guy waiting in the room looked… well, he looked like a bad memory. And I don't want to talk about it, but it wasn't the guy's fault. He just looked like someone I didn't want to remember, from when I was on the streets. And suddenly… I just couldn't. I started crying, and I couldn't stop. And John…." Jason heard the throb in his voice, and realized that the sadness he'd sensed inside was welling its way out. "John said that was okay. He told me to stay here, that he'd make sure I always had a place to sleep, but I needed to find something else to do with my life, because my time working at Johnnies was over."

Jason let out a sigh. Well, there went his fantasy of beating the shit out of the big exploitive porn mogul. Apparently the heart-of-gold thing ran fast and deep and all the way to the top.

"What have you decided to do?" he asked instead, hoping to pull Cotton out of the memory that was threatening to drown him.

"I have no idea," Cotton said with a sigh. He looked across the bed and gave Jason a weak smile. "I mean, taking care of you has been fun, but I have the feeling that as soon as you're on your feet again, you're going to dust the place and I'll be waving at you through your rearview mirror."

Jason stared at him unhappily. "Only because knowing me is dangerous," he said, his voice raspy. "Sometimes when I'm falling asleep here, I have to remind myself that I can't stay. I've got too many things to take care of. Too much shit to sort. That doesn't mean it's not fun to pretend this is my college fantasy come to life." He gave a half laugh. "Of course, it figures that I'm too sick to do anything about all the half-naked men running around. Just my luck."

Cotton gave him a better smile this time. "You say that, but I have the feeling you're probably too much of a gentleman to simply yell 'Air raid!' and jump on someone's ass with your dick out."

Jason spit tea and then snorted it up his nose. Cotton had to come help him with the tray and a napkin, and by the time he was done giggling, he fell back against the pillows weakly, completely worn out. Cotton made busy with the TV tray and the cup, and Jason put out a weak hand to stop him.

"What?"

"Could you… I mean, I'm going to be asleep anyway. But could you sit with me for a minute?" Because suddenly he *just couldn't*. He remembered Cotton using those words, and they came back to haunt him now.

"You want me to sit with you?"

His eyes were closed now, and he couldn't find any other way to ask. But he managed to free his hand from under the covers and hold it out, waiting until Cotton's weight depressed the side of the bed, and Cotton's grip—warm and a little moist, probably from when he was flushed and tearful—found his own.

"Yeah," he mumbled. "Thank you. Stay for a minute. Stay."

"Sure."

Sleep crept up on him with the stealth of a sunset, but Cotton's hand in his kept the chill away. He felt a soft kiss on his temple, and he didn't worry about why this beautiful, battered angel would kiss him, or if it was right or wrong. He only smiled a little and allowed the tide of sleep to pull him under.

WELL, THAT WAS UNEXPECTED....

COTTON YAWNED and wandered around the tiny kitchen. What was he doing again?

Oh. Yeah. Shit. Coffee. Cream. Ice.

Blargh.

It was after one in the afternoon, and he could barely get his shit together. Finally—*finally*—Jason had managed six hours with only a low-grade fever. His bandages had looked cleanly bloody and not infected, and the tension level around the apartment had gone from Defcon 5 to Defcon 1.

And to celebrate all of that good healing, Cotton had gotten to sleep for a whole six hours, and his body couldn't seem to handle all that good rest, because even though he'd woken up at eight, worked out, and showered, he was still operating at diminished capacity.

God, he could sleep for a week.

As he bumbled around the kitchen and tried to figure out how to deal with the reusable K-Cup pod so they didn't go through all the plastic in the world, he thought about the strange dissociative feeling of exhaustion that was swamping him.

It seemed to have something to do with relief.

It was like he'd been so worried, so amped with anxiety for Jason's well-being, that once some of the danger had passed, it was like he'd been the sick one, and he needed to catch up.

His musing was cut short when he hit the coffee cup against the sink with a clatter and swore, checking for cracks and working fiercely to *wake up.*

"Dammit," he muttered. This coffee cup—unlike the motley assortment of plates and silverware that sort of lived in the apartment—was actually *Cotton's.* It had been a Christmas present from Dex, who tried to give all the Johnnies guys Christmas presents, particularly if they weren't part of their families anymore.

The year he'd given Cotton this cup, it had been the only gift Cotton had received.

And—oh shit.

"God*dammit*!" There was a crack, down the side of the cup. Even as he examined it, the cup separated from the handle and crashed to the counter, where it gave up the ghost and disintegrated into eleventeen pieces, and he felt stupid, tired tears burn in his eyes.

"Cotton?"

Cotton looked up from his contemplation of the shattered coffee cup to see Jason stumble into the kitchen, in his boxer shorts and looking out of it.

"Hey," he mumbled, frowning. "What are you doing out of bed?"

"I heard a ruckus," Jason told him. "What happened?"

"I broke a cup." He shrugged, feeling stupid. "It was a gift from a friend, and I'm crazy tired, and never mind. Let me clean it up, and it'll be—"

"Hey," Jason murmured, his hand on Cotton's bicep comforting even if it was too warm. "What's wrong?"

Cotton tried to shake it off—the hand, the comfort, everything—but Jason was standing so close. He'd had his own shower the night before, and he smelled good. Sleepy warm man and somebody's expensive soap. Probably Curtis's, he thought in distraction. Curtis had good taste in smells.

"It's nothing," he said weakly. "I'm tired, and stupid things are getting to me...." His voice warbled, and he hated himself. "I swear, I'm not fragile!"

And there you go. The adolescent pitch that screamed, "I am *so delicate right now.*"

And then Jason did something unforgivable. He wrapped his arms around Cotton and hugged him. "No, no. You're not fragile," he murmured. "But you've had a rough week. I mean, I've had a rough week, but I've been unconscious for a lot of it. You've had a rough week, and you've been conscious for both of us."

Cotton gave half a laugh against his bare neck. Oh, this wasn't fair. He was in basketball shorts and a tank in deference to the late August heat, and Jason was *in his boxers*, and here he was, being held by the most interesting, most *desirable* man he'd possibly met in his entire life, and he was pretty sure sex was off-limits.

Wait. Sex *was* off-limits.

Jason was recovering, and Cotton was his caregiver, and that wasn't consensual, was it? This was pure comfort.

And with that tiny change of perspective, Cotton relaxed into the hug, letting the warmth, the kindness, and even the emotional strength seep into his body, making him relaxed and comforted as he'd never been by a sex partner.

He was safe here. He was *safe* here. He hadn't been safe since he was seventeen, and he was *safe* here, in Jason Constance's arms.

"You doing better?" Jason asked, voice gravelly.

"Yeah." Wow. Cotton wasn't short—five-ten, so not super tall, but not tiny. And he wasn't decked. Muscular, but his build was slender, so keeping bulk was almost impossible. But even sick, even thin, Jason was taller than he was, and his arms were longer and more powerful. This was a body that wouldn't let him down, Cotton thought muzzily, and while this moment, this hug, wasn't meant to be sexual, Cotton felt a tiny spark of awareness travel under his skin that told him someday, when Jason was at 100 percent and Cotton wasn't a bumbling mess, it could be.

"Thanks," Cotton mumbled, and he felt a little bit of heaviness in Jason's limbs that said he probably needed to be the one leaning against the counter. "Here." With a smile, he turned them and backed away, and Jason grimaced, embarrassed.

"Hey, I actually made it to the john myself today. Twice!"

"Well done," Cotton told him, laughing. Very carefully he stepped back and started picking up pieces of the mug from the sink.

"So who gave it to you?" Jason asked. "You said it was a gift."

It had been the dumbest thing—a unicorn on a yellow mug that said Back Off, Sugar-tits, I'm a Force of Nature! But....

"Dex. He's John's second-in-command. He... well, he tries to make sure everybody gets presents at Christmas. It's... a lot of us don't have families anymore, so it's sort of his thing. He sends out birthday cards and gives Christmas presents. It's like John does the dad things—food, shelter, health and dental, and Dex does the... you know."

"Mom things," Jason said, nodding. "Gotcha. So what do you mean no fami—what's that?"

Cotton heard it then. Shouting from the lawn down at the bottom of the stairs from their apartment and then pounding up the stairs and the unmistakable sounds of violence.

Oh God. Trouble was echoing up the stairway, banging on the metal rail, and he was barely dressed and Jason was *right there* in its way.

With a desperate lunge he threw himself at the knife block and pulled the chef's knife out exactly when the door splintered open and a pale pink fireplug charged into the room.

White, squat, all malevolent muscle, the bald man in the dark suit paused for a moment, panting, while Cotton stood in front of Jason and raised the chef's knife, wishing that just once in his entire life he'd ever held a weapon.

Their assailant glanced around the room. His gaze zeroed in on Cotton, and he raised his arm, an ugly-looking gun in his grip.

There was more pounding on the stairs, and a knife—smaller and deadlier and shaped more like an arrow—flew through the doorway and embedded itself in the killer's gun arm. His weapon-hand fell, and the assailant grunted, scowled at whoever was in the doorway, and switched the gun into his other hand.

Cotton stared at the chef's knife, and without knowing what he was going to do next, he pulled his arm back to throw it.

It bounced off the attacker's nose, leaving a long slash of blood and possibly hitting his eye. The man swore in a language Cotton didn't know, and he was repositioning the gun again when three shots echoed in the stairwell. The first hit him in the arm, and as he was turning to face the new threat, the next two hit him in the chest. He toppled over backward, colorless eyes staring up, mouth open as his last breath failed to come.

"Oh fuck," Cotton breathed, staring at the dead man. "Fuck. Jason. Jason, there's a *dead man on our carpet*!"

"Jason?"

Cotton looked up to the doorway, where a soldier stood. He walked to the dead guy and kicked the gun out of his reach before holstering his own weapon and glancing around the apartment.

"Jason?"

Cotton felt two hands on his shoulders, gentle and firm, pushing him to the side. "Lee?"

The soldier—handsome, round-faced, and square-jawed, with skin a dark-walnut color, and brown eyes that were soft in color but hard in expression—gave a tight smile in relief.

"Sir! Damn. That asshole broke ranks and charged the steps. I swear we didn't see where he was coming from."

Jason nodded and glanced around the apartment. "Well, props for being prepared," he said, shaking his head. "He would have had us. Thanks, Burton."

"Thank Ernie," Burton said. "But thank him later, after we get you somewhere safe. We've got to bug out, sir—"

"I'm coming with him," Cotton said, surprised he could even find his voice.

Burton looked at him in surprise. "You're what?"

"He's barely okay. I've been nursing him for a week. He's not going anywhere without somebody who knows what antibiotics he's taking and what painkillers he can have. He's not all right yet. You can't simply take him somewhere and expect him to do... to do—" Cotton waved his hands. "—whatever you did there. Not until he's better!"

Burton paused. "Sir?" he said, voice soft.

Jason's voice was trying to be hard, but Cotton didn't have to look over his shoulder to know the man was probably sweating, and probably shaking too. "I want him out of danger," he said. "He should stay—fuck."

Cotton turned in time to catch him as his knees went out.

"Goddammit," Jason muttered. "Not now. You should stay here."

"Not until you're better," Cotton said. "I get it. You're a hero. But you don't get to go be a hero until your body can keep up with the rest of you."

"Fuck!" Jason rubbed at his eyes with his palm. "Cotton, this is not going to be safe for you."

Cotton looked up at their soldier friend and supported Jason as he led him toward the couch. "I can have him dressed and ready in fifteen minutes. We've got go-bags packed. Jackson warned me. I just need to put together his medical supplies."

Burton nodded. "I've got a man down outside. I need to make sure he gets to the hospital, and Ernie can get him home. I'll be back." He grimaced. "And make it ten. I don't know where this asshole came from, but I don't imagine we've got much more time before another one shows up."

Burton's boots clanged in the stairwell as he went to talk to Ernie and whoever else was out there, and Cotton turned to the man who had just comforted him and was now sinking onto the couch and swearing.

"Goddammit, Cotton—"

"Jason? All due respect, man, but you can't order me around until we get you some pants."

Ten minutes—Cotton was proud of that. In ten minutes they had Jason in a pair of Randy's worn jeans, because they were comfortable, and the new tennis shoes they'd purchased Jason that week, and Cotton had changed into clean jeans and grabbed both their go-bags, handing them off to Burton, who was doing all the outside stuff while Cotton did the inside stuff.

He was under strict orders not to clean up: don't clean up the door, don't clean up the dropped mug, and definitely, by no means, was he to touch, step on, trip over, or freak out about the dead guy bleeding on the shitty carpet in front of the destroyed IKEA coffee table and the couch.

"But what will the guys…?" he started, stacking their bags and his phone and laptop cases in the shattered doorway. He'd thrown in a nylon mesh bag of hand-me-down paperbacks that accrued in the apartment over time. The basic policy was take one when you need one, leave one if you've got one, and don't feel bad if this is the book you absolutely can't live without. We'll deal. He didn't know if they were going someplace without internet or even television, and he hated being bored.

"They'll never know," Jason said firmly.

"But they're gonna know. I mean, even if there's a new rug, they're gonna know it's a new rug."

"Maybe it was new rug day at the apartment," Jason told him, and Cotton recognized those little pursed dimples in the corners of his mouth when he was unleashing what seemed to be a very dry sense of humor.

"They're not stupid," Cotton muttered, irritated.

"No, they're not," Jason said, and that suppressed smile faded. "But they're not going to jump to, 'Hey, did somebody get shot in here and did the government cover it up?' either."

Cotton let out an involuntary bark of laughter. "Randy might."

And that smile was back. "Yes, but given that Randy also wonders if he can hear the hair on his balls growing—at the top of his lungs, mind you—I think we're safe."

"Hey, there's a reason for that." Cotton finished the final stack of stuff, watching as Burton disappeared down the stairway with the first batch of go-bags and the medical bag.

"I'm interested to hear what it is."

Cotton gave him a level look. "Sure. Hey, let's go get you a shirt—"

"No time," Burton barked from the doorway. "Ernie and Jai are waiting by the car, and it's time to get this show on the road."

Cotton stood and put one shoulder under Jason's arm when Burton stopped him.

"Kid? Are all those muscles for show?"

Cotton winced. "Nossir." All one word, because that's what this man did for him.

"Then you hoist that man up like the princess of your dreams and follow me."

"Not the first time," Jason mumbled, allowing himself to be hoisted and wrapping his arms around Cotton's neck.

"Well, you know, a little food, a little PT—" Cotton paused to weave in and out of the doorframe. "—and you'll do the same for me."

Burton snorted in front of them but continued his brisk walk. Cotton kept up, a part of him relieved to be outside and walking after a week of having his only ventures out be into the apartment weight room or the laundromat.

"I can too carry him," Jason protested as Cotton slid him into the back of… well, a big old land yacht, really. Something huge and powder blue and clunky.

"Not right now, Colonel," Burton said crisply. "Now get in the Crown Vic like a good boy and let me take care of business."

At that moment, Cotton was surprised to see two men—one ginormous, with the same kind of knife sticking out of his shoulder that had been thrown into the dead guy's arm—pulling out of the parking lot in Lance's red Mazda.

"Oh my God! They're stealing Lance's car!"

Burton snorted. "No, they're *borrowing* his car, with… well, his forgiveness. Don't worry about it. Now climb in there, kid—"

"Cotton," he said, feeling naked and stupid and wanting this crisp, efficient, terrifying soldier to know he was a person.

"Cotton," the man said, his voice softening. "Don't worry, we won't steal your friend's car. I mean, he's our doctor, right? Took care of Jason? Yeah. We'll do right by him."

Cotton gave him a brief smile. "Thanks."

He slid into the back seat, and Burton closed the door. Almost unconsciously, Jason lifted his arm, and Cotton gratefully leaned against him. Yes, he was still sick and still weak, but he felt solid and reassuring and kind.

He made himself comfortable, safe in the heaviness of Jason's arm over his shoulders, while Burton made a series of short, terse phone calls, some of them to people Cotton knew. When he was done, Cotton gave him a few minutes to breathe while he negotiated the traffic on I-80 East.

"Tahoe?" he hazarded, and Burton gave a short nod in the front of the car.

"Small cabin off the lake, back from the road. I can get a couple of guys from our unit to watch over it. I'll feel a lot safer with you guys somewhere not here."

"Did you check the car for trackers?" Jason asked, and Burton swore.

"And that," he muttered, swerving off the road at the sign for Roseville, "is the reason you make the big bucks. Can I get an authorization on an expenditure, sir?"

"Sure," Jason murmured, yawning. "But you'd better drop us off at a hotel so I can put on a shirt and stop bleeding in the back of this vehicle."

"Goddammit."

THEY FOUND a hotel—not cheap but not the Ritz either—and Cotton used his credit card for the bill and some takeout while Burton traded in the vehicle for a new one.

"I'll reimburse you for this," Jason muttered as they both indulged in some In-N-Out. Cotton had gotten some for Burton too, because he seemed like he was having a stressful day.

"For In-N-Out?" Cotton laughed. "This is like holiday eating right here."

"You've got beef wrapped in lettuce with some mustard," Jason said dryly. "That's like diet food."

"Ground beef. If it was ground turkey, then we'd be talking." Still, Cotton took a delicate bite of his protein-style single patty and enjoyed the salty goodness. "Back in my modeling days, this would be two days' worth of food."

"Get out!" Jason stared at him. "Seriously? For as much as you guys work out?"

Cotton shrugged. "Well, it depended on how close we were to being on camera. Having defined muscles for the camera is a matter of fat-and-water balance to muscle mass. About three days before our scenes, we would pretty much go to liquid diet only—clear juice and broth and vitamins. By the time we were done filming, we were either starving or light-headed or both. So a couple of days restoring our electrolyte balance, then lots of working out and eating right, and then some more fasting." He took another happy bite of his burger. "Mm. Seriously, three months without fasting? Gotta tell you, it feels pretty decadent."

But Jason had stopped eating and was looking at him in concern. "But why? Why would you do all that?"

Cotton shrugged and took a sip of his diet soda. "Well, for one thing, there's comments. On the porn scenes. And if you so much as eat a tic tac, somebody'll pop up and call you pork-o the potbelly, and that's no fun. And...." He grimaced, wondering how much Jason remembered of his first three days. "There's, uhm, you know. Poop. I mean, cleans up, is no big deal, and still happens, but it's easier to film the scene if you don't have any bullets in the chamber, if you know what I mean."

Jason snickered and took another bite of his burger, but his gaze still rested thoughtfully on Cotton as they sat on the hotel couch.

"Still," he said, "wasn't that hard?"

Cotton's face heated. "Bulimia makes it easier. Enough that Bobby—he's a guy who lived at the flophouse before me—had to fix our pipes. And then after Bobby, Henry had to do it. And Bobby put the fear of God into everyone, so when Henry fixed the pipes, he managed to get a bunch of us in to see a shrink about food disorders. The shrink was sort of a snarky old codger, but nice. He said that once we moved out of the business, we might have an easier time seeing our bodies for the... what was it? 'The beautiful instruments of pleasure and utility they were meant to be.'" He smiled slightly. "That started to become a mantra, really. I'm not sure I understand it all, but, you know. I might someday."

Jason nodded soberly. "I get the utility, but, you know, that other thing. It's been a while."

Cotton's laugh held a little bitterness. "Sort of the other way around for me."

To his surprise, Jason's face flushed, and then, sadly, he put about half of a single-patty hamburger down. "I've only been back on solids for a couple of days," he apologized, and Cotton grimaced.

"Yeah, sorry about that. I guess I could have gotten some soup or something from that other place—"

"No!" Jason laughed. "No. It's been a while since I've done a good burger and fries. You made something functional into something pleasant. I appreciate that."

Cotton shifted in his seat, embarrassed. "You're really good at making the simple shit I do sound really cool," he said. "But, uhm, we both saw what happened today. Bad guy busts down the door, and first I freeze, and then I throw a chef's knife at him—badly. If your guy hadn't been staking out the apartment, we would have been dead."

Jason shook his head, and the thoughtfulness had turned troubled. "It was one of the bravest things I've ever seen," he said. "You, there, standing in front of me. You threw the knife because he had a gun and you'd seen it work. It was smart, and if you hadn't done it, he might have gotten a shot off. You saved both our lives. It's not your fault you don't walk around the house fully armed with a .45 in a pancake holster so you can kill random mobsters. You need to give yourself some credit, Cotton. You keep trying to tell me you're not great at shit, but I think you're trying all the wrong shit!"

Cotton rolled his eyes. "Whatever." He frowned, doing his own thinking. "Who were the guys who took off in Lance's car?"

Jason gave a smile. "Well, Jai and Ernie, if that tells you anything."

Cotton crossed his eyes. "It does not. Jai? Like, 'Hi, my name is Jai!'?"

"Yes. He is… well, hard to explain. But then, so is Ernie. They're Burton's people more than mine, but Ernie's had me over to dinner a couple of times."

Cotton winked at him coquettishly as Burton let himself in with the key. "Why, Mr. Constance, did you have a thing going on with this Ernie character?"

"He better not have," Burton said crisply, "or I would have skinned him alive."

Cotton stared at him in surprise as Jason held up the sack with Burton's food in it.

"Really?" he asked.

"Really what?" Burton opened his paper sack and his eyes rolled back in his head. "Are these fries animal style? Did you really get me animal-style fries? Because if you did that for me, then you were absolutely worth saving."

Cotton grinned, liking him a little better now that he wasn't barking orders. "Yeah, and that's exactly what I was thinking. Anybody who saves me from scary mobsters is definitely worth animal style and a double-double. But, uhm…." He risked a glance at Jason, who was midyawn. "Is Ernie, uhm, your, uhm…?"

"Boyfriend, Cotton," Burton said dryly. "And you live in a house with all the pretty gay boys in the world, so don't act like gay isn't a thing."

Heat was creeping down his neck. "It's just you—and Jason—you're so… uhm…."

"Butch," Jason said, laughing and yawning at the same time. "He's trying to say we're butch."

"I'm bi. Does that count?" Burton asked before biting into his burger.

"No," Jason said. "And I think it's hysterical because—" He yawned again. "—he knows Henry and Jackson, and they're pretty butch too."

Cotton shrugged. "Maybe the whole world needs to adjust its expectations," he said. "Go lie down, even for ten minutes. I'm going to be all alone, and if you get sick again, I…." He shuddered. "I mean, I could do what Jackson and Henry did by myself, but please don't make me."

"Fine." With not much more than that, Jason pushed himself up to lie on one of the queen-sized beds, curling into a ball on top of the coverlet.

Cotton gave a sigh and stood, grabbing the blanket at the bottom and pulling it to Jason's shoulders.

"I should have brought the blankets off my bed," he said disconsolately. "I didn't think. Jackson told me to pack for cold weather, but I didn't think about blankets or pillows or—"

"Hey," Burton murmured. "Stop. You did good."

Cotton looked down to where Jason had already closed his eyes and snuggled into the blanket around his shoulders, shivering a little. He held the back of his fingers against his forehead and sighed. Still a little warm. Not raging, but not healthy either.

"Do we have to get in the car right away?" he asked. "It's so hot outside, and traveling sucks when you're sick."

Burton took another bite of his burger. "No. In fact, we can wait until late. If there was a tracker on that car, they'll find it and assume we're going east and head out that way. We might be able to shake them if we head for the cabin after they've gone looking for us."

"Won't your people, or whoever, be able to track you?" Cotton had no idea how these things worked.

Burton shrugged, but it didn't look as nonchalant as Cotton thought he wanted it to. "I broke out an emergency ID. I've got a couple of them that the government doesn't know about, but they take some time to set up. I hate to burn one, but, well, it's Jason and it's important. I think we're safe." He yawned. "Besides, I have been stuck in that little apartment across from yours for a week and a half. There is something really exhausting about staking out a place for that long. And Ernie was there the whole time, and we couldn't even hold hands."

"Why not?" Cotton asked. "Regulations?"

Burton looked at him funny. "Rudeness! Jai put off a trip to see his own boyfriend to keep watch on you all. That would have been low-class to get all snuggly while he was there."

Cotton smiled. "Are all Jason's friends gay?"

Burton paused, thinking about it. "I think... I think all of Jason's friends know what it is to keep a secret," he said after a moment. "And because of when Jason and I started up in the military, that secret is being gay or bisexual."

"Was Jai in the military?" Cotton asked, suddenly hungry for all of this. His history was painful, and stupid, and probably boring, but Jason was a hero. Cotton wanted to hear who his friends were.

"Jai is… hard to explain," Burton said, thinking about it. "Let's say there's a gas station out in the godsforsaken stretch of highway between Las Vegas and Los Angeles that's almost a hellmouth for weird shit and gay men with a special set of skills. My boyfriend works there, my best friend runs the place, and all sorts of interesting people have gravitated that way, including Rivers and Cramer. And the people there may not always do things the legal way, but I'd trust pretty much all of them to do the right thing."

Cotton thought about that. "That's fair," he said softly. "I… I mean, sex workers aren't that great with authority because people assume we're criminals. But just because what we're doing isn't legal…." He paused, thinking about it some more.

"Doesn't necessarily make it wrong," Burton filled in for him before yawning again.

"Yeah," Cotton said, taking a sip of his soda. "Do you need a nap? I could stay up and read a book or something if you do."

Burton finished his burger and started on his fries. "Actually, that would be almost as fantastic as this animal style. Kid, give me ten minutes to finish this off, and I will take you up on that. Give me a couple hours, and we can leave when it gets dark. How's that?"

Cotton grabbed the bag of books and pulled out *The Cold Dish*, which Curtis had told him he'd like. "Sounds like a plan," he said, turning on the reading lamp. "Happy to be of service."

Burton paused. "Make no doubt about it, Cotton, Jason needed you this last week. I've… I've known him a long time. He lets his guard down around *nobody*. Maybe Ernie because Ernie's psychic and we all assume he knows everything anyway, but other than that, nobody."

Cotton was still trying to digest that Burton's boyfriend was psychic when Burton kept going.

"You could be the first person he's trusted close to his body in ten years," Burton continued. "And I've never seen him be with another soul as human as he's been around you. So I don't care if you're a unicorn, sex worker, you're the unicorn who made my boss—one of the best men I've ever known—happy, even for a short time. Make no mistake about it, your service is fucking important. To Jason, because he's needed that for a long time, and to me, because I've been worried about him for almost that long. So you take care of yourself, you understand me? You are literally the sunshine in that man's life right now. Have no illusions. You are needed."

Cotton stared at him, but he finished his speech and went to work on his fries, using a fork because they were messy. Cotton watched him eat for a couple of seconds before opening the book and pretending to read.

He had too much to think about to see any of the words.

BURTON TOOK them to Target before they lit out of town, and Cotton ran inside and bought fleece blankets, granola bars, and a flat of water.

"I'll stock the cabin before I leave tomorrow," Burton told them, "but this will do for breakfast."

"I got cookies too," Cotton told Jason as he snuggled in. "And some bouillon cubes. I figure most rentals have coffee, right?"

"Yeah," Jason mumbled. "Basic hospitality. How'd you know that?"

Cotton shrugged. "My family used to like to vacation when I was a kid. The coffee maker in the bedroom always seemed to be the coolest damned thing."

Jason chuckled. "My family went camping. Tents, propane stove, building a fire so you could defrost enough to go fishing."

"Heathen," Burton said succinctly from the front of the car as he pulled into the mild traffic of the humid, sweat-dripping night. "For us, camping was going without cable."

"We could go without cable," Cotton said confidently, the childhood memories holding the sweetness of nostalgia without the sting of having them suddenly ripped away, "but going without coffee was for barbarians."

"Mm. Instant coffee. My dad would give us instant coffee in the morning," Jason murmured. "I thought that's what coffee *was* until I went away to college. To this day I can't convince my father that Starbucks is a thing for a reason."

Cotton's throat was suddenly too swollen to talk.

"What?" Jason asked quietly.

Cotton just shook his head.

"What? I'm sorry, was it something I said?"

"I... I can never go back home," he mumbled. Most of the people at the flophouse knew. Henry knew the story, and so did Lance. Curtis and Billy had shared their own painful "getting kicked out of the house" stories, and they knew Vinnie had one tucked away somewhere.

Telling Jason seemed so much bigger somehow.

"Oh." Jason's arm tightened around his shoulders. "I'm sorry, Cotton."

Cotton shook his head, not sure he could say anything. From the front of the car, Burton spoke.

"My parents," he said, "do not know what I do for a living. I may take Ernie home to see them one day soon, but I may not. They think I'm basic Marine, still. They don't know about covert ops. They think I'm dating a girl. And it's not that I started out trying to lie to them, but you're not supposed to tell anybody about covert ops, and I met Ernie through my work there—"

Jason coughed.

"Shut up, Jason."

Jason coughed again.

"Oh God."

Cotton realized that they were trying to make it easier on him, so he played along. "What? What is he not saying?"

"Aw, tell him, Lee," Jason wheedled. "It's so cute. You'll die."

"It's not cute."

"Oh, it totally is."

"It's so not cute," Burton insisted.

Cotton was laughing, pulled out of his misery and grateful that the two total badasses who probably could have treated him like luggage were treating him like a friend.

"Please?" he begged, wanting to know now.

"You say it," Burton muttered. "It's your fault."

Jason breathed out. "Fine." He looked at Cotton, grimacing. "Although it feels wrong. You should see his eyes—he looks like a cartoon character."

"So does Ernie," Burton replied irritably.

"Fine." Jason rolled his eyes. "In a way it's funny, but maybe it's a soldier's sense of humor, so try not to be appalled, okay?"

"Sure." Cotton looked at him expectantly.

"Ernie was supposed to be a hit."

Cotton stared at him blankly as the words sank in. "A what?"

"A hit," Jason repeated. "A job. Burton's covert ops. We were given a dossier that said Ernie was a threat to national security and we were supposed to take him out."

"But Jason didn't like the folder," Burton said, like that meant something.

Cotton looked at him expectantly.

"The job didn't look legit," Jason admitted. "Ernie…. Nothing about Ernie's life said 'threat to national security,' so I told Burton to use his discretion. If he thought there was something wrong with the job, I gave him permission to walk away."

"You didn't walk away?" Cotton asked, enthralled.

"I wasn't the only assassin on his tail," Burton said, shaking his head. "There were three other guys about ready to take him out, and he killed two of them on his own. Self-sufficient and fearless. But innocent. He had to be self-sufficient because he really was that fucking innocent."

"Oh wow." Cotton wanted to meet him now. "But why? Why would you be told to hurt him?"

They both let out long breaths of air almost identically, through the nose. It was like watching twins, although they looked nothing alike.

"That's a long story," Jason said at last. "And it's how we met your friend Rivers. But... but it gave us both a taste for distrusting the orders we get. I mean, most of the men I'd recruited were recruited because they could think for themselves and because their moral centers were stronger than 'I was following orders.'"

Cotton was quiet for a moment. "Is that how you ended up driving the bus?" he asked.

"Yeah," Jason agreed. "And why we're running from mobsters without asking the military for help. Although...." He cleared his throat. "Burton, you *are* going to leave me some info on the people chasing us, right? Because it would be spectacular if we knew who to look for while we're hiding in the woods."

"I've got Henry and Jackson looking into the ID of the guy who broke ranks and tried to kill you," Burton told him, and even Cotton could recognize his "reporting" voice. "But we're going to need to talk more about what happened the night before you showed up so spectacularly in Sacramento. Anton is listening to pick up on who was buying and selling weapons on the inside. We need to see if it was someone buying *for* our guys, so, you know, getting a discount and pocketing the money, or if it was someone buying and trading and working the market. Owens is manning the coms, and we've got a couple of mics trained on command in Washington, and a few of them trained on San Diego to see if it was a local operation with someone who's got pull. Either way, we should have a list of enemies and potential antagonists by tomorrow evening, sir."

"Good job," Jason said. And his next words held the smile in them that Cotton recognized as a man talking to a brother, not a superior to his junior. "Think it's enough info to keep us alive for another couple of days?"

"Yessir," Burton replied. "Although if I could leave you up here and know you were safe while I used all our resources back at the base…."

"We might spend a little less time in danger. Understood."

"Seriously, Jason, show the kid back there how to throw a knife and hold a gun. I bet it would make you both feel better if he could do more than bounce a chef's knife off a bad guy's nose."

"What do you think, Cotton? Would it?" Jason was asking seriously—and respectfully—and Cotton felt like he had to give a respectful answer back.

"The knife," he said. "Not a gun. I… guns scare me. If I slip with a knife, I need stitches. If I slip up with a gun, I don't need anything."

There was a shocked silence, and then Jason laughed weakly. "D'you hear that, Lee? I think he fits right in."

WILLIAM TELL OVERTURE, INTROIT

JASON KNEW two things.

One was that he was warm and cozy under the covers, and the other was that it was ungodly cold out of them.

There was movement under the covers with him, and suddenly he knew *three* things.

Cotton was there with him on the bed. Shivering.

His eyes flew open, and he tried to shake off the lassitude of sleep. Cotton had fallen asleep on him as they'd traveled up the hill toward Tahoe, only to wake up when they'd arrived. Jason had been stiff, feverish, and sick again. He'd sat on a recliner in the small, admittedly cozy living room as Cotton and Burton had hustled around making the beds and turning up the heat. Gah! After two years of living in the desert, he'd thought he'd be more than ready to face the mountains, but even in early September, it got cold up there at night. Cotton had wrapped one of the new fleece blankets—it had something colorful and absurd on it that made Jason smile—around him, and by the time he'd spirited Jason to bed, Jason had no choice but to take his painkiller and his sedative and to fall almost immediately asleep.

He didn't remember much after that, but apparently the heat had gone off sometime in the night, and Cotton had ended up sharing the queen-sized mattress with him.

They weren't small men.

"Jesus," he mumbled. "Cotton, are you literally hanging off the mattress to not touch me?"

"I-I-I didn't want to p-p-presume...."

Oh dear God.

Jason reached out one arm and hauled him in, making sure he was covered by the three layers of blankets over them and flush against Jason's body, which was apparently still throwing off heat. Together, they gave one big collective shudder, and Jason had a rather dreamy moment to appreciate that muscular male body up against his.

"Presume away," he murmured, falling into sync with Cotton's breathing. "When do we need to wake up?"

Cotton reached out, rolling away long enough to check his phone to make Jason miss that amazing body next to his.

"It's only six," he murmured. "You've got another two hours before I check your vitals, and I've got another three before I absolutely have to get out of bed."

Jason chuckled, more than happy when Cotton returned to his arms without protest.

"Why? What makes you have to get out of bed?"

"Biology," Cotton murmured. "And calorie diary."

"You have to eat and… uhm…."

"Potty," Cotton filled in dryly. "Yeah. It's one of the things the shrink had us keep track of so our bodies were in our control."

"Mmm." His hair was so silky at his nape. Soft and sleep-scented; whatever bath products these guys used, they were amazing. Jason hadn't been so aware of smells since he'd first had to light candles in his college dorms when his sister visited to hide how much sex he'd been having in the times between.

Cotton's hand came up to where Jason's rested at his waist, and he tangled their fingers together.

"You don't mind me here?" he asked, his voice still sleepy. "There were two beds, and only so many blankets. Burton said you'd be fine."

"I don't know," Jason teased groggily. "I've been feverish. I might get deluded and wake up and fondle you. Be sure to slap my hand if that happens. Highly inappropriate."

Cotton's laugh was surprisingly bitter. "This body's been for sale before. Not sure anything really counts as inappropriate anymore."

And Jason was still falling asleep, dammit, but that needed to be addressed. "Any touch you don't want is inappropriate," he said, trying to sound stern. "Even mine."

The sigh let some of the bitterness out. "But I want your touch," he murmured, and the end of his words trailed off as he fell back asleep, leaving Jason to hold him as tight as he could, and wonder what they were going to do now.

APPARENTLY SLEEP some more. When he woke up, he was alone, but he had a vague memory of his vitals being taken and being made to swallow his medication. On the empty side of the bed, he saw a pair of jeans, clean boxers, and a T-shirt laid out, as well as a new gray fleece hoodie and a pair of new flip-flops.

Damn, for a group of kids who seemed to live in basketball shorts and bare feet, these guys apparently understood how to shop for someone else.

He was impressed.

He dressed hurriedly, the chill of morning still sharp, used the facilities in the luxuriously appointed adjoining bathroom, and followed his nose into the kitchen where Cotton stood, in an outfit much like his own but much more lived-in, and scrambled eggs on a well-outfitted stove.

The entire cabin, Jason had noted, was well outfitted. The bathroom had been done in white-and-cream tile, with a surprisingly large shower and big fluffy towels apparently standard. The bedroom he and Cotton had been in was lushly decorated, with a sturdy, warm wool rug and local art prints in frames on darkly stained wood-paneled walls. The sheets had been fine and soft, and the navy comforter had been the same. Cotton's fleece blankets—in the morning light coming from the window, he'd recognized a unicorn in rainbow colors and a giant anime cat, of all things—had contrasted starkly with the elegance and clean lines of the rest of the room.

But they'd made Jason smile, so he figured it was totally worth it.

And the kitchen had beige marble tile on the floor and walls, with black appliances—tasteful, elegant, a little plain, but definitely not "rustic."

"Where *are* we?" he asked, settling down at a solid oak kitchen table and a chair that didn't so much as register his weight.

"Ellery Cramer's mother's cabin," Burton said, watching his expression.

His eyebrows hit his hairline, so hopefully he didn't disappoint. "She just turned over the keys?"

"Mm-hmm. Ellery talked to her when you were still on the road from LA," Burton told him, his voice ringing with an unspoken "If you can believe that shit."

Jason really couldn't. "She what?"

"So it seems Rivers asked Ellery to rent a cabin, Ellery asked his mother for suggestions because the boy isn't stupid, and she bought the cabin and gave it to Ellery as a birthday present for Jackson that Ellery isn't supposed to tell Jackson about. He's supposed to produce the keys whenever they need a place out of town and say, 'My mother says this place is nice.'"

Jason breathed in deeply and there, under the smell of dusty pine trees, he caught a whiff of new building materials. "She had it renovated in a week?" he asked, feeling off-balance.

"Knowing that woman, she had it renovated two days after Ellery asked her if she knew of one he could rent." Burton shook his head. "You know how Rivers and Cramer keep showing up to fix the fucking world?"

Jason nodded.

"I guess Cramer comes by it honestly, and Rivers... well, he's like Ace, or Ernie. You know. A gift from the fucking gods."

"Who's Ace?" Cotton asked, dishing up a plate of eggs and sausage that Jason *craved*. Cotton gave it to Burton instead, but Jason knew there was more there *for* him, so he didn't fret.

"My best friend," Burton told him before shoving some eggs on a piece of toast and biting in, eyes closed. "Can we keep him, Jason? I mean, Ernie makes good donuts, but I'd give this kid a place to stay if he could cook breakfast for me. Pretty please?"

Jason laughed. "I'd love to," he said, meaning it, "but I'm pretty sure he has a life of his own."

"Untrue," Cotton told him crisply, plating up another breakfast Jason was pretty sure was for him. "Who knows? Maybe being a personal chef is the thing I was meant to do all my life."

"I don't know," Jason said dubiously. "That smells good and all, but I could swear you were meant to go into nursing. You're pretty much a natural."

Cotton turned toward the table and slid Jason's plate in front of him on a waiting cotton placemat. "I think you're biased," he said with an embarrassed smile.

Jason waited until the plate was settled before capturing Cotton's hand. "I think I know someone who's competent when I see him."

Cotton shrugged, pulling away. "I was doing pretty good in school before I got kicked out of the house. I mean, the GED was easy to get. I wouldn't mind going back to school. I just don't know if I'm someone you want in a high-pressure situation."

"Like when a mobster bursts through your door and you need someone to distract him so your rescue guy can shoot him?" Burton asked through a mouthful of eggs. He swallowed. "Yeah. I don't know anybody like that."

"You're very funny," Cotton told him dryly. "I'd be more impressed with myself if I could have gotten the knife to *stick*."

Jason had to work hard not to spit out his eggs, but after he'd swallowed the mouthful, he grinned at Cotton, tickled beyond all reason.

"We can work on that," he said soberly.

Burton grunted. "But first," he said, "you and me need to talk about what's doing."

"Cotton should be in on it." Jason sighed. "Because as soon as they find out he's with me, he's either going to be a target, or someone's going to try to convince him I'm Satan and he should turn me in."

"Would they do that?" Cotton asked. "More importantly, how would they do that? Would somebody call me up on the cell phone and say, 'Hey, that guy you're traveling with is the devil'?"

"Yes," Jason said, trying not to laugh. "That's pretty much exactly how it would work."

Cotton served himself a laughably small amount of scrambled eggs—no cheese, Jason noticed—with a single piece of bacon and some fruit. He frowned.

"Burton, did you go shopping this morning?"

"No, sir," Lee replied. "Did I not mention that Ellery had the place outfitted? Apparently he's got a place on call."

"Well, I'm not sure how secure that is," Jason mused, "but seriously. We've got food and drinks? That's amazing."

"You know what would be amazing?" Burton asked, his voice getting impatient. "If we knew who we could trust in the military and who to worry about trying to blow your brains out after I leave, so focus here for a minute."

"Sure," Jason sighed. "Ruin my vacation if you must."

"*Jason*! You were *shot*!"

Both of them looked at Cotton, who had practically thrown his plate down on the table and was standing, arms crossed, looking like Jason had kicked his puppy.

There was a shocked silence, and then Burton huffed out a breath. "Okay, the sad thing is, you're both right. He was shot, and he needs to take it seriously, and it's the first time he's been off duty in, what? Three years? And he had to get shot to do it." Burton turned from Cotton to Jason. "Which means that if we get these assholes off your tail, we might be able to let you stay here, chill out, and put on twenty pounds before you fly your scrawny sad ass back to the desert to start hunting down psychopaths again, which you're really good at and will probably not be done with any time soon."

"Understood," Jason said, mostly to take the aggrieved look off Cotton's face. These moments here, waking up with Cotton in his bed, having breakfast in a kitchen with a wraparound window overlooking the mystery of the forest—these were almost a fantasy to Jason. They were moments he could barely believe were real.

It was a little hard to grasp that to Cotton it was a frightening imposition.

"Anything to get Cotton back to his band of merry men," Jason said into the silence, winking. To his surprise, Cotton looked wounded. He looked to Burton for help, but Lee was shaking his head.

"Wow," Lee said.

"What?" God, he was confused.

"I'll explain later. Right now, what we know is this: Brigadier General Barney Talbot was the one who gave you the order not to return the kids to Sacramento. Douche move, yes, until you remember that you guys who make the big bucks operate off intel fed to them by people they trust. So let me ask you this—is Talbot usually a douche?"

Jason pondered a moment, thinking about those moments of knowing Talbot was in the hospital while two nurses snuck him and his young charges food and transportation and hope.

"He's... unimaginative," he said after a moment. "A hard-ass, yes, but not bright. He's the guy who watches *Cool Hand Luke* for pointers on how to make the prisoners behave."

Burton squinted at him and mopped up the last of his eggs with the last of his toast. "Is that even possible?"

Jason shook his head. "I swear, Talbot told me that men on his watch wouldn't be allowed entertainment. As far as he's concerned, all the problems in the movie stemmed from too much freedom."

Lee's eyes grew really, really large, and for once, he seemed at a loss for words. "Uhm...."

Jason gave a laugh. "You were lucky," he said. "You had a decent CO in the Marines, and then you had me."

Burton shook his head. "Me lucky, yes. But the rest of the world, unfortunate, definitely. So he's probably not our guy trading military weapons for mob money. Who lit a fire under his ass to make him so hot for yours?"

Jason bit his lip. "That's where I think our bad guy made a mistake. Because if it's not Talbot, we know it's got to be somebody *attached* to Talbot, since he was the one hunting me. So we know it's somebody who parties with the mobsters—"

"Probably Las Vegas style," Burton added, "because that's where the kids were headed and where the deals were going down."

Jason agreed. "So whoever you have on this—"

"Huntington and Owens, sir."

Jason nodded briskly, impressed as always by Burton's spot-on instincts. "Perfect. Huntington is, for some reason, very loyal, and Owens too. And they're both well-liked and in frequent contact with people off our base." He sighed and shook his head. "Makes people think we're a real unit and not a myth. Always helpful when you're looking for aid from other quarters."

"Why would they think you're a myth?" Cotton asked, and Jason glanced at him, realizing he'd been following their conversation closely.

"Nobody wanted to know," Burton murmured. "I worked undercover for months to bring down Karl Lacey and his buddy, Hamblin, the assassin broker. Once Lacey was dead, people would look at all my evidence and go, 'Oh, so that was bad.' But before anybody confronted him, they didn't want to know he was using the US Covert Ops budget and using behavior mod to turn soldiers into killers. So Jason comes in and he's part of the cleanup, and he's got a Covert Ops unit with all sorts of specialists, and…." Burton gave Jason a look that, frankly, he was uncomfortable with. "I don't know how you did it, sir. You saw the need, you co-opted the base, and you convinced us all that since we were the ones who saw the problem, we had to be the ones to go out and bring the renegade assassins back to ground." He nodded at Cotton. "It's dangerous. It made the other ops we used to take look like a cakewalk, because these are our soldiers, and they know our techniques and they know what to expect. And some of them have left bloody trails of dismembered corpses, and it is hard to see. But nobody else was going to do it. I sat in on some of those meetings. All these generals and shit, fiddlefucking around, trying to blame each other for how the guy responsible managed to con money from the budget to fuck with people's heads. But Jason says, straight up, 'We've got to take care of our own, even if that means taking them out. This is our mess. We need to clean it up.' And all of his men followed him."

Jason shuddered. "I tried to give you all a way out," he admitted, remembering the weeks following Karl Lacey's self-destruction. "I put a set of reassignment papers in front of every officer and enlisted man in my unit and told them where we would be situated and what we would be doing, and not one person turned those papers in."

"Why not?" Cotton asked Burton, obviously figuring that Jason wasn't a good reporter on his own self, which was probably true.

"Because of why he was doing it," Burton told him. "Jason had a staff meeting with his unit and told us that policing ourselves was the price of a free world and the largesse of our military budget. We could not call ourselves a moral nation if we didn't clean up our mistakes, and while the brass didn't seem to know what needed to be done, we had been taken into covert operations because we had a moral code that looked at the spirit of the law and not the letter of it. *We* knew what had to be done, and that was all we would need."

Cotton was looking at Jason with slightly parted lips and such incredible faith. "He believed the best in you all, and you helped him clean up the worst."

"It's a shitty job," Jason said gruffly, looking away from both of them. He was almost angrier at Burton, who should know better. "There's a reason we call it Operation Dead Fish. It stinks. I shouldn't have asked anybody to do it. It's… they were going to just… ignore it. Cross that bridge when we came to it. But Rivers and Cramer almost died, both of them, going above and beyond their jobs to find Lacey, doing what was best for the rest of the world. You, Lee, you risked court-martial refusing to take that contract on Ernie, because you knew it wasn't right. It would have been unconscionable to let an entire unit of killers loose on the world and not make an attempt to protect the civilians in danger."

"Only unconscionable to good men," Burton said pointedly.

But Jason shook his head, looking away, out the window, where the depths of the Tahoe National Forest beckoned to hide them all.

"You all—even Huntington—could have gone somewhere. Had a career. Climbed some ladders. I tried to warn you. Nobody in the government wants someone who's been with us sin-eaters. We know their secrets, and we have no respect for the ones who were going to leave the world to rot, and we have no power to fix anything other than what our unit was exclusively designated for. I was doing what was best for my conscience, but not what was best for my men."

"We made that decision," Burton said. "And if Ernie was here, he'd tell you that was the currency that bought our loyalty. He was given no choice at all to be a part of Lacey's unit. He knows what my life could have been. So no bullshit. Cotton, if somebody from the military tries to contact you and tell you Jason's the devil, you're free to say what you want, but—"

Cotton snorted, such an unlikely sound in the tension of the kitchen that Jason startled, turning to look at him.

"I know I'm not trained or educated," he said in the silence, "but I know good men who don't get credit. John Carey, my boss. You ask someone who doesn't know him and you'll hear 'sleezy porn guy' or 'drug addict.' But he gave us all a choice, and he gave us all respect, and we got to be in charge of our bodies and our lives in ways nobody had ever given us before. And he *was* an addict, but he's been doing the work to fix his life and atone for his sins, and even when he was using, he still didn't take advantage of us. He's not going to get any medals for that, but I think he's a good man. I think his business partner, Dex, is a good man. So I get it, Burton. Jason isn't going to be loved by the people who are supposedly in charge of him. But that doesn't mean he's not a better man than they are."

Burton smiled at Cotton, a full-out smile that dimpled the apples in his cheeks and made Jason think of fresh-faced young recruits out on their first leave. "Kid," he said, "You are all right. Jason, I think God was smiling down on you for once and you ended up with a guardian angel."

Jason couldn't help it. He looked at the lovely young man with the wide, sad eyes and the dimples that nobody got to see, and his heart broke a little, hope filling up the gaps.

"I thought that when I woke up," Jason said, giving Cotton a personal little wink. What would it hurt, he thought? What would it hurt to get personal with him? He was a beautiful young man with a wide-open future, and Jason was used up, discarded, worn down by hard choices and a hard job. Would Cotton even know Jason was letting yearning color his vision?

It could be Jason's secret. He'd kept crushes a secret before—quiet attractions go unremarked upon. He'd learned that if he acknowledged them in his heart and then let go of hope, the attraction didn't fester, didn't grow, didn't cause him to do inappropriate things or give away cards he'd learned to keep so close to the vest they were sewn under his skin.

God, that kid had felt good in his arms that morning.

Couldn't Jason savor that? Savor his long bare toes on the tile that morning, or the way his dimples tried to peek out when his eyes lightened to so much as a smile?

Cotton would go back to his room full of half-naked young hotties and a well-earned pathfinding mission to discover the rest of his life, and Jason would go back to the worst people in the worst places doing the worst things—and working to stop them.

What would be the harm in letting himself desire the young man when he knew that nothing would come of it?

Cotton broke into his thoughts. "You were delusional," he said dryly, "when you thought I was an angel. But that's fine. I don't think you're the devil, and I'm certainly not going to turn you over to the military if someone approaches me. Hopefully they'll take one look at me and think I'm too pretty for brain function and move on."

Burton and Jason both snorted. "That would be some serious underestimation," Burton said. "But fine. Let's move on to who *is* after you?"

"Well, we need to look at two things," Jason said thoughtfully. "We need to go back to who is under Talbot who likes to party in Vegas, and who was left over from the mobster blowout over that busload of kids."

"The Schroeders," Burton said promptly. "Dietrich and Karina. They were the only remaining scumbags. I have no idea who ambushed you on the road. That could have been Alexei Kovacs's men or that Ziggy guy's, both of whom are dead now so we don't have to bother with them. But Dietrich and Karina Schroeder escaped and so did Dima Siderov. So whoever is trying to get you is a confidant of Brigadier General Barney Talbot and partying with the Schroeders and/or Siderov."

Jason thought about it. "That actually narrows it down. We need to see who's been partying in Vegas, and we need to know who's surfacing in Sacramento. Can your sources manage that?"

Burton nodded. "Jackson and Henry have some time on their hands. Jackson's got that friend who's almost as witchy as Ernie too. I'll put them on it."

Jason closed his eyes and had a vague memory of his body feeling as though it were exploding with pain and fever, and Jackson Rivers, sweaty and stressed, calming him down and doing something medical while Henry assisted.

"Oh God. It's not like they haven't done enough for me. Hell, I hate to—"

"Oh shut up," Burton muttered. "Greater good, blah blah blah. Good people going above and beyond, blah blah blah. You don't have a corner on the good guy market, you know."

"They lanced my infected wound and irrigated it," Jason muttered. "It was so gross. I don't think you understand how truly gross it was. I won't be able to look them in the eyes after that. Just, no."

"Oh jeez, Jason," Burton shot back. "Ninety-nine percent of the time you're a thousand years old. Just this once, you need to grow up."

To Jason's surprise, Cotton made a noise, a cross between a bark and a chirp, and then, as he and Burton stared at him in surprise, Cotton made it again. And another one. And then a bunch of them in quick succession.

And before Jason understood what was happening, Cotton had buried his face in his arms and was laughing hysterically into the cave of his body, unable to stop.

Finally, when the noise had died down, Jason lowered his head to see how he was. In the quiet, dark hollow of his arms, Jason could see streaks of tears on his cheeks… and closed eyes. He was fast asleep.

Jason let out a breath and sat up. "I think maybe we need to put him back to bed."

"You too," Burton murmured. "You look exhausted. Here, let's walk him back and you guys crawl in together, and I'll get you some stakeout protection. I'll leave when it gets here."

Jason's stomach was full and his head was buzzing, but like Cotton, it felt like the strategy meeting had about tapped him of all his reserves.

He sighed and followed Cotton and Burton back to their bedroom, taking off his jeans and hooded sweatshirt and flip-flops as Burton undressed Cotton. It wasn't until Jason was sliding back in bed next to him, the young man curling up close, snuggling in his sleep, that Jason even wondered why they weren't using different beds.

He tried to say something like that to Burton before he left. "We should have split up," he mumbled. "Cotton probably doesn't want to get stuck with me."

Burton let out a snort and moved back to the side of the bed after turning off the light. "That's how you want to play this—*sir*?"

Jason heard the emphasis on his title and tried to work up the energy to bristle. "He's young," he mumbled, embarrassed.

"He's been absolutely devoted to you for a week and a half. I know *I've* aged in that time. I'm pretty sure he has as well."

Jason tried to snort, but it came out more as a whine. "I don't want to—"

Burton dropped down to his haunches so their faces were close together. "You need to, boss," he said softly. "You need someone in your life. You were tired and worn down and crumbling before our eyes. Ernie spent all our time together worrying about you. You get to have something—some*one*—who makes you feel better. That's not a crime, Jason."

"But he's an angel," Jason grumbled, not sure if he could get the enormity of the problem across. He was what he'd told them in the kitchen. A sin-eater. He'd seen such terrible things, given such terrible orders. How could he burden Cotton with knowing that he was a killer, just as bad but not as random as the people he hunted?

"So are you," Burton murmured. "An avenging angel, full of justice. But that's not a bad thing."

"You're impossible," Jason said, rolling over to his other side. Cotton was there, warm and welcoming and not shaming him for napping in the middle of the morning, and he was suddenly so weak and so tired he couldn't think of any other requirement in a companion.

Not a single one.

TWO HEARTBEATS

COTTON HAD to pee. He had to pee, and he was all alone in bed, and it was pretty much the only thing that was keeping him awake.

That and the air had assumed that odd, mosquito-y tinge to it that told him long shadows were falling. He had no idea why that made him feel like mosquitos were out there, but he knew the little bastards were somewhere.

It was time to get up and get dressed and face them.

His clothes were draped over a chair, and as he rolled out of bed, he was aware that his body felt lighter somehow, like that embarrassing hysterical laughter had unburdened him. He dressed quickly and made it to the bathroom, his body fighting to remember those moments cocooned with Jason under the covers.

Twice now, they'd been there together, snuggled on the small bed, Jason's arm wrapped around his waist, and he was suddenly wondering if he could sleep any other way.

After his trip to the bathroom, he found his way to the living room, where their comfortable kitchen table had been converted to an electronics store.

"What the—"

"Sh…," Jason muttered, using a screwdriver on a bank of monitors. "I'm teching."

"That's not a word," Cotton muttered. Squinting, he found the clock on the microwave and realized he'd slept for a couple of hours. It wasn't six or seven, as he'd imagined, but closer to four in the afternoon. The long shadows from the surrounding conifers made the world seem both safer and a more closely guarded secret.

He stepped toward the kitchen window. As he'd discovered that morning when he'd gone to fix breakfast, it was sort of a stunning beveled creation that stuck out about four inches from the wall, with a shelf that could be used for plants or recipes. It looked out over the slope of a hill that led to what appeared to be a branch of a small lake.

"Isn't Tahoe big and round?" he muttered, frowning. "This is small and sort of starfish shaped."

"It's Caples Lake," Jason replied. "We're on one of the branches. If you look out over to the left, you can see the resort. Lucky us, we just hit the off-season at the end of August/beginning of September."

"Why lucky us?" Cotton turned to look at him and noticed he was still "teching."

"Yeah, Burton wanted a contingent to keep an eye on us, but it's hard to be secret when you've got a bunch of special ops guys living in your cabin. So he rented one of those cabins off-season for cheap. The guys get to watch us in shifts, but they also get to enjoy the lake. He said there were people jumping for this assignment. They should be in place by tomorrow morning."

"Where is he now?"

Jason held up a finger and then tinkered with something on the table in front of him. "Hanging up cameras outside," he murmured. Then he picked up the cell phone lying on the table in the mess next to the monitor in front of him and said, "Camera three's a go. Could you point it thirty degrees north? That way there's not so much overlap with camera two, and we have a better view of anyone coming down the road."

"You're setting up security?" Cotton turned toward him and really took in what he was doing. A laptop sat open on the table, still charging, apparently from a cord that stretched to the wall behind where Jason sat. Next to that was an old computer monitor hooked up to… the hell was that?

"Is that a modem?" Cotton asked, surprised he even knew what one looked like.

"Internet is sketchy as fuck up here," Jason murmured. He had a small soldering iron next to him and a motherboard underneath it. Every now and then he'd take a wire and touch it to a contact point, and then, given what he saw on the monitor, he'd solder it on. "We don't have acres of cable to set up a good perimeter, but what we do have is…." He picked up the phone. "That's good. Camera three's a lock. Two more to go."

Burton said something Cotton didn't catch, but Jason answered.

"Yup. He's up. Asking questions. As he should. Yeah, we'll have breakfast ready for our guys tomorrow. Make sure you cross-reference them with Talbot's advisor circle. I don't want any conflict of—"

"They all hate Talbot, sir."

Cotton smirked. "Well, that came in clear," he said.

Jason arched a warning eyebrow at him. "Hush," he mouthed. "Did you make that a requisite?" He aimed the question over the coms.

"No, sir, but we did ask if they had any connections to him, and their consensus was that he was an asshole who thought anybody underneath his rank was expendable."

"Well, that's special," Jason muttered. "Wonderful. Are you putting up camera four now?"

"Yessir."

"Don't fall out of that fuckin' tree."

There was a sputtering on the other end of the line. "Falling out of trees is your job, sir."

"Fuck off, Captain."

"Yessir."

Cotton laughed a little, enjoying their camaraderie. Unbidden, the obvious question came out, and he could have kicked himself after it did.

"Why aren't you dating him?"

Jason swore and popped two fingers into his mouth. "Wha…?"

"He's got a boyfriend. Why isn't it you?"

Jason frowned. "I'm his superior officer. I can't sleep with him. That's unethical."

They both heard Burton snicker on the other end of the phone.

"And I thought he was straight until he met Ernie," Jason said loudly, mostly for Burton's benefit.

"So did I!" Burton shot back. "How about that one?"

"Gimme a sec." Jason did some more tinkering and then looked at his monitor. "Good. Five degrees right. One more. Good. Perfect. You can get down out of that tree."

"Yessir. Bit of a hike. Hanging up to save battery."

"Ten-four." Jason hit End Call and then stretched, yawning. "Did you have a good sleep?"

"Yes, thank you." Cotton caught himself midyawn and grimaced. "I had no idea how tired I was."

"Well, you've been nursing me back to health. It's been a full-time job. And yesterday was no picnic."

Cotton nodded and then remembered he was there for a reason. "How're you feeling?" He noted Jason's paleness, the high color in his cheeks. "Here." As Lance had trained him, he walked forward, put the back of his hand on Jason's forehead, and grimaced. "Still low-grade," he guessed. "I'll go get the medkit. I think you need your antibiotics too."

Jason groaned good-naturedly and took his hand before he could pull it back. "Yeah, I've only been up for a couple of hours, and I could sleep for another week. Once we get the cameras up, I'll feel better. The cabin has this great window over the lake and then a couple of them from the guest bathroom and the mudroom, but the living room and master bedroom are blind. If we could have a camera system in our room, I'll sleep much better."

Cotton paused, biting his lip, not wanting to state the obvious but not wanting it yanked away from him either. "Our room?" he asked, praying a little.

Jason looked away, releasing his hand before sitting down at the monitor.

"If that's okay with you," he said gruffly.

"Yeah," Cotton said, smiling a little. "I, uhm…." He bit his lip, and Jason looked up to meet his eyes.

"It was nice," he admitted. "Holding you. Probably not wise. You're very, very much younger than I am. Probably holding you is all I should do."

"You're not that old," Cotton said, thinking about all of the sugar daddies he'd hoped for while he'd been in porn. None of them—not one— had seemed as old or as grounded or as real as Jason Constance, though.

"Thirty-six," he muttered, with the same intonation he might have used to say, "One hundred and six," or "Three thousand two hundred and eighty-seven."

"Well, that's a whole fourteen years," Cotton said dryly. "Are you going to need a walker? Viagra? Let me know, old man. I can order what we don't have."

Jason snorted. "Condoms? Lube? An instruction manual? It's been so long since I've had sex with another person, I've probably forgotten how."

Cotton snorted and had just opened his mouth to ask how long it could have possibly been, but then the phone rang and Jason picked it up. He and Burton started their techspeak, and Cotton ran to the bedroom to find the medical kit he'd packed in that terrifying ten minutes.

When he was done there, he double-checked his own shaving kit, even though he knew what was in it already. Condoms, lubricant, PrEP meds. Safety and respect—John Carey, Dex, and every guy who'd lived at the flophouse or worked at Johnnies had been absolutely hammered with those concepts before the first shirt hit the floor. Cotton owed them all. Once his first few tests had come back negative and he'd been cleared to work for John, he had never, not once, taken his good fortune for granted. He'd been turning tricks on the streets, no lube, no PrEP, and he'd escaped with a clean bill of health. He knew other kids weren't as lucky as he was and that some of the kids he'd hung out with, leaning against the wall behind Goldies, the infamous porn store, hadn't made it to twenty-two.

For some of them, it was drugs, some it was violence, and some it was disease.

And until this moment, thinking about lying next to Jason Constance, being held like he was important, like he mattered, he wasn't sure if he'd ever been as grateful that he'd survived.

He met his own eyes square in the mirror then and tried to see what Jason saw when he called Cotton his angel. He'd seen himself a lot since he'd started porn—was vain enough to have watched his first couple of films to help himself get off, because, dude! There was a body he'd worked hard to make perfect drilling or being drilled by another perfect body, and watching someone else come inside him was such a rush.

But that had paled after a few scenes, and he'd started to recognize sex work as exactly that—work. And then he'd tried to date and realized that most of the guys not in sex work didn't see the work part. And most of the guys who were *in* sex work didn't want to bring their work home with them.

That moment Henry told him to stop dating, to try to fix his life before he invited someone else into it, had been pivotal for him, but he hadn't realized how important until he'd been forced to quit his job.

Sex and love were two different things. It sounded so simple to say it, but understanding that truth when everybody had their dick out and an open asshole was not so easy.

The last three months had made it much easier.

And the last week, caring for someone who had made his life mean something, had made him rethink everything in almost the same way. Everybody was worth love, but who was worth sacrificing for?

Not the young man with the limpid brown eyes in the mirror, but he was getting closer.

And he wanted to continue that closeness—right into Jason Constance's arms. He'd long ago given up on the idea that a lover would hold the secret of the universe or a way out of the incredible maze that was real life. But being held against Jason's body had given him faith in a way he hadn't had in a very long time. Perhaps—*maybe*—he had the things in himself that would find that secret, navigate that maze, fulfill that quest.

Stupid, maybe, but that didn't mean he was going to walk away from the possibility now.

A night by himself when Jason was only a bedroom away seemed unnecessarily cruel to both of them.

And he'd had enough cruelty for a lifetime.

But as he gathered himself, he reminded himself firmly that just because they shared a bed didn't mean they had to have sex. As the guys in the flophouse had taught him, sometimes simply having another body next to you was the best gift the world could give. And Jason was still recovering. Maybe he merely wanted to be kind. Maybe he didn't want sex. Maybe he just wanted closeness.

Cotton could deal with that.

It was loneliness he was tired of.

Resolutely, he went back out to do his job. And to find, however fleeting, someone to take the loneliness away.

Jason was clearing up the table by the time Cotton came back into the kitchen. Cotton scanned his forehead—a little elevated at 99.8, but not scary—and administered the medication. He repacked the bag and went to set it back in the bathroom by their bedroom when Jason caught his wrist.

"Cotton?" he said hesitantly.

"Yes?" Cotton smiled, hoping to send a message that he was completely amenable to anything Jason had in mind.

"I didn't mean to be forward. I mean, the sharing the bed is fine." A red stain took over his cheeks underneath the beard he hadn't attacked yet. "I only meant, with all that talk about Viagra, you didn't think I'd be... you know. Taking advantage."

Oh.

Cotton raised his hand to Jason's cheek and rubbed a thumb over the red stain, smiling a little at the prickle of the beard. "Do you really think you'd be taking advantage?" he asked.

Jason captured his hand. "You're just... really pretty," he said, rolling his eyes, probably at himself. "And it's been a while. It's not fair of me to hit on you or intimate we should be anything more than friends. I can't make any promises here. I... God, I can barely stand for more than long enough to take a piss, actually. I just... I like touching you is all. I can sleep in the recliner or on the sofa if you feel uncomfortable or—"

Cotton kissed him.

Fuck this "intentions" bullshit. Cotton wanted him. Cotton had wanted him from the beginning. Sure, they probably wouldn't be doing athletic, frightening sexual things that night or even anytime this week. But Cotton felt connected to Jason Constance in a way he hadn't felt connected to any man, ever, and he'd had a lot of men to choose from. He wasn't giving up any of their days in this little cabin when they could sleep under the covers together. He wasn't giving up even the opportunity to touch this man's skin in a sensual way instead of a practical one.

Cotton cupped the back of Jason's head, burying his fingers in the silkiness of his hair, and held his head at exactly the angle to ravish his mouth with every bit of prowess and finesse he had.

Jason whimpered, knotted both fists in Cotton's jacket, and clung, opening his mouth and letting Cotton in.

Cotton kept kissing, backing Jason up to a wall for the support and making free with his mouth, his lips, plundering the wet cave of Jason's mouth with his tongue and swallowing his groans, his whimpers, his little helpless begging sounds, until Jason didn't so much pull back as fall against Cotton's chest and tremble.

Cotton wrapped his arms around Jason's shoulders and held him firm and tight, like a lover who needed aftercare.

Long moments stretched between them, Jason locked in his arms, shivering, holding on for dear life, Cotton doing the unimaginable and supporting him, holding him, making him safe.

"I want you," he whispered in Jason's ear. "I want you healthy, and I want you willing, but mostly I want you to touch me in any way you can. You decide what you want us to do tonight. I'll be there. I'm not sleeping anywhere else but your bed, not while we're here. You need to decide what you're going to do with me, because you've got me until the world rips you out of my arms."

Jason gave a faint moan, and Cotton helped him over to the kitchen chair and settled him down again.

"Now, what do you want for dinner?" he asked.

Jason groaned and put his head in his arms. "A brain," he muttered. "A response. The willpower to say no."

Cotton crouched down beside him. "Have you found the willpower?" he asked seriously. "Consent is important to my people."

Jason gave a beleaguered little laugh. "Consent should be important to everybody. And to answer your question, not yet. The thought of sleeping on the sofa when you're in the other room makes me want to cry."

The statement was so very close to how Cotton had been feeling as he'd splashed water on his face that he found a peaceful smile stealing over his features.

"Good, then," he said happily. "We don't have to worry about it. We both know where we'll be sleeping tonight, and we both know that touching is very much on the table." His smile faded, and he gave Jason a stern look.

"Probably not much else until you're one-hundred-percent. There is a shit-ton of orange juice in that refrigerator. The fresh stuff too. You should be really excited about that, because it means we're *serious* about getting you healthy."

Jason gave a little hiccup, head still in his arms. "Good to know," he said.

Cotton flashed him a benign smile, recognizing his irony but dismissing it. "I think you're nervous," he said decisively. "Because it's been so long. Why has it been so long, anyway?"

"Because I got promoted," Jason mumbled. "I had my tech degree, I signed on for OCC."

"OCC?"

"Officer Candidate Course. It means I went through boot camp, and then I went through another boot camp, but that one training me about chain of command and how to lead men into battle."

Cotton caught his breath. "That's… that's scary."

"Well, there was a few months between them, but, you know. Had a double major. Electronics and business management. I'd planned to be a startup entrepreneur."

Cotton literally turned and stared at him. "You—I don't understand. Like, that's… that's not just a one hundred eighty degree turn in life, that's a one hundred eighty degree turn in *someone else's* life. What would make you do that?"

Jason blew out a breath. "My sister, Jessica."

"You have a sister named Jessica?" Cotton thought miserably of his own sister, ten years his junior. Did she ever miss him? She'd been seven when he'd been kicked out. He used to love to sit in her room and color with her because she'd say the most outrageous things. Did she remember that?

"Yes," Jason said with a smile. "Hey, thirty, forty years ago, Jessica and Jason were very en vogue as baby names. But she's about four years older than I am, and she's the first one who knew I was gay, and she held my hand during the whole coming out thing, which was horrific twenty years ago, I'm not going to lie. My parents were good, though. They didn't understand it. Awkward question time, but, you know. Parents." He gave a little grunt. "Anyway, she used to visit me when I was at college. She'd gotten her degree in nursing, and we used to joke that one of us was doing the altruistic thing and the other one of us was doing the douchey money thing, and I'd take her on fabulous vacations when she blew out her back on the floor."

Cotton snorted. "Well, at least you got along."

Jason looked sad. "Still do. I just…." He sighed. "I don't visit as often as I'd like. She… she doesn't know what I do now. Nobody does, outside of a small circle." A grin flitted across his mouth under his beard. "Of which you are one. But I miss her. She's funny. And a really good person."

"Is she still a nurse?" Cotton asked.

He grimaced. "Yes and no. She teaches nursing at a vocational school outside of San Diego. She got her professorship after the accident."

"Accident?" Cotton asked, suddenly concerned for this woman he didn't know.

"Yeah." Jason nodded. He'd set the monitor up on the counter by the door to the kitchen as they spoke. Now he stood and was wiping down the umber-stained wood and putting placemats on it in anticipation of dinner. The constant movement was automatic and precise. Cotton was suddenly aware that Jason's quiet competence was actually indicative of a rather amazing mind. He'd been bantering with Burton as he'd hooked up their surveillance equipment and had put away his tools neatly in what looked like a plain packing box that he'd apparently compartmentalized with cardboard left over from supplies Burton had brought him.

Cotton was lucky if he remembered to put on shoes in the morning.

He'd already been hanging on to every word Jason Constance uttered, but now he was doing it in desperation.

He really didn't want to screw up emotionally here when it looked like Jason was telling him something painful and important.

"Yeah, accident," Jason said, drawing near Cotton as he threw the crumbs in his hand into the trash can under the sink. He took a breath and leaned against the counter so they were side by side. "She came to visit me one weekend and stayed late to help me study. She sent me to bed and left for her house in the valley and got hit by a drunk driver when she was halfway home." He sighed. "I barely graduated, things were so touch and go for a while. And by the time she recovered, it became very, very clear that she would never walk again. Her spine had been crushed, and a lot of her internal organs had been damaged. Her entire life plan—things like hiking through Europe or having children—had been changed because one asshole decided to take two shots of tequila and drive home."

Jason's voice, always so even, so thoughtful, grew sharp and hard with bitterness, and Cotton couldn't help it. He grabbed Jason's hand as it rested against Jason's thigh.

"I'm sorry," he murmured, both of them staring at the gleaming stainless-steel refrigerator. A part of him was telling him he should probably start dinner, but most of him was saying holding Jason Constance's hand had become the most important thing he'd ever done.

"She's alive," Jason said. "And she's as ornery as ever. But I was pissed. I was beyond pissed. I… I could have thrown my whole life away, angry, aimless. It seemed so fucking pointless after that."

"What did she say to change that?" Cotton became aware Jason was studying the side of his face and smiling gently. "What?"

"How did you know she was the one who changed it?"

Cotton turned his head, frowning. "Because she's alive, and you love her. And that's where this story was going." He shrugged. "Some things you can feel"—he put his free hand over his stomach and rubbed—"here."

Jason put his fingers over Cotton's. "Only if you're extraordinarily intuitive," he said. "Because you're right. Jessie had a sit-down come-to-Jesus meeting with me from her hospital bed, for God's sake, and told me to snap out of it. She's really good at pointing out all of the blessings in my life, which is unfair, because she's one of the biggest. But she told me to find something that made me feel like I could control the world I lived in, to find a way to do some good."

"So you enlisted in the Marines?" Cotton asked, still in awe.

Jason shrugged. "You know. Sexy uniforms? I have to admit, I had some ulterior motives."

"Did you hit any of that?" Cotton had to know; he was as susceptible as the next boy.

Jason shrugged modestly. "Enough. Not as much as I hit in college, but, you know, not a monk. It was still Don't Ask, Don't Tell, so I just didn't tell. But…." He blew out a breath. "Right before my enlistment ended, before I signed my re-up papers, I got tapped for covert ops. The tap came with a promotion—one I hadn't really earned yet, to be honest. The reasoning was that my decisions had to be uncontestable by most of the officers on the ground. So suddenly, not only did I outrank everybody, I was everybody's asshole. And I couldn't afford to let anybody I was in charge of even know I had a dick, much less let them know which way it pointed." He let out a sigh. "And it got to be habit. God, there were so many awful things I saw. Some I was asked to perpetrate. Who… who wanted to sleep with a man who had to carry out hits? And then who had to order other people to carry them out? I… I was not a god. I had no business controlling life and death like I was put in a position to do. I couldn't let a single fucking thing distract me."

"Or be distracted by fucking," Cotton said, getting it.

Jason nodded, leaning his head back and closing his eyes. "And... and then Lee Burton came along. Best officer I ever trained. He was—is—extraordinary. I thought, 'He's only in it for three more years. I can be his handler for three more years. Then I can withdraw, have a pension, and hire a pool boy to take care of all my needs.'"

Cotton grunted and clutched his hand tighter. "That's a total lie," he asserted. "You wouldn't have."

"Well, no," Jason admitted, rubbing his thumb across Cotton's knuckles. "But, you know. It was my pet fantasy for a while."

Cotton let out a sigh, wanting him to know the truth. "I'm... I mean, for a couple of years, I *was* the fantasy. The fantasy is a bulimic, neurotic mess who's afraid of eating a tic tac and who kept thinking he was finding the perfect sugar daddy in porn. Uhm, maybe you need to find a real boy."

Jason's eyes shot straight to Cotton's. "What makes you think you're not a real boy?"

"I... I barely have a GED," he reminded Jason. "I think you're *amazing*. I will lie in bed next to you and let you do whatever you want to me. Or do whatever you want to you. But you need to know that when it's all said and done, I'll still be the kid who cried his way out of porn. And you need to know *I* know that. I don't get the cute guy in the red sports car. I don't get the knight in shining armor. If I'm lucky, I figure out how to get a good job to support myself and feel like I'm not a waste of skin."

Jason framed his face with both hands, and Cotton was mesmerized. His tired brown eyes, his heat, the kindness in the shape of his mouth and his touch—all of it held him in place, made him absolutely certain he couldn't move from this spot, not even if another mobster ran in with a gun.

"You're not a waste of skin," Jason said tenderly. "You *are* a real boy. And you *so* deserve the cute boy in a red sports car and not a dried-up old soldier."

Cotton closed his eyes, the words washing over him, washing away a layer of disbelief like dust, while the rubbed-in grime of pain and self-doubt remained. "You're not old," he said gruffly, their breath mingling, and then Jason put his lips on Cotton, and Cotton's entire concept of a kiss disintegrated into wonder.

Jason's lips were rough—he'd been sick, and they were slightly chapped—but his breath was sweet from orange juice. And none of that mattered. Heat, life-giving and blissful, poured from Jason's mouth into his, and Cotton opened up and became a vessel for all the tenderness, all the need, Jason Constance had dammed up in his soul for the last ten years.

It swamped him, dragged him under to a place where breathing was optional and the only thing that mattered was the stroke of Jason Constance's tongue against Cotton's, the pressure of his lips, and feel of Jason's chest under his hands.

Jason pulled back first, leaning his forehead against Cotton's, and for a few moments they simply worked at pulling in oxygen.

"My knees are wobbly," Jason said after a moment. "I can't even fucking believe this. My knees are wobbly."

Cotton smiled a little and kissed his temple. "Then you should sit down." He pulled Jason to the table and sat him down. "I'll cook. You get your strength up."

Jason gave one of his soft, bitter snorts.

"What?" Cotton opened the refrigerator again, grateful they had fresh foods. Salad-in-a-bag was always good, but so were fresh tomatoes and cucumbers. And look! A flat of boneless, skinless chicken breasts. He checked the spice rack, relieved to see it was fully stocked, and looked for a broiler pan. As he was assembling ingredients, he heard that bitter sound again, and looked up to see Jason shaking his head.

"What?" he asked, puzzled.

"Are you going to eat any of that?" he said softly.

Cotton shrugged. "I told you what I am," he said, unoffended. The whole reason Henry had made such a big deal about the lot of them—his own boyfriend included—going to see a shrink about their eating disorders was because Henry cared. Cotton understood that the fussing over food was a sign of affection. His own mother had done it when he'd been a kid and had grown faster than he could eat. That sort of thing could be amputated and die, he understood. It had with his mother. But he wasn't going to be cruel because someone was showing him that sort of interest in the moment.

"You're a beautiful young man," Jason said, sounding upset.

Cotton smiled at him, pleased. "That's kind," he murmured, stepping to the side and then back again. He resumed setting up the broiling pan and preheating the oven. "I keep a calorie diary," he said. "I eat as many calories as I promised to the week before." He let out a little huff. "Of course, Dr. Stevenson is going to be irritated because I've missed a couple of sessions. I'll have to text his office so he knows I'm coming back. He worries."

"Why does he worry?" Jason asked. His voice had that sort of sharp quality he had possessed when he and Burton had been talking about who might be after him.

"I think he became sort of the default shrink for the Johnnies guys. And the first kid who went to visit him made me look like a paragon of mental health. He worries about us. I mean, he's sort of sarcastic, and he's probably not all that professional—"

"What do you mean?"

Cotton thought about it and took a step to the side again. "Well, he gives us his opinion, and I *know* they're not supposed to do that. Like he told Randy that his heart might be twelve forever, but eventually he was going to have to use his indoor voice and not scratch his balls in public. Then he said that whoever thought he should be cut loose at eighteen should be shot. Then when Randy protested, he said he was retiring in a couple of years and he didn't have time to put us back together gently, but by-God he was going to make sure we went out into the world knowing we were decent kids with a decent future, so Randy could maybe stop yelling at him about why he had to rip all the hair off his balls, thank you very much."

Jason was trying not to laugh by then, and Cotton was proud of that, because he really didn't want to talk about himself. He didn't like his own stories; everybody else's were so much better.

"Well," Jason said after a moment, "I really do want to know about the hair on Randy's balls, but I also want to know how you heard all that. Did Randy tell you?"

Cotton's cheeks heated as he went about dinner preparations. "I, uh, was in the waiting room with Lance. We all went together and then saw him separately. Anyway, they were shouting at each other, and the walls were not made for that sort of abuse."

"Well, he sounds like a good shrink." There was a pause, during which Cotton tried to think if the three of them were going to need anything else to eat. "I hope you tell him more about yourself than you're willing to tell me."

Cotton almost dropped the salad bowl as he was fishing it out of a high cupboard.

"That's not fair," he muttered, shuffling his feet sideways.

"So's the fact that you apparently hate carbs. I see a perfectly good loaf of sourdough bread over that refrigerator. Any chance we could get some butter and garlic salt and a little bit of heat on some of that?"

Cotton went back to his job, soothed by the food prep and by the request. "Sure. I'll make some for Burton too."

"Make some for yourself too," Jason said, voice too soft to be an order. "As long as you're not allergic to gluten or anything."

"Nope. But, you know. Bulimic."

Jason let out a sigh. "Could you eat it and keep it down for me?" he begged. "I just… I mean, think about it practically, Cotton. You have dangerously low body fat. I've lost pretty much all my muscle and fat mass. If we want to have sex and not be like two arthritic joints grinding together, we need a little fat between us."

Cotton caught his breath and looked at Jason, not sure if he was serious or joking.

"Think about it," Jason said. He mock-thrust his hips. "It doesn't matter which one of us tops. If we're driving our hipbones into the other guy's butt bones, the best bone in the act is not going to remember its job!"

Cotton couldn't help it. He laughed. "That's terrible."

"Well, yes, but I was lying in your apartment for a week and a half, listening to you and your friends make jokes like twelve-year-olds, and I was stunned not one of you could think about that when you were all talking about carbs."

Cotton retrieved the sliced sourdough from the top of the refrigerator and proceeded to set up five slices of garlic bread. There wasn't any fresh garlic in the kitchen, but there was garlic salt, and he could make do.

Jason watched him working for a few moments and then said, "You know, you're pretty handy around the kitchen. Who taught you how to cook?"

"Henry," Cotton said, although that was only partly the truth. Henry had *reminded* him he knew how to cook. Once Henry started chivvying the flophouse guys into growing up a little and taking care of themselves, Cotton had been the one who'd gravitated toward cooking the most. Because he'd been seeing Dr. Stevenson, he knew everybody else's diet requirements as well, and he remembered how to make the lean stuff they all ate with a little bit of flavor to it.

"Henry?" Jason's voice sank for a moment, like he was pondering something. "That's odd. My mother taught me, and then my older sister. The way you move about in the kitchen—it's pretty ingrained. Not like you're trying to remember. From what I understand, Henry's only been in your life a little while."

"He's a good older brother," Cotton sidestepped, and Jason made the sort of "aha" sound somebody made when they were trying to get a key to fit in a lock. "What?" He turned. "What was that sound?"

"Your tell," Jason said softly, looking at him with troubled eyes. "I knew you were evading me about things, but you have a physical tell when you do it. Most people do. I had to figure it out so I'd know for certain."

Cotton shifted his feet again. "What... what do you mean?" But he knew. He must have evaded half a dozen questions in the last half hour, and thought he'd gotten away with it too. Jason struggled heavily to his feet, holding on to the back of the chair and the table, and Cotton felt altogether wretched, which sucked, because he'd been so happy! "No, don't. I don't need to know. Don't worry about it—I'm just not telling you the hard stuff. It's not important!"

Jason scowled and walked across the kitchen, putting his hands firmly on Cotton's shoulders and turning him toward his food prep and then moving them toward Cotton's hips.

"We're going to do this again," he said, voice gentle, and—oh Jesus—disappointed. "Let's start with, 'Cotton, how much of this meal are you going to eat?'"

"I'll eat with you—hey!"

He had no sooner finished saying the words than Jason's hands on his hips forced him back to his original position.

"Cotton, how much of this meal are you going to eat?" Jason asked again, his fingers tightening against Cotton's hipbones.

"One chicken thigh and the tomato I sliced with a little bit of salt on it," Cotton muttered. Jason's fingers relaxed against his skin, and he started to move a little more as his hands moved. "Why was that so important?"

Jason sighed. "Cotton, what did Dr. Stevenson say to you that was blunt but effective?"

"Same stuff he says to—what are you doing?"

Jason had put one foot on either side of Cotton's feet, and he couldn't shuffle them, couldn't side....

Step.

"My feet," he said flatly. "My feet were my tells. You're making me tell the truth by not letting my body lie."

"Yes," Jason told him, moving his own feet back and leaning against Cotton's back for a moment. "It doesn't work with hardened criminals, really, but it does work with people who don't like lying."

Cotton grunted. "Why do it at all?"

"Because you were leaving out the important stuff," Jason said, leaning his cheek against the back of Cotton's head. "I've told you more truth as a covert ops agent who isn't supposed to tell you *anything* than you've told me as a young man getting his life together who shouldn't have secrets of state pressing against his heart."

"It's dumb stuff," Cotton grumbled.

"It's private stuff," Jason corrected. He let out a breath and moved backward, hopefully to sit down. "Never mind. I'm sorry. It's probably wrong of me to force the private stuff. I just… I offered you my real stuff in good faith, Cotton. Why won't you tell me the real things too? I may not be able to promise you forever here, but I want what we do, what happens between us, at least to be real. Don't you?"

Cotton's eyes burned. "Yes," he rasped, looking sightlessly down at the chicken in the broiling pan. "Yes. More than anything."

"Then you're going to have to be brave," Jason told him, his own voice hurt and oddly tender. "You're going to have to tell me the real things or…."

"Or you might as well be having sex with the pool boy," Cotton said, getting it. He looked over his shoulder to meet Jason's eyes and was reassured, a little, to see they were bright and shiny too.

"I don't want the fantasy anymore," Jason said. "I'm old, and I'm sad, and it may not last, but it needs to be real."

And Cotton opened his mouth then to tell him everything—*everything*—but at that moment there was a heavy-booted footstep on the porch, and the front door, which led straight into the living room, which then led into the kitchen, opened.

Burton's voice boomed through the cabin. "Hello! If anybody's naked, I fucking quit!"

"We're in the kitchen, Lee!" Jason called back. Then he met Cotton's eyes and said, "Think about it," quietly, for him alone.

Cotton swallowed and nodded. "I'll think about nothing else," he promised, and then Burton strode into the kitchen and took in the preparations for dinner.

"That isn't fried?" he said in horror. "You had chicken, you had eggs, you had flour—"

"But I didn't have Rice Krispies," Cotton said. "That's what makes it perfect." His feet slid sideways—he felt them—but Jason didn't say a word.

He wasn't lying about the Rice Krispies making the fried chicken tastier, so he and Lee exchanged recipes for chicken he could probably never bring himself to eat while Jason sat and rested and Lee set the table.

SOMEONE ELSE'S LIFE

THAT EVENING was so normal Jason could almost weep for it. They ate dinner, and the conversation around the dinner table was about setting up the cameras and who would be arriving the next day and at what time—and about other things too.

Burton had seen a bear while he'd been up in the tree. In fact, part of the reason Jason and Cotton had gotten so many painful, wonderful moments alone together had been that Burton had spent part of his day up in that tree, hoping the bear and her two adolescent cubs would ramble on by. They did, but Burton must have recreated the moment a thousand times for a wide-eyed Cotton, who was enchanted to think there were bears in the surrounding woods.

"And deer too," he said happily. "I've seen a few, looking out the windows. And rabbits too."

"Yeah," Burton agreed, nodding. "I took pictures for Ernie."

"You don't have deer where you live?" Cotton asked curiously.

"We live in the desert," Jason said. "There's life there—more than people think—but a lot of it is hard life. Rattlesnakes, scorpions, jackrabbits that could rip you apart if you tried to catch them."

"Teeny mice," Burton said, nodding. "You would be surprised how many teeny mice there are. Ernie's cats...." He paused and added, "My boyfriend has a million cats. It's one of the first things I noticed about him that made me think he wasn't a serial killer or something. It's like I got us this nice house out in the middle of nowhere, and cats started a kitty exodus from all the corners of the earth just so they could show up at his doorstep and he could feed them. Anyway, so we've got fifty-dozen cats, and every now and then one of them will try to prove he loves Ernie best, so he'll bring a teeny tiny mouse to sit on the mat at the front door. It's so sad. There was this tiny mouse, going, 'Hey, desert sucks, but I haven't seen any rattlesnakes or scorpions today,' and *boom*! There's Ernie's cat, who shouldn't even fucking be there." He shook his head. "I told Ernie this, and he started singing 'Circle of Life' in full Broadway tenor. I was impressed by his range, but I don't think he got that cats are totally badass."

"He got it," Jason said. "You don't like to admit that even though Ernie looks like an anime character, he's got a streak of badass in him much like yours."

Burton gave a sort of fond, proud grin. "I know it," he said. "I just like to give him shit about the mouse population in Asschapped South of Hell is all."

"You live in Asschapped South of Hell?" Cotton asked, obviously curious.

"Did we mention the desert?" Jason said mildly. "We sort of co-opted an old military base. Burton lives within commuting distance."

"I have to stay at the base sometimes," Lee admitted. "But I got this house—it was like somebody thought they were going to put up this big housing tract of these million-dollar houses, but who in the fuck was going to buy them, right? Like the man says, 'You're out in the middle of the goddamned desert!' So they finished, what? Four? Five of them? And Ernie and I are the only people there."

"Really?" Cotton stared at him.

"It's amazing. There are four other perfectly good houses with their landscaping going to shit, but in between are the big vacant lots for houses that will never be built. There's even a giant pit about two miles away into the desert for all of the building materials they didn't want to cart across country, and another one for trash. I mean, I got this house for a song. I think the real estate agent wanted to have my babies, and he was way too old for that. It might have killed him."

Cotton looked at Jason, and Jason wanted to duck under the table because he knew what was coming. "Why don't you move out there?" he asked.

"Because he never leaves the base," Lee snorted. "He haunts the place like a zombie ghost, waking up in the middle of the night to go, 'This scumbag here! I think he's trying to obliterate a small city/state in the Ukraine!' And suddenly one of us gets woken up, and we know what *we're* doing that week."

Jason grimaced. "I get intel all day," he confessed. "We keep an eye out for things that might point to one of our subjects going rogue someplace he doesn't think he'll get caught. Anyway, I'll be in my room or the weight room or the pool, trying to relax from my fucking day, and all that intel suddenly has a train wreck in my head."

"And then one of us gets our week ruined," Burton confirmed.

"What are you sent to do?" Cotton asked, and Burton and Jason had a grim conversation with their eyes.

Finally Jason looked away and said softly, "Better he know me."

Burton shook his head. "It's not that simple," he replied. Then, to Cotton, he said, "It depends. We would love to be able to take these guys in, reacquaint them with the military, give them some counseling, debrief them. They signed up for a program that they thought would make them better soldiers, and they were tortured and brainwashed and basically taught to strip away their humanity and go out and kill to achieve an end. And *then* they were cut loose. When we got the guy who was doing this to them, they had nobody to turn to. Some of them went out to fulfil old missions, but political boundaries change, so even if what they're doing is appropriate by military standards, they're going to get into trouble. But these guys...." He shivered. "A lot of them aren't even human anymore."

"The Dirty/Pretty Killer," Jason said out of the blue, and Cotton caught his breath.

"Oh my God." Jason watched the color drain from his face. "Oh my God." Jason grabbed his hand as he started to shake. "That was last year."

Jason had done the math. Cotton had been off the streets for two years by then, but still, it must have hit him hard. The victims had all been young and beautiful, with just a little bit of street living on them. They'd turned a couple of tricks or done some drugs and were looking to score some more. Sometimes both. They'd recently started down the spiral where Cotton had probably been headed, and then they'd been murdered, brutally.

"Yes," Jason said quietly. "He... let's just say that after Jackson Rivers and Ellery Cramer brought him down, they followed his trail, and that's how the lot of us met. That, as they say, is how that happened. So sometimes— not often—we can bring them in. But most of the time...."

"You have to stop them," Cotton murmured. "Any way you can. I get it."

Jason looked away. He should have known. He couldn't make a case for them being real with each other if Cotton didn't know, down to specifics, what it was that Jason actually did. He ordered the deaths of former covert ops soldiers, and he had to look inside some really twisted minds to do it. Cotton was embarrassed because he was bulimic, because he'd been a sex worker, and because he was still getting his life together.

The bone-deep shame Jason felt for being a killer who sentenced other killers to death was like a black hole, devouring what was left of his soul.

Cotton's hand on his own was a blessing. "I wasn't on the streets when the Dirty/Pretty killer was out there, but I could have been. It could have been me. I was there the night Henry looked Jackson up on the internet, before they started working together. He… he was stunned that Rivers lived through that. So someone who is making sure that another Dirty/Pretty killer is being stopped—that's someone we need in the world, right?"

Jason shook his head, still not able to look him in the eye. "What should have been stopped was that he was made at all."

Burton's snort took both their attention. "Not even Ernie could do that, and he's witchy as fuck."

"You keep saying that," Cotton murmured, obviously as glad of the diversion as Jason was. "What makes him witchy?"

"For one thing, he said there'd be a storm at the end of August, and he wasn't talking rain. And look at us, finally seeing some of the clouds dissipate."

Jason glared at him. "Don't you dare say that. Have you learned nothing?" Back in college Jason would have eschewed the idea of psychic powers and laughed at Ernie's "witchiness," but soldiers were often superstitious. If you were risking your life as part of your job, you spent a lot of time talking to a higher power, whether you admitted you believed in one or not. Jason wasn't proud. He'd come to believe in the gods of luck, wisdom, and random fucking chance as much as the next soldier, and Ernie's abilities to simply sense the world around him out of sync with linear time was something he believed had saved a lot of lives—his included.

But part of jumping on board that train was not jinxing things by saying, "Looks like it's all clear, sir!"

Burton grimaced. "I said *some*! *Some* clouds! I didn't say all of them. I just meant that, you know, you managed not to die in a tiny apartment surrounded by porn stars."

Jason rolled his eyes. "That would *not* have been a hardship."

"It would have been for *us*!" Burton retorted. "You seem to forget that you are the glue holding our little enterprise together, Jason. You *have* to be healthy. You *have* to be well. So yeah, maybe it's been because I've had Ernie for almost a year, but I'm going to have a little faith. I'm going to hope. Do you fucking mind?" And with that, Burton shoved a bite of chicken and garlic bread into his mouth and chewed. He paused midchew, swallowed, and said, "Cotton, this is really amazing chow. You know that, right?"

Cotton gave a shy smile. "Thank you. You guys are fun to cook for. You actually eat."

Jason grunted. "And so do you," he said pointedly, looking at the half a chicken thigh and most of a piece of bread on his plate. "You promised."

Cotton sighed. "Of course," he said and began to eat determinedly, in tiny bites.

Burton raised an eyebrow at Jason, and Jason shook his head, mouthing "Later" at him. Ordinarily Burton's curiosity would be a violation; people had boundaries. But Jason and Burton had confided a lot in the young man in the past couple of days, and much of it was, in fact, classified. Information that Cotton—and good God, did they even know the kid's real name?—couldn't know.

But then Cotton had pretty much given his life over to keeping Jason alive, and Jason was reasonably sure that everybody who had been in the room with Rivers and Henry during the official debriefing knew most of what they'd told Cotton. The fact was, Jason and his team worked below the radar, were comfortable with being there, in fact, and so did Cotton. John Carey was never going to get a philanthropy award, but he'd apparently worked hard, purposely unnoticed, to make sure the kids in his employ were as healthy as he knew how to make them. Jackson Rivers and Ellery Cramer were never going to get medals for their work to bring Karl Lacey to justice, but they'd almost given their lives to do exactly that. Even Henry's boyfriend, Lance, and Jai's boyfriend, George, had risked their jobs and their freedom to take care of Jason when he'd needed them, and they expected nothing more than to know that the kids Jason had been transporting had made it home.

It was safe to assume that Cotton, much like the people who surrounded him, wouldn't be noticed in this lifetime or the next as the heroes they were, but Jason recognized the extent of their service, and of what they'd done for him personally. He couldn't give them all a zillion dollars and a new car, but he could give Cotton what everybody else had been given.

Jason's trust and the truth. And given Burton's freedom around Cotton, Jason figured it was a case of Jackson Rivers trusting the young man as well.

And of course, Ernie.

But trusting Cotton meant Burton needed anomalies explained to him. Since Burton was planning to leave the two of them alone in the cabin, with their watchers positioned nearby, Burton was trusting Cotton didn't have any medical or psychological needs that would render them both vulnerable if they were discovered and attacked.

So Jason got it, but he didn't want anybody but himself to know about Cotton's difficulties.

Cotton was, in a very personal, private way, Jason's. He tried very, very hard to keep up the illusion that his life started the moment John had found him, turning tricks apparently, but Jason wasn't fooled like that. He could see somebody had thrown Cotton away. Somebody had thrown *Jason's angel* away. Jason might need to leave Cotton when this was all over—he was certainly not in any position to make promises, and given how much grief he was getting while the government knew who he was, he certainly didn't want Cotton mentioned in *any* official reports, not as a spouse, not as a friend, not as a person of interest. But that didn't mean that Jason would throw him away too. Or throw away his privacy or his dignity or any of the things the young man worked so hard to protect.

Jason would tell Burton about the eating disorder, partly so when Jason was gone, Burton could help keep an eye on the young man. But he wasn't going to just dump the information out like it didn't matter.

It obviously mattered very much to Cotton.

Jason tuned back into the dinner table chatter and realized that Cotton was grilling Lee about the cats, and he had to smile.

Everybody except the allergic loved the cats.

"I'd love to have a cat," Cotton said wistfully. "And a dog. And a fish. An entire apartment full of animals." He grinned, hiding his face. "Animals don't judge, and as long as you feed them, they're very free with love. I like that in a roommate."

"Ernie's exact philosophy," Burton said. "And since I'm gone a lot, I told him the house was his to decorate as he pleased." He chuckled. "Imagine my surprise when I realized we were going for cats on every available surface."

"You weren't surprised at all," Jason chided, and Burton's smile was all fondness.

"Not even a little teeny bit," he said and then wiped his plate with the last of his garlic bread.

Jason glanced over to see Cotton had done the same, and he smiled gently. Cotton winked and got up to clear the table.

"Nope." Burton stood and took his plate. "My job. You guys go to the living room and cuddle on the couch and look cute. I'll bring milk and cookies." He gave Cotton a stern look. "One cookie?"

"Sure," Cotton murmured, smiling slightly.

Lee Burton would say he was the least personable, least kind, least amiable man on the face of the planet, but Jason knew better. All of those stories about Ernie—all of that affection for someone who wasn't conventional in any sense of the word—and Cotton now trusted him too. On the one hand, it was so smart it was almost cruelly calculated, but Jason knew Lee hadn't done it that way on purpose.

Burton wanted Cotton to trust him because Burton might have to save their lives again.

But it also had the side benefit of making their evening pleasant. Cotton came to Jason's chair and held out a hand. "Need help up?"

Jason grunted. He just might. He was exhausted already, and it was barely eight in the evening. "Fine," he grumbled, letting Cotton leverage him up and guide him to the living room.

The living room furniture was fittingly rustic—oxblood, to match the redwood paneling on the walls, with a smoke-colored Berber that would probably *will* stains to jump off the floor, out of the house, and into the lake. Cotton and Jason had been wearing flip-flops anyway, but Burton had taken off his boots before he'd sat down to dinner.

It was that kind of house.

There were thick wool throws in a big wicker basket at the corner of the couch, and as Jason settled into a spot where the arm could support him, Cotton grabbed one of the throws and the remote and settled in next to him, covering them both with the throw.

Jason raised his arm and let Cotton snuggle in, and something about his weight was so comforting, so sweet, Jason closed his eyes at it.

"Dinner was great," he said softly. "Thank you."

"Like I said, I enjoy it." Cotton held out the remote. "Any preferences?" He clicked the screen on and gave a pleased hum. "Apparently we have all the premium channels. All of them. Is there anything you've wanted to watch for the last thirty years and couldn't? It's here."

"*The Muppet Show*?" Jason asked, grinning.

"That's a real thing?" Cotton asked suspiciously. "I mean, I know they had Muppet babies and that movie with Jason Segel...."

"Heathen! Yes, it's a real thing! My parents loved them. Back in the day before dirt and dinosaurs when we didn't rely on streaming services and magic clouds to hold all our cultural treasures, my parents bought the DVDs. My sister and I still love them."

Cotton chuckled. "Don't sweat it. I can find them, see?" And sure enough, with the tech and media savvy of the young, he found the streaming service and the shows. He hit Play for the first one, and then, to Jason's immense satisfaction, he settled down against his chest, concentrating on the screen. A few minutes later, after doing the dishes, that's how Burton found them.

"Very nice," he rumbled. "I like men who can follow orders." He held out a glass of milk to Jason and a napkin of cookies to Cotton. "Share these," he said. "Because I'm too lazy to bring out another cup."

Of course Jason knew he wasn't lazy in the least. He seemed to want to encourage whatever was happening between Jason and Cotton, and Jason wasn't going to worry about why.

He was just going to enjoy the moment, Cotton tucked against him, the sweetness of cookies and the coolness of milk, and the gentle humor of old comfort TV.

HE WOKE up probably an hour later, missing the warmth of Cotton next to him. Burton was partially lifting him off the couch so he could move on his own power.

"Gah!" he muttered. "I'm helpless!"

"Yeah, you are. Remember that and listen to that kid when he tells you to eat and take your medication. I'm leaving in the morning after I introduce you to your security detail. I need to know you and that boy can function."

"We can," Jason said softly. "Where is he?"

"Straightening the bed and putting on his jammies. I asked him for a few minutes to talk to you alone, and he shadowed on out of here like that was his job. Creepy. I usually expect more backtalk than that."

Jason smiled a little and got his feet underneath him. "Let him get comfortable. You've seen him stand up for me—he's got backtalk in him."

"Yeah, I just…." Burton let out a sigh. "I like this kid. And you obviously trust him, and your instincts haven't let us down. But I need to know. Is he going to be okay? He looks a little fragile, Jase. I don't want to break him."

Jason nodded. "I think the world's tried," he said bluntly. "But he's dealing with the eating disorder—calorie diary and a shrink. And after all the shit that's tried to break him, he's still standing. I think he'll do okay. With any luck, this'll be a vacation, a week or two of sunshine and good food and maybe some hiking and swimming. It'll be like summer camp for the broken."

"You or him?" Burton asked, helping him break into a shuffling walk.

"Both," Jason said softly. "I'm so tired. I… I keep thinking, this can't possibly be because I got shot. I mean, I've been shot before, right?"

"It's mental exhaustion, you fucking moron," Burton told him, voice icy. "You were the one who told me I needed to have a place to heal outside of the base, and then *you* spend all your time inside the base, letting serial killers burn out your brain. Jesus, you were probably losing your will to live for the entire last year!"

Jason grunted. "Wow. That's, uhm, direct." He hadn't thought of it like that, but Burton wasn't far wrong. The perpetual exhaustion had been weighing him down so hard. That moment in the desert, looking at the kids who had been on their way to an unfathomable nightmare and hearing his superior officer telling him he had to take them there himself—that had been the moment he'd snapped. He'd literally chosen death, any kind of death, before doing one more morally reprehensible thing in the name of being a good soldier.

"Am I wrong?" Burton asked. "By the way, you must have lost forty pounds in the last two weeks. You two need to put on sixty pounds of muscle between you before I get back here. Carbs are not a dirty fucking word!"

"No, you're not wrong." Jason sighed as they cleared the living room and entered the bedroom. "Point taken. We'll have our very own camping retreat, right, Cotton?"

Cotton was coming out of the bathroom, dressed in basketball shorts and a tank top. He was shivering a little; the temperature had dropped in the evening and while the cabin had a heater, nobody had started a fire.

"Camping adventure," Cotton echoed, nodding. "It will be very after school special." He paused. "Which, you know, my generation has never actually experienced. Jackson had to explain it to me once."

"Shoot me now," Burton muttered. "I'm obviously too old to live, and I don't like icebergs."

"I'll take the iceberg," Jason said dryly. "I'm so old even the polar bears won't eat me."

"You're both hilarious." Cotton moved to help Jason down, holding the thermometer to his head briefly before checking it. "And you suck. Tomorrow, we sit out on the porch and read. The end. I'll bring you a blanket, we'll compare notes—it'll be scintillating, and maybe you can kick this fucking fever."

"Did he just say scintillating?" Jason asked dryly, feeling the low-grade fever exhaustion that he resented as much as Cotton apparently did. "Nobody's ever called me scintillating."

"You're a sparkling dinner companion, sir," Burton deadpanned. "Now stand up. I'm gonna unbuckle your pants."

"Kinky," Jason replied in the same voice. "Almost as good as changing my oil or vacuuming my barracks."

Cotton laughed and waited for Burton to help Jason out of his pants and hoodie before handing him his medication with a paper cup of water. "I'll remember that," he said. "Doing chores goes on the kink list."

"Well, sleep does it for me," Burton told them. "I'll be here in the morning to introduce you to your detail. Cotton?"

"Sir?"

"I'm bringing coffee, fruit salad, and pastries in when I go pick these guys up, so don't worry about breakfast. Is there anything you want me to shop for? The guys will be doing all your shopping from here on out, but I can get stuff tomorrow."

"Cottage cheese," Cotton said promptly. "Yogurt. Uhm…." He looked away, obviously embarrassed.

"What?"

"Uhm, I'm going to be done with those books in less than a week. I should have brought more."

"Give me the author's name and I'll see what I can do. There's some used bookstores in Tahoe. Here." He gave Cotton his phone. "Type in some other authors. If you guys are going to be lounging around like pampered poodles, you're going to need entertainment. Anything else?"

"A chess set," Jason said. He glanced at Cotton as he settled into bed, and Cotton seconded.

"You'll have to teach me how to play," he said shyly.

"Good." Burton confirmed. "Jason, I know you like coffee with those frou-frou creams. Don't even lie. I'll bring some. Cotton, the water here isn't great, but we've got bottled. Do you like sparkling?"

"Oh! Yeah, that would be great. All the smells." Cotton looked up from punching information into his phone. "Thank you."

Burton snorted. "Smells?"

Cotton looked embarrassed. "They don't really *taste*, do they? It's more like, you know, they made them smell really good, and your body pretends it's flavor."

"Jason, that's on the classified list. Now that he knows that, we have to kill him."

Jason's eyes popped wide, and he struggled to sit up, absolutely sure Cotton wouldn't think that was a joke. And then he heard a snort—the kind that came unwillingly from someone's nose and throat—and a dorky little giggle, followed by a suppressed "Hee!"

Worried, he turned to see Cotton covering his mouth like a little kid, and he grinned before turning back to Lee.

"He's gonna be fine," he said happily, and Burton nodded before backing out of the room.

Cotton giggled again and moved around the room, turning off lights. He paused when he came to the monitor, which Lee had moved to the end table by Jason's side of the bed. All of the screens were dark, but as they watched, one of them lit up, a dark flutter passing in front of the camera and disappearing.

"Owl," he said in wonder.

"Yeah. Wait...." Another screen lit, and two deer passed quietly, leaving the camera's range. In three seconds, the screen went dark.

"Will it be doing that all night?" he asked.

Jason sighed. "Yes, but it's set to chirp if something passes through more than two camera ranges. One happens, but more than that, we should know about."

Cotton frowned. "Are you going to be able to sleep like that? I mean, with one eye open?"

Jason's shoulder ached or he would have shrugged. "Have been for almost fourteen years now," he said softly.

Cotton's eyes narrowed. "Excuse me." And with that he stalked out of the room and knocked, politely, on Lee's door. Jason didn't hear the resulting conversation, but in a moment, Lee hustled back into the bedroom, giving Jason a bemused look.

"I'll be taking this until the security detail can have it," he said, sounding penitent. "You can't get better if you can't sleep."

Jason nodded, equally bemused, and Cotton opened both doors for Lee so he could set up the monitor in his room. Cotton returned to the bedroom, shut the light off one final time, and shivered his way into bed with Jason.

Jason rolled over and pulled him tight, that full-body human contact soothing nerves wrought fine with exhaustion. "Why'd you do that?" he mumbled, mourning because Cotton was here, he was willing, and Jason had at least one more day of recovery before he could do anything about that.

"Because you can't sleep if you're always on alert," Cotton said, with the practicality of someone who knew.

"You're right." Jason yawned. "How'd you guess?"

Cotton let out an unhappy little sigh, and down under the covers, Jason could feel the motion of restless feet. With a grunt he used one of his feet to trap Cotton's, and it was Cotton's turn to grunt.

"When I was living on the streets," he said after a moment, "you had to be alert or you'd get robbed or raped or worse."

Ah. "How'd you end up there?" Jason asked, wondering if this was going to be the moment Cotton told him.

"Same way everyone else does—dammit!" He'd obviously felt Jason's foot pressing against his shifting ankle.

"You're the one who keeps trying to evade me," Jason muttered.

"I'm tired!"

"So am I! Just talk to me like you trust me and I'll let you sleep!"

"Okay, fine." Cotton rolled over and scowled at him. "My parents kicked me out when they found me having sex with my boyfriend in my bedroom. Happy?"

"No. That's terrible. I mean, was it the sex or was it the gay or—"

"It was all of it," Cotton muttered. "But it's not even the worst thing."

Jason tried to study him in the darkness, but he'd closed the door to the hallway, and the tiny window in this room looked out into a moonless night. There wasn't enough ambience to see.

"What could be worse than that?" he asked gently, putting a hand on Cotton's hip.

"The worst thing was I was seventeen and my boyfriend was twenty. They tried to charge him with rape, which it totally wasn't. When I refused to participate in pressing charges—in fact, when I told the ADA that I'd seduced *him*—they gave me the choice of either living at home and following through or they'd kick me out."

Jason closed his eyes. "Oh, baby."

"Don't call me that," Cotton told him, voice choked and muffled. "I don't deserve it. It ruined his life, you understand? I showed up at his house, thinking, 'Hey, we can move in together, and I'll get a job and put myself through school,' and he'd spent two weeks in custody with the threat of being a registered sex offender hanging over his head. He didn't want a fucking thing to do with me, and I don't blame him. I had friends who put me up on their couches for a little while, but word got around, and parents thought I was some sort of pervert and…. God. Soon I was living in shelters, and I got pretty much everything I'd brought with me stolen in the first day. I swear to God, I turned my first trick to get out of the rain. He sprung for the hotel room, and I asked to use the shower, and…." Cotton's voice had grown sharp and angry, charged with bitterness in a way Jason had never heard from him before. But now it softened a little. "He washed my clothes and bought me new ones while I was trying to shower a week's worth of grime off. He bought me dinner and let me stay in the hotel when it was over, and... and he wasn't mean. Or entitled. Just lonely. He became a regular. Once a week. Same time, same place. It kept me sane, really, knowing that once a week I could pretend I had a home."

Jason's eyes burned. "I'd say 'good' or 'I'm glad,' but I'm so sad you had to deal with that."

"Wasn't the worst thing to happen to me there," Cotton said lowly. "I...."

Jason nudged his restless feet with his toe, letting him know that the truth was okay between them.

"The guy... the guy I couldn't do the scene with. He was a decent kid, you know? But he looked.... God, he could have been the little brother of a guy I knew when I was turning tricks. Basic bland white-guy looks—sandy hair, hazel eyes, square chin—not bad-looking, you know? Didn't *look* like a monster."

"Oh no." Jason's stomach dropped. He knew what was coming. How could he not? A teenaged boy turning tricks with no backup? "How many times?" he asked.

"Four," Cotton said, voice breaking. "He knew my corner. He'd show up, and I'd tell him no, and he'd drag me to the car and then dump me out when it was done. Never used a fucking rubber, never used lube. God. My regular—the nice guy—picked me up once afterward and spent the whole night with me in the shower as I cried. Sweet guy, you know? In his forties, but I was of age. I.... God. After John took me to the flophouse, I asked if I could go back and tell the guy goodbye. John did it for me. I guess the guy gave him money. John used it to start a bank account so I could keep the money myself. It's so weird. So weird. Like, there was the absolute worst of the world there on the street, ready to ream me up the fuckin' ass, but there was a sweet guy who only wanted company, and there was John who was strung out but trying to be a decent guy. I never knew who I was going to get." He let out a little sigh. "That's why I liked porn, I guess. They had, like, a list of items to perform, and you did each item until the other guy went 'Yes, that! Do that more!' It was, like, put in the quarter, get out the attaboy. I... I gotta tell you, I was *really* ready for some attaboys by then, you know?"

Jason rubbed Cotton's shins with his toes. "I get it," he said softly, suddenly too tired to keep his eyes open. "Cotton?"

"Yeah?"

"I'm glad you told me. I... I like who you are. I think you're strong... and kind, when you could have been a terrible person, a user. I was so tired, seeing all the worst things humans can do to each other, and suddenly, I was with you, and you've seen that too, but you still try your best. I'm falling asleep, but I need to tell you...."

Cotton reached for him, pulled *him* close, like he was giving the comfort, and Jason snuggled his head against Cotton's chest. "Tell me what?" Cotton murmured, like he really wanted to hear.

"You give me faith. You're the reason not everything is awful. There's people like you who do the kind thing sometimes, when people use shitty excuses to do the worst things, just because they can."

"Thanks, Jason," Cotton said softly. "Good night."

"Good night, baby. Can I call you baby now?"

"Only you," he said, and that seemed to be enough to send Jason right off to sleep.

TWO VOICES ECHOING

COTTON SMILED nervously at the three soldiers sitting at the kitchen table and tried not to flee for the bedroom. True to his promise, Lee had brought coffee and coffee drinks, with a fruit-and-ham platter and pastries, and the three men with buzzcuts and chests Cotton could only dream of achieving were currently eating all that food like it was about to sprint off the table.

Jason had jumped in and gotten Cotton a plate of fruit and ham, and Burton—who was running the show—had slipped him a carton of peach yogurt. They'd given him small portions, and Cotton was grateful. They wanted to help him, not pressure him, and given there was nothing in the military hero handbook that said "be kind to bulimia boy," he knew he could have ended up with worse people in his life.

But that didn't mean the guys at the table, to a one wearing hiking boots, cargo shorts, and olive drab green T-shirts, didn't scare the crap out of him.

"So," Burton was saying, obviously in charge of the op that *was* guarding Jason and Cotton. "We're looking for people connected to Dietrich and Karina Schroeder. Or Dima Siderov. Now, by all accounts Dietrich and Karina have heavy German accents, but Dima, who is Russian, has practically no accent at all. These are city dwellers. They are going to use city-dwelling tactics, and they're ruthless, determined, and organized. On the minus side, they don't appear able to think on their feet. The guy we encountered was wearing a black wool suit at the end of August, and you guys checked the surroundings. Did you see signs of anyone else?"

"No," said the smallest of the security detail, Briggs. He was African American, with pale brown skin, an apple-cheeked face, and tiny dark brown freckles. Cotton was a fan of freckles and apple cheeks. Ordinarily this guy would have turned his key, but right now, his attention was focused mostly on Jason and the quiet intensity he gave the briefing.

Jason was looking better—well rested, for once, and he had a little color. The fever was almost gone, and Cotton had a sudden irrational hope that maybe they could go for a walk that day. The cameras had revealed a wonderland of wilderness, and it had been so long since Cotton had been camping. If he excised the memories of his parents, he could recall the peace of being out in the woods. He'd once sat under a tree when his father thought he was fishing, and he'd read almost half of *All Creatures Great and Small*. His father had been irritated to find out he'd bailed on something "outdoorsy" and masculine, but Cotton remembered the wonder of that moment—the trees, the sounds, the breeze, the sun through the leaves—and it would always mingle with the images of a fallible human being struggling to treat animals whom he obviously loved in pre-WWII Britain.

Cotton remembered Jason and Burton talking about being out in the middle of the "fucking desert." He wanted Jason to have a good memory to take back with him when he returned to saving the world.

His attention was called back to Briggs, who was outlining what they'd seen and what he planned to do to keep watch.

"No people out here. Daniels spoke to the people in the cabin. They think he looks like Captain America. Children, pets, grandparents all love him."

Daniels indeed had a bit of a Chris Evans vibe. He gave an aw-shucks grin and took up the thread. "The cabins are run by a family—the Calendars senior, in their sixties, the Calendars junior, in their forties, and junior's three teenagers, who help out in the summer but are getting ready to move back to town and return to school. Once they move for the fall, it's going to be the three of us in one of the six-person cabins and two elderly couples sharing the other six-person. As of tomorrow, we should be the only guests, which means any cars coming or going are either going to be the two Chevy Tahoes owned by the Calendars, or somebody new. We've set up cameras at the entrance to the cabin road from the main road and at the entrance to your drive from the smaller road that leads to the private cabins. There are ten cabins, maybe, around the lake, and since it's too late for summer and too early for snow, they're going to be pretty sparsely populated as well. We'll be doing a lot of hiking and checking things out while we're here, but there will always be one person minding the cameras with a set of binocs trained on you guys here. If you see anything fishy on your own monitor or even get the prickles up your spine, give us a signal, any signal, and you should have backup." He gestured to the third member of their team, midsized, olive-complected, with wicked brown eyes and jet-black hair. "Medina here has the skinny on the coms and electronics."

Medina finished chewing in a hurry, then gave Burton and Jason an *un*hurried grin. "Gotta thank ya both for the chow," he said in an unabashed Texas accent. "Transpo here was a bear, and then we got here and I thought we'd be eatin' real bear shit for breakfast."

Briggs put his hand over his eyes in a pained gesture. "Texas, do you really have to share?"

But Daniels grinned. "I saw that episode too! Where the guys got dropped off in the wild with weird random shit and told to find their way home, and that one guy ate bear scat to survive?" He looked around the table, nodding. "See, bears have super bad digestive tracts so their food can sit in their stomachs and sort of… you know, do digesting things when they're hibernating. But that means when they're moving around, their droppings are like super rich in nutrients and shit, so you don't ever have to starve as long as bears still shit in the woods."

Medina grinned. "Right? So yeah, after learning factoids like that shit, getting fruit and pastry and coffee is a real treat. Thanks, Colonel, Captain."

They all nodded, and Cotton could tell by the strained looks on Burton's and Jason's faces that they were trying very hard to maintain an air of command around their troops.

Cotton had no such requirements. He gave a relieved smile at the three young men who would be holding his and Jason's lives in their hands. "Oh thank God," he said with feeling. "I thought I was gonna get, like, those guards at the Tower of London. I was so worried I was going to have to learn how to salute!"

He got three easy grins in return. "Just feed us now and then," Briggs said after shooting a quelling look at his two teammates. "I swear, we'll be almost civilized."

"And I'm used to living in an apartment with five other guys," Cotton said, nodding enthusiastically. "Seeing some friendly faces once a day will be super awesome."

"Five guys?" Medina asked, horrified. "Where'd they all fit?"

Cotton shrugged. "Well, we all worked in porn, so sometimes up each other's asses. But once you quit the business, you pay extra rent for that single bed, you know?"

Daniels spit out his orange juice and choked while Medina and Briggs pounded his back. For a moment, Cotton thought he might have ruined the moment of camaraderie, but they were looking at him with such open, engaging grins he sort of felt like he'd achieved a victory.

"This your friend, Colonel?" Briggs asked.

"He saved my life—a couple of times," Jason said, bumping Cotton's leg.

"I threw a chef's knife at a bad guy," Cotton told them, wanting them to know who they were working with. "It bounced off his nose."

"Killing me!" Daniels choked, head in his arms. "Love this guy!"

Briggs patted him a few more times between the shoulder blades. "That's the spirit. Tell you what, if Colonel Constance is resting and you're bored, you give us a holler and we'll have some weapons training. I love your energy. Throwing a chef's knife is using what's at hand, but let's see if we can make it stick, okay?"

Cotton smiled at Jason. "That way I can defend you for real."

Jason nodded. "You were doing pretty good on your own, but yeah, I think lessons would help."

Cotton's shyness had dissipated, and he finished off the rest of his yogurt while the guys completed the briefing. Burton had said this would be like a vacation for Jason, and Cotton was all for that. It occurred to him that this was like a vacation for *Cotton* as well, and he realized he hadn't so much as gone out of town with friends since he'd left home.

He got to have a vacation too—reading, hiking, swimming, and self-defense. It was like the day camp he'd always wanted but hadn't known how to ask for.

But mostly he was glad because Jason would be there with him.

Briggs, Daniels, and Medina all left shortly thereafter, but not before hooking their handheld monitors to the same feed that Jason was connected to. As they were walking out the door, Cotton asked them if Jason was needed to monitor the screen all night or if one of them could do it.

"He almost died of infection," he said seriously. "He's going to need his sleep or he'll never recover."

"Well, probably keep it in his room," Briggs said, thinking, "but one of us should be watching it at all times. If it's in the room, he can sleep and ignore it but wake up as soon as one of us buzzes him. He can also check it to ease his own paranoia."

Jason caught Cotton's eye and nodded to confirm.

"Because careful people are careful," Cotton acknowledged. "I get that. I just need to know he can sleep."

"Fair enough," Briggs said respectfully. "Go ahead and put it in the next room for a few more days—if he knows we're monitoring too, he might be able to get some real rest, as you said. Are you sure you're not a real nurse? I know Captain Burton said you'd been sort of roped into this whole thing, but you take this shit seriously."

Cotton rolled his eyes, feeling inadequate. "I'm sort of scraping the barrel," he admitted. "But if I'm what he's got, I'm what he's got, and I need to do my best."

Briggs's apple-cheeked face fell into sober lines. "We all work for Colonel Constance because we believe in him and what he's doing. You may not believe this, but I'm pretty sure he does. Your competence and hard work might be the things that get him through. Stay strong. Don't let him bully you into going back too quickly. We can't keep doing good work if he comes back only to get sick."

Cotton agreed. "Yeah, well, this is officially the most important thing I'll ever do. I need to do it right."

"You sell yourself short! You're what? Twenty?"

"Twenty-two."

"Go back to school. You could be something amazing!" And with that, Briggs turned toward his teammates, who were already walking, loose-limbed in the sunshine, toward the driveway that led down to the edge of the lake and their cabin complex. Cotton leaned against the doorframe and watched them go. They'd promised to give him a wave when they hit the dock so he could see what a signal looked like and knew to look out for one.

When Medina hit the dock, he tore off his T-shirt and waved it wildly in the air, making Cotton laugh a little before giving a brief gesture with his hand and moving inside. Burton was cleaning up breakfast, and he gestured for Cotton to take a seat.

"So…," Burton said, his voice leading.

"We're in good hands," Jason told him, sounding amused.

"Which means…," he prompted.

"That Cotton and I can relax a little, and I can rest and get better," Jason agreed.

"Good." Lee finished wiping down the counter and then turned to them both. "And it also means I'm going to leave. There is some snooping I need to do and may need some help, and I can't do it here. I'm driving down to Sac this afternoon, crashing at Cramer's place, I hope, and then continuing down to LA in the morning."

"Why crash at Cramer's—oh."

Cotton glanced up to see them having an eyeball agreement.

"Ellery Cramer?" he said. "Jackson's boyfriend?"

They both nodded.

"So you're going to ask Jackson and Henry for help," Cotton murmured. "Why didn't you say so?"

"Because the less we say, kid, the less we can be recorded," Burton said smartly. "Now I'm gonna go take a leak and grab my duffel and see myself out." He pointed a finger at Jason. "You may sit on the porch with a blanket and read." And then, surprisingly enough, he pointed the finger at Cotton. "You may join him, take his vitals, and feed him. Both of you"—and the incriminating finger made an inclusive little circle—"rest, sleep, confront your demons gently, and fall in love in ways nobody will expect. That's an order from Ernie to you. I'm out of here, because frankly, that shit makes me twitchy. Bye!"

Before he left he gave Jason one of those manly-man hugs, chest to chest, while Jason was still sitting, and then he disappeared into his room. A few moments later, they heard the porch door bang and Burton waved to him through the wraparound kitchen window.

"Alone at last," Jason said dryly, stifling a yawn. "I think I'll take my nap on the porch now, and if you like, you can take a hike around the lake. If we call up Briggs, one of the guys can come with you and show you around."

Cotton frowned. "What kind of shitty nurse would I be if I—"

"Left me alone for an hour in plain sight while being watched over by one of the finest reconnaissance teams I ever trained? You'd be a sane one." Jason's eyes crinkled kindly at the corners. "Go put on those cross-fit sneakers in your luggage. They're not hiking boots, but they're sturdy. I'll call Briggs."

Cotton sighed and felt the physical restlessness that he'd been too exhausted to acknowledge in the last week. "I really could use a good run or walk or something. If you're sure, let me take your vitals first and get you your meds and check your bandages. You're right. I'd *really* like to move my body."

TURNED OUT, Medina was the guy who accompanied him, and after securing water bottles to both their belts with some webbing, they were off. One of the features of Caples Lake was a great granite shelf that extended into the lake itself near the dock. Cotton wanted to take a look at it, to see if it was good for wading, which it was, but yikes! Walking on that thing in the early afternoon was like putting himself on a cookie sheet and setting it to bake. When they were done with that, they took a trail around the marina and along the water's edge and walked in the relative peace and silence of the forest shade. They'd gone around probably half the lake before Medina broke the silence.

"So you were really just sort of lassoed into being his nurse?"

Cotton gave a brief laugh. "Yeah. Knew the right people, I guess. Didn't have a job, and I can't start school until next semester. I was pretty much the flophouse cook and maid as it was. That's fine. Made me feel useful."

"Were you really in porn?"

Cotton laughed, because he'd expected the question. Medina may have been all military on the outside, but he got the feeling that on the inside, he was his unit's equivalent of Randy—his mouth always had a bullet in the chamber, and you never knew when he'd shoot it off.

"Yeah. Wasn't bad."

Because it hadn't been, not really. Not when he'd discovered that sex as a commodity didn't have to be cold and transactional. His first john—who never really gave Cotton his actual name—had taught him that.

"Were the chicks hot?" Medina asked, and Cotton couldn't help the sound he made.

"Not that kind of porn."

"Oh...."

They walked a bit more in the quiet, and Medina gave a hum. "Were you like that... you know, gay for the porn, or, you know. You like guys anyway?"

"I liked guys anyway," Cotton said. "Some guys get in there and take some sort of boner drug and get it on, but I think you can tell who likes it anyway."

"So all your roommates were...?"

"In porn," Cotton answered, and while he'd once dreaded this kind of conversation, thinking a normal person wouldn't get it, Medina was sort of fun. After Jason's compassion and steady acceptance, Cotton was ready to hope for kindness a little.

"And you all slept together when you wanted to?"

Cotton shrugged. "Sometimes. Sometimes we tried to date. That usually sucked, though. Once a guy found out what you did, he either expected you to put out all the time, and no, or he expected you to bring clown cars and acrobatics to the table and, also, no, or he expected you to cheat all the time."

"No?" Medina hazarded.

"No," Cotton answered, surprised at it. He would have thought he had no sexual morals, really, but it turned out, with the exception of porn, he'd been true to every guy he'd dated.

"Why'd you do it?" Medina asked.

Cotton gave him the short version. "Because I got kicked out of the house for being gay, and I wasn't qualified for anything else." And while the words rang true, he remembered that Jason knew the long version and had just held him and told him he was sorry, and was warm and kind anyway.

"Why'd you quit?" Medina continued.

"It was time," Cotton said, and again, the short version went to this cocky, fit young soldier, and it was okay. But the longer version sat with someone Cotton trusted, and that was important too.

The trail abruptly bowed into the lake, close to the edge, and Cotton took a moment to step out and look around. Across the water he could see the marina to his right, and his and Jason's cabin, farther back into the trees, in front of him. True to his word, Jason was right where Cotton had left him, curled up on the wicker couch on the front porch, under a blanket, a book in his lap. He had his chin on his fist, though, and was probably dozing.

Cotton started to wave anyway, ripping off his shirt and flapping it madly, and Jason startled and waved his arm back and forth, seeming happy to see him. After a quiet flutter of his hand, Cotton put his shirt back on and disappeared back into the trees to see Medina gazing at him fondly.

"What?" he asked.

"You make Constance happy," he said quietly. "Don't tell a soul I said that. As far as most of us are concerned, he's sexless, like a dragon or a whale or something. But you make him happy, and the last year has been hard. Most of us have wives or girlfriends or boyfriends to keep us from getting dragged under. He's got no one. It would be really good if he could have someone."

Cotton looked away. "I'm not in the military," he said softly. "I'll never get called into your secret base. There's not a spare hole in the middle of the desert he could keep me in like a little fieldmouse."

"Well, if there's a way, Colonel will find one. He's super damned smart, you know."

"I've noticed," Cotton said quietly. Then, to change the subject, "How cold do you think the water is?"

"Want to find out when we get back to the cabin?" Medina asked excitedly.

"God yes."

Cotton's shirt was soaked with sweat, and it sheened Medina's face and neck. The red dust kicked up by their shoes stuck to their ankles and calves, and every breath of air in the trees felt stolen from the shade, which was almost as oppressive as it was cool.

"Maybe if we hurry, we won't break and try to swim across the lake fully clothed," Cotton said, thinking he could probably do a couple of laps if he didn't have cargo shorts and trainers on.

"I'll take that bet."

Together they hustled along the narrow path, watching for bumps that might turn their ankles but otherwise keeping their eyes very much on the prize of jumping in the water when they'd walked the second half of the lake.

The last stretch, the stretch on the side with the cabins, had no trees at all next to the water, and by the time they'd drawn even with the front of Cotton and Jason's little shelter, they'd finished all their water and even Medina confessed to being a little dizzy with the heat. When they hit a good patch of beach, one not too tangled with vegetation but not littered with rocks either, the two of them stripped off their shirts and kicked off their shoes and socks, unloading their water bottles and wallets with their shoes. With a few strides and a bound, Cotton pitched himself hands first into the water and swam to the center of the lake before the chill could take his breath.

He turned in the water and had a thought.

"Wait, aren't you guys armed?"

Medina had surfaced a few yards away. "You mean besides my knife?"

"I was thinking a gun—I sort of thought you were my bodyguard."

"I am, sort of. But we've been under surveillance the whole time. I mean, you can't be on alert constantly. You get tired and mistakes happen. I got my first break, and you wanted a break too, and I figured, 'He's an okay guy—let's hike the lake together!'"

Cotton thought about that, thought about having a friend who wasn't and hadn't ever been in porn. Thought about how this young, adorable soldier should have turned his key in a big way, but all Cotton could think of was getting back to the cabin and drying off on the porch, and telling Jason that they'd seen three deer on the far side of the lake and, a little closer, a family of bunnies.

"It was fun," he said, because he was learning the value of having one person who knew all your secrets and how not all your friends needed to be up in your business. "If you want to take your break tomorrow, I'd love to do it again!"

"Excellent!" And then Medina swept his arm through the water, splashing him thoroughly, because apparently guys couldn't be friends if they weren't also assholes. Cotton met him with a drenching of his own, and for about twenty minutes they played "drown the asshole" or whatever game that was before they pulled themselves out of the lake, panting.

Medina put on his shoes and used his shirt for a towel, his bronze skin and tiny plum-colored nipples absolutely hot… but not at all as appealing as he would have been before Jason had called Cotton his angel.

"See you tomorrow about ten," he said. "Give Briggs a buzz if you can't make it."

"Dude," Cotton said, and they bumped fists before Cotton made his way back up to where Jason sat, watching the two of them with bright, curious eyes.

His cargo shorts were nearly dry as he hit the porch, but his skin remained lake cool. Jason gave him a heavy-lidded smile that Cotton interpreted with a throb in his groin.

This man—this decent man, whom the whole world moved heaven and earth to save—wanted him.

"Have a good time?" Jason asked.

Cotton grabbed his hand, not sure if he'd appreciate the familiarity, but Jason pulled it to his lips and held it against his cheek. "Cool," he murmured, closing his eyes.

"Still a little warm," Cotton told him, cupping his cheek and rubbing his thumb along Jason's cheekbone. "But getting better every day."

"Not soon enough." Jason held on to his hand but pulled it away from his face so Cotton could sit down next to him. "I was sitting here like a big jealous turd, watching you guys play down there. Not fair, I know. Medina's a good guy, and I don't think he swings our way, but still." He shook his head. "I wanted to be out there in the lake with you."

The throbbing in Cotton's groin grew into an ache.

"I wanted you to be," he said gruffly. "Medina doesn't do it for me, Jason. Not even a little. Briggs doesn't do it for me. Daniels doesn't. My roommates have been one-and-doned, and they've probably forgotten it even happened."

"I want to be better *now*," Jason muttered. "But I think I've got two more days of naps in me before I so much as try to walk around the lake."

"Then let's get you into bed so you can nap," Cotton said practically. It was his turn to bring Jason's knuckles to his lips, wanting to savor every second they got. "We'll call it foreplay."

Jason laughed softly, but he didn't argue, and together they made their way inside.

BIG SPLASHES

THREE DAYS after being forced to watch as Cotton jumped into the lake with the charming—and decked—Christopher Medina by his side, Jason was trying hard not to bounce on his toes.

"I'm ready, right?" he asked, positively giddy. "No fever since yesterday, my wounds are all clean and spiffy. We can go walking, right?"

Cotton gave him an exasperated look. "I told you, I'm texting Lance!" he said, laughing.

Jason could admit it; he'd been exhausted when he'd left the desert and probably at death's door for some of the last three weeks. But he'd been on the mend before they'd come to the mountains, and now, four days after arriving, he felt *so good.* It was like his body was remembering how to function when he wasn't always sick and sad. Good food, lots of sleep, and yes, antibiotics and painkillers that he was pretty religious about taking—as well as some vitamins that Burton had brought out of sheer hope, Jason figured—had begun to work some serious magic.

Yeah, he could still feel the lingering effects of illness. He didn't anticipate being able to hike around the lake and then swim in it for an hour, as Cotton had been doing over the last days, but oh please, could he hike on the path a little? Seeing the clear blue sky from the porch had been wonderful, but he wanted dust on his shoes and sweat down his back. *Clean* sweat, not sickly fever sweat. He was finally remembering what it was like to function above 70 percent, and he wanted *more*.

Cotton closed the medical kit—which Jason had to admit he kept antiseptically clean and organized—and tucked it under the bathroom sink. As he stood up, his pocket buzzed, and he looked at it and smiled.

"Your physician has cleared you for a *short* walk, Colonel Constance," he said pertly, a playful smile on his face, and Jason, excited and emboldened, ducked in and stole a kiss. Cotton grinned at him, comfortable and happy, and held a finger up to his lips.

"Are we anticipating something *else*?" he asked archly.

Jason couldn't help it—he giggled. "Yes?" Oh, he was hoping, so hoping. They had kissed in bed each night, like teenagers, their kisses growing bolder and more comfortable and passionate. Their hands had wandered, and while the paths had grown a little more familiar, they'd also grown exciting. So far they hadn't really done anything that would be considered untoward at a high school prom, but those moments, holding Cotton, tasting him, feeling his own body surging back to life, not just after his wound and his illness but after the long period of dormancy, was a pure, sweet, sugar-adrenaline thrill.

"Mmmmeeebe...," Cotton teased, biting his lip, and Jason snuck another kiss before turning toward the bedroom.

"Stop being so cute!" he begged. "I really want to get out of here for a little while!" Watching Cotton grow in confidence these last four days had almost been worth the wait. Jason had worried so much about taking advantage of a younger man, about being too old and too worn, and hell, about knowing better.

But sex didn't scare Cotton. Sex had been a commodity, a trade he'd made for food and shelter and even to an extent, for self-respect. What Jason had been offering him over the last few days—even the last week—had been kindness. Warmth. Physical intimacy without expectation.

And Cotton had blossomed into his arms, playing, smiling, teasing. And while Jason was pretty sure sex was going to be spectacular for *him* because he hadn't had it in so long, he was starting to hope that it would be wonderful for Cotton, because Jason didn't think he'd gotten a lot of sex that came with intimacy. Or without trade.

Jason was starting to hope that their touching was as special for Cotton as it was for him, and it was *so* amazing for him.

"Cute?" Cotton egged on now. "You think I'm cute? I'll have you know, I was billed as a power top."

Jason snorted as he bent down and pulled his socks on.

"No, seriously!" Cotton grinned. "I was the Dickinator. I saw a P-spot and destroyed it!"

Jason had to straighten up in the middle of tying his brand-new tennis shoe. "No, seriously?"

"You don't think I can top?" Cotton asked, eyes still twinkling.

"Well, yes, probably," Jason said, aware he was treading on thin ice. He shrugged sheepishly. "I just... I don't know. I kind of have fantasies about taking care of you. Is that bad? I mean, I know you can take care of yourself in bed. You had sex for a living. I'm sure you've got some tricks. It's just...." He took a breath, thinking about it. "I just... I feel like you need someone to hold your heart in their hands like it's precious. That sex is a place where you can have that. I mean, sometimes, yes, you're looking for Dickinator, destroyer of assholes, but sometimes…." He looked at Cotton hopefully, wanting the younger man to understand what he wanted and that he didn't want it to be a threat to Cotton's independence.

"Sometimes you want to be cherished," Cotton said in surprise. He sat heavily on the bed, close enough that their arms touched. "Is that what you want to do with me?"

Jason couldn't be sure if he was uncertain or excited about the prospect. "Is that so bad?" he asked, searching that angel's face.

He was only a little surprised—but oh-so-gratified—when Cotton kissed him, voraciously, taking all of their practice over the last few days and perfecting it, driving him into the bed and taking his mouth happily, again and again, while Jason ran his hands under Cotton's shirt and drank in the smooth skin of his back and down below his waistband, kneading the sweetly giving muscles in his ass.

Cotton groaned and arched against him, and Jason's eyes popped open. Three nights of necking and he hadn't once felt Cotton's, erm, erection.

"Oh my God," he said, the hard ridge of flesh arching against his hip. "Is that you?"

Cotton gave him a shy smile. "I'm, uhm… you know. It's sort of a requirement. You can't just be cute."

Jason laughed. "I knew you were more than a *very* pretty face from the beginning," he said, and Cotton tilted his head back and undulated again.

"Are you sure you want to wait until tonight?" he begged, and Jason used some of his new strength to flip them over so he was on top, kissing him and sliding his hand down the front of Cotton's cargo shorts.

"Do you want me to take the edge off?" he whispered. "I'm an old man, mind you. I might not be able to go twice in a night, but you, I bet I could take you in my mouth and—"

Cotton arched up against him hard, his body bucking, and he grabbed at Jason's shoulders with desperate fingers. His mouth opened soundlessly, and then he gave an agonized cry.

Jason let out a stunned breath as Cotton's entire body relaxed and he felt a warmth spreading against his stomach through Cotton's shorts.

"Oh wow," he said, shocked.

"I'm so embarrassed," Cotton told him, eyes wide. "I… I… I mean, I've never done that before. Not even when I hadn't had sex before!"

Jason's smile felt like it was going to take over his entire head. His *scalp* was crinkling into laugh lines.

"Oh *wow*!" he said again, feeling about twelve. "My God, Cotton, are you good for *my* ego!"

Cotton covered his eyes with his arm. "Can I go wash up and die alone now?"

"No!" Jason rolled to the side so they wouldn't both have to wash up. Cotton had done a good job packing, and there was a mudroom in the rear of the cabin with a washer and dryer and supplies, but they didn't have an abundance of clothing. "No," he said again, sliding off the bed and giving Cotton a quick kiss. "I'll be right back."

He returned with a warm washrag, helped Cotton out of his cargo shorts, and wiped him down thoroughly, impressed that he was not only really long and thick, but also still partially erect.

"I don't mean to keep harping on this," he said as he helped Cotton into another pair of briefs and went looking for the final pair of cargo shorts between them. "Because I don't want you to feel like an object here. But, uhm, is everybody—"

"Is everybody in porn that big?" Cotton asked wryly. "Yes and no."

Jason turned toward him, brow furrowed. "And you'll explain?"

Cotton let out a breath. "I never got to film a scene with him," he said. "He left right after I got to Johnnies, and he works as our off-site event promoter now. But he's… average. Average height, average build, average dick. Just… you know. Average. And…." Cotton looked pained. "I think he may have been developmentally disabled. Not a lot. Just enough to make school hard. He forgets things. He has to write everything down in his book, and we all remind him—gently—to do that. But he was one of their biggest earners for a while. John likes to say he was a reminder that the fantasy was for everyone, and I think he's right. Anyway, since Reg there's been a couple of other guys who aren't… perfect. But they're such great guys you have fun with them anyway. They're not as successful as Reg, but I sort of like that, you know…."

"You're not all gods and angels," Jason said, getting it. Then he thought of himself, of all the weight he'd lost, of his larger-than-average-but-not-supersized endowment, and sighed. "I hope you're okay with the fact that *I'm* neither a god nor an angel." He gave what he hoped was his prettiest smile, and Cotton managed to not look fatally embarrassed as he finished dressing.

"You're already out of my league," he said, rolling his eyes. "If you *were* a god—or an angel—I think we'd be talking overkill."

"Right," Jason said sagely, keeping his sense of humor. "I mean, you can't have two Dickinators in the same bed. They'd kill each other, badly."

Cotton cackled. "Yeah, but could you imagine the name of that film? *Dicked to Death: The Return of the Dickinator!*"

Jason covered his face with his hands to hide his laughter, but he couldn't. He ended up cackling while he and Cotton started a load of laundry and was still chuckling by the time he got his other shoe on and they started out the door. It was as though, by mutual agreement, they'd tabled sex and all of its intensity until they could hide in the shadows, because they were naked enough already.

THE WALK was harder than he'd expected, and as his leg muscles grew weak and his knees grew wobbly before they even cleared the first bend around the lake, he let out a groan.

"Oh, this is so depressing," he muttered. "I see why you didn't start me out toward the resort now. I wouldn't have cleared the cabins." Jason was thinking about their surveillance team, who was good about waving to them and keeping them in the loop. Those were his men—he'd recruited each one of them, even Medina who seemed like a big goofy kid until you watched him in action behind a rifle with a scope. He didn't want them to see him so tired he couldn't hike halfway around a very small lake.

"I mostly didn't want you to have to walk across that granite table that lines the lake's edge," Cotton admitted, keeping pace easily. "It's about six zillion degrees on that thing, and we agreed, no swimming in the lake water until your stitches are out."

Jason grunted. "Well, between you and the heat, I'm going to be taking a really amazing cold shower when we get back. Wow, it gets so cold out here at night. You wouldn't think it was so hot under the sun!"

"High altitude," Cotton said wisely, reminding Jason that *he'd* been the one to remind Cotton of this a couple of days ago, because Cotton had fallen asleep midkiss after two loops around the lake by foot and another *in* the water.

"Yeah, yeah," Jason grumbled. "Less oxygen, more sun, which is currently trying to fry my puny ass to a crisp before we even reach the trees."

"Well, let's get there and rest in the shade for a bit," Cotton said reasonably. "There's a fallen branch a little in from the tree line. We can sit there until you're ready for the trip back."

"You are *so* good at this nursing thing," Jason grumbled. "Are you sure you don't have a school you can apply to?"

"With a GED? Are you kidding?" Cotton blew out a breath. "I love that you have all this faith in me, man, but it's like you forget who you're here with."

Jason hated that note of self-recrimination in Cotton's voice. He caught his hand and squeezed.

"I know exactly who I'm here with," he said. "I'm here with the guy who's going to have to fireman carry me back to the cabin if I don't stop and get a drink of water."

Cotton eyed him. "That wouldn't be a bad workout," he said speculatively.

"Don't think about it, angel," Jason snapped. "My ego is fragile enough as it is!"

Cotton's mouth quirked, and he looked away. "Yeah, and it might rip your stitches."

"You suck," Jason told him, making sure to put one foot in front of the other.

"I do. I'm good at it! Want to try when we hit the shadows?"

"No!"

Cotton's laugh was good. When he wasn't cackling, it was a rolling, pit-of-the-stomach sort of sound, the kind that Jason often thought of as a "dad laugh." For not the first time, Jason wondered who would throw this kid out, who would force him to make that terrible choice? And he wanted to rail at the boyfriend, but he'd seen twenty-year-olds in the service who had wives barely out of high school. Being threatened with being put on the sex-offender registry was truly terrifying.

How resilient did someone have to be to have gone through all of that and still have a laugh that rang through the trees like bells, making them holy?

He didn't know how to say that—not now, when the echoes of the laugh were still fading, and he was short of breath anyway. Instead, he put out his hand and captured Cotton's, now that they were past the tree line, and together they made their way to the handy branch where he could sit and rest for the return trip.

COTTON ORDERED him to nap when they got back, while Cotton started dinner. They'd made it a habit to have two members of the detail over for dinner, although Cotton claimed he wasn't fooled. It was just an excuse for Jason to work.

In a way he was right. The guys kept contact with the base in the desert outside of Barstow, and there were usually two or three high-priority things Jason needed to comment on. Jason had *thought* they'd declare him AWOL and put a temporary commander in his place since he was gone, but Burton had been right. The brass—Barney Talbot included—really had no idea what he did there, and people were so anxious *not* to get stuck in "fly-swatting duty," as they called Operation Dead Fish, that there were no ranking officers there to take his place. Burton was acting CO, and he was apparently slipping coded messages on encrypted channels to Briggs, Daniels, and Medina to ask Jason for help.

"And nobody's figured this out?" Cotton had asked on the first evening. "Nobody? Everybody thinks that you've got a three-assassin detail vacationing at Tahoe and Burton is super interested in fish?"

"Are you kidding?" Daniels had said. "After all the work we put into encrypting that equipment? They'll be lucky if they don't think we're up here hunting *bears*. So don't worry. Nobody's going to figure out Colonel Constance is here through us, and Burton really *does* need help."

Jason was used to tracking multiple operations—and multiple possible "fish" sightings. His brain had always been on point when it came to keeping several different data streams straight. It had been what was going to make him such a brilliant coder and programmer in college. When he'd entered OCC, his abilities to process that much information so quickly in real time had been what had gotten the attention of covert ops. It was, as far as he could figure, his one talent. Where other commanders had to bark orders, fish around for information on tablets, and meticulously organize their chains of command, Jason's operations were literally "all up here!"

But it did make him damned hard to replace.

So Cotton's command to "Go rest up before your big tactical meeting with food," had been pretty on point, but it didn't mean Jason didn't resent the fuck out of recovery.

Still, as he'd trailed reluctantly to the bedroom, stripping his shoes and sweatshirt off as he went, he remembered that moment on the bed, the way Cotton's back had arched, the way he'd caught his breath.

They were going to have sex tonight. Or make love. Or bang. Or fuck. Whatever the kids were calling it these days when two consenting adults got naked and did beautiful things with their bodies. Jason was going to get him some of that.

With easily the most beautiful man he'd ever spoken to in person.

Wasn't that worth a little bit of coddling?

That thought got him to sleep like nothing else could have.

HE AWOKE to voices in the kitchen—Briggs and Daniels, if he wasn't mistaken—talking to Cotton.

Also the smell of chicken broiling.

Cotton was getting better about eating without prompting, but Jason had noticed he was so very good at making healthy meals. Yes, Jason had conspired with Briggs to get some steak and marinade into the refrigerator at the next shopping trip, and some baked potatoes would be great, but Jason got that if Cotton was going to eat and feel comfortable eating, he would have to eat the foods that made him feel in control of his own body.

His hard work at healing, at doing the right things to function in a frightening world, humbled Jason Constance to no end.

Jason had been given so many advantages—good family, good education, good ethos—and he'd cursed them so many times in this last year. He could have had a promotion, or been retired, or been rich, dammit, but instead he was tracing crimes across the planet and trying to pin down the one rabid soul responsible who had been twisted beyond humanity, and then sanction his death. His own soul had been withering, disintegrating under the pressure, but watching Cotton, he felt like he hadn't understood the depths of his own self-pity.

Cotton should have been loved. He should have been nurtured into adulthood. He should have never been forced to sell his sex, or his body, or his control over his own life. But he had been. And he wasn't bitter, and he wasn't vindictive, and he wasn't crying in a corner. Instead, he'd taken the scant blessings in his life and was looking forward to forging a better tomorrow with them.

And Jason found his only bitterness was that he wouldn't get to see what Cotton's better future might be.

But he refused to think about that right now. Instead he splashed some water on his face and made it to the kitchen, where Cotton was pulling dinner out of the oven and Briggs was setting the table.

"He must love us," Briggs said as Jason emerged from the living room. "He baked potatoes and had me buy butter and sour cream when I was in town today."

Jason made an ecstatic little "Ooh" with his lips, and Briggs laughed. Jason glanced up to where Cotton stood after setting the broiler pan on the top of the stove, and Cotton winked.

"I didn't say I was eating potatoes!" he protested. Then relented. "Okay, potatoes, yes, but not with butter and sour cream."

"I'll take it!" Jason said happily, and Briggs held his hand out for the down-low five.

Jason didn't leave him hanging.

He sat down in his usual spot—the one with his back to the corner of the kitchen and the full view out the wraparound window—and looked at Daniels, who was typing furiously on his laptop as he sat.

"Important?" he asked softly.

Briggs replied quietly, "Burton started listening for chatter on your mob guys, Karina and Dietrich Schroeder. Swear to God, Colonel, it's like listening to the same chatter when we're chasing down a target. Same stuff. We're looking for bodies, bodies are showing up. We're looking at drug trafficking to fund the criminal activities, and bingo. There was a murder at a meth lab in Auburn three days ago—methodical and clean, three bullets to three foreheads, the bodies lined up neatly out of the way. A substantial amount of product disappeared, and suddenly Coloma is flooded with overdoses. What does that sound like to you?"

"They killed a meth operation to take over the product and make enough money to keep moving," Jason said. "And they're headed this way. Why do you think they stopped to crime spree if they're only coming to take me out?"

Daniels paused to mull it over, and Briggs glanced at him with troubled eyes. "How would they know you're here?" he asked.

"We sold the car," Cotton said, surprising him. "Remember? Burton was afraid they'd tracked it somehow. We traded it in for whatever that was Burton used to get us here."

"We stayed in Roseville an extra eight hours," Jason recalled. "I remember. We were hoping that would throw them off track."

"And also hoping Burton could catch up on enough sleep to not crash the car," Cotton recalled. "You were both pretty wrecked."

"Now see, Colonel," Briggs said, grinning, "we need to keep this kid around more. He gives us *details*."

Jason sent him a killing look. "I'm sure he'll be excited to tell you about the night they had to lance my wounds too, but you may want to wait until after dinner."

Daniels and Briggs both groaned, and Jason went back to trying to figure out the conundrum.

"Let's go back to the beginning," he said as Cotton brought a platter of steak cuts to put in the middle of the table. Briggs followed up with salad and a basket holding potatoes, and he set them down as Cotton went back for fixings. Distractedly, Jason noted how Cotton seemed to blend seamlessly into any situation. He was smart—so smart—and he'd been devouring paperbacks at the rate of two a day. Jason didn't want to probe sore spots, but he suspected that when Cotton had been a high school student, he'd been in the academic track, probably headed for college. He was smart, personable, and he thought on his feet.

And kind. So kind.

All of that. *All* of that glorious potential, and it could have been flushed away. The thought made Jason want to cry.

"The beginning where?" Cotton asked, setting the last of the plates down and joining them. Jason took one of the baked potatoes onto his plate and cut a disk from it, setting it on Cotton's. Cotton smiled at him, and tapped a jar of salsa, and Jason got a lightbulb. Aha! Baked potato, no butter. So clever.

"I was shot by a gang faction from a gang that no longer exists, technically," Jason said in the clatter of people serving themselves. Cotton had already set aside a dinner for Medina. He'd done that every night as well, because he was Cotton.

"Yes," Daniels noted. "But part of the gang slivered off and is after you."

Jason frowned, and then Briggs frowned, and then Cotton frowned.

"What?" Daniels asked. "What am I not getting?"

"They would have no reason to pursue him this far," Briggs said thoughtfully. "But that's what it looks like they've done. Daniels, you and I have to comb the last week's news articles to see if there are any more crimes that look like that one. But we also need to figure out why they'd go to so much trouble. I don't think it's revenge. The mobsters wouldn't have any reason to know who drove the damned bus!"

"Unless someone told them," Cotton said guilelessly. "I mean, you've got someone working on the inside, you know that. So what if, instead of trading guns for children, they offered to trade guns to get rid of Jason? I mean, he got in everybody's way. Win/win."

Everybody stared at him, but he was looking determinedly at his potato. As they watched he broke off a nibble with a fork, dipped it in salsa, and snuck it into his mouth. With a blissful smile, he closed his eyes. "Almost like a cookie," he murmured.

"Colonel," Briggs said, meeting Jason's eyes, "get this kid a real fuckin' cookie."

"You do the shopping," Jason reminded him. Then he put a liberal amount of butter and sour cream on his own potato and took a bite. "But you know, he's right."

There was a collective deep breath, and Jason spoke up again. "I know Burton's monitoring coms, and Huntington is doing runs to other bases to pick up chatter. Is Owens still in charge of our supply lines while I'm gone?"

"Yessir," Briggs said.

"Good. Have him look for big movement of guns where there should be no movement of guns and see who authorized it." Oh, it felt so good to have a new lead on this! "Let me know as soon as you get something."

Briggs gave him a slow and measured blink. "Unless there's someone coming up the road to kill you, sir, I'll let you know tomorrow."

Jason gaped at him and turned to Daniels to reinforce the point. Daniels stared back at him.

"No," Daniels said, as though his silence weren't damning enough.

"Gentlemen, I know it's tempting to think of this as a vacation—"

"Not tempting," Briggs intervened. "Necessary. Sir, all due respect, but if we had to tear ass out of here overland at this point, we'd get about halfway around the lake before your boy here would be carrying you like a damsel in distress. And we get it. You've got someone after you, you need to recover, and once we take care of the credible threat, you're going to go back to the base all happy fine, and the government is going to do what it always does—pretend it didn't see what went wrong." Briggs snorted and made a gesture referring to his dark skin and the hard road he'd probably had to travel because people—and institutions—sucked that way. "They're good at that," he said blandly. "But in the meantime, we tapped into your camera feed so you don't need to sleep with the monitor in your room unless you get weird about flying blind. And my replacement is coming in two days, because, straight up, this has become the most sought-after vacation spot in Barstow."

Jason pinched the bridge of his nose. "I thought we were keeping this in a tight group of people," he said painedly. "So, you know, court-martial. In case that happens, it would be bad to take out our entire unit because you all knew."

Daniels made a rude noise. "Yeah. Fuck that." He reached over and snagged another piece of meat with his fork and another potato with his hand. "Chow's good, we get to swim in the lake, and I'm just waiting for the entire US Olympic swim team to decide this would be an *outstanding* place to train."

"You keep saying things like that," Briggs muttered, "but I have yet to see you stick your dick in anything besides crazy."

"Dude, the entire swim team, male, female, and trans? That would be *crazy*."

Jason gave them both an even look. "There are so many things I never wanted to know about any of my unit. That image? That is going to have to be sandblasted from my brain."

Daniels rolled his eyes. "We all have our fantasies," he said. "And right now, your entire unit is fantasizing about you being fit, tan, and relaxed. You're maybe twenty-five percent there." He nodded at Cotton. "We have even kidnapped you a nurse who can cook. I mean, male, female, that right there has *got* to be someone's fantasy."

"He didn't kidnap me," Cotton said mildly. "I was *recruited*."

Daniels hooted and then dug into the extra heaps of food on his plate. "And he's highly entertaining. No, Briggs is right. We're going to swap out your security detail with people we can trust. Burton is controlling the info there, and if he fucks that up, I'll eat my own toes."

"That guy is un*canny*," Briggs muttered. "Do you know how you ended up with the three of us as your security detail?"

"You lost a bet?" Jason hazarded, knowing soldiers, boredom, and the tendency of human beings to attempt to trade up into any given situation.

"No, even weirder. The three of us were set to go to Canada to take care of a subject. Burton texted us to ask if we'd be your detail, and we were, like, 'Sorry, man, can't make it.' He told us to sit tight for a minute 'cause he was getting another text. Do you know what happened?"

"No," Jason said, trying not to be frustrated, "because I'm not allowed to go back to work!"

Briggs ignored the last part. "Well, this particular subject was a super-urban animal. Like born and raised in the city, and he was killing people and bears—"

"Bears?" Cotton said, sounding stricken.

Briggs nodded. "I'm sayin'! Bears and wildlife. Leaving them to rot. Like some sickass shit. Anyway, Daniels, Medina, and I had been crewed up already. We were slated to move out in an hour, and Burton gets his text.

The next thing, he calls me, straight up, and tells me to check the subject's location. We've got him at a lake called Three Trees, in Canada. They've got hundreds of tiny lakes up there, and this subject has been haunting Three Trees forest, near the border of Ontario. So Daniels starts scanning our intel from Three Trees and he picks up on a call about 'SUV meets tree and bounces into the lake.' He follows up and... you tell it, Daniels."

Daniels jumps in. "So the SUV didn't just *meet* a tree. The subject *drove* it into a tree, running from a grizzly bear, because the subject was going to take out a half-grown cub with an AK-47 semiauto. But the full-grown bear took a swipe at him, and he shit his pants—swear to God, it's on the police report—and jumped into his SUV and proceeded to drive the SUV into a tree, where it bounced into the lake, and our subject drowned with a look on his face like this." Daniels mimicked pure terror. "Which is probably the most solid proof that God exists that I have ever fucking heard of. So there we are, go-bags packed for summertime in the forest near lake country—like, hot and cold together—and Burton asks us if we want to guard our boss, whom we don't particularly hate." Daniels let out a low whistle. "Un*canny*."

Jason slow-blinked. "Burton has some valuable assets," he said with a completely straight face, and he took a complacent bite of his steak. He absolutely, *absolutely* didn't look at Cotton, who was manfully hiding a covert smile, looking for all the world like butter wouldn't melt in his mouth.

DANIELS AND Briggs took off, bringing the little takeout plate for Medina as they went, and Cotton looked around at the kitchen they'd cleaned before they left.

"Want to go outside and read before the sun's gone?" he asked.

"No," Jason said softly. "I want to sit on the couch and watch a movie so you can lie on me and neck with me and we can touch each other's skin."

Cotton's tanned face went blotchily pink, and Jason smiled, closing his eyes.

"I made you blush," he murmured. "I will treasure that for my entire life."

"You and Burton trusted me with Ernie," Cotton replied, standing and offering Jason a hand up.

"You didn't let us down," Jason said mildly.

"Yeah, but you trusted me. And it was important to both of you. I mean, if you didn't tell those guys, you really do keep it quiet. That's...

that's amazing. Being part of your inner circle. That's the most trust I've gotten in my entire life."

Jason came to his feet, and they were standing, chest to chest, in the fading light through the wraparound window.

"Why did you do that?"

Jason knew the answer, and while it was manipulative on Burton's part, it was also very kind. "Because if we're going to do what I think we're going to do—if I'm going to have a lover, even for a very short time—it's got to be someone I have absolute faith in."

Cotton rubbed Jason's lower lip with his thumb. "That's scary," he admitted. "But I'd die to live up to it."

"That's what's scary," Jason said, licking the edge of the thumb and watching Cotton's eyes light up as he understood the game was on. "I hope I never let you down." He wanted to quantify that, to say again that this couldn't last. That he would recover, they would find the credible threat, and Cotton would go back to Sacramento and back to figuring out his life.

He wanted to make caveats, tell Cotton that they would only take this step if he knew Cotton would be okay when that happened, insist on some sort of "wellness test" to make sure that this step in the relationship wouldn't devastate him.

But Jason wasn't Cotton's father, or his big brother, or even, in this moment, his patient. Jason wanted to be his lover, and if he wanted that to be valid, the one absolute between them had to be trust.

Jason trusted that he wasn't a sugar daddy, that their touch wasn't transactional, that what they were about to do *mattered*.

And he had to trust that Cotton had enough agency to make this decision himself.

But something in his eyes must have given him away.

"Hey," Cotton murmured. "I'll be okay."

Jason closed his eyes, shivering at the first brush of Cotton's lips against his own. Cotton's tongue teased at the seam of his mouth, and he had no choice. He parted his lips and let Cotton in.

SUBLIMATION

COTTON HAD been swimming in Caples Lake for the past four days, and it was always a shock as the water, still chilled by the runoff from the very peaks of the Sierras, swept over his skin. There was a frozen moment in time when the things his body wanted—the cool of the water versus the reality he was living in, the uncomfortable sizzling heat and dust of the walk—collided in his flesh and his breath froze in his lungs while his nerve endings tried to decide if he had died or had been reborn.

Yeah.

Kissing Jason in this heartbeat, the promise of sex heavy between them, was like that.

Everything about this moment threatened glory, but Cotton had lived misery in his own skin for so very long. Every kiss of the last few days had been like dipping his toes into that strange, blessed water of rebirth, and even while they'd been glorious, he'd known that shedding the skin of the frightened confused kid he'd spent so much of his time being would be painful.

But nothing could prevent him from taking Jason's stubbled cheeks between his palms and plunging in.

Jason responded firmly but not forcefully. This wasn't a rough-play video or something with a little kink. This was two people who wanted to be together, and Cotton realized he was shaking with how much he wanted Jason's hands on his bare skin.

Getting his privates wiped down that morning had been clinical. Giving Jason sponge baths before he could shower had been clinical. *Every sexual act* he'd performed since leaving home had been clinical, even when he thought he was just putting out to keep a guy.

This was about being *personal*.

The kiss went on, and Cotton was being steered backward, to the bedroom, and given how quickly the two of them had vacated that morning, he thought he knew how important what they were planning tonight really was.

But as Jason's hands searched his skin, cruising his back, his waist, his backside, his thighs, he felt something grow from his stomach, from his groin, under his muscles, under his dermis. His breath came in short pants, and his movements had become jerky, uncoordinated. With a thump, Jason pushed him down on the bed and kissed his forehead.

"Hang out there for a sec," Jason murmured.

"Hang out?" Cotton tried to tease, but his voice cracked, and Jason gave him a wink.

"Yeah, hang out."

Jason turned and closed the door behind them, then locked it too, probably because someone in his job had the nth-level paranoia to do that. Then he flicked on one of the lamps and switched off the overhead light and, after helping Cotton up for a moment, pulled the covers down.

"No rose petals?" Cotton asked, still going for light and teasing.

"I was thinking wildflowers, but you know, grass stains," Jason said, turning into him. Cotton was reminded of the slight height difference, of the fact that Jason was, in fact, a little taller than he was. He was reminded of the heavy muscles that had once dominated Jason's chest and that would probably do so again as Jason struggled to recover.

He was reminded that Jason, for all his teasing and kindness, was older and wiser and had wanted to "cherish" Cotton, a thing Cotton wasn't sure had ever actually happened before.

Jason held Cotton's cheeks this time and plundered his mouth, his movements measured and passionate and sincere. Cotton whimpered and fell back against the bed again as Jason grabbed the hem of his T-shirt and pulled it over his head.

Cotton was going to yank down his own shorts next, but Jason was spending an eternity licking his chest, and Cotton was all for that.

Jason's lips skated along his smooth skin, barely skimming his nipples as he used his mouth, tongue, and fingertips to explore.

"So pretty," Jason mused. He raised his head to take Cotton's mouth again while his fingers continued to air-kiss Cotton's nipples. Cotton put his hands on Jason's hips, mostly to anchor himself while Jason investigated. He kept thinking he should be *doing* something, giving Jason a tour, pointers, anything. It had been *ten years* for Jason Constance, and he was choosing to end his celibacy with Cotton! But Cotton's body was telling him that while he'd thought he'd known what sex was all about, he'd been wrong, totally and completely wrong, and suddenly following Jason's lead was the only thing he could do.

Jason pulled back and lowered his head to Cotton's nipple, where he sucked lightly and then a little harder. Cotton moaned and melted into the mattress, because his muscles were a joke and nothing could support him now.

And Jason kept kissing. He found the fly to Cotton's cargo shorts and tugged it open. Cotton managed to lift his hips while Jason stripped him down, and then Cotton was naked on the bed while Jason pushed him back against the sheets.

"You're still dressed," Cotton complained breathlessly.

Jason grimaced. "I'm not as pretty," he said, completely practical.

Cotton shoved himself up on his elbows. "Wait a minute—"

"You've seen all of me!" Jason laughed. "At this point, I've got as much sex appeal as a carton of milk!"

Cotton growled a little and was surprised because he usually only made that sound on camera, not in his private bed. After pushing himself up farther, he grabbed the bottom of Jason's zipped hoodie and his T-shirt, pulling them both up and over Jason's head before he could protest.

And Jason was right that Cotton had seen all of him, had given him sponge baths, knew where his bandages were and what the stitches looked like underneath. But right now, in the glow of the lamps, knowing that the body in question—stringier now than it had been, but still defined, still vital—was pulsing with desire for Cotton, it looked very much different.

It almost glowed.

Cotton paused in wonder to touch the same skin that he'd tended with a washcloth and antiseptic, but now with sex in his fingertips. The difference was extraordinary, and Cotton had to swallow past a dry mouth as he realized Jason's nipples—pale and tiny—were erogenous zones now, and Cotton had been given a pass to play.

He tasted, and tasted again, suckling as Jason had. This time Jason was the one who moaned, and Cotton licked and teased some more.

Jason's palm in the middle of his chest, pushing him down, was not exactly unwelcome, but Cotton still gave a sound of protest.

"Mine!" he said, allowing himself to be gentled.

"Me first," Jason said, laughing, and then he positioned himself sideways on the bed and kissed down Cotton's body, pausing to lick playfully at his navel and then, oh thank the stars, making his way to Cotton's cock.

His orgasm that morning had been a surprise, but it also hadn't been that deep or far-reaching. A preliminary or appetizer, Cotton guessed, for what they were doing now. Thick, fat, and long, his cock rested against his thigh, and Cotton had learned to be grateful it functioned so well but otherwise to not attach a whole lot of self-worth to the thing. He'd learned over the years that if a guy let the size of his cock define his personality, he would be, at best, a big fat dick. At worst, he'd be a little petty dick. But either way he wouldn't be all that fun to be around.

Jason's firm grip around him made his entire philosophy skew a little.

Jason stroked him with wonder, but he also kept up the kissing on his stomach and around his hipbones. The clench and release of his body took him by surprise, and Cotton hissed as his cock spat precome. Before he could control himself, he heard his own voice, begging.

"Lick me? Please? Oh God—"

And Jason complied immediately, licking, sucking, pulling Cotton's length into the wet heat of his mouth and squeezing with his lips and tongue. Cotton thought fleetingly of touching himself, of pinching his own nipples, but he couldn't even concentrate on that. Instead he crumpled the sheets in his fists and cried out, bucking, thinking he could hold back, make this a small peak, but Jason's hand grazed his balls gently, and Cotton's vision went white with a full-blown orgasm as he came into Jason's mouth.

Jason swallowed—twice—and pulled himself up the bed, still wearing his cargo shorts, looking supremely pleased with himself as he rested his head on Cotton's shoulder.

"That was amazing," he said, using his palm to wipe some of the glaze off his lips.

Cotton wanted—*needed*—to kiss him again, and he captured Jason's swollen, come-covered mouth with his own. Jason let out an ecstatic little gasp, and Cotton plundered some more, mad for Jason's taste, his happy sounds, his pure joy in something Cotton had written off as fun but not profound.

Jason's hums of pleased surrender were some of the most tremendous things Cotton had ever heard.

Cotton rolled him over to his back and fumbled with his fly. He yearned to see this body naked again, but active, excited, a holy temple for the man who had made him feel useful and smart and desired.

And it was just as beautiful as Cotton remembered: thick, long, but more than that. Jason almost purred as Cotton stroked him, and when Cotton looked up at his face, his tongue extended, Jason gave a happy little wriggle.

Jason wanted his touch. Not just wanted it—needed it. And not just any touch.

Cotton's.

Ten years of holding off, waiting for someone he could trust, someone who would care for him and make it important, and Cotton was that person.

Cotton closed his eyes and took Jason into his mouth and sucked gently, plying his tongue, playing and titillating and arousing, until Jason gave a moan and then pushed Cotton off.

"I have plans," he said.

Cotton stared at him, surprised. "Yes?" Oh, he'd loved to be topped. *Ached* for it. But topping was physical and demanding and….

"If I have to sleep all day tomorrow," Jason swore, "yes." He shoved himself up and cupped Cotton's cheek with his palm. "Come on, sweetheart, I swear, I won't hurt you."

Cotton thought of telling him that of course he would; he was going to leave, and Cotton was never going to be okay again.

He forced that out of his mind and his heart. Jason didn't want to leave him, of that he was sure.

"Okay," Cotton murmured, lying back, tacitly hoping they could do this face-to-face. He pulled his knees up, splaying himself out, and smiled a little into Jason's eyes. "It's your playground. You already tried the swings."

Jason's low laughter made him smile, and he reached for the lubricant Cotton had shown him in the end table the night before.

They'd talked about being safe—Cotton had been tested with absolute clockwork when he'd worked for Johnnies, and he was still on PrEP now. Jason was on PrEP too, and while he hadn't explained why, Cotton had guessed.

If you had contact with other people's blood a lot, being protected was a good idea.

But that's not what they were doing here. Jason had grabbed the lubricant and was slicking him up, one finger stretching him sweetly, and Cotton tilted his head back and allowed the warm ache to take him over.

This wasn't about hurting at all, Cotton thought, as Jason added another finger. This was all about healing, and Cotton's body, electrified and buzzing from want, completely agreed.

"Please," Cotton breathed. "Please."

Jason moved, shifting so he was between Cotton's splayed knees, notching himself into Cotton's stretched entrance.

"Please?" Jason murmured, lowering his head for a kiss, and another, and another.

And while he kissed, he slid in, slowly, arching his back so they could kiss while he entered. With a lunge, Cotton scooted forward, taking him all in and wrapping his legs around Jason's hips to hold him tight.

Oh God, he had this man inside him, this amazing, strong man who seemed to care for him and touched him with such reverence Cotton could cry. And he was *inside Cotton*, and Cotton never wanted to let him go.

Jason gasped softly and pumped once, experimentally, until Cotton cried out, needing.

Again and again Jason pumped his hips, thrusting deep and pulling back, the rhythm as necessary as heartbeat or breath. Cotton's entire body shook, and Cotton began to beg. *"Harder, oh please, harder, faster, oh God, my skin, it's going to explode, I need you inside me, all of you, fill me, oh please, Jason, please!"*

Jason grunted, hips thrusting, and kept up the solid, powerful fuck that didn't just take Cotton over, it *owned* him. He didn't say anything but scowled, concentrating, as he took Cotton places Cotton swore he'd been but had never seen for the magic they really were.

Up! Up! Up! until Cotton's body quaked and Jason shoved inside him one last time, crying out, filling him, scalding and real and—oh God, Cotton couldn't, he couldn't, his heart, it couldn't—

"Augh!"

He was too breathless for it to be a scream, but it was loud, and he could have no more controlled the sound than he could have controlled the weather. He started to come again, his entire body shorting out, synapses firing out of rhythm and rhyme, body moving spasmodically as he lost complete control in orgasm.

He'd never, ever done that before.

By the time he came down, he was still shaking, almost sobbing, and Jason had pulled the covers around them and was murmuring soothingly into his ear.

"Oh God," Cotton said finally, the first coherent thing he could remember saying.

"Yeah." Jason's voice was gruff, tender, and Cotton's throat ached. Could he ever remember tenderness like this?

"I, uh, didn't do anything embarrassing, did I?" Cotton asked, almost afraid.

"God no," Jason replied, nuzzling his temple. "But you did come apart."

Cotton heard a note in his voice that made him smile. His eyes burned, and his ears ached along with his throat, and his body was trying to figure out how something he'd thought he'd known like the stroke of his own hand was now colossal and terrifying and overwhelming. But he recognized that sound in Jason's voice.

"You're damned proud of that," he said, his teeth chattering a little.

"Best damned thing I've ever done," Jason said, like a vow. That was the last thing they said for a little while as Cotton shuddered out the last of his climax in his lover's arms.

JASON'S EVEN breathing told Cotton he'd fallen asleep, and Cotton rolled out of bed to go wash up. Jason surprised him by rolling over and pulling him close.

"No," he mumbled. "Don't leave yet."

"I'm messy," Cotton said, thinking about his stomach and backside, both caked with come.

"I know. I'm proud of that. Let it stay a minute."

Cotton's breath caught, and he rolled into Jason's chest as Jason nuzzled him some more.

"Is that weird?" Jason asked, but it didn't sound like he cared. "Weird that I want you on my skin too? I want us to be a memory we can't lose."

"No," Cotton whispered. "Not weird. I don't want you to ever go away." He paused. "You're so young. In your heart. All the awfulness in the world, and you've seen it firsthand. How are you so young?"

"My heart hasn't gotten much use," Jason confessed. "All the awfulness in the world, and very little of it has been perpetrated against me personally." He pulled Cotton close, close enough that Cotton could hear the beating of that heart. "Besides my sister's ordeal, I think the most awful thing to happen to me is going to be losing you."

Cotton made a hurt sound, and Jason added, "But that's only because having you is the most wonderful thing. I need to be grateful for this moment, right here."

"Me too," Cotton mumbled, and this time, they really did fall asleep.

COTTON WOKE up close to morning to use the bathroom. When he came back, he found Jason propped up on his elbow, regarding him with wide, shiny eyes as he emerged.

"Hurry up and let me in," Cotton mumbled, and Jason lifted the covers for him.

"Chilly?" Jason asked, sliding his arm around Cotton's bare stomach and pressing up along his backside again.

"Yes!" Cotton laughed, welcoming Jason's warmth along his back.

"But you didn't put on any underwear." Jason's hand splayed possessively over his stomach, and Cotton wriggled, enjoying that.

"Nope."

"Were you, maybe, counting on me to keep you warm?"

Cotton smiled, loving the play, the way the words made him laugh. "Maybe."

"Mm...." Jason bucked his hips, pushing his stiffening erection up against Cotton's bottom. "How warm?" he purred in Cotton's ear.

"Incendiary," Cotton replied, thrusting back.

Jason parted his cheeks and Cotton propped his knee up and ah! His length, his girth—a teeny bit of slick and he slid right in. This time was warmer, slower, luxurious. Cotton took his time to remember the feel of him, the width of his hands across Cotton's stomach, and his smell. When climax washed over the two of them, it was warm, cleansing, and gentle, and Cotton drifted off to sleep with Jason still inside him, like that was how it always should be.

FALLING LEAVES

"YOU CAN breathe now," Cotton said, his voice only shaking a little.

"You did fine," Jason told him, wanting to reassure him somehow—pat his hand, kiss his forehead, something. But Cotton's hands were encased in poly gloves, and he'd sterilized all the materials he'd needed. Very carefully, a stitch at a time, he'd removed the stitches from Jason's side. Jason was surprised to realize they weren't the stitches from the bullet wounds. Instead, they were stitches from where the flesh had been split to lance the infection underneath. The scars weren't little puckers with the eruption of scar tissue beneath, but instead were bumpy tears, the imprint of the stitches very apparent.

"Yikes," Jason said, looking at his flesh in the mirror. He had other scars—a couple of knife wounds, some bullet grazes—from his time deployed before he'd been promoted, but these were thick and deep and inexpertly tended to. "That's not pretty."

"You were being operated on by two PIs and an ex-porn model," Cotton said tartly. "It was never going to be."

Jason frowned. "I don't remember that. It was sort of a blur." He gave an apologetic smile. "I'm sorry."

Cotton shook his head, rounding up the last of the bandages into a waste bag and setting the scissors and clamps aside to boil later. Jason had seen him do this and had been impressed. For a guy who professed to have had no working knowledge of medical procedure a month ago, he was damned sharp about it now.

"It was awful," Cotton muttered. "You were out of it, and Lance was in the middle of surgery and couldn't come. It was Jackson, Henry, and me, and all we knew was if we didn't do something, you weren't going to make it, and if we called an ambulance, you'd probably get shot or imprisoned." He shuddered, looking away, but Jason could see his face was pale and his eyes red-rimmed.

"I'm sorry," he said again, drifting a soothing touch down Cotton's backside. "That must have been so brave of you—"

"I was terrified," Cotton said flatly, finishing his cleanup and turning toward Jason. He didn't come close enough for Jason to touch, though. Instead he leaned against the counter as though he was trying to be casual. "None of us knew what to do, and you were in so much pain, and your temperature was going up and up and—"

"Hey," Jason murmured, standing up and moving toward him.

Cotton shook his head, but not like he was saying no, and not like he was trying to shake off Jason's touch, but like he was trying to shake off the memory.

"Hey," Jason said, crowding him, sensing the need for comfort like an ache under his own skin. "I'm okay. Look at that. You saw me at my worst, and now I'm all better, and you helped do that. Isn't that amaz—"

"You almost died!" Cotton burst out. "I didn't even know you then, and I was afraid. And now I know you, and I know it could happen again, and most of the time I can forget, but I'm *terrified*, and what if I lost you?"

Jason went still, the part they hadn't spoken about in the last week catching up with both of them, but Cotton shook that off too.

"No, not that you go away. What if I don't know you're out there? I can be okay if I know you're out there, that this guy who really cared about me is out there, but his stupid job saving the universe is taking him away. I *get* that, but what if you're not out there? How do I *live* if you're not out there in the world?"

His voice broke, and Jason pulled him close, his own eyes stinging. "You live," he hissed harshly, although his hug was gentle. "You live. Whether I'm out there or not, you *live*. Because leaving you is going to be like ripping my arms off, and my lungs, and all the other things, and the only thing keeping me from bleeding out is going to be knowing *you're okay*. So you find a purpose, you start school, you fall in love again, but you *live*!"

And there it was, the unspoken thing between them, what they both knew to be true.

"I will *never* fall in love again," Cotton sobbed against his chest, and Jason held him tight, his own shoulders shaking, and he made a promise when there were no promises to be made.

"Me neither," he whispered. "You take all the lovers you need, but I will never fall in love again."

"I don't want anyone else," Cotton said brokenly. "So you need to live too."

"Okay," Jason said. Oh, this was worse than the first promise, but he'd make it if he had to. "I'll live knowing you're out there."

"Me too."

And that was it, all the words either of them had, and for a moment they just held each other in the bathroom, the scars on Jason's body forgotten.

It was the scars on their hearts that were going to be much harder to bear.

AN HOUR later Cotton and Jason made it all the way around the lake, partly at a run.

September was nearing the end of her dance, and the mornings were becoming sharper and more bracing, the afternoon shadows stretching longer and darker, but in the heat of the day, when the sun was pressing hard on their heads like a flatiron, the lake still beckoned, even if it was chillier now than it had been when they'd first arrived.

But Jason had pushed Cotton to take his stitches out just so he, too, could go swimming in the damned lake, and this time, when Cotton left his shoes and T-shirt and small daypack on the shore, Jason left his too, and together they whooped and hollered and screamed as they jumped into the freezing water.

A few minutes later they were treading water as their teeth stopped chattering, and Cotton shook his head. "I swear, it's gotten colder in this last day. I'm not sure I want to jump in tomorrow!"

"Don't care," Jason panted, grinning. "I had to watch you swim with Daniels, Briggs, Medina, and then Perez, Klausner, and Goldfarb. Dammit, *once* I wanted to get to be the one half-naked with you in the lake."

Cotton laughed. "Perez and Klausner are women," he reminded Jason. Trina Perez and Greta Klausner had come up with Collie Goldfarb to replace the first team. Cotton had been sorry to see Briggs, Medina, and Daniels go—Medina, in particular had been teaching him to throw a knife, and Jason knew they'd become friends—but he'd welcomed the second team with just as much graciousness and had been as helpful during the daily dinner/strategy meeting as well.

"Don't care," Jason said pertly. "I wanted to swim with you. That's all."

Cotton laughed, and Jason's heart throbbed a little in relief. That sad, fraught moment in the bathroom had been sweated away with the run and then rinsed off in the lake, he hoped, although he knew that wasn't possible. While he still wasn't at 100 percent, that didn't matter. All their intel pointed to the fact that their time here was coming to an end.

Cotton swam the length of the lake, but Jason knew he wasn't going to make it that far. He clambered out and was drying himself off with his

T-shirt when Trina Perez walked up to him, her easy, swinging stride almost an affront to how hard Jason had needed to push himself to get around the damned lake.

She barely refrained from saluting, and he grimaced. They'd covered the whole "covert" thing when the new group had arrived, and he'd once again asked them if they needed to bow out, like he'd asked the first group while Cotton had been napping.

The results were the same, but Jason wasn't sure how to make the case that nobody was there in an official capacity; the military was still actively searching for him, and just because the mob was too didn't mean he was out of the woods yet.

But Jason had first recruited Trina for his unit when she'd taken out her would-be rapist, who was, unfortunately, her CO. Jason had heard about the incident through the grapevine and had been appalled when he was told she was filing papers for a dishonorable discharge because she'd pretty much been told her career was over.

It wasn't right. He'd offered her a place in his unit on the condition that she could opt out at any time, but he thought anybody who could dislocate both her attacker's knees and then fireman carry him to the brig while he moaned was someone he'd want in a tight spot.

She'd been a natural at covert ops. She'd started out in coms but had eventually been running independent operations of her own. He'd acted as her handler until he'd been put in charge of Operation Dead Fish, and then she'd come on board working reconnaissance and action. This meant she was given a subject's location and profile, and she'd go scope him out, looking pretty and sweet and like a tanned, sloe-eyed soccer mom, and then determine whether to take the subject out or bring him in.

She was adept at both. People underestimated Trina Perez at their peril.

"Sir," she said briskly, that soccer-mom image not tarnished in the least by her terry-skirt wrap over a floral one-piece, like any woman on vacation.

"Jason," he corrected. "We're trying not to make me look like anyone's CO."

She rolled her eyes. "Have you tried body paint that says Don't Look Here? Because otherwise you might as well send up a signal flare."

He grimaced. "Yeah. Well, from a distance, I'm supposed to look like a guy recovering from a car accident," he muttered.

She raked sharp brown eyes over his body, taking in the unbandaged wounds. Her lips pursed in a low whistle. "That was a bad wreck," she said, a hint of gentleness in her voice.

"The 'accident' was through and through," he told her truthfully. "It was recovery that was the wreck. Don't get me wrong, I hate hospitals, but I gotta tell you, when it comes to fighting infection, they're usually better than cheap apartments."

Her eyebrows hit her hairline. "I just bet!" Her eyebrows lowered into a concentrated scowl and she got down to business. "Which brings me to why I'm here. We've got some urgent intel from Burton and Briggs. Apparently he's put the guys on some incognito recon missions in the, erm, nearby social gathering place of other military personnel."

Jason took a moment to digest this. "You mean after sending the guys on a week's vacation in Tahoe, they got to put on a Navy uniform and go experience shore leave in San Diego?"

She grinned. "Yup. Apparently Medina got to the hotel unannounced the other night and found Daniels in a bondage threesome. I guess you could hear the screams of 'My eyes!' for two counties, sir."

"Oh dear God," Jason responded, horrified. "You assholes really do need me, don't you?"

Trina looked serious. "Dead Fish isn't the same without you, sir. And we've got maybe a week before *somebody* realizes you and Burton have been phoning the whole op in and they try to replace you, so we need to process this new intel, stat." Her eyes drifted out to where Cotton sliced through the water with the graceful undulations of an otter. "Although if I may speak freely, sir, I think your nurse is going to miss you." She gave him a shrewd glance. "And vice versa."

Jason swallowed, and his face went cold. "We are both aware this is a temporary situation," he said roughly.

"Well, that's a shame, sir," she said. "Sometimes civilians allow us to be human. They remind us of what we're trying to do."

Jason compressed his lips into a flat line. "We're trying to keep killers away from the civilian population," he said in measured tones. "Let's start by keeping them away from our civilian here."

Perez met his eyes. "Understood, sir. But you are our package. *You* are the one we're keeping safe."

Jason shook his head. "I will be rendered obsolete if that civilian is neutralized," he said. "Is that clear?"

She chewed her lower lip and spoke in the direction of the lake. "I have a boyfriend in Las Vegas," she told him, shocking him badly. "He's so sweet. He's a high school science teacher. Can you imagine that?"

"No," Jason said, smiling a little.

"I haven't told anybody at Dead Fish about him. I haven't told him what I do. But I show up one week a month, and we fuck like bunnies, and I cry when I have to come back, and he's the only person who's seen me cry since my mother died. If anything I ever did came back to hurt him, I would be 'rendered obsolete.'"

Jason let out a breath. "And you spent your week off here?" he asked, horrified.

She gave him a brief smile. "Well, I'm hoping I'll get permission for two more week's leave when this is over, sir."

"Granted," he said.

Her smile faded. "If I didn't get that week, or that weekend, or that text, or that phone call, I wouldn't be… human enough to do my job, sir. Pretty soon you'd have to send a recon and recovery unit after *me*. Do you understand?"

Jason nodded, his heart giving a pained thump in his chest. "He needs to get his life together," he said softly. "I can't deny him a chance to see who he'd become without me."

She rolled her eyes. "Fucking lonely. That's what he'd become. But seriously, it's none of my business. Call him out and we'll go up to the cabin—Goldfarb is back with the coms, and Klausner started lasagna in your kitchen already."

Jason grimaced. "I'm not sure if he'll eat lasagna," he muttered.

She gave a one-shouldered shrug. "He's a sweet boy," she said, her ten years of seniority over Cotton showing. "If a nice woman like Greta Klausner makes him lasagna, he'll eat it. Trust me."

"Yeah, but I hope she's making salad too."

"'Course. It's what she's gonna feed her kids when she leaves this gig and has twelve. Anyway, I'll watch you from the porch, and you call him back. We got shit to sort."

Jason sighed, then turned to see Cotton finish his first lap before waving him toward shore. As he eyed that lean body emerging from the water, the goose pimples apparent even from fifty feet away where Jason stood, he thought sadly that at least he got the last swim of summer.

At least there was that.

THE LASAGNA was in the oven by the time they'd gotten back and changed, and they sat around the table with phones out, tablets at the ready, and the camera monitor on the counter behind the table.

Jason realized that the calm before the battle was over, and his troops were ready to go to war.

"So," Trina said, pulling up the notes she'd written on the tablet, "here's what we've learned. Briggs was in the officer's club, because he rocks the Navy stripes, and he overheard a couple of people talking about a buddy of theirs who owes them money. At first he lets the chatter wash over him, but he hears one of the guys say, 'Talbot has no idea how deep he's in.'"

"Talbot?" Jason asked sharply. "So this guy works for my CO—"

"The one who tried to stop you at the hospital," Cotton said.

"Yeah. The one we figured was a tight-ass but not a douchebag—he had advisors working for him who were probably steering him wrong."

"Yes," Trina agreed. "So Briggs starts listening harder, and he actually picks up on a name: Deavers. Turns out Master Sergeant J. Frederick Deavers, who works under Talbot and is responsible for gathering all his intel, has gotten in way deep in Vegas, and he owes not only his men money but some bad guys in Vegas as well."

Electricity crackled along Jason's spine. He knew this feeling from the hunt, and he'd been good at the hunt once upon a time.

"So Burton put Owens on Deavers's coms…, Jason prompted, because Burton was whip-smart and knew how Jason thought.

"And we got to hear him get tongue-fucked via cell phone by a woman who purred in German," Greta Klausner said, rolling her eyes. "She sounded exactly like my grandmother from the Old Country. It was fan*tas*tic."

"What was so fantastic about it?" Jason asked, a little horrified.

"My grandmother was not a very nice person," Greta said frankly. "Picturing her as a mobster's moll trying to suck this guy in was really gratifying to a lot of my worst childhood memories."

Next to him, Cotton hid an amused snort behind his hand. "I had one of those," he said apologetically. "Not German, though. Just sort of awful."

"Yeah. Not all grandmothers knit and give out cookies," Greta said, nodding with all sincerity. "Some of them play 'Only my favorite grandchild gets to lotion up my bunions.' So hearing Karina whatserface—"

"Schroeder," Cotton and Jason filled in.

"Yeah, that bitch. Hearing her promise this guy to lick him like a lollipop if he could only get them the guns early…."

Jason sucked in his breath. "Wait—is he going to do that?"

"No," Greta said. "Because Medina and Daniels are genius. They tracked down the shipment of guns he was going to use to pay her with, like you said to.

And then they rerouted it through Fort Dix. So the guns Deavers is going to use to pay off the bad guys are on their way. He has receipts, but…."

"Not getting to Southern California until after this is almost over," Jason said. "Well done, team! How did Karina take that?"

"Not great," Trina chimed in. "Let's say she had several unflattering things to voice about her surroundings. Collie, do you remember her exact quote?"

Trina had left her secure cell phone open to Collie Goldfarb, who had the cabin under surveillance.

"She said that until he got them the guns, they were stuck knocking over shitty stores in the ass-end of nowhere," Collie supplied, his light tenor crackling over the line. "And according to Owens and Medina, she said it with*out* the German accent. In fact, Medina swore she went full Brooklyn."

Jason grunted his appreciation. Was it true? Possibly not. Was it amusing? Yes, very.

"Did you run the local po-po intel to see if you could spot a trail?"

Collie grunted. "Sir, not to be a killjoy? But spotting their trail is like smelling death with your head up a corpse's ass. Six days ago, you had a couple of possibly unrelated crimes to go on, am I right?"

"A drug ring takeover and a stop and rob," Jason confirmed. "What do we have now?"

"Right now we've got a series of drug overdoses in a casino on South Shore, Lake Tahoe, and a couple of convenience store robberies with casualties in each one. The police are trying not to panic people, but you can tell they're flying blind. It's one of the biggest crime sprees in the area in years."

Jason sucked in a breath. "Dammit," he muttered. "I hadn't realized they'd passed us up."

"Frankly, sir," Goldfarb said, "You weren't fit enough to get out of our way if we'd gone after these guys. You and Mr. Harris are our biggest concerns."

Jason blinked. "Mr. Harris?" he said, because of all the names that had been thrown at him, that one was the most unfamiliar.

"Your nurse?" Collie said. "Mr. Carson Harris, aged twenty-two, resident of—"

"Stop," Jason said, watching as Cotton curled in on himself. Jason reached under the table to take his hand and found it was clammy and cold. "Cotton?"

"It's my real name," Cotton whispered, not meeting his eyes. "I... I haven't used it in years. John had my ID made out to Cotton Carey. I told you that."

Jason nodded and squeezed his hand. "I forgot." He grimaced. "And I'd not counted on my team's thoroughness." He said out loud, "Cotton Carey, and if we could make sure *all* his IDs are made out to that name, he'd be much obliged."

"Oh," Collie said through the phone, sounding temporarily off-balance. "Yeah. Sure. Sorry, Cotton."

"You're keeping Jason safe," Cotton mumbled. "It's all good."

"So," Collie went on, obviously trying to find his stride again. "We needed you to be in decent condition, because if you weren't, and they went after you, we'd be spending all our firepower defending you and none of it taking Karina and Dietrich out. They have a couple of goons with them. We've caught at least three different guys on camera doing the jobs like ripping off the liquor stores or selling the drugs. If the criminal behavior wasn't organized like it is, we'd assume they were having a very busy day, but we ran them through some facial recognition, and they're known associates of Dima Siderov, which means the Schroeders got them by default. In fact, they're some of the few surviving members of the Siderov gang after the goings-on a month ago, the ones who laid you up and put you in hiding."

"Has it only been a month?" Jason muttered. "I could swear it's been at least a year."

"Well, I understand a good vacation is like that, sir," Goldfarb said, tongue firmly planted in cheek.

"Is he always like this?" Cotton asked. "Because I see why he's the one giving out information from across the lake."

"I am, in fact, a goddamned delight," Collie said, and coming from the stout, prematurely balding man who had deadpanned his way through six days of meetings with Jason and Cotton—not to mention his prior three years in Jason's unit—there was a good reason everyone around the table let out a chorus of "Oh my God!" and "Dear Jesus, why?"

"Notwithstanding," Jason returned dryly, "we need to know where they are and if they've made us yet. Because if they haven't made us or are about to come crashing into our little wilderness with a bunch of semiautos, we need to go hunt them."

"*We* need to go hunt them, sir," Trina said, voice flinty. "We were waiting until you're mobile, which you are. But you're at roughly eighty percent. You wouldn't let one of us out like that, and we're not letting you go hunting like that."

Jason opened his mouth to protest, but Greta laughed. "Oh, watch him, his ears are turning red. It's adorable. Colonel," she said, eyes big and guileless, "we get that you want to stop the bad guys from hurting innocent civilians. It's what you do. But you need to stay in the tower for this op and guard your own civilian."

Jason took a determined breath to explain to them—civilly, and not like a roaring bear, which he'd been told he could be—about how this was his unit and his mess, and he wasn't going to sit there and let bad things happen to his people when—

"And one of us is staying with you," Collie said, with more authority in his voice over the phone than he'd ever had in his entire life. "Burton's got reinforcements coming up early tomorrow morning, and we'll run a five-man unit. We figure covert, and by the day after tomorrow, the Tahoe area wakes up safer with a few extra dead people in it. 'Does that sound like a plan, Collie? Yes, Collie, you're brilliant, we should *always* run with your plans.'"

Goldfarb's basic "ness" derailed what Jason was going to say next, and he breathed out some of his frustration. "We can't do that," he said, his voice gritty. "If we want the military to clear me so I can come back, we have to keep at least two living scumbags to confront Deavers with. Otherwise we just went off the rails and took out random criminals with our superpowers."

"Ugh!" Goldfarb groaned. "And this is why you get the hot red convertible, chief. Because you think about things like how not to go to Leavenworth."

"It's a good thing he does," Trina said pertly, "or I'd be so on that car."

Jason's eyes went wide, remembering the bright red Maserati GranTurismo convertible, his one—*one*—indulgence, back at the base in the desert. "It's, uhm… I mean, you kept the tarp on her, didn't you?"

"No, we've been using it for target practice," Goldfarb retorted.

Greta patted his shoulder. "Don't mind them. Yes, we kept the tarp on her. In fact, we put her in the hangar to keep her out of the elements, and I think Burton's friends even came and did some maintenance."

Jason's eyes went wide. "Burton's friends?" he asked, not actually wanting to know.

"Yeah, that yummy guy with the hazel eyes," Greta said, "and his scrawny little sidekick."

"Sidekick is my speed," Trina said.

"Sidekick is psychotic," Goldfarb quelled. "I've seen eyes that jumpy in subjects. Besides, girls, cool your jets. I think they're a couple."

"They are indeed," Jason said, keeping his smile to himself. "And, uh, be kind to the sidekick. He's a good guy, but he is... jumpy."

"That is just my luck." Trina sighed. "But we're getting off track. Chief, you're right. We need to stop the bad shit now, but how do you want to keep from killing all the bad guys?"

"Well, if we kill or capture the soldiers—to be delivered to the proper authorities of course—the generals will have no choice but to come after us here."

Cotton stared at him. "Like, say, the way the dead mobster *crashed through our apartment* when you could barely stand? That's fine. That's totally fine. Of course we should do that again." Cotton's hand in his had grown bony and clammy, clinging for dear life and not seeking comfort.

"I can stand now," Jason said, his voice steely. He noticed Cotton didn't flinch from that, and a part of him rejoiced, because that meant Cotton knew all of him.

"Yeah, but how long's it been since you shot anything?" Greta asked and then held up a hand. "No. Don't answer that. Look, I say we split the difference. Tomorrow, after your run around the lake, one of us will take you to a shooting range the guys scouted when they were up here and you weren't moving much."

"And as discussed, while that's happening, the rest of us will go hunting," Trina said with satisfaction. "Goldie's got some addresses scouted, some possible targets, and a witness to interview. We flash our ID, look like a big deal, and we might make some arrests."

Jason let out a grunt. "We won't be able to let local LEO know we're here until we start stepping on their toes," he said unhappily. "I don't like that. We usually rely on them for backup."

"Why can't we?" Cotton asked. He obviously liked the idea of backup.

"Because we don't have the only coms system in the military," Greta said, grimacing. "But I really don't like the idea of not telling them."

Jason thought for a moment. "Guys, let me make a phone call...."

JACKSON RIVERS sounded like he was in the middle of running somebody down. His breath came in short bursts, and Jason could hear footfalls on the pavement as it did. Jason was impressed by the man's willpower. And willingness to answer his phone.

"I can call back later," he began, looking through the darkened living room to where Cotton and Greta were moving around in the kitchen.

"No, no. We've lost him." And then Rivers called out, "Henry, is he gone? Yeah, fucker's not here either. That's okay. I know where he'll be. We'll get him on the way home."

"Suspect?" Jason asked.

"Witness who can clear our guy," Rivers panted. "Fucking coward. Doesn't want to tell his mom he was in a bar at the magic age of seventeen. Which means, guess where he'll be in an hour?"

"Home doing his homework?" Jason hazarded.

"Give the man a cigar," Rivers laughed. "Which means we got time." Then, obviously to Henry, "Yeah, it's Jason. No, he's not dead." He paused for a moment and asked into the phone. "Cotton still okay? The guys have been asking about him."

Cotton was, in fact, clearing the table so they could all eat. "Yeah," Jason said thoughtfully. "He's fine. In fact, my guys have been teaching him how to use a knife, in case shit gets hairy."

"Wait a minute," Jackson said. "You can barely fucking move. How hairy is shit gonna get if you can barely fuckin' move?"

And this time Henry's voice came in loud and clear. "Ask your two psychotic cats!" he said. "The little one has enough fur for two whole other cats."

"You have another cat?" Jason remembered the first one. During that week he and Burton had been tracking Jackson and Ellery, he'd seen the battered, torn-eared, three-legged beast glaring at him through the bedroom window on more than one occasion.

"Yeah, we got it from Ernie, who had a party without you, and he and Burton worried about you the whole time. And you, apparently, were trying to be woodsman of the fucking year!"

"I have to be," Jason said defensively, remembering why he'd called. "Jackson, the Schroeders are up here, and they're leaving civilians in their wake trying to find me. We've got their gun connection ready to hook, but we need help bringing down the rest of the Siderov army."

Jackson let out a low whistle. "LEO?" he asked, thinking like Jason that local law enforcement officers might come in handy right now.

"If I briefed them, their coms could give us away," he said. "Do you have any contacts up here?"

Jackson grunted. "Maybe," he admitted. "Or I can get some guys here up there. Would that be okay?"

Jason let out a breath. "Yeah. Yeah, that's okay. Can you get back to me in an hour?"

"Sure, what's in an hour?"

Jason looked over his shoulder from the living room into the kitchen and sighed. "My last meal as a free man," he said, hating the idea of going back to work for a moment.

"It might not have to be," Jackson said gently, and Jason wanted to smack his head against the wall.

"He deserves his own life," he said stubbornly.

"Yeah, but maybe he wants you in it."

"Look, Rivers, I gotta—"

"Yeah, you gotta stomp down on your emotions until they rise up, grab you by the throat, shake you around a little, and then grind you into the pavement. I've done that. It's not fun. You enjoy yourself. I'm going to see if some folks can come up and maybe save your ass for you. Bye."

"Prick," Jason muttered as the phone went dead. It wasn't fair; he knew it. Rivers, Cramer, and Henry had all put themselves out for him and had risked their own injuries and backlash to protect him, but he couldn't help fuming. Really? A scrawny alley cat of a man who couldn't avoid trouble if it came with detour signs was going to tell *Jason* how to run his own personal life? It was just that the quick jab about stomping down on his emotions until they rose up and took a guy by the throat had been so damned...

True.

He sighed and pocketed his phone, putting on a smile as Cotton walked in.

"Who pissed in *your* Wheaties?" Cotton asked, raising his eyebrows.

Jason's smile relaxed a smidge, became real, and he resisted the urge to put a hand on Cotton's hip and draw him close. "Nobody," he murmured. "I'm brooding."

"It's because you're in the living room with the lights off. It's like setting the stage. 'Now I shall brood! Commence the brooding! The brooding is in session!'" Cotton turned a grin toward him, and Jason returned it, years dropping from him like weights, landing at his feet.

"I should either turn the lights on or go eat," he said.

"Probably eat." Cotton gave him a brief smile, but Jason caught the edge of sadness there too. It hit him. Cotton wasn't stupid. He knew what the coming events could mean.

"Cotton—"

He shook his head, as if to ward off Jason's words. "It's okay," he said gruffly. "I... I knew it was coming. Every minute I get in the meantime is a good one." He flashed that brief smile again, his eyes shiny. "C'mon. Greta made me promise to gain two pounds with dinner. I think it's some sort of challenge she set herself. I don't want to disappoint her."

And Jason didn't want to push it, didn't want to make those shiny eyes spill over, not for all the "I'm sorries" in the world.

A FLASH ON THE MONITOR

THE CABIN seemed quieter after Greta and Trina had left, and Cotton wiped off the last counter and started the dishwasher. He was staring thoughtfully out the window, trying to still a heartbeat that had hummed threadily in his ears since seeing Jason in the darkened room.

It felt like such a metaphor.

Cotton would go back to his regularly scheduled life and work valiantly to get his shit together. He had roommates and friends who would help him get into junior college, and he was still getting residuals from Johnnies—not to mention the constant offer to go do off-camera work such as editing or even filming that was always on the table. He'd resisted so far. Some of that felt like a pity offer, since he'd exhibited no inclination or even talent in either area. But he knew if he needed the money, John would be there to let him help.

The point was, even if Cotton ended up bagging groceries or working reception in a gym, he would have a way, a life, a path. He was young, and while that hadn't meant much to him in June when he'd had to walk away from porn, it meant something to him now. He had *so much time* to get his life together, and after the last couple of weeks of taking care of another human being when he was at his lowest, Cotton thought he might be up to the job of taking care of himself.

For the first time since that terrible moment in his bedroom at home—Brent yanking his dick out of Cotton's mouth, the light flaring, his father yelling about getting his gun—Cotton thought he was going to be okay. In fact, he had the *right* to be okay. He could do that.

But leaving Jason, alone in a darkened room, Cotton wasn't sure he could do *that*.

He was going to have to. He knew that on one level. But in the past month, sitting with the soldiers who worked under Jason in his unit, Cotton got two feelings. The first was that these people would die for him—no questions, no hesitation. Jason inspired that sort of loyalty, and Cotton could see why. He was smart, but he was also compassionate. He made decisions easily and with a measured consideration of all the angles. But he was not afraid of input, or even good-natured teasing.

And he didn't allow his staff to take risks that he wouldn't take himself.

The fact that there were people begging to be put on his security detail—and spend their vacation time doing so—told him all he needed to know.

But the other feeling that wouldn't leave Cotton alone was that Jason, for all his personality and good qualities as a boss, was still the boss. The buck *did* stop with him. He didn't *allow* the fuckups of his superior officers to color the good work he felt his crew did.

That's why Jason had ignored his misguided CO and had taken those kids to safety himself.

That's why he'd given Burton, who had been in the field, the freedom to choose whether or not to take a contract on a man who might be innocent.

And that's why he'd taken on an assignment—sin-eating, he'd called it—that would all but destroy his career but was the only thing he could do that made any sense.

That was why he was the world's loneliest man.

And Cotton, who had gotten to be in his arms for the last few weeks, who had made love to the Colonel, the man in charge, the CO to all the ubercompetent, really amazing, super fun soldiers in their security details, was so far out of his sphere of influence, so far out of his scope, that Cotton was, in fact, the perfect man to keep him company.

Cotton didn't want to rule the world. He didn't want to eat anybody's sin. He just wanted to make sure he could take care of himself so he could take care of the people he loved.

Like Jason Constance.

He loved Jason Constance.

He wouldn't say it. He'd fallen in love about a hundred times in the past three years. Once, he'd been in love with John. Another time with Dex. For a heartbeat, it had been with Henry. And that didn't even count the men he'd thought he'd been dating, who had wanted to use him, his pretty body, his pretty face. But he'd begun to realize that summer that this wasn't really "in love."

Sure, he *loved* the people in his life who had been good to him—John, Dex, Henry. They cared for him in return, all of them, and he was starting to realize how much he owed them for the person he was becoming.

But he hadn't *loved* the sugar daddies who'd just wanted to use him. He hadn't *loved* the other porn models who wanted to hook up because sex was cheap, easy, safe, and free. He certainly hadn't *loved* the boyfriend who'd gotten him kicked out of the house, although he hoped Brent had been able to pick up his life and move on after he'd almost had everything ripped apart by Cotton's parents.

He had loved his little sister, though, and thinking about her, he still did.

And he was pretty sure he loved Jason Constance.

At the very least, he'd die for the man. But God, by all Cotton had begun to learn about the world in the past few months, he really didn't want to leave him alone in a darkened room.

His musings were interrupted by the feel of Jason's hands on his hips, the heat of him along Cotton's back, the pressure of his groin against Cotton's backside. Cotton closed his eyes and tilted his head back, reveling in being alone with him, in his heat, in their touch.

"You're brooding," Jason whispered in his ear.

"Not possible," Cotton told him, not able to smile. "I didn't turn off the lights or make the announcement."

Jason laughed softly and kissed the side of his neck. Cotton let him, enjoying that for a moment. Jason liked to do things—touchy things—that had nothing to do with "This will get your dick hard" and everything to do with "This will make your heart beat and your chest swell and your stomach erupt into butterflies, and you will weep wanting to be touched like that some more."

Cotton had felt a little like a fraud when he realized that kisses on his neck or a nibble on his ear or fingertips along his waist to his hip could make him fully ready, cock dripping, asshole clenching, begging and needy for sex in a moment's time. Wasn't he supposed to *know* about sex? Wasn't sex his *trade*?

Except there was nothing worklike about the sex he had with Jason. There were no "Hey, this trick usually gets a guy off with maximum intensity and minimum effort, so let's do that so I can sleep tonight" moments.

With Jason, sex wasn't about *trade* at all. In fact, it was all about *wonder*, and Cotton hadn't known he could still feel wonder, but he did.

Jason continued to kiss down his neck, his bare hands shoving up under Cotton's T-shirt and spanning his waist, stroking his stomach, teasing the skin on his ribs not quite enough to tickle.

"Jason?" Cotton asked breathlessly, lost in the swirl of wonder that always threatened to submerge him.

"What, angel?"

Ah! Even his breath in Cotton's ear was like light and sound and electricity, all of it zapping straight to the erogenous zones.

"Your touch makes me fly," he said, hoping he was even coherent. "I want to make you fly too."

And with that, he turned in Jason's arms and took his mouth tenderly, but took it nonetheless.

Jason melted, allowing himself to be walked backward, led to the darkened bedroom.

"You have something in mind?" Jason asked breathlessly.

"Yeah." Cotton had so little power in his life, but this, *this* he could do. "I want to make you feel cherished."

The sound Jason made then was fat with promise, heavy with need. "You don't have to."

"I'm good at this," Cotton whispered. "Let me be good at it for *you.*" He didn't say that he wasn't sure he'd ever want to do it with anybody else again. He wouldn't put that on Jason's shoulders—or even on his own. But he knew that Jason Constance had waited for ten years to make love again because the life he'd chosen for himself, the things he'd wanted to do in the world, had made living without sex worth the sacrifice. Cotton would never again have sex for any other reason than touching someone being worth changing his life to be with that person.

He'd change his life again and again to be with Jason Constance, but he knew that wasn't possible. He wanted to show Jason what the time they *did* have together meant.

"Okay," Jason murmured, and there was an edge of sadness in his voice. He was already missing them, and Cotton couldn't change that.

He could only give him memories to sustain him.

He kissed Jason with everything he had—powerful kisses, but not masterful. He wasn't trying to dominate or bend Jason to his will. He wanted Jason to feel what he felt every time they kissed.

Jason seemed to know that and let him lead. Their clothes went first, all in a rush, because they knew each other's bodies by now, and the surprise wasn't in the unveiling.

It was in the touching.

Cotton gorged himself on skin. He kissed the places *he* loved to kiss, mostly because Jason made the good sounds when he kissed them. He spent an eternity on Jason's nipples, because they were sensitive, and he loved the helpless noises Jason made, the way his hips arched, thrusting his full cock into space, and even better, the way he mastered *himself,* forcing his ass against the bed to wait for the next touch.

Eventually he moved to Jason's cock, loving the startled gasp when he closed his mouth over the bell. Jason's fingers tangled in his hair—long and curly these days—and Cotton teased the harp string with his tongue while fisting the shaft, not too hard, not too soft.

"You're killing me," Jason whispered as Cotton stroked with his lips and tongue. "But in a good way."

Cotton chuckled, letting the vibrations rock him, and kept up the blowjob, using barely enough pressure to arouse him, but not enough to make him come.

"Cotton?" Jason begged, after spurting a particularly wicked jet of precome into Cotton's mouth, "Do you want me to, uhm…?"

Cotton pulled back and blew gently across the head, smiling when Jason's entire body—getting tanned and fit and healthy—shuddered.

"I'm going to fuck you," he said, making sure there was no equivocation. "And I'm going to do it for a long time," he promised. "And you might come, but I'm going to keep going. So if you need to come in my mouth now, I would love to swallow. We've got more to do tonight."

And with that, he took a spit-slickened finger to tease Jason's entrance, and Jason bit down on his palm as he screamed, shooting hard and thick into Cotton's mouth.

Cotton swallowed it down, shuddering, his own cock aching with the taste. He used some more spit and some more come and played with the pucker some more.

Jason made a sound of discomfort, so Cotton pulled off, cleaning as he went, and parted Jason's cheeks, rimming him happily.

Jason had stopped begging—stopped making words, actually—and it was like his body had accepted the floaty, subby place where it could endure pleasure after pleasure with greedy urgency.

He made a particularly needy whimper, and Cotton pulled reluctantly away. Oh, Jason liked his ass played with. Unashamedly too. Some men didn't want to talk about it, or ask for it, or even mention that they liked it done, but Jason was unapologetic. He'd said at the very beginning that he liked to bottom, and Cotton would be taking him at his word tonight.

As Cotton sat up on his knees and wiped his face on his shoulder, he took stock of his handiwork.

Jason Constance, Colonel, a covert ops specialist with hundreds of people under his command, was splayed, knees spread lewdly, cock growing thick and fat again, face sweaty, lips swollen with kisses, wanton and ready for hard use.

Oh wow. He was *Cotton's*. Cotton was going to have him and use him and fuck him and… cherish him. Love him.

Cotton shuddered, the thought alone almost making him spill. With practiced movements, he smoothed slick over his cock and then fitted himself between Jason's spread knees.

"I might be," Jason panted, "a little tight… oh… oh God. Oh God. Fuck… yes. Please. Please don't stop. Oh…. God. *Yes*."

Cotton had stretched him out thoroughly, probed with his tongue, then his fingers, and now Jason expanded, stretched to fit around Cotton's cock, as Cotton slid inexorably in.

Finally, after an eternity, he was all the way in, and Jason's entire body gave a terrific shudder.

"Yes," he begged, almost tearfully. "Oh, angel, I need this. I need this. Please…. I need this."

Cotton took his mouth first, kissing gently, and then as Jason returned the kiss with more power, and more, Cotton began to move.

He kept his thrusts smooth and even at first, a strong power fuck, but Jason didn't let him stay in control that long.

He begged so sweetly.

Stronger, harder, hips rocketing, thrusts growing uneven. A shudder rocked Jason, and his ass clenched down hard on Cotton, making his vision explode in white light. His own urgency, want, almost consumed him then, and he realized how much he'd been holding back, trying to possess Jason with everything he had.

But that one moment, shocks of pleasure sizzling along his nerve endings, told him he couldn't do this alone. He couldn't just fuck the man he loved into submission. He had to be subsumed himself.

So he closed his eyes and let it happen. Let the pleasure override his caution, his synapses, let his thrusts grow frenzied, harder, allowed Jason's cries of pleasure to drive him.

"Yes! Oh angel… oh please… yes! Oh please…. *Yes*!"

And with that one thrust, Jason's body convulsed, an orgasm ripping through him, clenching down on Cotton's cock like a vise. Jason shot spend for the second time that night, and Cotton drove into him one final time, his spine arching as his orgasm took over, blinding him, consuming him, sweeping him away into an ocean where there was only Cotton, Jason, and the briny release.

Cotton pulled out reluctantly, the rush of spend coating his thighs and Jason's backside. That wasn't enough. That couldn't be the end. His cock was spent, but his heart still pounded, still hungered, and he pushed Jason's knees over his shoulders and sprawled on the bed, parting his cheeks and licking, tasting, rubbing Jason's sensitized rim as Jason moaned incoherently. The two of them together hit his senses potently, and he shuddered, needing more.

Jason started to shudder again, his hands splaying, his body clearly out of his control. Cotton thrust three fingers inside and paused.

"Jason," he said, voice serious. "Jason, baby, focus."

Jason turned bleary eyes down the length of his body, and Cotton regarded him soberly.

"I want to keep going, but if you're too tender, you need to tell me to stop. Nod your head yes if you understand."

Jason nodded his head.

"Now do you want me to stop?" he asked, and his heart shuddered when Jason shook his head in the negative.

"No," he slurred. "More."

"Good."

He pumped his three fingers in and out, spreading them, watching as Jason spiraled, ever more undone. He entire body arched, and he threw one knee over the other, turning sideways in a protective gesture, but Cotton had done this before and kept his fingers where they needed to be.

Inside his lover, feeling the pulse and heat of him.

He kept fucking, and Jason moaned, shuddering some more.

Cotton added another finger, and Jason turned his face into the mattress and howled, a dry orgasm racking his body before he went absolutely limp.

"More," he mumbled, and Cotton's cock had stiffened again. He hoisted himself up over Jason's quaking form and slid in easily, the slickness tempered by the slight swelling of overuse.

The result was Jason locked around him like the fist of a god, and it took one, two, three strokes before a slow-rolling burning scald of an orgasm ripped through him and into Jason.

This time when he collapsed on top of his still-trembling lover, he knew they were done.

IT TOOK Cotton half an hour before he could stand on wobbly knees to go fetch a washcloth and some clean sheets. He wrapped Jason in a towel while he changed the bed and then spread him out, as docile as a sleepy bunny, on the towel so he could clean the come that matted him everywhere—chest hair, groin, backside, thighs. All of it, Cotton thought, all of it was because Cotton had taken him someplace not even Jason Constance had ever been.

He bathed Jason's body tenderly, speaking softly to him, telling him the truth with every breath.

"You're so beautiful," he murmured. "So beautiful. You're kind and smart and the best lover I will ever have. And I love you. And you probably don't believe that and think I'm too young, but I've believed I was in love a thousand times, and this is the first time it made me better. Made me stronger. Made me someone who can really love and not someone who is constantly begging for what the world won't give me. You did that." He kissed the inside of Jason's knee and then his thigh. Jason quivered, so he went back to his task—and telling the truth.

"I've spent the last few years bouncing up and down and going from here to there, because I didn't think I had any control over my life. But you've given me control here, and you'll never know—never—what that means to me. And you've trusted that I'll be okay when you have to leave, and that's such an amazing gift. It's big... and important... and that's how love feels this time. It feels real."

He finished his task and stood, still naked, to roll Jason off the towel and then back into his place on the bed before covering him with the quilt and blankets because he was starting to shiver. He'd taken a step toward the pile of laundry, planning to put it in the washer that night so they could dry it in the morning, but then Jason stopped him with a hand on his wrist.

"I love you too," he whispered, and Cotton could see a silver track running from the corner of his eye into his hair.

He hadn't wanted to say it, Cotton figured. Hadn't wanted to bind Cotton to him any more than they were already bound. But Cotton really had unraveled him, and Jason had trusted Cotton when he'd been completely unable to look after himself.

He'd done it willingly, and Cotton would take the words, which he needed so desperately, he could admit that now, as the best gift of all.

He kissed that silver tear track and went back to the last parts of cleanup, putting the sheets in the washer.

On his way back, he saw the perpetual glow of the monitor in the guest room, where they'd kept it since Burton had left, and Cotton's newfound sense of responsibility, of participation in his own life, reared its head.

With a lump in his throat, he unplugged the monitor—which ran on a fairly decent battery even without a power source—and moved it into the bedroom he and Jason shared.

He set it up on the end table on Jason's side of the bed, glad Jason was turned away from it, tucked into himself in aftermath, too exhausted and floaty to realize the monitor was even there.

Cotton climbed into bed next to him and snuggled, shivering for a couple of minutes while his body got used to the warmth again and keeping his eyes on the monitor.

Nothing for a moment, and then one of the panels lit up as an owl flitted across the screen. The panel went dark in sixty seconds just as another panel lit up with the same animal. In another moment, a panel lit up to show a parade of possums, white as ghosts with the night-vision cameras, making their stiff and awkward way through the trees. That panel went dark, and the possums disappeared outside their territory, and the screen was blank.

Cotton stared at it, wondering what wonder would show itself next, and right after he thought, "Hey, maybe I'll see a bear or something," he fell asleep.

SPEEDING UP THE RUN

"NOT A word," Jason said, scowling, as he limped around the lake that morning.

"Sorry," Cotton said, but he didn't look sorry. Nor should he be. Yeah, Jason was sore, but damn, what a way to go.

"My fault entirely," Jason said, slowing to a stiff walk. "Forgot how long it's been. Those were some muscles that hadn't been, uhm, worked in a while."

Cotton laughed softly. "You work them every day," he said coyly, and Jason laughed.

"It's really not the same."

And finally, his angel, the man who had literally fucked him onto another plane of existence the night before, gave a self-satisfied smirk. It was well earned. Jason may have been walking a little stiffly—and running was not as much fun as it had been the day before—but damn if his heart, his *soul*, didn't feel infinity to the nth power less lonely.

On the one hand, it was stupid. They still had to face down the mob, arrest Deavers, and convince Talbot to not prosecute Jason. And the situation hadn't changed in the least regarding Cotton. Jason was still going to have to go down to the desert near Barstow and Cotton was still going to Sacramento where he had friends who could help him as he started school and got his life in order.

But the situation between Jason and Cotton was radically different, in a way. Cotton had taken control and pushed Jason to his absolute limits the night before, and Jason knew why. It was his way of proving that he was strong enough, *whole* enough, to accept what they were—who they were—for the time being, and that he would be okay when their brief liaison ended.

Which was a soft balm on Jason's soul, because he'd been worried, but it was also a chafing, painful realization, because the hard truth was that Cotton might be okay without Jason, but the time without Cotton stretched before him like Death Valley itself.

Except worse, because sometimes, in the evenings, when the sun was going down and the sky looked as though God had broken out the good oil paints and textured canvas, Jason *liked* the desert.

"Yup," Jason said now, ignoring the ache in his chest. "You're pleased with yourself."

"Well *yeah!*" Cotton's laugh—young, exuberant, happy—added years to Jason's life. Or maybe that had been the sex, but either way, it was Cotton. "But I will be even more pleased with myself if we can get you to run a little farther. It's only a little farther!"

Nurse, caretaker, personal trainer, gym coach…. Cotton's future was an endless vista of opportunity. Jason needed to respect that and let him go when their time was up.

"Isn't that what the big bad wolf said to Little Red Riding Hood?" Jason retorted.

Cotton howled, and they continued their run around the lake.

It really *was* too cold to swim that morning, and Trina was waiting for Jason when they got back.

"You can keep going," Jason said, when Cotton made a disappointed noise because their morning workout had been cut short. They'd already talked about Cotton making another loop around the lake since the swim was no longer feasible.

"No!" Trina said sharply, and Jason's eyes darted to her.

"Tell me," he said, ten years of command falling onto his shoulders like a ton of bricks.

"In the cabin, sir," she said tightly. "It's not safe out here."

It was amazing how quickly Jason could move with the right motivation.

JASON HAD Cotton shower first while Trina briefed him.

"Goldfarb and Klausner moved on a tip-off this morning," Trina said. "Two soldiers. They'd spotted them on the security feeds of the casino where the ODs happened and one of the liquor-store murders. We tracked the soldiers down to a crappy hotel, and they went to do recon. They got shot at. Klausner was hit. They called me from the hospital. She's stable but sedated. Goldfarb won't leave her side, not even to give a statement, and for the same reason you didn't go to a hospital in the first place. He does not trust local law enforcement, and any communication with Barstow is likely to be compromised. We are not sure if they were tracked down here or—"

"Jason!" Cotton's voice held the edge of panic.

Jason and Trina met eyes and darted into the bedroom, where Cotton was staring at the monitor on the end table.

Jason had seen it there that morning, and a part of him had mourned that his life was no longer his own, but now he was grateful Cotton was thinking about more than the two of them.

"Oh hell," Trina muttered. "Shit, Colonel, we need to get you to safety."

The entire monitor was alight, with three operatives, a woman and two men, closing in on the cabin from different angles.

"That woman is Karina Schroeder," Trina said dispassionately. "See the bandage on the shoulder? Goldfarb said he winged her."

"Is there anyone else coming?" Jason asked.

She shook her head. "There was a rockslide south of here this morning." This happened often—usually when fires had taken out the ground cover and the landscape shifted. Any rain at all could send the roads that carved through the Sierras into a disaster. "The team that was going to accompany us got stranded. It's why we went in a man light. As for *them*, I don't know. Greta got Karina's husband, Dietrich. He's stable and in the same hospital. Goldfarb isn't going to sleep, I shit you not."

"So are these the only three we have to worry abou—hey! Did you see that?"

Karina Schroeder and her soldiers were dressed in black. It was probably fashionable mobster wear in the middle of the city, particularly if she was committing crimes at night, but in the daytime in the trees, they stood out in stark contrast to the faded greens and khakis—even on the black-and-white monitors.

But something had moved in the periphery of one of the screens, something Jason had not been able to pin down.

"No," Trina said. "No, I didn't see what it was, but—oh fuck. Who is that?"

"No," Jason said.

"No!" Cotton said.

"What the…? I told them to get us in contact with LEO!"

But Jackson Rivers and Henry Worrall had apparently not been able to make those contacts, because they were driving down the road in a very classy cream-colored Cadillac Seville.

"That's a nice car," Jason said, stunned.

"It's probably John's," Cotton said. "His boyfriend was in a car accident and doesn't move well. Henry works as his driver sometimes."

"Who's John?" Trina asked.

"A porn mogul," Jason told her, because this was his life and he was going to own that. "He's apparently a very nice guy."

And then there was a flicker on the monitor again, one that Jason couldn't make out, and he swore.

"Someone else is out there," he muttered. "Okay, let's look at our options."

"We could escape out the back window," Cotton pointed out. "Look, they're moving in on the sides of the cabin. Karina is moving around to the front. See this part of the monitor over here? It's free. They wouldn't spot us."

"But what if there's another one out there," Jason muttered, torn. "We only have a guess there were four, and Karina's husband was wounded. She's going to be pissed."

At that point, Jason's phone rang, and he pulled it out of the running pack at his waist.

"So are you guys trapped in that indefensible cabin?" Jackson Rivers asked. "Because that was a bad move."

"It was either that or be a duck in a lake," Jason retorted. "Lake's cold. Warmer in here. I thought you were going to hook us up with LEO!"

"We were going to, but your unit moved early, and now Ellery is in Tahoe, keeping your guy out of jail for obstruction of justice. He's also briefing the sheriff's department on why they should keep Dietrich Schroeder handcuffed to his bed rail. You're welcome."

"This is so not fair," Jason muttered, glaring at Trina. "You were *not* supposed to move without my go-ahead!"

Trina grimaced. "Recon, Colonel. I swear, we were doing a drive-by so we could give LEO their location. It was not supposed to get dire!"

"Well, it's pretty fuckin' dire," Jackson said from the phone. "Look, we've got a bead on their vehicle. They've got a driver parked back from the road—you might not have it in your cameras. I'm leaving Henry here to disable their vehicle."

"Nice instincts," Trina said with a grimace.

"That's why they pay me the big bucks," Jason told her. "So I can lay odds that there's other bad guys we can't see."

"Talk to me about the ones you *can* see," Jackson said. "We saw the black SUV off the road. What do you have?"

"Three subjects, moving in on the cabin from the north, east, and west sides," Jason said. "The south side appears not to be covered. Possible escape for our civilian through there?"

"Wait," Cotton said, sounding confused. "Am I the civilian? Why aren't you escaping with me?"

"Because, baby," Trina said, while Jason and Jackson continued to plan over the phone, "it's time for Jason to go to work."

COTTON DIDN'T like this. He didn't like it, he didn't like it, and he didn't *trust* it. Every instinct he had said he and Jason needed to stay together to survive, but then, the last time he'd faced off with an opponent with a gun, he'd thrown a chef's knife at the guy's nose.

He didn't even have a chef's knife here, and while he'd had a few knife-throwing lessons, they equaled nothing that was going to make him hot ninja shit since then. They'd been planning to go to the shooting range that afternoon so Jason could practice, but apparently the bad guys were in a hurry.

And even he could see that the three people wearing traditional bad-guy black were moving in on the cabin in position to take out anybody inside.

"Why would they leave the south side open?" he pondered.

And Jackson said over the phone, "They didn't."

"Repeat that?" Jason said, sounding surprised.

"It wasn't open. Now it is. And we have a great place to get Cotton out and you guys too."

"Where we can circle around and take them out," Jason said with satisfaction. "Trina, are you armed?"

She patted the pancake holster in the small of her back, and Jason nodded.

"Fair enough," he said. "Excuse me, all, I need to fetch my service weapon."

Cotton had packed it. He remembered that because besides the clothes they'd purchased for him, the service revolver, holster, and boots had been pretty much the only things Jason'd had that were salvageable after Lance had cut off all his clothes to treat him.

It was the one and only time Cotton had ever held a gun.

"Please tell me he's cleaned it in the last two weeks," Trina said as Jason ran to the back bedroom.

"Yes," Cotton told her. "After breakfast this morning. Why?"

"Because those things don't fire right if they're not cleaned regularly," she said. "And the only thing worse than having to fire one is having it misfire because there's too much debris in the chamber."

"This morning," Cotton repeated, remembering Jason's quiet concentration on the task before their run. He'd said much the same thing Trina just had, but the incident had served as a reminder—yet another one—that as much as he loved this man, Jason had never really been his.

"Good," Trina said. Her lips quirked up. "He really is an amazing marksman, particularly with handheld. With rifles, I'd prefer Goldfarb or Klausner, but Colonel Constance is nearly as accurate with small arms as a lot of soldiers are with a scope. Don't worry, Cotton, we're in good hands."

Cotton didn't tell her that he'd known that from the beginning. Even sick and feverish and helpless, Jason Constance had never not cared for the people he was with.

"Where are you going?" Trina asked as he turned away.

"If we're dodging out the back window and running through the woods, I'm going to want my cargo shorts and my wallet," Cotton told her. "And maybe a hoodie."

"Good thinking," she said, and her face was soft. "Get what you need, kid. I have the feeling we're hitting the ground in five."

COTTON CHANGED from his board shorts—which he wore in his loops around the lake in the morning so he could run and then swim—into dry clothes while Jason slid into jeans, his boots, and then his holster. He put it on over a camo T-shirt. Randy had bought it, thinking for some reason it was the only color Jason could wear. Cotton had no idea why, but suddenly, Jason looked very dangerous.

"You okay?" Jason asked as Cotton snagged his hoodie and got situated.

"Yeah, sure," Cotton told him, and he couldn't have stopped the betraying shift of his feet if he'd had a giant there to hold him in place.

"Aw, baby," Jason said with a sigh, coming close to pull Cotton into his chest. "You don't need to lie to me."

Cotton laughed slightly. "Understood," he said. "I'm scared. And I'm worried for you. And I don't want it to end like this."

Jason nodded and kissed his forehead. "Look," he said softly. "I can't tell you how I'll do it, but... but if we get separated, my first priority is going to be to get you back to your real life. And after that… just look for signs, okay? Like secret-agent stuff. I'll try to let you know I'm okay."

A coldness that Cotton hadn't wanted to acknowledge had been seeping into his chest eased up, warmed. "I'll watch for it," he said, smiling a little, "and hope."

"Colonel," Trina called from the guest room, which held their escape window. "We're running out of time."

"C'mon," Jason said, grabbing his hand. "We've got to exfil, and we've got to do it now."

Cotton had noted before that the smaller guest room had a decent-sized window, although it didn't have the nice attached bathroom that made up the master suite. Trina was looking at the monitor, making sure their way ahead was clear, and talking on the phone with Jackson as Jason lifted the sash and scrambled out over the ledge, dropping heavily into the loam close to the house. As Cotton did the same, he saw that Jason had drawn his gun and was holding it facing the ground, eyes shifting left to right, sweeping the ground for enemies.

The road to the cabin angled down into the lake's valley, and Cotton realized for the first time how steep the hillside was behind them. They were going to have to run overland without a trail, but more than that, they wouldn't be running a level loop. They would be running *up*, and Cotton wanted to beg Jason not to do this. It was too hard, too hard and too far, and Jason was barely recovered.

But they had no choice. Even Cotton knew that.

In another moment, Trina had discarded the monitor and hopped out the window as well, her weapon drawn, ready to bolt. She grunted quietly, then pointed to herself, pointed forward, and moved into the point position while Jason trailed up behind.

"We're heading for Jackson's car up on the road about a mile and a half," she whispered, and Cotton and Jason both nodded. Then they heard a twig snap in the direction of the cabin itself.

"Run."

Cotton was pretty sure that years later he'd wake up drenched in sweat, dreaming of running uphill through rough forest terrain, catching his toes on old roots, fallen limbs, and rocks, trying to keep his feet.

After the first couple of missteps, he locked his eyes on Trina, watching where she placed her feet, and for a few breathless moments, his life became following her, step for step, as fast and as hard as she was running, staying ten steps behind her, letting her sure footing and training lead them to safety.

And then a soft gasp far behind them caught his attention, and he turned his head for a moment.

"Jason!" he panted.

Jason was still running determinedly, but he was lagging far behind Cotton and Trina. "Keep going," he breathed, waving his hand, and Cotton turned uncertainly, trying to trace Trina's sure steps through the mountain. In the few heartbeats it had taken for Cotton to check on Jason, she'd gotten a good fifty feet ahead, and he gritted his teeth and took a few strides in her direction before he saw her stumble and fall.

He was racing to help her when the small pop of a handgun hit his ears, and he realized a giant red bloom was flowing across her back as she fell face first into the dirt and leaves of the forest floor.

"I'd advise both of you to stop moving," came a precise female voice, "or I shall kill the unarmed boy first."

Cotton's first instinct was to jerk his head around to check on Jason, but another report jerked him to a stop. He swiveled his head wildly to see where she'd shot, only to determine her handgun—he had no idea what type—was aimed in the air.

"Nein! Do not check on him. Look only at me!"

Cotton swung his head slowly, searching the forestscape, until he saw the woman, possibly twenty yards away, almost directly up the hill, holding something black and lethal in classic shooting stance.

While he'd been lost a lot while Jason and the others had been discussing strategy, he definitely recognized this person. Karina Schroeder had black hair pulled tightly back, as well as severe features and a square jaw.

"Good," she said, voice shaking. "You can follow orders."

"He's a civilian." Jason's voice rang hard and cold from behind him. "This is between you and me. You need to let him go."

"This is *not* between you and me!" she declared passionately. "It was *never* between you and me! It was between my husband and the guy with the guns. Why you had to get in the way of that payment of children, I will *never* understand. Now put your weapon down, or I will shoot him. I've got the clean shot here. I know you don't!"

SIGNS

OH GOD. Of all the stupid things. While part of Jason knew they would have been trapped in the cabin, as he sighted down his shaking hands to where Karina stood, he was still blaming himself for being trapped *here*.

Dammit, he couldn't get a clean shot! Cotton was standing directly in front of him, Karina slightly to Cotton's right. He needed Cotton to shift— God, just a little. A step or two.

C'mon, Cotton, please read my mind. Please please please please….

Jason's heart was beating so loud he almost couldn't hear his own voice. "Cotton," he said through a dry throat, "it's all going to be okay."

"Of course it is," Cotton said, sounding as serene and as trusting as Jason had ever heard him. "You'd never lie to me."

Cotton hit the word *lie*, inflected it, and that quickly, Jason knew exactly what he was planning. Jason didn't even have time to scream, "Baby, duck!" before his angel's feet made their telltale shuffle to the left.

And Jason had a clean shot.

He barely registered the kickback, the report, before Karina Schroeder dropped into the dusty leaf mold at her feet, and another bullet *thunk*ed into the tree to his right. He swung smoothly, sighting the target, also in black, and pulled the trigger of the Glock semiauto twice in quick succession.

The target staggered back and Jason swung to his left, finger poised on the trigger once again, only to see that the target was being thrust toward him, chest first, hands tied behind the back, by a skinny asshole in cargo shorts and tennis shoes who was holding a tire iron in his left hand while he held the secured prisoner with the right.

"Whoa! Whoa! Whoa!" Jackson Rivers cried out. "Hold on there, chief, I'm a good guy!"

Jason swallowed, his adrenaline ebbing enough for him to take stock. "Is that all?" he said. "Are we clear?"

Before Jackson could answer, Cotton said, "Jason, Trina's down. I need to go check on her. Help me check!"

"Stay put," Trina moaned, and the rush of relief he felt almost sent him staggering to the ground.

Jason looked hard at Rivers. "Are we clear?"

"As far as we know," Jackson said. "You three made a lot of noise crashing through the brush. I watched this guy talk to his buddies and turn from his assault to the front of the house."

"Jason!" Cotton called, anguish in his voice.

"You're clear," Jason said, holstering his gun and leaning forward to rest his hands on his knees. "Go check on her, angel. I'm gonna stay here for a moment, and Rivers here is going to call Burton to come take care of the bad guys."

He took stock of the guy to his right, whom he'd hit center mass, and at Karina Schroeder, still and dead from a shot right between the eyes. "And get rid of the deceased too," he muttered.

Jackson grunted. "I can do that," he said. "But how about you deal with this guy and talk to Burton instead, and I'll get Henry to come help me move the bodies closer to the house." He grimaced. "God, what a shitty job."

Jason had to laugh. "Bailing my ass out of the fire or what you do for Cramer?"

"I meant yours," Jackson said sincerely. "I couldn't do what you did, but I sure am glad you did it."

Jason nodded wearily and pulled his cell phone from his pocket. As he did so, the guy in Jackson's grip struggled hard enough that Jackson kicked him from behind with enough force to send him to his knees.

"Before you start moving bodies," Jason said, the adrenaline leaving him in a rush, "do you think you could tie that guy to a chair? We need to have a few words."

"Your operation," Rivers told him, which considering how much of it was random and how much was a clusterfuck, was not exactly a sign of respect.

EXFIL

AN HOUR later, Cotton was tending to Trina, who had a through-and-through bullet wound in her shoulder, and Jason was wondering how to tell him it was time for him to go.

He'd been so competent: bathing the wound in antiseptic, using every trick he'd learned watching Lance tend Jason, making sure she had some painkillers first. Cotton had carried her into the cabin by himself, proving all those muscles really *weren't* for show, and then quietly set about dressing the arm and making his friend feel better, speaking only to give terse orders to Rivers, which Jason and Henry heard from the other room.

They were interrogating the two surviving suspects, both of them sullen and angry and tied to chairs in the kitchen with actual nylon cord from Henry's car and not with zip-ties, which Jason didn't like because they could be broken.

The suspects—both men in their thirties with dark hair and eyes and features as severe as Karina Schroeder's had been—were giving them information, but doing it bitterly.

If Jason had to hear "Why should I tell you, you killed my boss!" one more time, he was going to pull out his Glock and clock them each behind the ear so he didn't have to think about them for a while.

Finally, Henry Worrall gave him a little wave. "Hey, can I try?" he asked.

"Knock yourself out," Jason muttered. He pulled out his weapon, still appalled that Rivers and Henry had launched themselves into this operation without small arms of their own, and handed it to Henry, who took it with the grace and assurance that told him soldiers didn't forget.

"Better me knocking myself out than you knocking them on the heads," Henry said frankly. "I mean, you seem like a decent guy and all, but you're gonna kill them if you have to keep doing this." He kept his voice raised so both the captives heard him, and Jason grunted affirmative.

It wasn't true—at least he *hoped* it wasn't true—but they didn't know that, and it made sense to give them time with a guy dressed as a civilian who might not scream in their faces like Jason had been about to do.

He was exhausted.

If nothing else told him how much he'd needed time to recuperate, being ready to curl up in a little ball to fall asleep after the last two hours did. He resisted the temptation to look out into the sparkling waters of the little lake outside their cabin and beg his team for another month to stay there with Cotton, alone, making love and growing stronger, until Jason felt like he could do this again, could make hard decisions, could pull the trigger in more ways than one.

But he had a mess on his hands, and the one thing he'd promised his sister after that long-ago accident was that he'd take his responsibilities in the military seriously. He'd never let her down.

He needed to help clean up this mess.

"How's the patient?" he asked Rivers, who was hanging out in the hallway, waiting to see if Cotton needed any help while apparently making three hundred phone calls to fix Jason's life.

"She's stable," Jackson told him. "I talked to Burton, and he's got medics coming up from Sacramento who can transport her back to the base. Apparently you people and your secret-agent bullshit think that's a good idea."

Jason nodded. "Mostly I don't want her someplace I can't watch to keep her safe," he said, meaning it. "I'm a control freak that way."

"I've noticed," Jackson said dryly. "That doesn't mean she doesn't need some blood and some antibiotics and industrial-strength painkillers, although your boy managed an IV bag for fluids with some mild ones, which I find a little frightening. Apparently Lance has schooled him in everything but how illegal it is for him to give that kind of help without a license."

Jason sucked air through his teeth. "Well, he will probably need to be broken of some habits before he goes into medical care as a vocation," he said. "But if he can make her more comfortable before the medic chopper arrives, I'm grateful."

"How's your scumbags?" Rivers asked.

"Talking, but they're being assholes about it," Jason replied. "For instance, I know that they were going to kill me to get guns from Deavers, but I don't know when or where they're supposed to meet up. Your boy is trying to help me out there, so that's nice." Jason gave a glance over his shoulder and saw Henry involved in earnest conversation. Maybe he could do it, Jason thought. Well, good. Jason was not on his game today, and he could admit that.

"Well, lucky you," Rivers said, "Karina's husband caved when Ellery told him she was dead. Apparently she was the driving force behind their little crime spree, so he's ready to go cry in prison now. I've got a time and a place tonight. Deavers is apparently going to be in Tahoe because you're a lucky bastard. Now that Dietrich has a guard, Goldfarb would like to get Greta released so they can come here and debrief. I told Ellery to go for it. They should arrive a little before Burton does, so you're doing okay."

Jason nodded. "I am," he said, "thanks to you."

Rivers shrugged. "De nada."

De nada. It meant "It was nothing." But it was everything, and Jason knew that more than most people. And still, he was going to ask for more.

"If it was nothing," he said bitterly, "you wouldn't mind doing me one more little tiny favor, would you?"

Jackson met his eyes with compassion, but his words were harsh. "You're going to make me break that boy's heart, aren't you?"

"No," Jason said, watching Cotton, confident, kind, talking to Trina reassuringly and telling her she was going to be okay. God, he was gorgeous. Not just the curly dark hair and the enormous eyes with the cheekbones and the dimples and chin. His smile, his calm, his compassion, his humor—all of it was beautiful, and Jason swallowed hard, thinking he'd had that beautiful creature, that angel, in his bed, in his *life*, for a blessed, blessed time.

"No?" Jackson asked, sounding hopeful.

"I'll break his heart," Jason said, dashing those hopes, he knew. "But I'd really appreciate it if you could take him home."

"No," Cotton said after Jackson had told him Jason needed to talk to him.

Jason ignored who might be watching and cupped his cheek. "It's time, Cotton."

"But Trina—"

"We've got medics on the way, and the rest of the team. It's time for my crew to leave this place and to clean it up and to make it look like we were never here. Too many questions otherwise. Our final op is tonight, and we'll be running it from a hotel room in Tahoe. It's time for you to drive away and resume your regularly scheduled life."

Cotton shook his head, his shiny eyes overflowing in a way Jason hadn't seen since those very first days when he'd been almost too sick to remember.

"I want to stay with you," he whispered.

And Jason's own eyes burned. He needed to be honest, he thought, with a lump in his throat. "No, you don't," he rasped. "Because it's going to hit you eventually, what you watched me do today, and I don't want to be here when you look at me like I'm a killer. I'd rather have you leave now, when you still remember me as your lover and you think I'm an okay guy."

Cotton shook his head, rejecting the words, and captured Jason's hand where it rested on his cheek. "That's a shitty excuse," he said, voice thick. "Because I know exactly what you did today. You saved our lives. And that's the man I love."

"And you jumped into the breach and took care of my soldier," Jason whispered. "And that's the man *I* love. And you need a chance to fulfill all that promise, do you understand me?"

"No—"

"Please?" Jason said, eyes spilling over. "Please don't make this hard? As soon as the medics get here, you and Rivers and Henry need to go. Grab your stuff now, baby. You don't have long."

"God*dammit!*" Cotton managed, before Jason captured his mouth, their hot tears, their moments together, their love.

This kiss was bitter and salty, needy and sad, and Jason finally pulled away with a sound he wasn't proud of.

"Watch for signs, okay? I'll let you know when I land."

Cotton nodded and met his eyes. "And I'll be waiting when you're ready for me to land with you."

Jason should have told him no, to forget that dream, to let this moment be it, but Cotton stepped away from him, spinning on his heel, obviously determined not to hear it.

And Jason knew the words would have frozen in his throat.

Ten Hours Later

WATCHING DEAVERS cry when Jason strode into the back room of the casino with Burton and two MPs on his six was satisfying, he had to admit.

It wasn't just that the lanky, dark-haired serviceman *cried*, it was that he turned pale first, and then he put on a ghastly smile and said, "Imagine, you taking your vacation at the same time I am!"

"Oh Jesus," Burton growled. "Can I kill him?"

"Well, you *can*," Jason told him dryly, "but the real question is *may* you kill him, and no, you may not."

Deavers wiped his nose on his shoulder, leaving a big glossy slug of phlegmatic contrition.

"Please?" Burton said dryly.

"I didn't mean for you to get hurt," Deavers said, looking hopefully back and forth between them, and Jason wasn't sure what happened next.

One minute, he was standing next to Burton, watching in an almost detached fashion as the serviceman who'd betrayed him was cuffed and frisked and effectively neutralized by two men who might have been doing the same to *Jason* if Ellery Cramer hadn't gotten Dietrich Schroeder's confession on tape and into the record books… and the next minute Burton was hauling Jason off the man, but not before Jason heard the *thunk* of cartilage as he broke Deavers's nose.

Deavers howled, and then Jason lost his cool.

"Kids, you asshole! Those people were paying for your guns with *kids*! And then the kids got away and they were paying for them with *me*! And then they couldn't find *me*, and they were killing their way up through Northern California and Nevada out of sheer rage! *What was so fucking important that people needed to die?*"

And Deavers started to sob in earnest, and Jason heard something about a child with an illness and expensive treatment that the military's TRICARE wouldn't cover, and he had to turn around and walk away.

The last thing he heard was "*You would have done it too!*" and Jason fought the urge to throw up.

"No, you wouldn't have," Burton said.

"But does that make me better or worse?" Jason asked painfully.

"Sir, you need sleep. Are you sure you don't want to spend some more time at the cabin? Cotton could catch a ride back up just as easy as he caught one down the hill."

Jason's eyes burned, and he shook his head. "There are probably at least sixty-eleven things on my desk right now that absolutely can't be put off," he said. "Tell me I'm wrong."

"I'm better than that," Burton retorted, stung. "There's only eleventy-twelve."

Jason laughed a little as they made their way to the SUV that would take them to the military plane that had been sent to apprehend Deavers after Jason had made his call to Talbot.

"No," he said, the words weighing about twelve-thousand pounds. "I'll go, be a good boy, and get back to work." *It's not like you have anything better to do.*

"No offense, sir, but I don't think there's a medal for sexual martyrdom."

Jason did a spit-take, and then covered his mouth with his hand. "I beg your pardon?" he said, staring at his subordinate—and his friend.

"Why can't you bring him out to the desert?" Burton persisted. "Remember when you told me to go fetch Ernie? Best thing I ever did. Added years to my ability to do this job. What, you're not good enough to get laid like someone in the lower ranks?"

"It's not about me," Jason said doggedly. "It's about *him*. He's barely twenty-two. Did that escape everyone's notice?"

Burton snorted. "Nope. We just thought that twenty-two years was a long enough time to feel alone in the world, and maybe you could sort of fix that for him."

"By practicing job and lover polygamy?" Jason snapped. "What kind of man would that make me?"

"A human one! But never mind. I'll start looking for the sexual martyrdom medal in the mail for you, sir, because we all know that's the next best thing!"

Jason groaned and scrubbed his face with his hands. "Twenty-two," he muttered.

"Yeah," Burton replied. "But that doesn't mean shit if you love him."

Jason growled into his hands, and Burton patted him on the back. "Think about it, sir. But, you know, maybe after a little bit of sleep."

TWO WEEKS later, Jason sat up in his tiny officer's bunk room, Cotton's name clawing to escape his throat. With a deep breath, he wrapped his arms around his knees and shook, trying to remember what had scared him so badly.

Had Cotton been in danger? Was that what the dream was about? Because if Cotton was in danger, maybe Jason should do what he promised and reach out? He remembered reaching—reaching for that slender, capable hand, needing to feel it clasped around his own, needing to hold on to it, pull himself up, so he could breathe past the murky water that threatened to suffocate him, so he could remember what the sun looked like again.

"Shit."

Cotton hadn't been in danger. *He* had.

That had been the dream. That had been what had awakened him, fighting with his covers and swimming in sweat.

Just his own subconscious, trying to save his soul.

The next morning he left Burton in charge.

"Where are you going, sir?" Burton had asked, taking the tablet with all of the active targets and their retrieval teams. Burton hadn't launched any new campaigns while Jason had been laid up, which had been a canny move on his part because Jason was really the only one authorized to decide which targets could be brought in and which ones needed to be neutralized, and Jason didn't want his friend with those decisions on his head. Unfortunately that meant they had a record number of people in the field at the moment. It was really not a great time to leave.

But Jason was tired of fighting.

"To see my sister, in San Diego," he said.

"Your sister?"

"I'm not sure I ever told you about her," Jason said with a slight smile. "She teaches nursing at a junior college on the outskirts of the city. She's also," he added, face flaming, "Dean of Student Admissions."

Burton's smile was wolfish. "Godspeed, Colonel."

"Thank you, Captain," Jason responded. He gave a slight smile. "I don't know if he'll even come," he added.

"And you won't until you try. Now hurry, before any of this shit explodes and leaves me with a big mess. Go!"

San Diego Medical Training College was the ungainly lettering across the front of the administration building, but other than that, the graceful stucco buildings of the campus projected a stolid sense of purpose against a San Diego blue sky. The October weather was scorching and humid, and Jason was grateful he'd changed into civvies before he'd left.

More specifically, he'd changed into the cargo shorts and camo T-shirt Cotton had packed for him before they'd even known each other. Turned out, Cotton had figured out exactly who he was before he was even conscious.

Jason had been there to visit Jessica before, but he checked in with the admin building to see where she'd be. He arrived as her lecture was ending and had a moment to appreciate her delivery from the top of the stairs.

Before the accident, she'd never been able to sit still, and not much had changed as she lectured from her specially designed wheelchair. She worked out copiously to be able to maneuver, and she darted back and forth in front of the podium, a small microphone clipped to her collar, as she called on students to answer questions and gestured to the diagram on the board.

She was so animated. He felt the usual glow of pride in her watching her work.

"Mm… no," she told a student. "No, we can't really say the limbic system operates independently of anything else in the body. I mean, it's the *brain*, right? And the brain runs the show! You overrun your limbic system with pain, and the whole works shorts out and shuts down. And if you think I'm kidding, try taking this class with a hangover!"

There was general laughter and she went on, finishing the anatomy lecture on a high note before dismissing the class. Jason stepped aside as the students filed out, thinking for a moment that they all—even those in their thirties—looked impossibly young.

Then his eyes fell on a couple of students Cotton's age specifically, and he almost turned around and called the whole thing off, but by then, Jessica had already seen him.

"Jay Jay?" she cried happily. "Oh my God, is that you!"

He gave a sheepish smile and clambered down the steps, feeling the weight he'd yet to put back on acutely.

"Heya, Jess," he said, taking her hand and bending down to kiss her cheek. "Long time no see."

Jessica frowned up at him, her rich brown hair only streaked a little with gray and pulled back in a messy bun to stay out of eyes the same dark brown as his own.

"For a month it was no hear," she reminded him, and he grimaced. As soon as he'd been back at the base, he'd answered his family's increasingly frantic texts. They'd even called Brigadier General Talbot, but Talbot—still under the assumption that Jason had gone rogue for no good reason—had refused to answer, saying only that his whereabouts were a matter of proprietary information. Apparently Jessica had given the man a good earful about how Jason always texted before he went under so nobody worried, but Talbot hadn't budged.

Well, to be fair, he really *hadn't* known where Jason was.

"Sorry about that," he said again. "That was… unexpected."

"Unexpected, my ass," she snapped. "Look at you! What happened?"

He laughed shortly. "It's a long, long story that you really don't want to hear. I… uhm, can we talk in your office? I have a favor to ask."

"A favor," she said blankly.

"Yeah. You know. Like, you do something for me for no other good goddamned reason than you love me and I need help."

She nodded. "I'm familiar with the concept, Jay Jay. I've just never heard it coming from *you*."

He sighed. "Well, it's not really for me," he apologized. "It's sort of for a friend."

She grunted and stowed her laptop and cables in the quilted, flowered briefcase on the table, then tucked the case in a saddlebag at her side. "Figures," she said. "Follow me and we'll catch up. I've got an hour before my next lecture. I can't *wait* to hear this."

A few minutes later, Jason sat in the horribly uncomfortable chrome and lime-colored vinyl chair in her office, fidgeting as she digested his proposal.

"A full ride?" she asked again.

"I can, uhm, fund it," he said, his face burning. "I have money saved. It can go to tuition—"

She waved her hand to cut him off. "I've got access to scholarship funds," she said, her two dark eyebrows coming down in a stern V over her nose. "I don't want your *money*, Jay Jay, I want an explanation. I know this is a small college, but we've got some prestige. You just want me to admit this random kid and give him a full ride because...."

"Because he needs a break," Jason said, swallowing. "Because he'd be good at it." He tried his best little-boy smile to see if it held the weight it had when they'd been teenagers.

Her frown deepened. "We're not the only nursing school that gives out scholarships," she said.

"He... he'll be giving up the only security he's known for the last four years," Jason said, squirming. "I... he'll recognize your name. It might help."

"Jason, is he even qualified?"

"He's got a GED," he said honestly. "But I think he was an honors kid before he got kicked out of the house. He, uh, reads a lot for pleasure. He's smart, Jess. He's smart and he thinks on his feet and he's compassionate and organized—" He saw her start to shake her head "no" and a sudden desperation took over him. "—and he kept me alive for two weeks when I was just some stranger dumped in his bed."

She gaped at him. "Jason!"

With a growl of frustration, he ripped his shirt off and showed her the scars with their rough stitch pattern on his shoulder and side. "He and his friends field-operated on me with not much more than a medical kit and their courage when I was about to die of infection," he said, his voice aching with the need for her to understand. He pulled his shirt on, feeling twelve again, and added, "For a month he monitored my vitals, administered my medication, and even learned how to install an IV. And his life could have been shit—do you understand? He was kicked out at seventeen and given a chance to press charges against his twenty-year-old boyfriend or live on the streets. And he chose living out on the streets because his boyfriend had done nothing wrong. He's got integrity like you can't believe. And he could have been a mess, or a train wreck, but he's so goddamned sweet. He's got friends and protectors, and he's so grateful for them, but he needs more. He…."

"Does he love you back?" she asked, voice soft.

He slumped defeatedly in the damned chrome chair. "He says so." Jason shrugged. "It doesn't matter if he does or not. I want him to have better. Please?"

She sighed. "When he fills out the application, under 'Employment' what's it going to say?"

Oh God. "John Carey Industries," he told her, hoping she wouldn't—

"Seriously?" she asked, her voice squeaking.

"You know what that is?" he retorted, and his own voice had a few cracks in it too.

"I lost the use of my legs, not my sex drive!" she said defensively. Then she took a breath, and another, and another. "Fuck. Well, it's not like we don't have some students here funding their education on webcams. And I understand the better film companies test copiously."

Jason nodded. "They do. And John Carey sort of took the kid in. He could have exploited him, but he gave him a place to stay and food. Cotton is the one who insisted on modeling to pay his way."

She tilted her head back and closed her eyes. "This is *so* seedy," she muttered before pushing herself up and giving a small smile. "But it's also the first time you've ever really been in love."

"I'm so old," he admitted, scrubbing his face with his hands.

"You want me to send him this offer out of the blue?"

"If your name is on it, he'll know," Jason said. "I told him to look for signs." He bit his lip, hating the uncertainty, hating to wait. "You'll, uhm, tell me if he says yes?"

"Why?" Jessica asked. "What will you do?"

"I've got some ideas," he said with dignity. He didn't want to put a voice to it, to the hope, to the culmination of all the "what-ifs" he'd put in motion by asking his sister for such a monumental favor.

"Jason," she said, her voice softening.

"Yeah?"

"You deserve everything. You're a good man, and you work a hard job. Even if you can't give me details, I know that. You deserve a house, a family, a picket fence, a dog. At the very least, you deserve someone who loves you enough to save your life."

"A dog?" he asked wistfully. "I don't know if I'd be home enough for a dog."

"Maybe a cat," she conceded.

He smiled, thinking of Burton's boyfriend. "Turns out I know someone with lots and lots of cats."

"Well, it's a place to start."

He left shortly after that, buoyed by his sister's promise that she'd tell him as soon as she heard back from her offer. His step felt a little lighter as he ventured out into the sodden sunlight, and while he tried to keep the hum of making plans out of his mind, he did allow himself the tentative feeling of hope.

CHOOSING BLUE SKIES

COTTON STARED at the thick information packet in his hand, looking for the angle.

"What's doin'?" Henry asked, barging into the flophouse like he lived there, with Randy, Vinnie, and Curtis on his heels. Billy had moved out while he'd been gone, apparently finding his own bliss with a friend of Jackson's, but Chale had taken his place, because that's how things went there. Chale's chirpy optimism felt a lot different than Billy's brooding sarcasm, but then, he'd chosen "Chale" as his porn name, and that seemed to indicate a guy with rainbows shooting out his ass. So far, he'd been a decent roommate— not oversexed, and he didn't wear his damage on his sleeve.

And Cotton understood his porn was fan*tastic*.

Cotton looked up from studying the brochures and the seemingly improbable letter that came with them and frowned. "Does this look legit to you?" he asked, shoving the whole mess at Henry.

Henry read the letter, his eyebrows and eyeballs doing an intricate little dance between disbelief and excitement.

"Oh my God," he said. He stared at Cotton. "A full ride? Did you even apply to this place?"

"No," Cotton said, although he *had* applied to a few junior colleges in the area, for reasons. For missing Jason Constance beyond-all-reason reasons, which were, as far as he was concerned, perfectly legit. "I never even heard of the place until now."

"Well, it *is* nursing school," Henry said. "A three-year vocational program, with the option for a BA if you want to take that track. And this Jessica Constance person sure seems to want to give you a scholarship, with student housing inclu—"

"Wait, what?" Cotton asked. He hadn't gotten to the signature at the end; he'd been too stuck on the too-good-to-be-true in the middle.

Henry paused, thought for a moment, went back to reread the person on the header, and then flipped the page over to read the signature. "This Jessica *Constance* person," he said, his voice dripping with meaning. "Does that name mean anything to you, Cotton Carey?"

Cotton bit his lip, trying to keep the smile from taking over his entire body. Signs. Jason had promised him signs. A letter from his sister offering him an education in nursing—something Jason thought he could do and love doing it—seemed like more of a giant neon beacon, but it was *definitely* a sign.

"Yes," Cotton said, failing his battle against the smile. "Yes, it does."

SCHOOL DIDN'T start until January, which gave Cotton a few months to say goodbye, and he used them to get his shit together. He spent time taking placement tests on a laptop he used his savings for, as well as taking some online science refreshers from the local adult outreach programs. Nothing that would get him units, but enough to make him remember all the stuff he thought he'd forgotten in high school.

And he spent time being there for his friends—consoling *them* over breakups, being the workout buddy they needed, doing the dishes and cleaning house to help pay the rent nobody would let him pitch in for. He felt useful and needed and loved, and it was funny how this should have made it harder to leave, but it didn't. It made him realize he could leave and the love would still be there. The *people* would still be there. He'd still have Henry's cell number, and John's, and Lance's, and even Jackson Rivers's. Leaving here was not like getting kicked out of the house. He wasn't being cut off from his support system, he was being supported to go out on his own.

He spent Christmas at the flophouse, but John had a big party at a local park clubhouse a couple of days beforehand for all his boys, and that was fun too. The clubhouse itself wasn't fancy—linoleum floors and folding chairs—but John and Dex, his second-in-command, had worked hard to decorate it nicely, with gold foil and glitter and red velvet and a big tree with presents underneath for all the models and the people who worked with them. And even the kids of some of the former models and staff. It wasn't a "porn" party; it was a work party, and everyone dressed in their best slacks and chinos and put on their best sweaters to go eat cold shrimp on the boss's dime and be with their friends.

Cotton knew a lot of places had parties like this, but he wondered if any of them were as warm or as kind. Sure, there were going to be guys hooking up at the end of the night, but they did that shit all the time. While they were there, they got to be young professionals who took each other seriously and talked about school and their other jobs and their families and boyfriends—and some girlfriends—and generally celebrated without excess.

There couldn't be any excess. All of John's models were over eighteen, but about a quarter of them weren't over twenty-one, so it was pretty much soda only. Since John and Galen were in recovery, that was appropriate too.

Cotton got a lot of pats on the back and "We'll miss you, man"s, which sort of made the moment bittersweet, but also, mostly sweet. He'd been cared for here. His family at the flophouse, his family with this company, it hadn't been bullshit. He'd been loved. He'd left an imprint other than his porn videos. People would remember his kindness and his smile.

It was funny how he hadn't realized what had made him stay there until he was ready to leave.

At the end of the party, John called the whole staff to the front of the clubhouse to make a speech, which he hadn't done since Cotton had started working for him. He stood, Dex on his right, Galen on his left, wrapped in a sweater on the frosty lawn in front of the parking lot and shivering.

"So," he said, looking embarrassed and uncomfortable as he bounced on his toes, "our friend Cotton here is going off to college, and that happens a lot with my guys, and I'm always glad to see it. I mean, I worked damned hard to build up a porn company, but Dex and me, we also worked to build up an 'after-porn' company. We wanted our guys to have options when they were done making pretty movies for us to enjoy, and you all know that. Some of you even work there."

He winked and there was generalized laughter before he went on. He'd been working to buy a retail franchise so he could hire from the model pool for life after porn—apparently he had a thing for pet stores. "And while I think you're all meant for great things—and you all deserve the best happy ever afters in the world—there are some of you...." His voice dropped, and he searched Cotton's eyes out, his own eyes growing bright in the soda lamp that watched over the lawn. "Some of you," he repeated, his voice growing husky, "that I worried about more than others. And one of those boys is getting ready to fly, and at first I was thinking that I was the only one who wanted to do something big for him as he left. But the more you all talked to me, the more we realized that all of us were so damned proud of him that we wanted to do something big."

John paused and Cotton looked around and realized that his roommates were all gathered around him, including Billy and his new cop boyfriend. They huddled close enough to jostle, to put their hands on his shoulder, or, in Chale's and Vinnie's case, to make "Eeeeeeeee...." sounds of excitement like little kids.

And everybody—*everybody*—was looking at him.

And John kept talking. "As we were looking for something big to do, we realized our boy was going far away with no means of transportation to get him back home if he needed to return. So we pitched in and got him a present so he could go out and make the world a better place." He reached into his pocket and pulled out a key fob, which he clicked.

A small Nissan Sentra, not brand-new but not on death's door either, lit up in front of the curb near where they were standing.

"Cotton," John said, holding out the fob, "come get your present, kid. And promise you'll come visit when you can."

Cotton couldn't remember a whole lot of that night, but he knew he was crying for a good long time after that.

A week later, his roommates—his brothers—helped him pack the car with his bedding, his laptop, and his clothes, and then they all hugged him hard before sending him on his way.

SCHOOL WASN'T easy, but then, he hadn't expected it to be. While his dorm roommate—a fresh-from-high-school kid named Brad who was really excited by the ease with which his classmates could buy beer—spent a lot of his time getting drunk and getting laid, Cotton spent his time remembering how to be a student. He read the textbooks, did the homework, and went for the extra credit. He *did* remember—in fact he remembered how to be a *good* student, but now he had a goal beyond pleasing his parents.

He was out to please himself.

After two weeks, he left his last class of the day feeling exhilarated and exhausted... and strangely let down. It wasn't that he'd thought the whole thing was a ruse for him to see Jason. He was very cognizant that this was a chance for him to do well, to earn a good life for himself, to keep growing.

But... well, he thought he'd at least see Jason a *little*.

And beyond that, while he did have some homework, he also was coming to realize that he had room to breathe. He didn't have to spend every waking hour swimming for his life. His newly awakened academic skills were reminding him that he could do this, and he could do it without quite so much sweat.

He sort of wished he had someone to spend the weekend with.

He wasn't willing to go dating again, but he would really like a friend.

And that's exactly what he was thinking when he walked down the steps of the classroom building, heading across the street for the on-campus student housing, and saw the dark-haired guy in the chinos and the plaid shirt, leaning against the red sports car.

Cotton came to a complete halt, all his breath stopping in his body as Jason raised his head and smiled.

"Hey."

"Hey," Cotton said, remembering—barely—to look both ways before crossing the street. He walked right up into Jason's space, ignoring propriety, ignoring his fellow students streaming to their cars and dorms. Jason was *there*, and he looked good—fit and tanned and fully recovered, his warm smile showing the crinkles in the corners of his eyes.

"You got homework this weekend?" Jason asked, like it was the most logical thing in the world.

"Some," Cotton admitted.

"Could you do it somewhere else?" he asked, biting his lip.

"Hell yeah. Let's go."

"Do you want to pack a go-bag?" Jason laughed, and Cotton shook his head.

"I'll fit into your clothes," he said confidently. "I've got my laptop, I've got my books. I'm not giving you a chance to get away."

Jason laughed some more, tilting his head back and letting the sound wash over them both. "Pack a go-bag," he said softly. "We can't have sex the whole time. We're having dinner with friends."

Cotton squeezed his eyes shut, giddy, floating, ecstatic. "Where are we going?" he asked.

Jason brushed his lips quietly against Cotton's, and Cotton sighed, wanting to fall into the kiss but keenly aware that once he did they'd be having sex in the back of the sports car right there, where it was parked, and that wasn't the impression he was trying to make.

"Pack for two days," Jason whispered. "Including swim trunks. I'll have you back Sunday night."

"Okay." He tasted again, and Jason slid his tongue in enough to make him moan before Jason pulled back.

"Go," Jason said. "I'll be here when you get back."

He was.

FOR A while, they just drove, the Maserati handling like a dream as they cleared the congestion near the suburbs and hit the open road. Cotton tilted his head back and let the wind blow through his hair, taking in the sun on his face and power of the car. And the man at his side.

After an hour Jason stopped at a hole-in-the-wall taqueria for them to eat, and they started talking. Jason told him what had happened with Deavers, and how Talbot had pretended like Jason had never left his post in the desert, and how Jessica was so pleased with Cotton's progress so far.

"Your sister's a great teacher," Cotton said, enjoying his carne asada salad very much. "She's making me remember why I liked school in the first place."

"Has she said anything to you?" Jason asked. "About me?"

Cotton shook his head. "Nope. If I hadn't realized who she was when the paperwork showed up, I wouldn't know we knew someone in common."

Jason winked. "She might be more human after you graduate. Three years?"

Cotton let out a breath. "Yeah. Seems like forever."

"You don't have to spend it all at the dorms," Jason said.

"What does that mean?" Cotton's heart began to thrum.

"Do you trust me?"

"Yes," Cotton said, unequivocally.

"Then wait a little. I'll show you."

The next hour and a half went by fast. Jason pulled the top up, and they hit the desert highway still talking, as though the months between them had never been. They had been driving down a long stretch of absolute nowhere when they passed a gas station on one side and a garage and what looked like a little house on the other. About a mile beyond that, Jason slowed and turned left on a road that meandered behind the small hills that lined the freeway, and Cotton looked around curiously.

"Is this a… a neighborhood?" he asked.

"Mm… sort of," Jason told him. "It was going to be, and they got about a third of the houses built before they ran out of money. But one house in every three lots, maybe, was fully hooked up and ready to sell."

"The houses are great," Cotton said appreciatively, remembering Burton saying something about this place back at the cabin. But he hadn't talked about the houses themselves. Big, with four bedrooms at least, he'd wager, along with vaulted ceilings and second stories and pools in the backyard, if the glittering water behind one of the fences was anything to judge by. "But who would want to live out here?"

Jason shrugged. "Well, in fact, it's only about forty-five minutes from my base," he said.

Cotton took a breath, the implications hitting him, the thrum of his heart becoming almost overwhelming. "Jason. Is one of these houses yours?"

Jason pulled up into a driveway of one of the more modest houses, a ranch-style one-story but with solar paneling on the roof. It had a pool—Cotton could see the telltale glimmer—and drought resistant landscaping in the front, as well as a couple of hardy shade trees.

"Yes," Jason said, swallowing, and it hit Cotton that this was a big deal for him.

"It's… it's amazing," Cotton breathed. "I—"

"It's ours," Jason said, in a rush, and Cotton stared at him. "I made keys for you. You can drive out here on the weekends even when I can't make it. You can live here, with me, during holidays and over the summer, and after you graduate. And as long as you want to and as long as you love me, it's ours."

"Ours?" Cotton said, feeling dizzy.

"Please?" Jason was looking at him now, his face pale but determined, and Cotton wanted him—wanted all of him. Wanted his terrible job and his kindness and the sanctuary he was offering and the life. "I can offer you a job when you're done with nursing school. Civilian medic, if you like. Or there's a tiny hospital nearby. I have some friends who work there. You'll meet them. Or you can commute and live in another apartment and come here when you have days off or—"

Cotton stopped him with a kiss, hard, insistent, no bullshit, and needy. Jason returned it, his mouth beyond needy, on to begging and desperate.

These were the kisses his body had craved during their long months apart. This was the pent-up desire he had banked with the hope—the barest hope—that someday it would be fed again and allowed to flame.

"I will always come back here," Cotton promised, not caring what he'd have to do to make that happen.

"I need you," Jason whispered. "I need you to come back here. I need you in my house and my bed and my life. Can you do that?"

"It's all I ever wanted," Cotton gasped, and then with a wrench he pulled himself away and threw the door open, barely remembering his go-bag from the back. "Come on, let me see my new home."

They made it just inside the big white pine door.

Cotton turned his head as Jason closed it and threw the bolt, and then he dropped his go-bag and they were on each other, kissing, panting, pawing at each other's clothes with such intensity that Cotton heard something rip. It was probably his shirt, but he didn't care.

They only made it to the bedroom because Jason kept steering him there; probably because that was where the lubricant was.

Jason entered him slowly, eyes focused on Cotton's face, hips thrusting in carefully. Once he was fully seated, he bent and they kissed, but Cotton's body was too amped to stay there long.

"Now," he whispered. "Now."

What followed next was explosive... and blissful. Their bodies heaved, slapping, and the sweat ran down Jason's torso, down his face, as he powered into Cotton, reasserting himself, making Cotton his.

Cotton could never be another man's, not after this.

When Cotton's crest came, he arched breathlessly, not even touching his cock, and as he shuddered, Jason gave a shout and climaxed inside him, both of them spending hotly as they shivered in reaction.

Jason pulled out reluctantly and hit the pillow next to Cotton, still breathing hard.

"That wasn't enough," he panted.

"No," Cotton agreed, closing his eyes and gulping air.

"I promised myself I'd let you do homework." He looked so earnest.

"Tomorrow," Cotton said, nodding. "Tomorrow. I'll do homework. You sleep in. Now we need more of what we just did."

Jason closed his eyes, smiling slightly. "You'll have to see the house eventually."

"Sure. Not now." Cotton wanted him all over again. Wanted to take him this time, wanted to drive him out of his mind. He wanted Jason loose and sloppy and incoherent, because only Cotton could make him that way.

"Not now?" Jason asked, raising surprised eyebrows at him.

Cotton lifted his head and took his mouth with purpose, his body waking up already, telling him it had been too long and they had more to spend.

"Later," he murmured. "We have time for the future later. But I have a home now, and it's with you. And that's what I want to do with my time."

"Me." Jason was laughing as he said it, but Cotton took his mouth again, and the laughter faded, replaced by gasps and another rising tide.

Later, now, it didn't matter, Cotton thought as he took his lover apart piece by piece. What mattered was they were *there*, in a place meant for them both. What mattered was they had a future there, and Cotton could make a home. Never again would he be lost or adrift. He had purpose now, and some of that was school and his vocation, but so much of that was this man and the life they would build together.

There would be surprises and friends—Cotton already knew there was a dinner in their future, and he looked forward to it. But right now, he had everything he'd ever wanted and the only man who could make that happen, and he was old enough now and wise enough now to take the moment in both hands and make it his, just like Jason had.

They were each other's now, and Cotton would always have a home in his heart, and Jason would always be there to fill it.

AUTHOR'S NOTE: INTRODUCING *CRULLERS*

THERE IS a shape to any story and any subgenre. Contemporary romance has a shape, romantic suspense has a shape—to change the shape of the story is to change the subgenre, and readers get cranky when that happens. As writers, we try to stay as consistent as possible to the expected shape. We can tell many, many different stories, but if they're in the expected shape, readers forgive us the variety.

That said, the Fish books and their spin-offs, the Flophouse books, and the pre/sequels *Racing for the Sun* and *Hiding the Moon*, have become vast and unwieldy. I can write the main stories in the expected shapes, but everybody has their favorite characters.

"That's great. But what was Sonny doing while Ace was gone?"

"Oh! I bet Ernie had something to say about that!"

"Jai's so stoic—he needs a sweetheart. Who's he seeing that the others don't know about?"

I get these questions—and more—all the time, and I'm curious about the answers too, so I write the stories in little pieces. Just for fun. Just for the long-term readers on my Patreon. And then, when the stories are attached to a book—or two, as in this case, or three, when the third Flophouse book is written—they become their own massive enterprise.

Not easy to put into book form; the shape is sprawling and not really newbie friendly. But people who love these characters, are invested in them, have read every book in the series—they really want to see those stories.

What follows is two-thirds of a group of stories I called *Crullers*, mostly because it started with Burton and Ernie from *Hiding the Moon*, and Cruller is Burton's nickname. The stories are "gap fillers." They're not necessary to *School of Fish* or *Constantly Cotton*, but they're fun little moments that got some play. They're assembled in chronological order, and many of them tie into this book, *Constantly Cotton*. If this is your first book in the Fishiverse or the Flophouse series, these are characters you've seen mentioned.

This is a glimpse of their private lives.

The other third of *Crullers* actually forms its own plot arc. I'm planning on putting most of that at the end of the next Fish book.

One chapter at the end of this addition is really the final chapter of *Under the Stars*, a novella posted mostly on my Patreon that closes out *Racing for the Sun* and *Hiding the Moon*, and written because people didn't want to see Jai without a mate. It will be a part of *Under the Stars* when I make that available, but it wasn't needed here.

So yes, that explanation was complicated and messy—but then, so are people. If you're a fan of *my* people, I hope this series of ficlets is enjoyable after you've read about Jason and Cotton.

That's really all I hoped for all along.

CRULLERS

A Hiding the Moon Story

PART 1

ERNIE SAT up so abruptly that Lee Burton was startled. Burton rolled out of bed, grabbed the gun from under the mattress, assumed a crouch, and aimed at their bedroom door before Ernie could tell him to calm the fuck down.

"What is it?" Burton demanded.

"Next week," Ernie said. "You have to leave in two days. The big boom will be next week."

Burton did a slow pan to where Ernie sat up in bed. "So I've got time."

Ernie nodded and then took a deep breath, his shoulders slumping. "Sorry, Cruller."

"Yeah, well, not your fault," Burton said, his heart twisting a little. There had to be a joke out there about a psychic and an assassin. *Did you hear about the psychic who hooked up with a hitman? The poor guy never saw it coming.* Truth was, Ernie was at the mercy of his visions—he didn't know when they were coming or how, or even what they would be about. Because he loved Burton, they often centered on him, and Burton was grateful for the times a call or text from Ernie had given him a heads-up—or even saved him from injury or worse.

But getting jerked out of his sleep in the dark of the night, heart pounding, sweat soaking his body from fear, was a hard price sometimes.

Lee put the gun back into its hole between the mattress and the box spring and crawled back into bed. "C'mere," he rumbled.

Ernie tucked up against his body, sighing.

"Bad one?" Lee feathered fingers through Ernie's damp hair, and Ernie nodded against his shoulder.

"Something's brewing," he mumbled. "Jackson, Ellery, Ace, Jai, George—it's gonna be big."

Oh, that was *not* good news. "Anything I can do to prep?" Burton asked.

Ernie shook his head, his voice breaking. "Nothing. There's never anything you can do. It's all chaos."

"Oh, baby." Burton held him tighter, wishing for the release of sex, but knowing that Ernie needed hard, steady touches right now. "Not chaos. Remember that. Just by warning me, you made us ready, okay?"

"Jason," Ernie said brokenly. "Cruller, he's gonna need us."

Burton frowned. "Jason?" Ernie had been trying to adopt Burton's CO, Jason Constance, since they'd moved into their house, which sat within walking distance from Ace and Sonny's gas station in a little forgotten suburb that only had five finished houses. Four of them sat vacant. Their isolation was Ernie's salvation—the emptiness of the desert helped keep Ernie from overdosing on too many people, too many psychic connections, but the result was that Ernie's strong clairvoyance focused on the people he cared about. Ace's small family in the middle of the desert was well watched over by the powers that be.

The isolation also served to make Constance comfortable enough to… to reach out. To have friends. He'd been Burton's handler in special ops since Burton had been recruited from the Marines. Burton trusted him, which didn't come easy, and Constance?

The more they'd worked their current mission—Operation Dead Fish, which was to track down and bring in serial killers who had been trained by a rogue military commander—the more Burton had watched Constance become isolated. Worn. Sad.

During a recent op, Constance had admitted to Burton that he was gay. And he hadn't had a lover in over ten years. The confession still made Burton's heart raw; no wonder he responded so kindly to Ernie's overt attempts to mother the full-grown badass. Constance didn't have anybody else. Even if he had family—and he did have parents and a sister—that man or woman you poured your fears out to in the dark of night was a whole different person.

Jason Constance may have rank on Burton, but as far as Burton could see, he had the support system Constance did not.

Even if his support system consisted of one flaky baker/psychic/gas station clerk, two criminals, a psychopath, and a college student who texted them from Los Angeles at least once a week to let them know she was keeping on the straight and narrow, it was still better than the vast echoing vault filled with the voices of the people you'd failed to protect and the demons that killed them. Burton had the feeling that's all Constance had.

So he was okay with Ernie pulling Constance in. He was hoping to pull him in a little further. Ace had made the winter holidays a thing in the past two, three years, and Burton thought his boss could use some warmth when the desert grew cool.

Unfortunately it was the end of fucking August and 120 was not uncommon in their desert. They had a kickass AC system: Burton had some money socked away, and since property values weren't great and they'd had to do most of the power hookups themselves, he'd been able to spare the expense to keep an army cool in their house. However, the heat made asking someone to drive an hour for dinner because you were worried about them sort of an imposition.

At least Constance, knowing that Ernie was very, very off-books and probably officially dead, had allowed Burton to set up an encrypted coms system in his home office. Three days a week he drove the hour to outside of Barstow, and sometimes he got sent on ops. But he got to spend a lot of time at home, doing his own searches for one of the hundred or so trained criminals who had been turned loose on the world.

Which was good, he admitted, pulling a shivering Ernie closer into his arms. He used to wonder how Ace could live with Sonny, because Sonny was so very needy. But Ernie, who seemed as self-sufficient as the many cats he fed and cared for, seemed to need him too. Ernie wouldn't lose his shit. Wouldn't freak out and yell at customers and tank the gas station business or the racing gigs that kept their little family solvent—not like Sonny might, if Ace was ever gone too long from his side.

But the thought of Ernie waking up alone in this house and yelling for Burton when Burton was off chasing a bad guy squeezed Burton's heart until it threatened to stop. So far, letting him sleep at Ace and Sonny's when Burton was out on an op had been working, but God. Being home, being a part of someone's life, had never seemed so very important to Lee Burton, until he'd heard Ernie Caulfield call his name in the dark.

"Cruller?" Ernie whispered, sounding hazy and dreamy, like he was about to go under.

"Yeah, baby?"

"Don't worry. Sonny knows how to use a gun."

Oh *fuck* no—like Burton was going to get any sleep *now*!

"SO," LEE asked super casually the next morning over a breakfast of granola and fruit. "What did you mean by 'Sonny knows how to use a gun?'"

Ernie shifted from one foot to the next. He always wondered how much Lee heard when he was shot through with psychic lightning. "You know what we haven't had in a while? Donuts. I could make cake donuts for everyone at the station. Jai's going to see George this weekend. I'll make some for everyone and Jai can take some to George."

He turned his back to Burton then, which was hard, because now that they were keeping house together, Burton liked to eat breakfast in his white boxers and nothing else, and the sight of that amazingly muscled, smooth-skinned body was... well, it was a gay boy's dream to have a lover who looked like Lee Burton, that was for sure.

But Lee was going to ask about the dream and Ernie... well, Ernie didn't know enough to pony up, not yet.

In a clatter, he started pulling out his deep fryer, the oil, which he bought by the gallon, and the big industrial mixer that Burton had mounted to the end of the counter for him. He was going to make a *fuckton* of donuts.

"You can bring some of them to Jason," he said, seeing Burton's CO in his mind's eye. Jason... wasn't eating well right now. He was restless, moving his hand over his stomach like he was developing an ulcer. Oh no. Another one had disappeared. "Jason's going to call with another name for you to run down," Ernie said. "Wait for me to finish the first batch before you leave town."

Lee groaned and stood, his hot body aligning itself with Ernie's as he kissed the back of Ernie's neck. His hands, battered, dark, and capable, slid around Ernie's waist, and Ernie closed his eyes and accepted all of Burton's calm, steely-eyed power wrapped around him like a cloak.

"You sure you don't want to do something else while we wait for that call?" Burton asked.

Ernie turned in his arms and tasted him... ah! So sweet! "You loved me real good last night," he whispered. "We've got to take care of your guy now, okay? And...." He shivered. "There's something brewing, Burton. A perfect storm. Lots of lightning strikes. We've got to start the day off with donuts."

Lee pulled away and cupped his face. "You'll stay with Ace and Sonny at night?" he asked, to make sure.

Ernie smiled a little. "And feed the cats during the day, I promise." He swallowed. "Hey—you know that batch of kittens bunkered down with the black cat in the garage?"

Lee struggled not to cross his eyes. "Yeah?"

"Jackson and Ellery will be ready for one of them soon. Don't worry. It'll all work out."

Burton dropped his head against Ernie's shoulder. "Baby, you do realize that talking to you is like talking to a runaway ceiling fan?"

Ernie chuckled at the image and then sobered. "And there's going to be a boom."

Burton's eyes got big and at that moment, his phone—sitting on the table, where Burton had been using it to scroll through his feeds—buzzed. Burton closed his eyes and walked toward it, grimacing when he got close enough to see who was calling.

"Burton," he said tersely. He listened to the answer with narrowed eyes, and Ernie turned back to the donuts. "Yessir. I hear you. Long op. I'll head out within the next two hours."

Constance said something that made him grunt.

"Why two hours? Well, sir, because my boyfriend says you have to have donuts before I go."

Ernie could not imagine what Jason Constance would say to that, but it must have been something encouraging.

"Yes, sir," Burton replied. "I will thank him for you. And yes, sir, I will do my best to keep him safe."

Ernie gave him a relieved smile. "Thank you," he mouthed.

Burton signed off and set the phone on the table. "Baby, I hope you know what you're doing, because I am all sorts of worried."

Ernie gave his lover his best smile. "Don't worry about me, Burton. I'm just powdered sugar on the wind."

Grumbling to himself, Burton headed to the bedroom to shower and probably pack his go-bag, and Ernie set about assembling his ingredients. In his mind's eye, he had four different action-adventure movie films going, all of them featuring different people who he knew personally, over an overlapping time period.

One of them featured him and Sonny, and a really bad guy, and a gun being fired.

PART 2

"YOU SWEAR they'll be okay?" Sonny asked, fractious-like.

Ernie chewed on the inside of his cheek. "I swear," he said weakly. "Honest, Sonny—I've got nothing bad about them at all."

Okay, so that was sort of a lie.

He saw lots of *violence* about Ace and Jai—it was swirling around them, like a sirocco, hot dry wind and sand that had been heaved up in a choking wave. But through it all, Ace and Jai continued to walk, eyes squinted against the sand, bandanas covering their mouths and noses—it wasn't that they were unaffected, it was that they were unthreatened by it. Not this time.

But even mentioning that there was violence could be the trigger that sent Sonny Daye off into the wild blue.

But sometimes, Sonny surprised Ernie.

"You think them kids'll be okay?" he asked fretfully, leaning against the car he'd just finished repairing and gazing off into the direction in which Ace and Jai had disappeared. The sun was starting to lower, and the eastern sky was already purpling in the August gold.

"I can't tell," Ernie said, also fretting.

Burton had left that morning, and that had sucked. But Ace, Sonny, and Jai had enjoyed the donuts, and Ernie always felt a very satisfying sort of pride about that. It was like he did have a life skill—baking (or deep frying, because that's what donuts were!) really had been how he'd made his living before Burton had saved him from assassins. His life may be better now, but a little bit of autonomy was nice.

Still, Ernie had been half-expecting the moment when Ace looked across the street, where a filthy RV had been parked, and peered into the back window. One at a time, peaked little faces had pushed up against the glass. The RV had been left sweltering in the sun, and the guy driving had been disreputable to say the least.

After Jai and Ace had counted more than ten children, all about the same age, in the RV—and the driver had gotten into the vehicle without so much as a water bottle for the kids in the back—Ace and Jai had gone off in pursuit.

Sonny had asked Ernie before they'd left if Ace and Jai would be okay. Ernie had said yeah, sure, the blood would happen to someone else.

And then Ernie had called Jason Constance to make sure that's how it went down.

Jason had the kids now—he'd gotten a military-issue transport to take them to Sacramento, where they'd been kidnapped from. Ace and Jai had brought the RV back to the garage, souped it up a little so it wasn't burning quite so much oil, and then taken off again.

Ace had grabbed Sonny before he left and disappeared into the back corner of the garage. Ernie couldn't hear what he was saying to calm Sonny down, but he apparently hit the magic words. The roiling mass of explosive confusion that Ernie had sensed from Sonny's slight, wiry body had faded, leaving the usually volatile man sad and still.

"Think it was the right call?" Sonny asked. "Sending them off with that Constance guy?"

Ernie gnawed at his thumbnail. "Jason's good," he replied. "He's brave and kind. I just… it's like all the stars in his sky just changed. I can't explain it. But I think sending them to Jai's boyfriend was a good idea."

Sonny let out a frustrated groan. "What do you suppose Ace and Jai are going to do now?"

Ernie sighed. "I think tonight they're going to get to Vegas and sleep, then figure out a plan in the morning." He brightened, and like his gift sometimes manifested itself, this came out of his mouth before he knew he was going to say it. "I think Burton's going to be there to meet them."

"Burton?" Sonny said, perking up. "Really? Aw, Ernie, that makes me feel a helluva lot better."

"Well enough to bring Duke with me to go feed the cats and check on the kittens?" Ernie asked kindly.

Sonny's entire countenance melted. "Think maybe if we locked Duke in the house, I could pet the kittens?"

"Yeah, Sonny. I think that's fine. I think locking Duke in the house would be really courteous to the mama cat. I'm glad you thought of that."

Sonny sent Ernie an unguarded smile—the kind of smile that let Ernie see what Ace saw in him—and Ernie breathed a sigh of relief.

His job was to keep Sonny calm. He was pretty sure he could do that—until tomorrow night, at the very least.

Unfortunately, as he and Sonny locked up the garage and got ready for Sonny to drive Ernie home for an hour, Ernie got glimpses of what else was going on that night, and it wasn't nearly as peaceful.

"YOU'RE JASON Constance?"

Jason looked at the very average-looking man in scrubs, his blond stubble unimpressive, his gray eyes mild. He was hovering in the bay of a hospital, where Jason had been instructed to drive the shuttle-style bus filled with recently rescued, mostly preadolescent children. George was supposed to meet him and give all the kids the once-over to make sure nobody was sick or spreading something hard to cure, but looking at this small, very average man, Jason couldn't possibly believe he was at all related to the disreputable lot of Burton's hidden friends—

"You're George?" he asked. "Jai's George?"

—particularly the seven-foot Russian with the scary smile.

But Jai's George apparently didn't see it that way. His averagely pretty face split into a blinding smile. "You've seen him? He's okay?" George asked, standing on the ground in front of the steps up to the bus. "He said he had something important to do and the kids needed me."

Jason nodded and flashed his military ID. He'd changed into civilian clothes when the bus had arrived—he was currently wearing faded jeans and an OD-green collared shirt. George frowned and studied the ID and then pulled back, his smile just as pretty as it had been before.

"Great! My friend Amal is here to help—"

"Nobody is supposed to know we're here!" Jason hissed.

George scowled at him crossly. "Jai said we needed to hurry, so you get two of us. Amal is my supervisor, and he's promised not to document this. I need his help to get it done. You understand?"

Jason closed his eyes, feeling keenly that he'd been awakened at four a.m. with news that a rogue operative that they'd been tracking might be ready for retrieval. Actual retrieval and not assassination, which was a plus— that's why he'd called Burton for the job. Killing people who'd been warped by their own military didn't sit well with any of his crew. He tried to spread out the captures as opposed to the kills equitably. Everybody needed a win.

"Yeah, sure," he muttered. "Doesn't matter. Do you have anyone you can send to get them food? They've had water and peanut butter and crackers earlier today, but I have the feeling they're going to need more than that."

George looked over his shoulder at the terrified group of kids. When Ace and Jai had taken out the driver of the shitty RV, they'd been dressed in filthy rags and scared. Jai, who spoke Russian and Ukrainian apparently, had calmed them all down, and both men had provided the water and the peanut butter and crackers, as well as—miraculously—some clean clothes, which apparently Burton's boyfriend had stocked up on. They'd been good as gold for the long drive from the garage to this bustling metropolitan hospital in LA, but they were also confused as hell.

Jason didn't blame them.

"Amal!" George called. "We need food, stat. Can we snag one of the orderlies?"

Amal nodded. "I'll have Jenny raid the cafeteria—we can get them some fresh fruit too. You start with the physicals. Give me ten minutes."

"Groovy!" George looked at Jason to see if he was good with that, and Jason wasn't sure what showed in his eyes but George looked behind him and added, "And a big carafe of coffee, with some fixings. Even if he doesn't like sugar, I have the feeling he's going to need all the stimulants we can give him!"

Jason let out a little laugh. "You're Jai's boyfriend?" he asked again.

"Yup! How's my giant Russian bear?"

Jason felt a bright smile spread to his cheeks. "Taciturn and terrifying," he said honestly. Then he sobered. "And just like Ace, he's doing good works and not telling the world about it."

George nodded, like he expected nothing less. "There's nothing sexier than a hero," he said happily. "Now if you'll excuse me, I'm going to take some temperatures and write down some vitals."

Jason gave himself permission to tilt his head back and close his eyes while George was there. Per the military, he wasn't sure when he'd get another chance to nap, right?

He must have been out for more than ten minutes—maybe it was closer to thirty—when George interrupted his snooze by crouching next to him and shaking his arm.

"Constance?"

Jason blinked hard. "What? What? Are the kids all right?"

"Kids are fine," George said and nodded over his shoulder. "Jenny's giving them all fruit and sandwiches and milk and water. That's not the problem."

"What's the problem?"

"There's military guys here—they're in the front of the hospital, being total dicks, and I told Amal that you might have violated some protocols to get these kids back to their homes. Am I right?"

"Yeah," Jason said, every fiber in his body alert. "Shit."

"Okay—here's the thing. Amal's okayed you to grab a hospital transport. We usually use it to bus patients to and from the nearby convalescent hospitals, but this one's a little older, so it won't be missed for at least a week. Me and Jenny will take you and the kids, but you need to be quiet. Your dick general or whoever came in through the front, and this bus is over in the wing close to him. We're literally going to be crawling under the windows to get to it, and we have no time. Are you game?"

Jason remembered Brigadier General Barney Talbot's voice as he'd told Jason to keep the children where they were because they were valuable assets in an upcoming op.

Ace had needed to keep him from flinging his phone across the desert.

These kids had been freaked out and stunned. They'd been dragged from their home neighborhoods, stuffed in a stifling, filthy RV, and deprived of food and water for what Jason suspected was a number of days.

He wasn't putting them through anything else besides a ride home.

"I'm game," he said. He took a breath. "Sophie? Maxim?"

Two of the kids—they looked between twelve and fifteen, and related, with dirty blond hair and enormous gray eyes—stepped forward from the back.

"Mr. Constance?" Sophie, the more gregarious of the two, asked him.

"We need to sneak off this bus and onto another one," he explained. "I need you and Max to help me keep the kids from making noise."

"Can we keep the apples?" Max asked, sounding pained.

Jason managed a smile for the boy, who seemed frightened but functional.

"Of course," he said gently. "Go get everyone ready. I'll get out first."

He grabbed his phone and his small go-bag, which included a first-aid kit and a change of clothes. After looking at George to lead the way, he glanced behind him and made sure the kids were following.

Then he pocketed the key for the damned military transpo because making shit easy for Talbot was not on his list of things to do.

The next ten minutes were incredibly nerve-wracking, mostly because they were so silent. In a deadly serious game of follow-the-leader, George took them behind the parking garage, back toward the hospital. At one point in time, they really did have to crouch, bending over so they could pass unnoticed in front of the windows, because Talbot could be heard on the other side, bullying staff members about how could they miss a bus full of kids.

Jason knew he'd lost a few years of his life before they'd all managed to pass that wall and make it back to the barbwire fenced-in area that marked hospital transport. George had the key for the gate, and past that, he led them to a red shuttle bus that had seen better days. He unlocked it, and then he and Jason ushered the children—all of whom were clutching their apples and sandwiches and water and milk for dear life—back up into the new bus.

Jason breathed a sigh of relief, and George pressed the keys into his hand. "Hurry—but not too fast," he said. And then he grinned. "And if you see Jai, tell him I'm fine and no regrets, okay? The guy's awesome, but he worries too much."

Jason nodded. "I will. And if you get into trouble, tell them I lied and told you this was a legit op, okay?"

George shook his head. "Negatory. Amal and I will tell them we don't turn our back on kids. Now go. Be safe." George turned toward the children, who were now back in their seats and dutifully buckling their seat belts. "Be good for Lieutenant Colonel Constance, okay?"

"They'll probably court-martial me," Jason said. "Maybe just have them call me Jason."

"Nope," George said, and then he gave a very passable salute. "They're going to know that someone with honor worked super hard to get them home."

And with that, Jai's very un-average, very *very* impressive boyfriend hopped off the bus and ran back toward where Jason had abandoned the military transport.

Driving very mildly, and praying to be invisible, Jason made it out of the hospital parking lot and back onto the road.

"Mr. Constance?" Sophie said from the seat behind him. "Are we going to keep driving, or are we going to stop sometime tonight?"

Jason looked at his watch and saw that it was barely nine. If he was going to rest, he should do it in the darkest part of the night—sleeping in the bus in the middle of the day was no good, and he was pretty sure he couldn't make it to Sacramento, not now, when he had to cut through LA traffic and then probably drive up toward Lancaster to stay off military radar.

"We'll stop in a couple of hours," he promised her. Then he smiled slightly. "Hey, Sophie, do you see what that little cubicle is in the back of the bus?"

Sophie's entire face lit up in smiles. They'd been able to make one stop between Victoriana and LA, and the kids had been miserable, and it hadn't been enough.

"Oh, Mr. Constance! You're so wonderful! You got us a bus with a *bathroom*!"

Jason had to chuckle. He was being chased by his own military, and, very probably, by local mobsters, all of whom wanted their hands on these children. But this girl had managed to find a silver lining.

"You're a hero!" Sophie told him, eyes wide, and he winked at her and told her to tell the others they could only use it one at a time, and everybody had to buckle their seat belt when they weren't going to use the facilities.

A little part of him whispered that it had been a long time since he felt like his job made him a hero.

It felt pretty good.

PART 3—KABOOM

THEY'D STOPPED at the garage to fix the RV, but what Ace really wanted to do was take a sandblaster to it and erase it from the earth. The interior was squalid and filthy and smelled like the piss of a thousand sweaty cats, and thinking of them as cats and not terrified children was the only way Ace could even stand to look at it.

He'd texted Ernie quietly and had him get Sonny out of the way so he and Jai could get in there, tune the fucker up, buy a shit-ton of ice to shovel in the back to keep them cold, and then drive off. Ernie texted him right before Ace and Jai were ready to get back on the road, telling him to relax, Sonny had stayed for dinner, and since they had Duke with them, he might just stay with Ernie until the next morning, when they went back to the garage.

Ace was so relieved he could have cried.

"What?" Jai asked as Ace started the thing up. Yup, ran better. Ace still wanted it dead. "You have never heard of sleeping on a friend's couch? Yours almost had my ass print on it, before George started coming to my apartment."

"As far as I know, Sonny ain't never had a friend he could have a sleepover with," Ace said shortly. "It's like a part of his childhood he might get back. Sue me if I am excited about this."

Jai grunted. "That is entirely fair." Then his face fell. "Even I had friends as a child," he said. "What do you know of Sonny's life—"

Ace swallowed and shook his head. "I... I can't. Not when we're cruising down the road in this... this fucking abomination, okay?"

Jai's silence was hard to read, and Ace snuck a look at him. He was gazing out the passenger window. "I carried such a torch for Sonny for so long," he said wistfully. "But every so often I get a glimpse that shows me you are the better man for him."

Ace grunted. "Well, I may be the better man for *him*, but I am definitely not the better man." He gave Jai an assessing look and tried to decide if he could crack a joke. "Besides, you've got a pretty nurse who has broken the law a couple of times, just for you, and you know that's sort of a fantasy."

Jai grunted in return, but Ace could tell he was pleased.

"I shall tell him," Jai said. "He will be surprised. He thinks he is very ordinary."

But Ace knew better. George had spent a lot of his own time in the past two months helping Alba's community, being someone they could turn to for their medical needs and who wouldn't call ICE, staying completely off the radar. It wasn't like criminality was a *requirement* for a life partner if you knew Ace and Sonny, but Ace was beginning to see how it could be a perk.

Together they rumbled through the night, pulling up to rest at the big casino just inside the Nevada border, the one with the scary clowns.

Although it was "family themed," the place was almost deserted, and Ace pulled around toward the back where nobody was parked, and the only thing that could see them was acres of desert. They broke out the sandwiches they'd bought for the trip and ate and drank lots of water, rolling down the windows of the RV and opening the door to let the hot desert wind cool them off.

"What is the plan?" Jai asked.

"Well, Burton was going to try to get the address of the place where this thing was going. We need to scope the place out, make sure the bad guys are bad guys, and, I don't know. Return their RV I guess."

Jai raised an eyebrow. "That's it? Return the RV?"

Ace looked at him levelly. "I did text Burton to bring us some C-4 and a detonator," he said. "I mean, we don't *have* to return it the same way we found it."

"You mean," Jai said slowly, "that you would like to kill it with fire."

Ace's mouth twitched. "Can you think of a better way to kill it?"

"Christ no," Jai said thickly. "Do we mind if it takes out some bad people when we do?"

"*I* don't," Ace said, truth at the forefront. "But," he added loyally, "we do have to see if Burton has a plan."

"Heh heh heh…"

"What are you laughing about?"

"I don't think Burton ever has a plan for us, Ace. I think you have turned Burton's life into a life without a strategy."

That was ridiculous. "I don't see why you're blaming me for that and not Ernie." Ace sniffed. "I mean, you gotta admit, Ernie does send plans to shit."

Jai shook his head. "Ernie is like a weather app. He's very good for plans. He's very bad for surprises."

"Mm…"

"Or very good for surprises," Jai corrected. "It depends on if you like surprises."

"Not with my C-4 and human trafficking sleazeballs," Ace assured him.

"Well, then he's bad for them. But he does come with surprises. There is no arguing that."

There was not, and they turned to other topics, eventually settling down to sleep.

The last thing Ace did before he closed his eyes was take a picture of the night sky, where you could see the demarcation from the light pollution from Vegas, which was nearly thirty miles away, and the clean desert that he and Sonny were used to. He sent the picture to Sonny without a caption, but Sonny sent back, *Missing you too.*

Well, nobody said Sonny Daye was stupid.

THE NEXT morning, they were saved from dying of heatstroke in the RV by a knock on the window.

Lee Burton, dressed in motorcycle leathers and a shiny black helmet, was standing right outside, two giant iced coffees in his hand.

"Ooh!" Ace said, giving one to Jai. "I love these. They're like morning dessert."

"Yeah, Ace." Burton always sounded like he was dryly laughing. "That's what they're called. Morning dessert."

"Don't be shitty," Ace told him, sharpness in his voice. "Do you have any idea how horrible it is in here?"

Burton grimaced. "Sorry, Ace. I was just… you know."

"Looking forward to some time with your boy," Ace said. "Welcome to the club. Membership: everybody here, plus their boyfriends, so that's six. What can we do for you?"

"Well, for one thing, you can come with me into the hotel, because I've got us a suite, and if you like, you can take a cold shower and we can figure out what the fuck to do with this thing. How's that sound?"

Ace beamed at him, then got quiet. "Sounds good—but we'd better not tell Sonny. He likes hotels a *lot*. He'd be downright sad to be left out."

"Understood." Burton and Jai both nodded, and he breathed a sigh of relief. Knowing that would make the difference between enjoying a cold shower and some clean sheets that night, and feeling awful every second of the day.

They took a second nap to make up for the shitty sleep in the RV, and Burton got them room service breakfast, which Ace enjoyed, and then Burton brought out a map and they started planning.

"Now see," he said, "the kids were bound for this place here. I scoped it this morning while you two were snoring in the RV and it's one of those estate places out in the middle of the desert. You take what looks like a side road, and suddenly you're surrounded by trees and landscaping that is just sucking down water and does not belong there, and then the driveway turns to gravel, and there's a roundabout in front of a fountain and a mansion the size of Victoriana."

"You are shitting me," Ace said, and Burton pursed his lips and shook his head.

"I am most assuredly not shitting you," he said. "And I almost shit my pants when I got that far. I was on my motorbike and it wasn't quiet. There were cameras and everything—but practically nobody there. Jason apparently has the entire base working on where those kids were supposed to go, and I'm telling you, something super hinky is going on. They were heading to this place—the chatter we were picking up is that there is some sort of auction there *tonight*, but there is now cross chatter about something major going down—some sort of big power transfer up north, and it looks like all the rats have jumped ship. So, we've got a conundrum here."

Ace and Jai looked at each other, and Jai narrowed his eyes.

"Is not such a conundrum," he said. "Are there bad guys in the house?"

"Yes," Burton said, holding out his hands. "That house is run by one of the most bloodless Russian mobs in the southwest. There's no sweet unsuspecting family in there—I climbed a tree and got pictures, and I'm telling you, it's not quite the mansion from *Scarface* but it's not *not* the mansion from *Scarface* either."

"I have not seen this movie," Jai said. "Is good?"

Ace shrugged. "Super violent. You know all those memes and shit of Al Pacino with the big machine gun and the face iced in cocaine going, 'Say hello to my little friend'?"

Jai's eyes widened. "This is the house the children were going to?"

Burton nodded, and Ace knew he and Jai were on exactly the same wavelength—but he wasn't sure if Burton was, so he wasn't going to warn him.

"Why?" Burton asked. "Do you want to see it?"

Ace and Jai exchanged a longer glance.

"I think we need to drop the RV off there," Jai said. "Do not worry. If you were caught on camera, you can wait back before the estate starts. It will just be Ace and me. We will not get into any trouble."

Well, Ace figured, that was probably right. They'd either do what he was thinking they'd be doing, or they'd be dead.

BURTON DID not like this—he did not like this one bit. Thirty-six hours after finding Jai and Ace asleep in a hotel parking lot, he lay under some of that unnaturally placed foliage, a signal jammer in his pocket making damned sure none of the cameras caught his image, or Ace and Jai's either. He was about a quarter of a mile from the house with the fountain, watching as Ace parked the RV in front of the giant architectural monstrosity and trying not to rethink his life choices, when his phone buzzed.

Don't worry, they're fine.

Oh, thank God. Ernie—even when he said woowoo shit, it was usually a comfort.

What about Jason? he asked.

Not so fine. Will need your help, but I don't know where or how.

Fuck. *Fuck.* Goddammit.

Thanks, Ernie. How're you and Sonny doing?

There was a long, long pause, and Burton's heart froze in his chest.

Is anything wrong?

And another pause. For a moment, he thought about screaming Ace's and Jai's names, throwing them all in the tiny rental car Ace had suggested he get, and hauling them all back to Victoriana.

We have it handled, Ernie finally texted. *Don't worry. It's all good.*

Burton stared at the phone in his hand and caught his breath.

Have what handled? he asked when his fingers could work. Dammit, Ace—where were you—

At that moment his phone rang.

ACE HADN'T been a good boy growing up. He'd broken into a few places— usually liquor stores to steal beer, and once an enemy's house to leave a note to say not to fuck with Ace's little sister, or Ace and his big brother, Jake, would give them their just deserts. It took him less than two minutes to spot the servants' door on the east wing of the house and break in.

The place was empty—at least downstairs.

Upstairs, they could hear two people arguing in Russian, and Ace looked to Jai, who smiled unpleasantly as they made their way through the kitchen.

"They know where the children are headed," Jai translated. "And they don't want them to go back to Sacramento."

"Why not?" Ace asked. Then, "Damn. That's not what a dining table is for."

Through a couple of french doors, they could see a pricey marble dining table, except instead of food, it was heaped with drugs and C-4.

"I do not want the drugs," Jai said. "But that other thing…"

"Yeah—I don't think Burton brought near enough." He'd brought enough to take the RV out, this was true. But seeing that there weren't that many bad guys here—and that they were going after the kids Ace and Jai had rightfully saved—he thought maybe he and Jai should have bigger plans than that.

"You take the C-4 back to the RV," Ace said. "I'll check around to make sure nobody else is here but the two assholes upstairs."

Jai's gaze shot back toward a door behind the kitchen. "Nyet—I have a better way."

Two minutes later they were in the security room, because Jai's instincts were spot-on. And looking from camera to camera, Ace didn't see a fucking thing.

"I really don't want to get a batch of kids if they're here," Ace muttered, "but see—" He aimed a camera at an empty room that had mattresses on the floor and one toilet. It was in the basement, unsurprisingly, and the door to the upstairs was wide open. "—it's us and the two assholes upstairs."

"Then we go," Jai said. "This C-4 wants to become something else. It has a feel that way."

JESUS. JACKSON fucking Rivers, private investigator and general badass, was on the phone, and he had some bad fucking news.

Jason and the bus full of kids were on the way north still, but he'd been waylaid by mobsters, which might explain where they'd all gone for the moment—but also by his own military, which was pissed that Jason hadn't brought the shipment of children here, to this deserted fucking house.

And Jackson knew that Jason was headed his way because Jackson and his boyfriend, Ellery Cramer, defense attorney at large, were working on a case involving two of the kids on that bus.

Seriously. Burton could not believe their fucking luck, both good and bad.
But right now, it was mostly bad, because he and Ace and Jai were—

He watched in disbelief as Jai and Ace hopped into the RV again and
fiddled.

"Burton?"

"Uhm…"

The RV made a circle around the fountain and off to the side a bit,
crushing some of that unbelievable vegetation. Then Ace and Jai leapt from
the vehicle and Ace reached inside and did some quick work with his hands
on the pedals and the steering wheel.

And both of them came hauling ass up the hill.

"No," he shouted, figuring out what in the fuck they were doing before
the RV even got past the fountain again. "No, you assholes, this isn't what
I told you to—*fuck!*"

The RV crashed into the house just as Ace and Jai got to his hiding
spot, and the explosion that came next shook the world.

PART 4—SONNY

I DIDN'T like it when Ace was gone, nosirree, I didn't. But he was gone, and he was gone to help kids, which I got. When bad stuff happens and you're a kid, well, it sticks. It makes it so you're not a kid no more but it's hard to grow up too. You're stuck, half the time thinking it's all bad and half the time hoping someone will save you, even if you *are* saved, and you *been* saved going on five years now.

I think that's how long it's been. I was like eighteen or something when I joined the army and I saw Ace. God, I wanted him then. Wanted him to keep me. I didn't know then that he wanted bigger things for me, wanted us to keep each other. I try—every day I try—to be the guy who can do that. Can be a lover you want to come back to when you gotta go be a hero.

It's a good thing Ace is Ace, and solid as they come, or I'd be sorta scary when he was gone.

Like the second day he was gone—I think it was the second day, because even though I was at Ernie's that first night, me and Duke and all the fuckin' cats, I didn't sleep great. Day sorta bled into night and into day again and I woke up not with Ace, which hadn't happened much since we decided to keep each other, so you can see my confusion.

So by the second day after that, I was sorta tired. I had to make Ernie talk to the people who came in to get their cars fixed, because the first time I shouted over my shoulder for Ace to come help me and then when I remembered Ace wasn't there, I tried to explain that Ace wasn't there and, well, those people probably would have driven off into the road with half their car dragging behind them if Ernie hadn't come and made it better.

So yeah, it's probably a good thing I stick to cars, right?

Anyway, I do stick to cars, but in the afternoon Ernie brought me water and lunch and then asked me where we kept the guns.

I told him they was locked in the end table in the TV room and then I gave him the keys while I guzzled my water. I finished my water and went back to the Audi I was working on for the crispy pink man who was waiting patiently for it across the street. He was a sweet guy, but probably should not've been driving a convertible in this heat, certainly not in August. I mean, alls I was doing was fixing the latch, but I'd felt so bad for the guy, I was double-checking his engine coolant and shit because if he broke down after we got the top back up, he'd cook like a dead worm on the asphalt, and I'd kinda liked him. He'd offered to bring me a soda and I do love my sweets.

Anyways, there I was, double-checking all the checks, when it occurred to me to ask why Ernie needed a gun.

I finished up with the Audi and found Ernie in the air-conditioned clerk's cubicle. I knocked on the door gently before I said something.

He practically grabbed the ceiling and that was my first notion that something mighta been terribly terribly wrong.

"What?" I yelled. "What happened? Why do we need the guns? Jesus fuck a rabbit, Ernie, the hell is wrong with you?"

Ernie's face was so tense it was white under his tan. "Why did you scare me like that!" he yelled, his voice breaking.

"Why'd you jump like a fucking kangaroo, Ernie! What's going on?"

Ernie held a hand up to make me shut up and then stood for a moment, his other hand on his chest while he calmed himself down.

He was down to steady breaths when I saw the pink crispy guy walking back, a big soda in his hand that I think was for me.

"Gimme a sec," I told Ernie. "I gotta take care of this."

I didn't charge the guy none—it took me like five minutes, and the soda was appreciated. I told him he needed to stock up on zinc oxide 'cause that's what we used in the military, and he said he appreciated that. Then he wrapped his head in a towel and smeared cream all over his face and got into the car. Good—maybe the cream would help the blisters.

I came back and Ernie was standing behind the door, one of the three Berettas Ace and I kept in the drawer pointed down like maybe Burton had taught him how to use it.

"The fuck?" I asked, because it was starting to dawn on me that no matter what Ace and Jai were doing right now, something else was going down.

"They're pulling up," he whispered. "They're violent men, Sonny. Tell them we're closed."

Fuck. Oh fuck. We'd done this before—but Ace and Jai had stood in the bay, one of them holding the gun while the other one'd worked on the car.

"Yeah, fine," I said. "Gimme the other gun. I know how to use it."

"You startle easy," he said, his breath coming in quick pants.

"Did we or did we not have to peel you off the ceiling?" I asked. Jesus, it should be clear to even Ernie that if someone was gonna do the killing, it should be me because seriously, motherfuckers who want to hurt my family aren't real people to me, and that's the finger you want on the trigger.

I checked the gun over and had just shucked my coveralls down to my waist so I could shove it under my belt when a dented black SUV sped its way past the drive to the front of the shop and around the back to the garage bay.

I looked at Ernie and said, "Hide under the counter," before I ran out to greet whatever bad news just pulled up.

They got out and started talking quickly in words that sounded like Jai's, gesturing to each other and then to me. I waited patiently with a stupid expression on my face because it helps sometimes if people think you don't get what's going on.

These assholes were obviously debating whether I was the one they were supposed to kill or someone else was.

"Can I help you?" I asked when the sun had about pounded us all flat. Them more than me 'cause they were wearing suits in the sun, which is dumb and I felt sort of vindicated for thinking I could probably shoot them easy.

"We are looking for man who owns this garage," one of the men said thickly, and I blinked real slow.

"Ace," I said. "He's not here."

"Where'd he go? Our contact says he and a big Russian guy work here. They did bad things."

Like saving children. I got it.

"He went up north," I said, figuring I was steering these guys away from Las Vegas, which was really the only other direction they had. "There's a car up in Bakersfield he's gonna go look at. Took Jai to see if it could be raced. You gotta go now, I'm closing up."

The two guys looked at each other, ugly expressions on their faces, and then quicker'n rattlesnakes they both reached for their pieces.

I had mine out first and shot one guy in the leg and then had the gun on the other guy before he even knew what was going to happen.

For a long, sweaty moment, we stared each other down while the guy I'd just shot writhed in the oil-soaked dust that marked the entrance to the garage bay. He was making a whole lot of noise, and I admit, it was making my hands shake a lot more, but still I kept the gun trained on the guy who was trying to inch his fingers toward his own.

Both guys were midsized, the wounded guy shorter than the nonwounded guy, and both had dark hair and dark eyes, with the sort of high cheekbones that Jai had.

"You need to put your hands out right now!" I shouted, seeing the guy reach for his gun again. "Out! Out! I'll fuckin' put the next one in somebody's head!"

"We're just here for that Ace guy!" he yelled back. "Give us Ace and we kill him and it's all—"

And then Ernie yelled, "*Augh! Fucking boom!*" and shot the guy in the head.

I stared, stunned, as the guy fell to the ground, brains leaking out of his ears, and the other guy whimpered and put his hands up over his head as he curled up in the dust.

I kept my gun out and called to Ernie without looking away, "Ernie? Ernie, why'd you go and kill him?"

"'Cause he was gonna kill us both if I didn't," Ernie said shakily, walking out from the cubicle. He'd had a real clear shot from there, and I don't think the dead man ever saw him.

"You know that for sure?" I asked, my gun a little shaky but still trained on the wounded guy.

"Saw it real fuckin' clear," Ernie muttered.

"What about this guy? Do we get him to a doctor?"

Ernie made a rasping sound in his throat. "No. And George can't know."

And that's what clued me in that this was really bad. 'Cause George was good. He was a good guy. We all knew Jai's boyfriend was sacred or something. We only involved him in good things, and this was a bad thing.

Ernie had taken this mobster's head off.

"I…" I lowered the gun a little but still kept it midway. "Uh, Ernie?"

"Yeah?"

"Ace wouldn't want me to kill this guy when he's helpless."

Ernie stared at the guy. "I know."

"What do we do with him?"

"Shit. Well, first, let me get his gun," Ernie said. Then he blinked. "All of them."

The guy moaned and put both hands flat on the ground and Ernie walked over and took a semiauto, two Glocks, and a knife bigger'n Ace's off the guy before doing the same thing to the dead man.

"Maybe put those in the SUV," I said.

"What're we doing with this guy?" he asked.

I looked at the garage and the coils of rope in there. "Tie him up?"

So that's what we did. We put the dead guy on a tarp and rolled it up and put it back in the SUV, and then we tied the wounded guy up super tight, bandaged his leg, and stashed him in a corner of the garage. We weren't mean. We gave him water. Ernie went and got the oxy we had left from last time someone got super hurt and we gave him that. The gunshot in his leg was through and through—washing it in the sink and wrapping it good wasn't easy, but we did it.

And then we gave him more water, and Ernie left me in charge with a gun and a big soda while he fed and watered Duke and took him out to crap. He came back and watched the guy while I peed and then, because it was dark and cooler, and he was used to walking in the desert, excused himself while he took the car for a drive.

That was when Ace called me.

"Ace?" I asked, voice shaky. "You comin' home?"

He made a pained sound. "Naw, Sonny. Not yet. We finished shit up here in Vegas—that worked out fine. But Jason's in a heap of trouble and we need to make sure he and the kids get to Sacramento. I'm sorry. I... I want to come home, you know that, right?"

And for a whole minute, it was like I was Ernie. I saw that if I said shit went down, he'd come home, Jai too, and those kids and that guy who'd helped us a lot in the past—they'd be swinging in the cold. And for a minute, I didn't care. Ace was *mine*, and we took care of each other. He kept me and I kept him, and that's who we were supposed to be.

"Sonny?" he asked, his voice full of worry. "You okay?"

But they were kids. Kids like I had been. And Ace didn't want them hurt 'cause he knew I'd been hurt and he felt like rescuing them was rescuing me from a thing that had happened a long time ago but still happened sometimes in my head.

He wanted to make sure those kids didn't have it happen in their head too.

"Fine," I said, voice shaky. "Call me when you're done tomorrow. I need you home when you're done."

"I don't like being gone," he said fretfully. "You and Ernie getting on all right?"

"Yeah," I said. "Ernie's got kittens. Spent the night last night and saw 'em. Was like I was a real kid, yanno. Sleepovers."

Ace chuckled. "Yeah. Well, hope you have as good a night tonight."

I gave a sad look at the sweltering garage with the asshole bleeding on the floor and drinking his umpteenth bottle of water. More than they'd given those kids, I remembered. Yeah. Fuck him. I'd shoot him if I had to, so Ace could go do a big good thing.

"It should be quiet," I said, hoping I wasn't lying. "You take care now."

"Yeah, you too."

We signed off, and I thought someday we'd have to learn to say "Love you" 'cause it sure would have made me feel a damned sight better, even if I knew it was true without the words.

Anyway, Ernie showed up two hours later, sweaty and exhausted. I was tired too, but I figured he needed first nap.

It was gonna be a long fuckin' night, but before he walked up to the house and left me in charge of the whimpering guy with the leg wound, I just had to ask him.

"Ernie, when you said, 'Fuckin' boom!' what the fuck did that mean?"

Ernie blinked. "Ace and Jai just blew something up," he said, sounding just done.

I sucked in a breath, and was about to get mad at Ace for not telling me, but then I realized Ernie had just dumped a dead guy's body and I was watching a bad guy in our garage.

"Fuckin' figures," I muttered. "Get some sleep. Keep your phone by your bed. I'll buzz you if I start nodding off."

We switched off about three hours later, so I was fast asleep when Ace called me in the morning to let me know he was on his way home.

PART 5—ERNIE

ERNIE SAW it.

All in one moment—in a heartbeat, really.

Sonny was going to lower the gun, because he didn't want to kill anyone, and he really didn't want Ace to be mad at him, and Ernie's gift hit him like a giant wave.

Ernie was tumbled about in that wave like a dryer sheet in the dryer, and he'd look up one way and see what would happen if he did one thing, and look the other and see that timeline too.

He looked one way and Sonny lowered the gun and the bad guy shot him. In the head. Ernie had seen his misshapen skull and had known that the man who had once been his friend and had known... he was gone. He'd seen Ace, mad with grief, taking on the mob alone, not letting Jai or Ernie back him up.

He'd seen Ace die too.

He'd seen their little group of family here in the desert frayed, scattered. He'd been all alone in the big house with Burton, and they'd been together but Burton's friend Jason hadn't made it, because Ace hadn't been there to help.

Jai had been cut loose, adrift without his friends, and he'd run away from George, who had never loved again.

All of that because Sonny Daye, who had more right to be a psychopath than anyone Ernie had ever met, had not wanted to kill a man in cold blood.

And then Ernie had seen himself pulling the trigger, and none of that other stuff had occurred.

He didn't even recall making the decision after that. He'd learned shooting in the army, and he'd learned when someone was full of bugs. He could feel the bugs clickety-clackety-crawling around in this guy's brain from where he'd stood, hidden. A smooth motion, gun out of the back of his pants, sight, aim, shoot.

Boom.

And oddly enough, he'd felt Sonny's horror at what he'd done—but he didn't feel his own.

And watching Sonny pulling himself together to do what had to be done—that had kept Ernie steady. Sonny didn't look at him like he was crazy. He didn't give him any "Oh, poor Ernie, he had to kill a man, he must be shook."

Sonny Daye treated Ernie like an equal, and like a grown-up. As far as Sonny was concerned, Ernie could make that decision of his own free will, and if Ernie had done it, he must have had a reason.

Sonny's simple faith had given Ernie the confidence in his own judgment to not be taken out at the knees.

He'd done the awful thing then. He'd rolled the body up in a tarp and, with Sonny's help, had put it in the SUV. Sitting behind the wheel had been... vomitous. He'd had a front row show to every horrible deed perpetrated by the driver who was currently leaking brains in a tarp in the back, and the man gave bugs a terrible, terrible name.

He had no problem driving the car into one of the old quarry pits out behind the housing tract he and Burton lived in, the only residents in what was supposed to be an upscale block of desert living jewels.

He'd soaked the car in a generous amount of gasoline and had lit a fuse made of twisted toilet paper as he'd sent the thing hurtling into the quarry. It had hit the bottom with a decent explosion and flameout, and Ernie had been mildly impressed.

Jai was so proud of himself for blowing shit up—but hey, Ernie didn't do bad either!

He'd even been able to stop off at the house and wash off before walking back to the gas station, and when he'd gotten there, well, he'd been fairly impressed that Sonny and the guy he'd shot were both still alive.

Sonny looked wired for sound—but surprisingly enough, not psychotic and not catatonic, so Ernie took him up on his offer of sleep, knowing the entire time that sleep was not what he needed.

He climbed into bed and called Burton from their room built into the back of the house, keeping the lights off. Duke was cuddled in his arms, but only because the little dog was really good at not making a sound when the lights were off.

"Hey," Lee said, his voice mildly muffled in that way that said Ernie was on a helmet com. "How's things."

And Ernie had been so good those months, when Burton had been undercover and Ernie had been living with Sonny and Ace. He'd kept his mouth shut, he'd tried not to worry Lee, not for the small shit. But that one little question, now, after having killed a man, and Ernie's throat closed.

He'd killed before—Burton knew he could. Burton had walked into an alley expecting to find Ernie hurt, assaulted, dead, and had found Ernie standing and his enemies dying instead.

But this… this had been rawer than that. Maybe because he'd been offered a choice in his head, and had made it. Before, that night in the alley when Cruller had come to rescue him and had found he wasn't bad at rescuing himself, he'd reacted. He'd been high and lonely and desperate and he'd known Cruller had been out there but hadn't known when he'd act. He'd shoved that one guy's nose into his brain pan without thought and without mercy and he could live with that.

Here, he'd made a choice, and he'd done it coolly, and he'd done it because Sonny Daye was a friend and Ernie didn't want to see him dead.

"Ernie?" Concern—lots of it—laced Lee Burton's voice. "Ernie? Baby? You okay?"

"Fine," Ernie said hoarsely. "Just… some guys came by the gas station today. One's wounded. Sonny's watching him. One's dead. He was gonna kill Sonny and—" He couldn't say any more.

"You killed him first," Burton said, his voice flat.

"I'm sorry," Ernie told him, hating the crack in his own voice.

"Oh, baby—don't be sorry. Do I have to turn around—"

"No!" Ernie's voice cracked some more. "Jason needs you—man, you gotta catch up with him. He… he's gonna need you. And everybody. Every one of you. Sonny's lying to Ace—don't… don't tell him until tomorrow, okay? Just… you'll know when. But…" He palmed the tears that made his face hot. "Love you, Cruller."

"Love you too, club boy," Burton said softly. "Here, you wanna hear about how Ace and Jai were heroes today?"

"Yeah."

"You can't tell 'em I said that, though, because I really wish they would stay out of this shit. Worries me sick, I can tell you. Anyway—so they were just supposed to do recon…"

Ernie knew what Lee was doing, even as he closed his eyes. He was distracting Ernie, making it so he didn't focus on the scary thing he'd just done. He made the story funny, because Ace and Jai weren't super-slick assassins, but he also let Ernie see how proud he was to have friends who'd do the brave thing, the smart thing, the thing that needed to be done.

Ernie's eyelids felt heavy, his soul as tired as his bones. Burton wrapped up his story and started on another one about Ace in the desert that Ernie had already heard before but loved. Before he knew it, Cruller was whispering, "Love you, club boy. You did the right thing," in his ear as he drifted off.

"Love you, Cruller. Come home soon."

"No reason to stay away."

And Burton signed off, leaving Ernie to slide into a few hours' sleep, content in the knowledge that this was true. Lee Burton knew exactly who Ernie was—he'd known since the beginning. And he'd loved him and had been proud of him for exactly those things.

Good. Ernie probably couldn't change—but he'd try if it meant keeping Cruller happy. He was glad he didn't have to, not yet.

PART 6

ACE BLINKED through sandy eyes as the soldier next to him shook him awake.

He felt a little bad about leaving Jai and Burton in Sacramento, but they'd needed to make sure Jason was okay and that all the bad guys had been rounded up or shot.

Or knifed in the chest. Ace wasn't sorry about that either—the bad guy had been aiming a gun at Rivers and Rivers was a good guy. Ace *was* sorry that he'd only gotten *close* to the guy's heart and he'd needed to hit a car door before he drove it in completely and died. But the guy had been a scumbag, and it was no skin off Ace's nose when scumbags suddenly had problems breathing 'cause they accidentally shoved a knife further through their heart than it needed to be.

In fact, the op in Sacramento had been fun, but no sooner did they have Jason Constance tucked away some place that needed guarding than Burton had gotten a call that said Ace was needed back at the garage, and Ace had remembered that Sonny was his priority.

There was something going on that Burton and Sonny hadn't been telling him. He knew it. He knew that they probably kept it a secret for the same reason he wasn't going to tell Sonny about blowing up that ritzy disgusting palace in Vegas or about how really out of control that morning's op had been. Ace got it. Sometimes you just didn't want people to worry, that was all.

By the same token, sometimes just knowing someone was trying not to worry you was worrisome as it was.

Burton had tapped a helicopter to fly him to Victoriana. It had been waiting at a private airfield outside of the former Mather Air Force Base, so while all the drama in Sac had gone down before six-thirty a.m., it was not even ten by the time the helo set him down in a patch of sand about two hundred yards behind the gas station. Ace thanked the guys who'd given him a ride, fed him a breakfast sandwich, and then let him sleep, rocked by the motion and the *whup-whup* of the chopper's blades. Then he slid out of the bay doors, keeping his head down as he ran. Behind him, Burton's special ops brethren had slid the bay door shut and taken off, and Ace wasn't even sure if they knew what he, Jai, and Burton had done that day.

Which made him happy, mostly, because seriously, the less the military people knew about him and his gas station, the less he and Sonny would be bothered by shit like this when it didn't travel right to their front door.

As he trotted in the still-scorching morning heat, he took in the gas station and felt his hackles start to rise.

The garage bay door was shut and a Closed sign was in front of the clerk's cubicle. Approaching the side door, he saw Ernie stumble out of the house, looking tired and wonky and like he'd slept under a helicopter, because his hair was a curly, bristly tumbleweed.

"Sonny's in there!" Ernie called, trying to get his long, loose limbs to make a run. "Don't go in without saying who you are! Sonny! It's Ace! No shooting!"

Shooting? Who in the name of all the little green fucks had given Sonny Daye a gun?

And for the little green fucks' sake, *why*?

Before Ace could voice these concerns, he heard the click of the chain and dead bolt locks on the inside of the garage, and Sonny—looking exhausted and crazy-eyed—opened the door.

"Ace?" he said with a smile. "That sure was fast. You called me super early in the morning and I sent Ernie back for some more sleep. We ain't got much sleep, you know—we had some things happen."

From the depths of the sweltering garage came a moan, and Ace was pretty sure his eyes about jumped from his skull.

"Uhm, Sonny? Who's in there?" And, oh God. "And why do you got a gun in your hand?"

Sonny grimaced. "You got your knife on ya, Ace?" he asked.

Ace, in fact, did—he'd pulled it from the bad guy's chest himself. Leaving evidence was never a good idea.

"Yeah—do I need it?"

"Well, I'll give you the gun, but I think the knife might be better. Nobody with a knife ever shot someone on accident."

His hands were shaking, and Ace used tender fingers to take the gun from Sonny's clammy hand and shove it in the back of his jeans with the other one he'd used during the op.

"Sonny? You gonna let me in there to see what's what?"

"Yeah. He's looking a mite feverish, Ace. I got no idea what to do with him."

Ace took a deep breath and shoved the door open, allowing sunlight to penetrate the murky, oil-scented depths of the garage bay.

There was a bad guy there. He was bound and gagged—but he'd been given a pillow and water, and judging by the bottles filled with yellow water, had been allowed to relieve himself when necessary. He had a clean bandage wrapped tightly around his calf, and he was a little pale, but generally looked well cared for, and when Ace walked through the door, he started struggling and protesting from behind the gag.

Sonny kicked him in the wound, which surprised the hell out of Ace, and said, "Hush now. This is the guy you were sent here to kill, so now *he's* going to have to decide what to do with you."

The guy turned gray, and his eyes rolled back in his head and he passed out.

Ace stared at him. "You wounded him?" he asked, struggling for context.

"I wounded him," Sonny admitted. "He and his buddy were going for their guns and I wounded him. And then his buddy was gonna shoot me, so Ernie shot him in the head and got rid of the body and the SUV. But see? Now we got a problem."

"Yeah, we do," Ace muttered. He strode to the guy without preamble and tore off his mask, which brought him abruptly back to consciousness. "Who in the fuck do you work for?" Ace demanded.

"Why the fuck do you care?" the man snarled weakly.

Ace smacked him on the side of the head. So help him, it had been a rough and ragged three days, and he got here and this asshole is bleeding in his garage? And lookit, Sonny and Ernie—they were *toast*. They were exhausted. And as far as Ace could tell, this asshole was the reason why.

"'Cause if you been shut up in here since yesterday, I know a bunch of shit you don't know. Like, I know which mob bosses are dead, which ones are in prison, and which ones are in the wind. So you give me the name of your mob boss and I'll tell you what's gonna happen to you. That simple."

The guy slow-blinked. "Uhm—"

"And you gotta tell me where he got his information. 'Cause that's real fuckin' important. We're not exactly Grand Central here. How did he know who in the fuck we were?"

"'Cause one of his coyotes carrying a shipment of kids asked the people at the gas station store across the street," the guy said sullenly. "We been losing people, and there's been weird shit happening on this stretch of road. He said he'd look to see what was going on. Ivanov said he'd pay extra."

Ace gave a narrow grin. "We got nothin' to do with weird shit goin' on here," he said. "We're just a bunch of people tryin' to make a living."

The guy's mouth worked, and Ace kept his expression serene because he knew the reality of all those times Ernie had known someone was a bad guy and Ace and Jai or Ace and Burton, or sometimes Jai all by himself, had gone off into the dark of night and done invisible deeds was carefully shielded behind his hooded eyes.

"How am I going to explain my dead partner?" the guy asked, the disbelief dripping from his voice.

"You don't need to explain jack to nobody," Ace told him. "All the people *you're* worried about are dead. If I dropped you off in the middle of the night at a shopping center with an urgent care, you could feel the fuck free to forget we existed. You might even want to crawl back into whatever hole you came from and find a different life." He pulled the gun from the back of his pants and shoved the muzzle under the guy's chin. "That might be the only way you get to keep your life at all."

The guy nodded wearily, and Ace took a breath and sized up the situation.

"Either of you sleep?" he asked.

Ernie and Sonny both shook their heads negative.

"Then here's what we're going to do." He had to think a minute because they'd set fire to Ernie's car in the desert, and it wasn't like they had burner cars wandering around. But....

"Sonny, grab the spare plates from the work counter over there and put 'em on your car. I'll put this guy in the trunk and go make the drop. While I'm doing that, Ernie, you watch the front office and tell them we'll be gone until this afternoon, and Sonny, you'll go to bed and sleep for real this time. When I get back, you two switch off and I'll help with the backlog if we get any. How's that?"

They nodded their heads wearily and they got to work.

Ace drove the guy to the bus station in San Diego. There were a lot of homeless people hanging out there—the guy wasn't going to stick out any, and Ace figured one of the officials in the terminal could get him to an urgent care center.

As Ace helped him out of the trunk under a series of overpasses, he made sure the guy was square on the details.

"So," Ace said, slicing through the duct tape Sonny had used on his hands. "What happened to you?"

"I was walking by a stop and rob and got hit by a stray bullet," the guy repeated dully.

"Where was the stop and rob?" Ace continued to probe.

"How in the fuck would I know! I'm from Vegas!"

"What happened to your car?" Ace wasn't clear on this either, but what mattered was what the other guy thought.

"It was stolen," he said. Then he shuddered. "It was a piece of shit anyway."

"And who in the fuck am I?"

The guy looked at him, his eyes sunken into his head. "A guy who's not going to let me walk away again if I bring trouble to his door."

"My boyfriend spared your life," Ace told him. "He didn't have to. Wouldn't have bothered him particularly if he didn't. But I figured you got given a second chance here. Nobody knows who you are. You don't owe markers to anyone. And you and me never fuckin' saw each other. Are we clear?"

The guy nodded dispiritedly, and Ace figured he'd probably lost family in the last two days. Apparently the entire mob world had been turned upside down, and that blown-up house outside of Vegas had been part of it. Well, that was not, strictly speaking, Ace's fault. He cut the ropes holding the bad guy's ankles together, got in the car and merged into traffic, leaving him there among the tent city with a lot of people who had no idea who Ace was and would never care.

Then Ace took off. Ace got takeout on the way home—he figured Ernie and Sonny were probably past cooking, and had to admit, he wanted an early night of it himself.

But not too early.

That night, Ace and Sonny lay in their room, the air conditioning on so loud that Ernie, sleeping in his little add-on room they'd built for Burton probably wouldn't have heard a helicopter if it had landed on the roof.

That was real good because Ace hadn't touched Sonny in nearly three days. Ace ran a hand from this throat down between his pecs to his groin again and again and again, while Sonny closed his eyes, arching his back as Ace moved his palm. Sonny really did like knowing he belonged to Ace, all of him.

"Ace?" he said, his voice getting quavery like it did before Ace absolutely needed to fuck his scrawny little body into the mattress. "I don't like it when you go."

Ace paused midstroke, rubbing a palm over his nipples just to hear Sonny gasp. "Me neither."

"But when you do, we need to do something different from now on," he said.

This was good—Sonny didn't usually say things like this. He waited until Ace figured he needed them.

"Sure. What do we need to do?"

He rolled over to his side and kissed Ace, hard and whole and pure. "We need to say 'I love you' when we're on the phone. I needed them words real bad last night but I knew if I said 'em, you'd be on the next plane home. We need to say 'em even when we're not scared. Just to say 'em. Can we do that?"

"I love you," Ace said, voice almost breaking. God—of all the things he didn't think Sonny had learned yet—he'd learned *this* one, a habit that could feed Ace's soul over days like the last three had been for both of them.

"I know now," he said grinning, "but I meant other—"

Ace lunged across the space between them. "I love you," Ace whispered gruffly, manhandling Sonny until he was underneath Ace, naked, his legs spread. Ace loved foreplay with Sonny Daye, but not tonight. Tonight, Ace grabbed the lubricant from under their pillow and slicked up two fingers while he was still talking. "I love you," he said again, thrusting fingers into Sonny's asshole and shuddering when he groaned.

"I love you too," Sonny muttered, and those words, from him—they made Ace harder and more achy while his chest felt like it was dissolving, and his throat felt too tight to breathe.

Ace shoved his cock inside Sonny, and said it again. "I love you." His voice broke so hard all that came out at the end was a cracked whisper.

"I love you too—fuck me, Ace! Fuck me hard!"

Ace did. So hard. All that worry and fear—and that pride. Oh God—so much pride, 'cause look at Sonny, all that growing he'd just did! All of it went thrusting into his narrow little body while he wrapped his legs around Ace's hips and cried out. "Ace!"

And then Ace couldn't talk anymore, because his body had ramped, raced, reached two hundred miles in six-seconds flat, just like the Ford SHO. Ace was ready to burst inside his man—he wanted Sonny to be filled with everything Ace felt inside his chest.

Sonny moaned, his come spattering between them and that set Ace off, spurting hard, filling Sonny up with all that pride.

They came to on their backs, the air conditioner drying the sweat and come from their bodies, their hearts too full to speak.

"Ace?" Sonny said, his voice rough with passion and love—Ace never doubted it.

"Yeah?"

"How come once I realize it's okay to say the words, it feels like we don't need no others?"

"We'll need 'em eventually," Ace reasoned. "But right now, they're the only ones that're important. Say 'em again."

He chuckled. "Love you, Ace."

"Love you too, Sonny Daye."

It wasn't the name he was born with, but it was so much the man that he was.

PART 7

JAI HAD never been thrown into an op with Burton—but he'd known something was up when Burton sent Ace back down south.

Still, he knew better than to ask questions after the children were all placed in Ace's purloined eldercare shuttle bus and taken somewhere to be reunited with their families. He just took Burton's proffered helmet and folded himself up on the back of the motorcycle, letting Burton whisk him away from the scene with all of the police cars and the big rainbow school bus.

He was unsurprised when Burton pulled into a used car lot, walked in, then came out with the keys to a ten-year-old Crown Victoria.

Jai blinked at the car—powder blue—as Burton flipped him the keys. "I appreciate the leg room, but I hope I don't have to outrun anything faster than an aging beagle."

Burton's lips twitched. "No promises, man. I get some cash to flash on ops, but we're going to need food, so this is what we've got."

Jai sobered. "Your friend, Jason—will the government be angry at you, because you came to help him today?"

Burton shook his head. "I don't see it playing out that way," he said grimly. "Because once somebody tries to go in and do Jason's job..." He blew out a whistle. "Nobody wants that. Jason was like the government's sewage worker. Everyone can crap on him until they realize he's the only one who can make their shit go away."

Jai frowned at him. "That is a terrible way to treat a good man," he said, troubled.

Burton swallowed and nodded. "Well, we're going to do him better than that, but first we need to find a place close to Henry's. I want us close to that place until Jason's at one hundred."

"Da," Jai acknowledged, and then, a little wistfully, asked, "May I call Ace when we are settled? And..." He swallowed. He knew Burton knew about George, but how many people must he be vulnerable in front of about his little nurse?

"I don't see why not," Burton told him. "But I'd call George first or he'll get jealous."

Jai pretended to roll his eyes—but inside he was appreciative. He had been alone for so very long, but being "given" to Sonny and Ace had changed his life in many ways. One of them was that he had friends who were *not* Sonny and Ace. Lee Burton was a good man.

"George does not get jealous," he said. "George knows I want nobody else."

Burton wrinkled his nose and swung one leg up over the back of the motorcycle. "That's good to hear. But maybe you should tell him and not assume he knows. I assumed Ernie knew I would eventually come around, and then you two showed up without any eyebrows at an op you shouldn't have touched with a barge pole, and suddenly I felt the urge to tell him."

Jai grunted. "You are very wise. I am tired and hungry and ready to start our watch from someplace without noise. Where am I going."

Burton gave him hurried directions to a big apartment complex on the Fair Oaks side of J street, a few blocks down on Hurley. He parked his bike in a visitor's slot, then strode in and came out with a key and a number.

"I had the boys in the shop set us up with a safehouse we have here," he said, handing Jai the key. "There's a king-sized and a couch, you can go catch a nap and I'll go talk to Jackson's friend and get some food." He looked Jai up and down. "And some clothes so you can shower. Jean size?"

Jai grimaced. "Thirty-eight-forty," he said, embarrassed. Big. His waist was trim, and that was nice, but he was a tall, big man.

"Must be nice," Burton told him. "I'm a twenty-eight-thirty-two myself."

Jai gave a short laugh. "Sonny has a twenty-six-inch waist. I could snap him like twig."

"Right? Ernie's a twenty-eight, but I swear it's a different twenty-eight." He shook his head, and Jai realized that they had been gossiping like women, and it had been almost fun. "Anyway—I'll be back with supplies. Sleep now while you can, and then you can shower and keep watch while I'm sleeping." Burton sighed. "I am saying, sleeping on a helicopter is not a great way to relax."

"Agreed." After they'd blown up the house with all of the drugs and only a couple of mobsters in it, Burton had told them that Jason was going to need help in Sacramento in a matter of hours—as were Jackson and Ellery. To facilitate *that*, he'd called in a helicopter for transportation and had a motorcycle waiting for him as well as a disposable car waiting for Ace and Jai. It was Ace's idea to trade the disposable car in for a shuttle, so they could get Jason's charges to safety. Burton had not been pleased, but he had to admit, it had worked out well.

"So, you find our digs, shower if you want to—I'll be back in two hours. Deal?"

"Da."

Jai didn't miss the reference to the shower more than once. He agreed. Too much time in the grime and heat and… well, he had a big body and probably a big smell.

By the time he'd gotten out, his phone had charged and he called Ace first because if he talked to Ace, he knew what he could say to George.

"How is it going?" he asked without preamble.

"Buddy, you do not want to know." There was a certain grimness in Ace's voice. "And if you talk to Burton, tell him next time I want a heads-up about what's waiting for me when I get back. I'm not a little kid and Sonny's stronger than he looks."

That alone had Jai sitting up in bed, the sheets wrapped around his waist, alarmed. "What in the—"

"Have Burton tell you when he gets back—and tell him that the thing that went down is settled now. I dropped our straggler off near an urgent care and with a shitty story. I'll give Burton his name later, but right now, I gotta get home. Sonny and Ernie are more fuckin' tired'n I am right now."

"I am boggled as to how this happened," Jai said, not even wanting to hear the story before he flew down to Victoriana. "What should I tell George?"

"Tell him you'll be there after Burton's done with you," Ace said, sounding surprised. "Man, all I'm saying is you have earned yourself a week off. Sonny and Ernie held down the fort just fine, so, you know, sleep. Scare small animals. Tell George hi from Jai." Ace snickered at that last one, and Jai tried not to smirk. It was hard, though, when his boss—his friend—was giving him carte blanche to be with his boyfriend in spite of a whole lot of trouble that had just tromped through their house.

"My head hurts," Jai admitted, surprised because he didn't admit to physical discomfort unless it could hinder him doing his job. "I don't know how you're moving."

"I caught a nap on the helicopter down," Ace admitted. "I'll be fine. You nap now if you got the chance. Burton's probably got shit all figured out."

"We are currently in a safehouse where—" He was going to say it—he was going to say "near Constance"—but then it occurred to him that a parabolic mic was pretty damned easy to use and that could be a reason Ace didn't want to give Jai details about what happened with him and Sonny either. So he finished with "A safehouse where I can sleep."

Ace's grunt told Jai he wasn't fooled. "Good. You do that. Give George a holler, though. I'm sure he's worried."

"Da," Jai told him gruffly, and it was a sign of how tired he was that he let what happened at the garage go for the moment, accepting Ace's reassurance that he had it under control. Ace would tell him if it wasn't. He might downplay it, that terse military man's vocabulary serving him in good stead. *Not a big deal, Jai, but half my leg and most of my kidney is blown across the desert, you wouldn't want to come here and calm Sonny down while I go into a coma, right?* "You tell us if anything else happens."

"If it comes up," Ace said, his voice so mild it almost put Jai to sleep. Almost.

He signed off, tired, and instead of talking to George, which could get long and comforting, he texted him instead.

Children are back where they belong. Burton and I are staying to look after friend.

George's response was so very *George*, really.

Was he hurt?

He'd been shot—Jai had seen that. His shoulder and arm were bloody, and he was bleeding through his Kevlar, which indicated some knifework there too. And his face looked like he'd been through a war.

Da. He risked much to get those children to their parents.

Are all the bad guys taken care of?

He sighed. Probably not, if Ace had dropped one of them off at an urgent care and Jason had been attacked in transit.

Nyet. That is why we are staying for a few.

Oh! I have a few days off—I could trade some shifts, turn it into a week, and come stay with you!

Jai stared at the screen, a part of him getting so excited about having George by his side, being a quiet hero in his own way, that his eyes actually burned. More and more, the long weekends with George were not enough. More and more, Jai wanted George to come home to Jai, in his neat little apartment, so they could eat together or watch movies. But why would George leave a job in which he was respected to live in the desert?

Until Jai could answer that question, he wouldn't ask the other.

It is not safe, little George, Jai replied regretfully. *We are here as weapons and surveillance. If you are to take vacation days for me, I would rather we spend them doing fun things. Like camping.*

Or getting a hotel by the beach, George filled in. Jai stared at the words hungrily.

Da. When I am done here, perhaps we can do that. He pressed Send and then paused, feeling shy even as he typed the words. *I would love a vacation with you that does not involve tents and bonfires.*

Me too. Love you, Jai—don't forget that.

One does not forget a miracle. Good night, little George.

And then he turned his phone off and fell hard and fast asleep.

He slept for a solid two hours, awakening when Burton shook his arm. His eyes shot open, but he knew where he was. Asleep, yes. Dead to the world? Not so much.

"You smell better," Burton told him dryly. "Now it's time for me to do the same. There are fresh jeans and T-shirts in the bag on the chair. I set up a camera and a scope through the window to keep an eye on the place where the boys are staying. We're inside the complex, but their staircase can be accessed outside. It can't be helped. Take a good look while I'm showering, and don't forget to eat."

With that, Burton disappeared into the bathroom, a duffel over his shoulder, and Jai rolled his eyes. Smart man, Lee Burton, but he often forgot his friends weren't in the military and didn't take orders well. Ace could give a good order too, but Ace was also good at assuming Jai wasn't stupid and wouldn't starve with a perfectly good pizza sitting on the cheap Formica table in the apartment.

Jai felt marginally more charitable after he'd dressed and eaten. The clothes fit well and the pizza was excellent, and there was a chair set up in front of the camera on a tripod, so Jai was very much in a good place.

When Burton emerged a few minutes later, also fresh and clean, water droplets sparkling on his shaved black curls, Jai could ask him in a *civilized* fashion about what had gone down at the garage.

"Oh God. Yeah, that," Burton muttered, getting a bottle of water from a flat he'd brought in. "Yeah—Ernie told me while we were driving up this morning. On the one hand, it was good because it kept me awake, but on the other…." He shuddered and smothered a yawn. "Apparently the coyote you guys intercepted had time to call in you and Ace to his bosses, the guys we blew up in Vegas and helped to take down this morning. Anyway, two yo-yos showed up at the garage last night ready to take Ace out. Ernie killed one, Sonny wounded the other, and they kept him in the garage waiting for Ace to get there and deal with it. That's why I sent him back." Burton grimaced. "Otherwise, I wouldn't have minded three of us. Rivers told me his assistant, Henry, lives in the apartment downstairs and kitty-corner from the one where Jason's staying. I've got his number—he's the guy—"

"Who drove Constance away," Jai interrupted. "I remember. So that makes sense, why we are here. Like you said, good fortune the military had a safehouse. Sonny and Ernie were unharmed?" He may not carry a torch for Sonny anymore, but he did still care for the damaged little man. And Ernie had become a good friend.

"Yeah—a little freaked-out, and I honestly don't know what Ace is gonna do with the wounded mobster—"

"Let him loose by an urgent care," Jai informed him. "After letting him know his bosses are all dead, and he will be too if he shows up again."

"He did *what*?" Burton demanded. "Are you kidding me?"

"Nyet—you talk to him."

"Oh my God. Fine." Burton let out an exhausted sigh. "After I wake up," he muttered. "Ernie wouldn't have let him do that if the consequences were bad."

"Da," Jai agreed.

"Bed," Burton told him.

"Da," Jai agreed.

Burton's mouth twisted. "You know, you could be one of my favorite op partners. You and Ace are like, my favorite team." And suddenly Jai could read the thing he wasn't saying.

"Besides Constance, who is also your friend."

Burton nodded, yawning again. "Yeah," he said, dispiritedly. "I'm trusting you with my brother's life here. Let me know if you see anything."

Jai nodded, eyes wide and sincere.

He got that, having brothers you would die for. He hadn't in the mob, but he sure did now. With a little grunt, he settled himself into the chair and started his share of the surveillance. In the corner of his mind, he wondered if they could pull Ace and Sonny up here too.

PART 8

ONE WEEK after Jason Constance had been placed in the apartment with Henry's friends, Burton was tired, cranky, and feeling very bad about dragging the stoic Jai into this mess.

Ace had sent Ernie up to help, and Ernie, at least, had been able to tell them when they could sleep because he knew in his bones that nothing would happen that night. Unfortunately, Ernie's witchy thing was on high alert too.

"There's eyes out there," he'd say. "They're not doing anything tonight, but they're out there."

"Whose eyes?" Burton would ask—they had it down to a ritual by now. "Ours or theirs?"

"Both," Ernie said, like he was thinking hard. "There are soldiers *looking* for him, and they're not sure why, and there are mobsters who know where he is, but they're afraid of all the muscle he's got around him." Ernie laughed the last time he said this, like he'd just read a funny meme on his phone. "He doesn't know they're porn stars."

"I find it difficult to believe myself," Jai had interjected, sounding just as laconic as always.

Burton blew out a breath through his nose. "Man, I should send you home," he said, not for the first time. "You have a week with your boyfriend waiting, and you have been like, a colossal good sport here—"

"Your friend is a good man," Jai said, and Burton was glad he'd gotten to know Jai in the past few years, because he knew he was sincere. "He deserves friends to make sure it is all well."

Which is exactly what Ace had said when Burton had apologized for leaving Ace and Sonny without two employees in a shoestring operation. Then Ace had blown his mind by saying they'd actually asked Alba for a recommendation for someone they could pay under the table. The girl they'd rescued earlier on in the summer, the one whose parents had been taken away by ICE—Alba's mother was fostering her, and the girl didn't start school for another couple of weeks. She'd been asking to earn her keep, and while it wasn't something Burton couldn't understand—his parents had been solid middle-class and he'd grown up thinking that room and board were a given—Alba's mommy had gotten it completely. According to Alba, her mother would have been fine if the girl had just hung out and been a girl, but when your whole world has been displaced, it was hard to trust in that type of kindness. So Ace paid the girl, the girl paid Alba's mother, and Alba's mother put money away to help the children travel when their parents could be found.

Burton got it—but that didn't make him feel any less guilty.

"Well, if nobody makes a move soon, he's going to be a good man with only Henry to have his six," Burton muttered to himself. "We can't do this much longer." It was easier with three of them. Everybody got eight hours of sleep if they needed it, and a chance to go out and exercise. They took four-hour shifts, two hours at a time, one person at the scope or binoculars and the other standing back from the window taking the long view. On the one hand it was as thin a stakeout as Burton had ever been on, but on the other, it felt like overkill. It wasn't like anything was *happening*, was it?

Of course, there really *were* a lot of super fit, handsome young men coming and going from that apartment. Not *this* morning, of course. This morning, Henry was out on a case with Jackson, his boyfriend was at the hospital, and most of the young men were either at school or at a number of jobs that each one seemed to hold. The only exception was a sloe-eyed, dark-haired, slender young man with a quiet smile who Henry had identified as "Cotton."

"Cotton?" Burton asked, surprised. "That's a name?"

Henry had given him a flat look. "Yeah, Lee. All sex workers use their real names when performing. It's totally safe."

And for the first time in a *long* time, Lee Burton felt his cheeks heat in a blush. Oops. There were some things he knew, but apparently lots of things he did not.

But Cotton was the only name they had for the kid—and he seemed dedicated to Jason Constance like nobody Burton had ever seen. He only left the apartment when somebody else was there to care for Jason, and he seemed to be the one on for getting him supplies. Burton had seen him come in loaded with extra clothes, extra bedding—even food, which was only notable because Burton didn't see a lot of food going into that apartment. He didn't even want to think about how they all stayed that impossibly muscled and thin at the same time.

And this afternoon, at one-thirty p.m., Cotton was the only person in the apartment with Jason Constance, and Burton was thinking this whole idea was a bust.

Until Ernie fell out of his chair and said, "They're making a move! Now!"

Jai was up like a shot away from the scope and out the door, and Burton ran hot on his heels. Across the quad, they could see a couple of squat, muscular legs hammering up the staircase of the porn stars' apartment, and while Jai and Burton were both running full-out, Burton knew they weren't going to make it.

He screamed, "*Jason, get down!*" as the guy hit the landing, and then Jai rounded the corner to go up the stairs and staggered back, a knife in his shoulder.

Burton was surprised enough to pause, because this man had become his brother in the last week, but Jai was shooing him up the stairs. "Go!" he shouted. "Go!"

At the top of the stairs, the guy with the knife was shouldering his way through the door. He was built like a freight train, and apparently he was motivated, so with a wrenching, splintering sound, he went cracking through the door and tumbling into the apartment. Burton—knife drawn—raced hot on his heels.

He hit the landing and pivoted and saw the man standing, legs apart, in the process of aiming his gun. Burton didn't even need to see where he was aiming it to throw his own knife cleanly at the man's gun arm before he could fire.

The guy grunted, but stayed standing, switching his gun to his other hand. Burton was raising his own Beretta when he saw another knife—this one a chef's knife—come flying through the air to bounce off the guy's nose.

That made him stagger, and Burton had time to aim his own gun and call, "Drop it, or you're over."

The man—squat all over, nose, eyes, ears, neck, legs, torso, all of it compressed into one mean muscle—gave him a dismissive glance and then turned to shoot again, and Burton dropped him in his tracks, and even with a silencer, the gun's reports seemed unnaturally loud in the quiet apartment complex.

He turned his head to make sure everything was okay and saw, to his surprise, that shadow-eyed wraith of a kid standing in front of an exhausted, dead-on-his-feet Jason Constance in the tiny apartment kitchen that sat practically behind the door.

He'd damaged their dead guy's nose with a thrown chef's knife just before Burton had shot.

"Oh fuck," the skinny kid breathed, staring at the dead man. "Fuck. Jason. Jason, there's a *dead man on our carpet!*"

"Jason?" Burton queried.

The kid glanced up at him, and Burton grimaced. Not a bad-looking kid, but fragile—Burton had seen that from surveillance.

Burton held the gun pointed up and grunted at the dead guy at his feet before kicking the gun out of his hand, holstering his own weapon, and glancing around the apartment. "Shit," he said. "Jason, do we have any idea who this is?"

Jason put two hands on the kid's shoulders and pushed him to the side. "Lee?"

Burton gave a tight smile of relief. "Sir! Damn. That asshole broke ranks and charged the steps. I swear we didn't see where he was coming from."

Jason nodded and glanced around the apartment. "Well, props for being prepared," he said, shaking his head. "He would have had us. Thanks, Burton."

"Thank Ernie," Burton said. "But thank him later, after we get you somewhere safe. We've got to bug out, sir—"

"I'm coming with him," the kid—Cotton?—said.

Burton looked at him in surprise. "You're what?"

"He's barely okay. I've been nursing him for a week. He's not going anywhere without somebody who knows what antibiotics he's taking and what painkillers he can have. He's not all right yet. You can't simply take him somewhere and expect him to do… to do—" Cotton waved his hands. "—whatever you did there. Not until he's better!"

Burton paused. "Sir?" he said, voice soft. A civilian, but one apparently familiar with the sitch. It was Constance's call.

"I want him out of danger," Jason said, and Lee could hear him desperately trying to assume command. "He should stay—fuck."

Cotton turned in time to catch Jason as his knees went out.

"Goddammit," Jason muttered. "Not now. You should stay here."

"Not until you're better," Cotton said. "I get it. You're a hero. But you don't get to go be a hero until your body can keep up with the rest of you."

"Fuck!" Jason rubbed at his eyes with his palm. "Cotton, this is not going to be safe for you."

Cotton looked up at Burton, supporting Jason as he led him toward the couch. "I can have him dressed and ready in fifteen minutes. We've got go-bags packed. Jackson warned me. I just need to put together his medical supplies."

Burton nodded. "I've got a man down outside. I need to make sure he gets to the hospital, and Ernie can get him home. I'll be back." He grimaced.

"And make it ten. I don't know where this asshole came from, but I don't imagine we've got much more time before another one shows up."

When he got down the stairs, Jai was struggling to get to his feet, Ernie at his elbow, snarling at him. "No—no, don't take it out. No, don't. Don't. Because I said so. Dammit—*Dammit, Cruller, make him listen to me!*"

Jai gave Ernie a pat-on-the-head sort of look. "It is in my shoulder," he said patiently. "If I take it out, I will not gush blood and die."

"But it looks serrated," Ernie snapped. "Which means you *could* irreparably damage something. Goddammit, could you just listen to me, you big doofus? I *like* you and I would rather you not *die*."

Jai looked at Burton in frustration. "Can we not do something about him?"

Burton nodded. "Yeah. Ernie, I'm going to give you keys to Lance's car—and you're going to take Jai to the hospital."

"What are you going to do?" Ernie asked, confused.

"I'm going to get Jason the fuck out of here, and then I'll contact you with more info later."

For a moment, Ernie's expression was Burton's greatest fear. Lost, like one of the kittens he protected with such dedication. And then, just when Burton's heart was going to crumble, when he was sure he'd lost Ernie's devotion, that the last cranky week of close quarters and no physical contact had broken him, Ernie's dark brows snapped together and his spine straightened.

"Get me the keys and I'll clear out mine and Jai's stuff," he said. "I don't want to leave him in a car without AC."

Burton almost cried. All the shit he'd seen, all the shit he'd done, and watching Ernie pull himself together and be *that guy*, he almost wept in gratitude.

"I owe you so much, baby," he said, not caring who heard him. "So much."

Ernie flashed a grin. "Don't tell me that," he chided. "I can do so many things with you, you have no idea."

Burton squeezed his eyes shut and then opened them and pivoted on the wooden staircase landing, trying to get a move on.

IT TOOK them ten minutes to clear out, which, considering the extent of the flustercluck, should have earned them all medals.

Ernie and Jai were gone first, but after checking the area for other assassins and loading Cotton and Jason into the Crown Vic with emergency duffels packed, including everything Constance would need medically,

Burton called one of the members of his team back in the hidden base and gave him the low-down.

"My package has been retrieved," he said shortly, knowing that Owens would understand. "Must hide until Christmas. Shopping center is a bit of a mess."

"How big of a mess?" Owens asked, and in the background, Burton could hear the clicking of the keyboard.

"A body that needs to be identified, in an apartment that's going to get very busy very soon," Burton said, glancing at Cotton in the rearview for confirmation.

The young man nodded and then checked to make sure Jason was propped on enough pillows to be comfortable. For his part, Jason had his arm extended, like he expected Cotton to curl up in his embrace.

When the kid did exactly that, Burton almost swerved into an oncoming lane.

He pulled his attention back to traffic—and the matter at hand.

"Can you maybe keep people out of there for an hour?" his contact said, sounding a little panicked.

"Well, yeah. But I gotta get off the phone now and make some calls."

"Where are you delivering the package?" Owens asked, and Burton blew out a breath.

"I'll let you know," Burton told him, and was half-expecting the "Hey!" on the other end of the line.

"Yeah, sorry," he said, clipped. "But I want the package safe and anonymous and guarded. I'll tell you when I'm certain it's all okay."

Owens blew out a breath. "I hear you," he said. "I'll have your cleanup in an hour—if you can keep it all clear for us, that'll be great."

"Roger that."

Burton's next call was to Henry.

"'Llo. Who's this?"

And Burton was on his last nerve. "Who do you think, dumbass!"

"Oh! Burton! Sorry about that. Dude. What's up?"

"I've got Jason and Cotton, but there's a dead guy in the front room of that shitty apartment. I've got someone working on it, but I need you to keep your guys clear of there."

"Jackson, duck!" Henry called out and then swore. "Goddammit, doesn't anybody tell the truth? 'No, Ellery, I've gone straight, Ellery!' If he's so straight, why's his place guarded by the shiny dome and kilt mafia!"

"I can see you're busy," Burton said, voice dry.

"Fuck!" There was the sound of flesh on flesh, and then a *whoomp!* "Nice," Henry said, his voice carrying. "So I take it we're not representing this asshole?"

"Wait," Jackson Rivers could be heard over whatever they were doing. "I need to talk to this guy first. It's not his fault he's seven feet tall and pissed off!"

"Sure it's not," Henry muttered into the phone. "So, dead guy in the flophouse? Are you sure?"

"Well, he won't be there if you can keep your kids out of there for an hour or so."

Henry grunted. "Well, the only one who might be iffy is Randy. He's shooting a scene today, and he's always done early, because that kid could come six times in an hour and still be ready to hump a hole in the sink, you know what I mean?"

"I wish I didn't."

"Yeah, so do I. But don't sweat it. I'll call up John and see if we can't make sure he stays at the studio for a while. Everyone else *should* be gone until five-ish."

Oh, thank God. "Awesome," Burton said sincerely. "Also, Ernie took your boyfriend's car. You said he could, and he did, and now Jai's probably got blood all over it."

"What?" Henry's voice cracked. "I'm going to have to explain blood in his car to *Lance*? Are you kidding me?"

"Uhm, yeah. Sorry, Henry. I'll see if we can get that cleaned."

Burton's head was starting to hurt, so he didn't even bother to end the call—he just clicked Off. Behind him, he heard Jason chuckle weakly.

"Today is just not your day," he said.

Burton was at a stoplight, so he checked in the rearview mirror. Constance was sitting, eyes closed, face an ashen gray, and the kid leaning on him was touching his forehead worriedly.

"He got a fever?" Burton asked. He knew that infection had been a problem, because Lance had kept him updated, but seeing his boss—usually hale, hearty, and active—look this weak sort of shook him.

"It's gone down in the last two days," Cotton muttered. "Where are you taking us?"

In the back of his head, Burton remembered asking Ellery Cramer for a favor before everything had shaken out. "I've got one more phone call to make," he said. "And by then, we'll already be on the road."

PART 9

"I WAS holding the knife," Jai said evenly. "And I tripped and fell."

The doctor gave him a flat-eyed glance, and Jai tried to smile. Like most people when faced with that smile, the man turned a little pale, and then he made an irritated notation on his tablet.

"Fine—I can put that in our records, but a police officer will have to sign off on it. You can't just walk into the ER with a bowie knife embedded in your shoulder and not expect questions, Mr....."

"Sartov," Jai lied, because that was the fake ID he had on him. "Dmitri Sartov."

The doctor gave him another narrow-eyed look. "Sure. Sure that's your name. Look, let me get our local officer here to—"

"He's fine, Connaghey," Sean Kryzynski said, limping in with a buffed and polished younger man at his side. "No need—Sartov is a department asset. Is he going to be okay?"

The doctor—a thin, balding, worried man in his fifties who had probably seen too much, gnawed at his lower lip. "Yes—the wound will need care, though. Is there anybody at home who can change a bandage?"

Jai thought yearningly of George, and how they'd been texting madly about taking some time off together when this op ended.

"Da," he said, not sure if he could keep the wistfulness out of his voice. "There is someone, yes."

"Then if you could sign this off, Sean, we'll be okay."

Kryzynski—a friend of Jackson Rivers and Ellery Cramer—took the tablet and gave the requisite signature, then waved the doctor off.

"There," he said quietly to Ernie and Jai. "I just expensed your medical bills. He'll be back with some pain meds and antibiotics, and then we can play musical cars and you can go."

Jai regarded Kryzynski narrowly. "Last I heard, you were in a hospital bed. What are you doing here?"

"Killing himself," the young man at his side said bitterly. "Did you really have to—"

"This man is a hero, Billy," Kryzynski said softly. "You weren't there when Rivers told the story. This man, and this young man's boyfriend, just saved a busload of kids—and I'm pretty sure they saved Cotton's life."

Billy's eyes got large. "Cotton—?"

"I'll tell you later." Kryzynski took the careful breath of one for whom breathing is a new luxury. "Right now, let's get me to their car and them to ours. I promised Ellery we'd clean the blood out of their car and give them something that would let them get to LA today."

"Except our car is your doctor friend's," Jai said.

"You got blood in Lance's Mazda?" Billy asked, aghast. Then understanding dawned. "Which is why we need to get the upholstery cleaned. Okay. I get it. It's all coming together." He shook his head. "You live a very interesting life, Sean. But you still need to get home for your nap."

Sean gave the kid an exasperated look. "We're getting there," he wheezed.

Jai eyed him with quiet disgust. "Everybody. Must everybody be a hero?"

"You are telling me," said the man at Sean's side. "Anyway, here." He dug into the pocket of his faded jeans, the action stretching his T-shirt across a chest that had been molded out of marble. "Here." He dropped the keys in Ernie's hand. "Now you give me Lance's."

"I can't believe I'm giving up my car for a week," Sean said weakly. "Love that car."

Jai grinned at him. "What kind of car is it?"

"Dodge Charger." He sighed. "I only wish it was circa 1970, but no. Modern model."

"You should try a Ford SHO," Jai told him, missing Ace's beautiful celebration of metal, oil, and will. "But we will treat your car well."

"Trust us," Ernie said. "This is the guy who helped Ace and Sonny make Jackson's car." He paused. "Before, you know. The thing."

Sean's eyes lit up, and Jai knew how they'd pay this nice policeman back.

The doctor returned with the prescription then, and Sean and Billy made their way out.

"Lovers?" Jai asked idly, his shoulder aching. He was looking forward to the pain medication very much.

"Not yet," Ernie said. His narrow face—tense and worn after this last week—relaxed slightly. "But soon. They're good for each other."

"Those are good stories," Jai murmured. "I am glad to hear." He was tired. A week of sitting, with only the occasional PT for any sort of outlet, had taken its toll. And when he did go outside, it was to a suburb/city. No large buildings, only cracked roads and strip malls, trees and hurricane fences. Lots of stores, the occasional park, and too many boring cars stuffed between stoplights like sausages. Jai had been born near St. Petersburg—big buildings, many people, great wealth and great poverty cheek by jowl, and long winters of bone-crushing cold. So odd that in this suburban no-man's-land, he found himself missing the desert instead. His apartment building was much like the one Burton had secured for them. It housed a cluster of two-story squares with stairwells and no discernible rhyme or reason to the layout. But he knew—always knew—that outside the environs was the desert, stretching to the small shopping center and the block that encased the schools. The three levels of grammar, middle, and high school all sat on the same stretch, sharing a track and a football field with a small side-yard marked for toys for the younger children.

And beyond that was more desert.

A man could get lost in the desert. A man could be free there. And while Jai was not nearly so solitary as to want to wander out into Death Valley and become one with the sand, he was soothed by the idea that the only people who knew who he was were the people he wanted to know—and that there weren't so many people out in the world as to fill up all that space.

He missed his desert. He missed his job. And he really, really wanted to see George.

"I'm glad to tell them," Ernie said, yawning. "And I'll be super glad to get back home. You ready, big guy? I've got some driving to do."

"Da," Jai said on a yawn of his own. "Some painkillers, and we are good to go."

The Charger was comfortingly loud and it had some leg room, and bless Ernie, he knew how to fly down I-5 like policemen weren't a thing. He wasn't as reckless as Ace—and he certainly never pushed the car to its limits—but once he put on some music, he seemed to lapse comfortably into the Ernie zone, and he'd be slowing the car down before Jai could see the red lights in front of them. He probably didn't even know he was doing it, but Jai could close his eyes and sleep as he did with nobody else besides Ace. There was just trust there.

As there was surprise and a little disappointment when Jai opened his eyes and saw that they had swept past LA and had gone all the way down to I-15 and were in Victoriana.

"Oh," he said, his voice falling leadenly. "I thought we would be stopping in LA."

"Yeah, well, I called ahead to make sure we wouldn't be wading through traffic," Ernie said. "George isn't at home right now, so we thought it would be better if I brought you here."

"Who is we?" Jai asked, feeling grumpy.

At that moment, there was a tap on his window, and Ernie unlocked the door.

And George practically fell into his lap.

He didn't kiss and wiggle like a puppy—George was a relatively sane human being. He just sat there for a moment, head on Jai's good shoulder, and breathed.

"Stabbed?" he asked carefully, like he was keeping his voice in check.

"It was only my shoulder," Jai mumbled. Oh, he felt good. So good. "What are you doing here?"

"Ernie called me. I called my boss, he gave me the time off, and I grabbed my cat and came over. A week, big man. You and me get a week."

Jai wrapped his good arm carefully around George's shoulders and almost groaned with the decadence. "But first," he said, tired and hungry and hurting, "I need to get out of this car."

It took all three of them—Ernie to push and George to pull—to help him out of the low-slung vehicle. His legs ached and he felt a little woozy.

"Whoa there," George said, concerned. "Let me guess—no food, too much pain meds?"

"Is like you are medical professional," Jai said sourly.

"Yeah, well, I've just seen how you work. Which is why I stopped for supplies on the way here—and by the way, I had to take Jingle into the store with me in the carrier, so you can imagine the bitching."

"From the cat or the management?" Ernie asked curiously.

"The cat," George said, nodding. "Walmart did not even fucking notice, if you can believe that. Anyway, we've got lots of premade pizza, already cooked for tonight, and all you've got to do is make it up those stairs."

They got Jai up the stairs and onto his couch, where he sagged with relief. "Gah!" he muttered. "I am useless. Ernie, are you okay to drive home?"

"Going to Ace's," he said briefly. "Already cleared it with him. Sonny and Ace have been looking after my cats—had to call and check."

Jai managed to give him a questioning glance. "The cats are good?" he asked carefully.

Ernie gave a sweet smile. "Spoiled rotten. Apparently every night while Ace is closing up, Sonny goes out there with Duke and locks Duke in the bathroom and makes love to every cat that will let him touch it. Ace says the kittens in the garage are doing great—running around, getting into trouble—and Sonny moved them inside to the spare bathroom because he kept fretting about it getting too hot in there. I tried to tell him that I'd parked them by a vent and they were getting lots of air and shade, all they needed was water, but Sonny wasn't having it."

Jai felt something in him loosen. "Sonny—he will surprise you sometimes."

"In the best of ways," Ernie agreed. He stood from his perch on the corner of Jai's couch, and, unexpectedly, clasped Jai's hand in both of his.

"Enjoy your week off, Jai. Let yourself be cared for. You're a good friend and a good colleague, and you have earned your rest."

"Pizza?" George asked, because he'd been bustling in the kitchen this whole time.

Ernie smiled slightly and shook his head. "Sonny made me mac and cheese with hot dogs. He thinks it's my favorite—he missed me."

And with that, he slid out the door. Jai listened, eyes half-closed, and heard his feet patter down the stairs and the roar of the Charger, and then George presented him with a plate of food, which he demolished before he could even acknowledge it was there.

THAT NIGHT, they lay in bed underneath the ceiling fan and each told his story of the past two weeks. Jai had not realized George had been so close to danger when the children had been in his care. George had not realized that the tired officer who had been driving the busload of children had been wounded so badly that he was still sick.

Jai's voice and story wandered in and out—he was aware, but much like he trusted Ace and Ernie to drive, he trusted George would not make fun of him for being tired and loopy from painkillers and thoughtful.

"I missed you," he said baldly, after a silence had fallen. "You being here, in my apartment, it is a miracle."

"I think so too." George let out a breath. "Jai?"

"Da?"

"Why don't you ask me to move out here with you?"

Jai closed his eyes, the outline of his tiny apartment still imprinted on his eyelids. "Because I live in a small apartment, and my friends are all criminals—"

"But good men," George said.

"But you have a good life," Jai told him. There was a "whump" and the cat leapt onto the bed and made his big fluffy self comfortable between the two of them. "You are respectable, and you have friends, and—"

"There is a small hospital out here," George said, interrupting. "It's mostly an emergency room, a birthing room, and a couple of ICU equipped rooms, with a would-be surgery. It's got maybe fifty people working there—doctors, nurses, support staff, custodial staff, total. I put in an application and they said they might have an opening in a couple of months."

Jai made a soft moan. "You would do this?" he asked, his eyes hot and bright.

"Of course I would," George said, his voice choked. In the darkness he felt George's touch feathering across his cheek. "I… I mean, we could look for a larger place, but Jai—you and your criminal friends have become a very big part of my life." George cupped his cheek. "I… unless you don't want me here—"

Jai couldn't help the wetness that slipped through. "More than anything," he said gruffly. So many reasons not to ask George to do this. So many reasons this was a bad career move, a move that took George from his family, from his friends—from civilization.

But Jai was on empty after the last couple weeks of missing George, of wanting his touch, his voice in the dark. He'd seen Burton and Ernie touch each other casually as they'd moved throughout the surveillance apartment, and his heart had hurt, each time.

His entire body ached with the need to have this person near him.

"So, I should prepare to move out here?" George tested again.

"I should say no," Jai murmured, thinking of Sonny and Ernie and the bad men showing up at their door. Thinking about the blood and the violence he'd seen in Sacramento, the random assassin charging up those apartment stairs to splatter Jason Constance's brain like a watermelon. He captured George's hand and placed a tender kiss in the palm of it.

"Will you?" George asked, and Jai could tell his heart was in his throat with the fear of this.

And that's what put Jai over.

"Nyet," Jai rumbled, cupping George's hand to his cheek again. "I will not say no. But… but you need to respect my friends' needs, da? To not ask too many questions? To be willing, should the police come one day, to say, 'I did not know, officer. He seemed like such a good man.'"

George let out a broken chuckle. "How about, 'He wouldn't tell me what he did, officer, but I assume he had a good reason. He's the best of men, and I trust that what he did, he did to protect someone. That's the way he works.'"

Jai's bitter smile was also sincere. "You must acknowledge that this might not keep me from prison."

"If you acknowledge it's true," George murmured. He pulled his hand away from Jai's cheek for a moment, and with some rustling and a heave, he lifted the indignant Jingle off the bed and onto the floor. Then he wriggled closer to Jai, close enough to spread his hand against Jai's heart.

"Such a good heart," George said gruffly. "I need to know *you* know it's good too."

"You love me," Jai murmured.

"Da." Jai didn't have to open his eyes to know George's lips were carved into a slight smile.

"Then my heart must be good. I will protect a man with such a good heart."

"Good," George murmured, and then he captured Jai's mouth with his own, their kiss salty and hard. Jai opened his mouth, drifting in and out of sleep for a moment, but George pulled away, laughing.

"Sleep," he mumbled. "But you'd better be ready to put out tomorrow."

Jai smiled even as he felt himself drifting away. "We will need a gag, little George. I will make you scream, just for me."

"No man I'd rather scream for," George told him, and Jai wanted to chuckle, but he was already asleep, dreaming of delights to come.

Keep Reading for an Excerpt from
Fish Out of Water
Fish Out of Water Series, Book #1
by Amy Lane

ELLERY CRAMER knew his tie was perfect, but he checked it anyway as he got off the elevator on the fourth floor. Pfeist, Langdon, Harrelson & Cooper was one of the best criminal defense firms in Sacramento, and it didn't get that way because its employees neglected details.

And Ellery wanted his name on that list of partners so bad.

When he'd first gotten his degree, he'd dreamed of opening his own practice, but no. His sister had run numbers on that—she was an actuary—and had determined that his best chance for financial success lay with hooking up as a junior associate and working his way up to partner.

Six years after signing on with Pfeist, Langdon, Harrelson & Cooper, he was one of their most trusted trial lawyers, and he was conscious of the honor.

He was also conscious of his suit.

Today he wore the silver pinstripe, which, although it didn't complement his dark hair and eyes at all, *did* make him look severe and imposing, and he was all for that. He'd spent two hours cross-examining a witness that day and had enjoyed making the guy—a police officer, no less—crumble like a cookie.

Ellery did so enjoy his petty torments.

But as much as he enjoyed destroying police officers on the stand, he wouldn't ever mess with Leonard Pfeist's secretary. Nope—Ellery was *very* good at knowing who to toady, and the secretary was the heart of the firm.

"Good afternoon, Jade," he said pleasantly and was greeted with a heavy-eyed scowl in return. Ellery gaped at her, uncertain of how to respond. Granted, he and the firm's legal secretary weren't close. Jade was a little too rough around the edges for Ellery to really warm up to. He got that Leonard Pfeist, the most junior of the partners, did the hiring, and *he* seemed to rely on Jade's street-smart, tart-mouthed presence, but Ellery had been brought up conservatively. Between Jade's unapologetically vibrant appearance and the female sexuality that rolled off her like perfume, her whole presence made him *very* uneasy.

But he'd never seen her look like she could rip someone's head off with her bare hands, and that was the way she was looking at him now.

"Took you long enough," she snapped. "Did or did your schedule *not* say you were supposed to be in the office an hour ago?"

"I was in court!" Ellery objected. "It went—"

"I know when it went to. And I know you stopped for coffee and probably to schmooze that judge you're always trying to flirt with. What you *needed* to do was to be *here* because you've got someone here who needs your fucking help!"

Ellery stared at her, his mouth opening and closing in surprise. Smart-mouthed, yes, but never insubordinate—never *rude*. "Uh—"

"Take it easy on him, J—he didn't know."

Oh great. *Him.*

Ellery stared at Jackson Rivers with a distaste that had nothing to do with the man's looks. Dark blond hair, green eyes, and a square jaw—if the remains of an adolescent acne problem hadn't roughened his skin, he'd look like a movie star. As it was, he appeared weathered and capable—stringy, no-bullshit muscle and an uncompromising glare. Jackson was the law firm's head PI, and while the job was not supposed to be as glamorous as television made it look, Ellery had always wondered if maybe Jackson Rivers didn't break a few rules to be so goddamned good at what he did.

Need a witness background? Yeah, sure, he was there. But he was there with the *dirt*—the stuff that made the witness unreliable, the stuff that Ellery could use to keep a client out of prison.

But it was just not fair that he was so goddamned *beautiful*. That broke a rule or two that Ellery really loathed. Jackson was good-looking and personable. He and Jade had history and kinship; they seemed to speak a different language sometimes. Jackson would swagger into the office and shake hands with Leonard Pfeist and flirt with the other secretaries and face the clients, confident and unafraid....

It made Ellery feel like he had in school. Exceptionally singular, unexceptionally alone.

"He don't know and he wouldn't care if the problem didn't end up on his lap," Jade snarled, making Ellery wince. Well, he'd always thought she harbored sort of a dislike for him, and she certainly wasn't bothering to hide it now. "Are you *sure* this is the guy we want?"

Jackson's gaze raked Ellery up and down, and Ellery had to remind himself that Jackson was a *PI*—he had no say in how the firm was run or who got which cases. Leonard Pfeist might think he walked on water, but there were three other partners who had a say in things, and Ellery was in good standing with all of them too.

"He's not afraid of the cops," Jackson said, pinning Ellery hard with a green-eyed glare. "Everyone else worked at the DA's for a few years—they've got ties. This guy doesn't give a fuck about anything but winning."

"Yeah, for *himself*."

Jackson's shrug rankled. He apparently thought that was fair.

"J, does it matter why he wants to win as long as he wins for K?"

"Yeah," she muttered. "Unless he thinks it's better to cut and run. He'd better not bail on my brother—he needs us, Jacky!"

Jackson's jaw tightened and his glare intensified. Ellery's hands were sweating, and he hated himself desperately for wanting this man's approval. He drew himself to his full six foot two and pulled his lips back in disdain. "Whatever your little family matter is," he sneered, "I'm sure you can deal without me. What makes you think I even *want* this case?"

Jackson snorted and rolled his eyes. "Don't stress yourself, Pinstripes. If you've got the guts for it, you're going to want it. No self-respecting shark would turn this one down."

"Let me be the judge of that. Do I even get an explanation?"

"I'll tell you on the way to the jail."

ELLERY'S FAMILY considered themselves liberal, but that didn't mean they wouldn't have pressed the locks on their doors for reassurance if a man who looked like Kaden Cameron had approached their car.

Easily six foot five with skin of darkest brown and a head shaved bald, Kaden dominated the small bare conference room of the county jail. The bandage taped behind his ear didn't make him look the slightest bit vulnerable either. He had craggy, ageless features, a scowl that could shake mountains, and shoulders that looked like they wouldn't fit through a door. He appeared to be every inch a badass, from his Lakers sweatshirt to his black Converse, but his file told another story.

That didn't mean Ellery's hand didn't shake as he took a quick sip of water and set his cup back down on the plain steel table.

"So you can put your house down for collateral," he said, because the first order of business was *always* making bail.

"My house," Jackson said promptly. "Not his. It's a duplex. I have a renter on the other side—"

"That racist asshole still live next door?" Kaden interrupted, but the look Jackson shot him wasn't annoyed.

"He's not racist, K, just old."

"Yeah, he's an old *racist*," Kaden grumbled. "Seriously, Jacky, did you *hear* him arguing against Kobe Bryant being one of the greatest ever?"

"It was at my house over Thanksgiving, dumbass," Jackson said, rolling his eyes. "You two had to be threatened with a potato gun—and your own wife did the threatening. You remember that?"

Kaden flashed a nostalgic smile. "Heh. Yeah. Rhonda was *pissed*."

"She should have been. You were all up in his face when he was trying hard to be your friend. He was playing with your children—he won't even talk to his *own* kids. Just because he doesn't like your pick of basketball players doesn't make him a racist. And you have a *daughter*, K—do you really want Kobe Bryant to be a hero? Mike's a good guy."

"He's not going to be so good when he gets evicted because you gambled his home on me," Kaden said, and Ellery made a quick reassessment.

He'd assumed that Kaden had gotten distracted because—like a lot of Ellery's clients—he was in denial of how much trouble he was in, but that wasn't the case at all.

"Not a gamble, K, 'cause you're not going to run. And you know what? Even if you *did* run, I'd rather get an apartment than know Rhonda and the kids were out on the street."

The man who looked Jackson Rivers in the eyes was obviously capable of meeting reality. "They're going to be on the street anyway," he said. "If I can't work during this bullshit, we can't make payments."

Ellery didn't blurt out "Pro bono?"—but he wanted to. He must have made some sort of noise, though, because Jackson sent him a glare that was probably meant to shrivel Ellery's manhood, root, stalk, and berries. Ha! Little did the man know he put on Kevlar undershorts in the morning.

Figuratively, of course.

"Your sister's moving in," Jackson said, pulling Ellery back from the shoring up of his self-esteem. "She'll help Rhonda with the payments until you can. Don't worry, K, your people gotchu." Jackson glanced back at Ellery. "You got anything else to say?" he demanded.

Ellery glared at him. "You know I do. The bail hearing is tomorrow, first thing in the morning. I need something to give the judge besides just who's going to help with the payments."

"I'm not going to run," Kaden said. "I've got a wife and two kids and a fuckin' dog who thinks I invented the morning crap. I own a house and part of a business. I've lived my whole life in this city. I'm not a flight risk, and I didn't kill no fucking cop!"

Ellery sucked air in through his teeth and looked at the anemic file, which featured the single crime-scene photo. That alone was weird, because there shouldn't have been a photo in the file at this juncture anyway. Even if he normally *did* have photos at this point, the fact that there *was* only one bothered the crap out of Ellery. Jesus, a hundred CSIs in Sacramento, and they get one lousy photo and some even blurrier pics of fingerprints? Something horribly wrong was going on here.

But the image bothered him more than the lack of evidence. The image was of Kaden slouched down against the counter of the gas station franchise he owned a piece of. His eyes were closed, and a trickle of blood leaked from under the black stocking cap he'd been wearing.

A SIG Sauer P229 handgun lay near his outstretched hand, pointed in the direction of the police officer who lay sprawled dead with a hole the size of Texas in his chest. A blood pool spread luridly over the floor.

"Now see," Ellery said delicately, "we may be able to get you out on bail, but I think it's that last part that we're going to have trouble with."

When he looked up from the brief, it was not Kaden's hard look of resignation that punched him with the most grit. No—it was Jackson Rivers's blistering look of accusatory fury that made him think that Kevlar undies just weren't going to be enough.

"I think maybe you need to tell me what happened," he said deliberately. "And don't leave anything out."

Kaden Cameron met his gaze straight on, and Ellery wasn't imagining the hostility there. "There isn't much to leave out," he said, voice flat. "Because I don't remember *crap*."

Yeah. And if that was true, that was going to make things *so* much more difficult.

"Well." Ellery resisted the urge to shove his chair back and fidget. "This is going to be a real short meeting."

From the twin looks of disgust he got, he figured that was the wrong thing to say.

Award winning author AMY LANE lives in a crumbling crapmansion with a couple of teenagers, a passel of furbabies, and a bemused spouse. She has too damned much yarn, a penchant for action-adventure movies, and a need to know that somewhere in all the pain is a story of Wuv, Twu Wuv, which she continues to believe in to this day! She writes contemporary romance, paranormal romance, urban fantasy, and romantic suspense, teaches the occasional writing class, and likes to pretend her very simple life is as exciting as the lives of the people who live in her head. She'll also tell you that sacrifices, large and small, are worth the urge to write.

Website: www.greenshill.com
Blog: www.writerslane.blogspot.com
Email: amylane@greenshill.com
Facebook: www.facebook.com/amy.lane.167
Twitter: @amymaclane

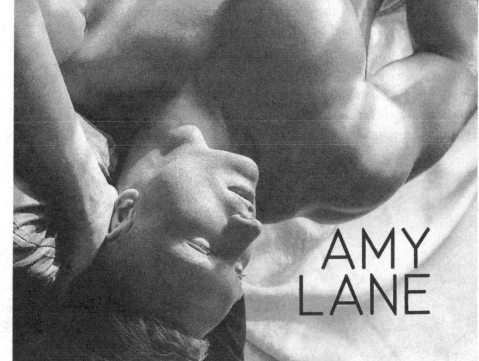

SHADES of HENRY

AMY LANE

A Flophouse Story

One bootstrap act of integrity cost Henry Worrall everything—military career, family, and the secret boyfriend who kept Henry trapped for eleven years. Desperate, Henry shows up on his brother's doorstep and is offered a place to live and a job as a handyman in a flophouse for young porn stars.

Lance Luna's past gave him reasons for being in porn, but as he continues his residency at a local hospital, they now feel more like excuses. He's got the money to move out of the flophouse and live his own life—but who needs privacy when you're taking care of a bunch of young men who think working penises make them adults?

Lance worries Henry won't fit in, but Henry's got a soft spot for lost young men and a way of helping them. Just as Lance and Henry find a rhythm as den mothers, a murder and the ghosts of Henry's abusive past intrude. Lance knows Henry's not capable of murder, but is he capable of caring for Lance's heart?

www.dreamspinnerpress.com